The Witching Hour

Elizabeth Laird has been nominated five times for the Carnegie Medal and has won numerous awards, including the Children's Book Award. She is the author of many highly acclaimed children's books.

She and her husband divide their time between London and Edinburgh.

Praise for *The Witching Hour*:

'A tale told with drama, feeling and maturity' *The Times*

'Meticulously researched and beautifully written, this is Elizabeth Laird at her best' *Scotsman*

'Another superb ripper . . . *The Witching Hour* has a delightful solidity that harks back to an earlier era' *Telegraph*

'An epic adventure given teeth by historical accuracy and Laird's trademark humanity. I really couldn't recommend it highly enough' *thebookbag.co.uk*

Also by Elizabeth Laird

Lost Riders
Crusade
Oranges in No Man's Land
Secrets of the Fearless
Paradise End
A Little Piece of Ground
The Garbage King
Jake's Tower
Red Sky in the Morning
Kiss the Dust
Secret Friends
Hiding Out
Jay
Forbidden Ground
When the World Began: Stories Collected in Ethiopia
The Wild Things *series*

The Witching Hour

Best wishes to Nicole

ELIZABETH LAIRD

from

Elizabeth Laird

MACMILLAN CHILDREN'S BOOKS

For the Laird family

First published 2009 by Macmillan Children's Books

This edition published 2010 by Macmillan Children's Books
a division of Macmillan Publishers Limited
20 New Wharf Road, London N1 9RR
Basingstoke and Oxford
Associated companies throughout the world
www.panmacmillan.com

ISBN 978-0-330-47210-4

3 5 7 9 8 6 4

A CIP catalogue record for this book is available from
the British Library.

Typeset by Intype Libra Limited
Printed and bound in the UK by CPI Mackays, Chatham ME5 8TD

I would like to thank:

Alistair Laird McGeachy, who first told me about
Hugh Blair, our mutual ancestor

The Riis family who welcomed me to Ladymuir

My husband David McDowall, who inspired me with
his enthusiasm for the Isle of Bute

Lindsey Fraser for her interest and encouragement,
and, as ever, Jane Fior for her invaluable help and
guidance.

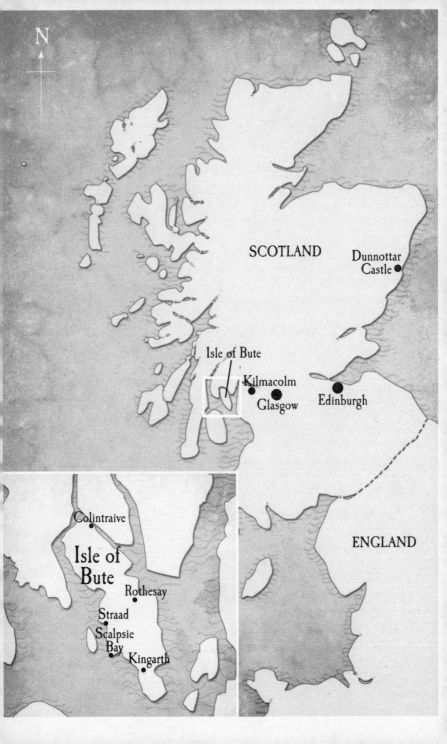

Preface

Scotland was a rough and violent place in the seventeenth century. In the north, the Highland clans were at each other's throats. In the southern Lowlands, fiery Protestants had swept away the old Catholic religion and created their own Presbyterian Church.

These Presbyterians were filled with enthusiasm and a sense of their own rightness. They didn't want anyone else to appoint their ministers or interpret the Bible for them. They wanted to pray and run their Church in their own way.

Four hundred miles away, down in London, King Charles II and his government felt threatened. They saw the Presbyterians' spirit of independence as a rebellion. The King decided to choose bishops to rule the Church in Scotland so that he could control the turbulent Scots through them.

The Presbyterians were infuriated. The King had no right, they said, to interfere with their religion. The most determined of them banded together and signed documents called 'Covenants', in which they promised to remain true to their Church and resist the King. These men and women were called 'Covenanters'.

The government in London decided to crush these rebellious people. As the years passed, and the Covenanters continued to reject the King's bishops, Charles's soldiers hunted them down with increasing cruelty. The Covenanters resisted, slipping out into the hills to worship in the open air in their own way. Those who were caught were imprisoned, fined and sometimes even executed. This tragic period in Scottish history is known as the Killing Times.

Several of my own ancestors were Covenanters, and three of them feature as characters in this novel. Their names were John Laird, Stephen Barbour and Hugh Blair. Of them all, most is known about Hugh Blair, who lived on a farm called Ladymuir near Kilmacolm in Renfrewshire. Most of what I've written about Hugh Blair happened to the real Hugh Blair.

When I visited the Riis family, who now live at Ladymuir farm, they showed me round their land and took me to see a hollow by the stream. It was here that the famous Covenanter preacher, James Renwick, came to speak one day in 1684 to a crowd of brave people who risked everything to hear him, even as the dragoons scoured the hills all around, their muskets primed to shoot.

The religion of both Catholics and Protestants in those days was harsh rather than consoling. Being in the right and doing one's duty were seen as more important than showing love and mercy to others. Religious men and women believed that the Devil was a real presence, stalking the world, seeking to tempt people away from the truth, and that those who sinned in thought or deed would be sure to go to Hell and burn in everlasting fire.

At the same time that the King was pursuing the Presbyterian rebels with merciless violence, there was a fever of witch-hunting in Scotland. Scared by the violent forces at work in society, people turned on each other. Those most commonly accused of being witches were elderly women. Many were arrested, tried for the crime of witchcraft and strangled, after which their bodies were burned at the stake.

In my family there was a woman called Margaret Laird who was accused of being a witch in 1698. The records of the parish of Kilmacolm describe the fits and fainting spells she suffered. In those excitable times, that was probably enough to make people suspicious of her. Though the accusations came to nothing, it was the thought of her, and what she had suffered, that helped me to create my own Maggie in this book.

Chapter One

Chapter One

I was the first one to see the whale lying dead on the sand at Scalpsie Bay. It must have been washed up in the night. I could imagine it, flopping out of the sea, thrashing its tail and opening and shutting the cavern of its mouth. It was huge and shapeless, a horrible dead thing, and it looked as if it would feel slimy if you dared to touch it. I crept up to it cautiously. There were monsters in the deep, I knew, and a great one, the Leviathan, which the Lord had made to be the terror of fishermen. Was this one of them? Would it come to life, and devour me?

The sand was ridged into ripples by the outgoing tide, which had left the usual orange lines of seaweed and bright white stripes of shells. The tide had scooped out little pools around the dead beast's sides and crabs were already scuttling there, as curious as me.

It was a cold day in December, the sun barely risen, and I'd pulled my shawl tightly round my head and shoulders, but it wasn't only the chill of the wet sand beneath my bare feet that made me shiver. There was a strangeness in the air. The early mist was clearing. Across the water I could already make out the Isle of Arran, rearing up out of the sea, the tops of its mountains hidden as usual in a crown of clouds. I'd seen Arran a dozen times a day, every day of my life, each

1

time I'd stepped out of the door of my grandmother's cottage. I knew it so well that I hardly ever noticed it.

But today, as I looked up at the mountains from the dead whale in front of me, the island seemed to shift, and for a moment I thought it was moving towards me, creeping across the water, coming for me, wanting to swallow me up, along with the beach, and Granny's cottage, and Scalpsie Bay, and the whole of the Isle of Bute.

And then beyond Arran, out there in the sea, a shaft of sunlight pierced through the clouds and laid a golden path across the grey water, tingeing the dead whale with brilliant light. The clouds were dazzled with glory and I was struck with a terror so great that my legs stiffened and I couldn't move.

'It's the Lord Jesus,' I whispered. 'He's coming now, to judge the living and the dead.'

I waited, my hands clamped together in a petrified clasp, expecting to see Christ walk down the sunbeam and across the water, angels flying on gleaming wings around him. There would be trumpets, the minister had said, as the saved rose up in the air like flocks of giant birds to meet the Lord, but down here on the ground there would be wailing and gnashing of teeth as the damned were sucked down into Hell by the Evil One.

'Am I saved, Lord Jesus? Will you take me?' I cried out loud. 'And Granny too?'

The clouds were moving further apart and the golden path was widening, making the white crests on the little waves sparkle like the clothes of the Seraphim.

I was certain of it then. I wasn't one of the Chosen to

rise with Jesus in glory. I was one of the damned, and Granny was too.

'No!' I shrieked. 'Not yet! Give me another chance, Lord Jesus!'

And then I must have fallen down because the next thing I remember was Granny saying, 'She's taken a fit, the silly wee thing. Pick her up, can't you?'

I was only half conscious again, but I knew it was Mr Macbean's rough hands painfully holding my arms, and the gruff voice of Samuel Kirby complaining as he held my legs.

'What are you doing, you dafties?' Granny shouted in the rough, angry voice I dreaded. 'Letting her head fall back like that! Trying to break her neck, are you? Think she's a sack of oatmeal?'

Behind me, above the crunch of many feet following us up the beach towards our cottage, I could hear anxious murmurs.

'The creature's the size of a kirk! And the tail on it, did you see? It'll stink when it rots. Infect the air for weeks, so it will.'

And the sniping tongues were busy as usual.

'Hark at Elspeth! Shouting like that. Evil old woman. Why does she want to be so sharp? They should drop the girl and let the old body carry her home herself.'

Then came the sound of our own door creaking back on its leather hinge, and the smell of peat smoke, and the soft tail of Sheba the cat brushing against my dangling hand.

3

They dropped me down on the pile of straw in the corner that I used as a bed, and a moment later Granny had shooed them out of the cottage. I was quite back in my wits by then, and I started to sit up.

'Stay there,' commanded Granny.

She was standing over me, frowning as she stared at me. Her mouth was pulled down hard at the corners, and the stiff black hairs on her chin were quivering. They were sharp, those bristles, but not as sharp as the bristles in her soul.

'Now then, Maggie. What was all that for? Why did you faint? What did you see?'

'Nothing, Granny. The whale . . .'

She shook her head impatiently.

'Never mind the whale. While you were away, in the faint. Was there a vision?'

'No. I just – everything was black. Before that I thought I saw . . .'

'What? What did you see? Do I have to pull it out of you?'

'The sky looked strange, and there was the whale – it scared me – and I thought that Jesus was coming. Down from the sky. I thought it was the Last Day.'

She stared at me a moment longer. There wasn't much light in the cottage, only a square of brightness that came through the open door, and a faint glow from the peats burning in the middle of the room, but I could see her eyes glittering.

'The whale's an omen. It means no good. It didn't speak to you?'

4

'No! It was dead. I thought the Lord Jesus was coming, that's all.'

'Hmph.' She turned away and pulled on the chain that hung from the rafter, holding the cauldron in place over the fire. 'That's nothing but kirk talk. You're a disappointment to me, Maggie. Your mother had it, the gift of far-seeing, but you've nothing more in your head than what's been put there by the minister. You're your father over again, stubborn and blind and selfish. My Mary gave you nothing of herself at all. If I hadn't delivered you into this world with my own hands, I'd have thought you were changed at birth.'

Granny knew where to plunge her dagger, and twist it for good measure. There was no point in answering her. I bit my lip, stood up and shook the straws off the rough wool of my skirt.

'Shall I milk Blackie now?'

'After you've touched a dead whale? You'll pass on the bad luck and dry her milk up for good. You're more trouble than you're worth, Maggie. Always were, always will be.'

'I didn't touch the whale. I only—'

She raised a hand and I ducked.

'Get away up the hill and cut a sack of peats. The stack's low already, or had you been too full of yourself to notice?'

Cutting peats and lugging them home was the hardest work of all, and most times I hated it, but today, in spite of the rain that was now sweeping in from the sea, I was glad to get out of the cottage and run away up the glen. I usually went the long way round, up the firm path that went round and about before it reached the peat cuttings, but today I plunged straight on through the bog, trampling furiously through the mass of reeds and flags and the treacherous bright grass that hid the pools of water, not hearing the suck of the mud as I pulled my feet out, not feeling the wetness that was seeping up the bottom of my gown, not even noticing the scratches from the prickly gorse as it tore at my arms.

'An evil old woman. They were right down there. That's what you are.' Away from Granny, I felt brave enough to answer back. 'I *am* like my mam. I've the same curly hair, so Tam says.'

Most people called old Tam a rogue, a thief, a lying, drunken rascal, living in his tumbledown shack like a pig in a sty. But he was none of those things to me. He'd known my mother and I knew he'd never lie about her to me.

I don't remember my mother. She was Granny's only child and she died of a fever, when I was a very little girl. I just about remember my father – he was a big man, not given to talking much. He was a rover by nature, Tam said. He came to the Isle of Bute from the mainland to fetch the Laird of Keames's cattle and drive them east across the hills to sell in Glasgow. He was only meant to stay on Bute for a week or two, while the cattle were rounded up for him, but he chanced on my mother as she walked down the lane to the field to milk Blackie one warm June evening. The honeysuckle was

6

in flower, and the wild roses too, and it was all over with him at once, so Tam said.

'Never a love like it, Maidie,' he told me. 'Don't you listen to your granny. A child born of love you are, given to love, made for love, and you'll not rest till you find it for yourself.'

'Granny said the sea took my father,' I asked Tam once. 'What did she mean?'

I'd imagined a great wave curling up the beach, twining round my father's legs and sucking him back into the depths.

'An accident, Maidie. Nothing more.' Tam heaved a sigh. 'Your father was taking the cattle to the mainland up by Colintraive, making them swim across the narrows there. He'd done it a dozen times before. The beasts weren't easy – lively young steers they were – and one of them was thrashing about in the water as if a demon was possessing it. Perhaps a demon was, for the steer caught your father on the head with its horn, and it went right through his temple. He went down under the water, and when he was washed up a week later, there was a wound from his eyebrow to the line of his hair deep enough to put your hand inside.'

There's nothing like hard work in the cold of a wet December day for cooling your temper, and by the time I got home I was more miserable than angry. My arms were aching from the weight of the sack. I was wet through. The mud on my hem slapped clammily against

7

my ankles, and I wished I'd been sensible instead of running through the bog.

I was expecting another scold from Granny as soon as she saw the state of my clothes, and the rips in my shawl, and my face all streaked with peat and rain and tears, but she only said, 'Oh, so it's you come home again, and a fine sight you are too. Running through the bog like a mad child – *I* saw you.'

She took my wooden bowl down from the shelf, ladled some hot porridge into it from the cauldron and put it into my hands.

'Take off that soaking shawl and put it to dry, and your gown too.'

It wasn't an apology exactly, but it was all I'd get. I could see that she was sorry for what she'd said by the way she set a stool and told me to sit down by the fire of peats that were smouldering on the hearthstone in the middle of the room. I was feeling chilled now, shivering, and I crouched low over the weak flames, never minding the thick smoke that curled up into my face, grateful for Sheba, who jumped up into my lap and let me warm my hands in her soft black fur.

The days are short in December. It was soon time to fetch Blackie in for the night and shut her into her byre, which was no more than a room beside the kitchen. For once, Granny went out to find her herself, and to milk her too. As she came back towards the cottage I could hear her talking to someone, and laughing. There was only one person who could draw such a happy sound from her.

Tam, I thought, jumping up with delight.

Blackie's hoofs clopped on the stone threshold of her byre, and then came a thud against the thin wooden partition at the end of the kitchen as she butted at her manger with her head. The kitchen door opened, and Granny and Tam came in.

Tam's shirt was dark with sweat, his short breeks were ragged at the ankles and torn at the knees and the plaid he wore wrapped round himself was so dirty and stained that the wool's once-bright colours had gone for good. But that meant nothing to me. His front teeth were as few as the posts of a rotten fence, his face was pitted and scarred with the smallpox, his long, tall body was as thin as a stick and the hair under his blue bonnet had mostly fallen out, but there was no one who cared for me as Tam did, and no one else that I loved.

'Look at the girl now,' he said, setting a black bottle down on the table. 'She summons monsters from the sea with the power of her beautiful eyes. It was you who sang to the poor whale, was it, Maidie, and lured it up to its death on the beach?'

'I did *not*.'

For once, I didn't like Tam's teasing. The whale had been too grand and strange for jokes.

Granny had gone outside again to fetch water from the burn.

'Why do you always call me Maidie?' I asked Tam. I'd meant to ask him often but never dared while Granny was around.

9

He looked over his shoulder but Granny was still filling the bucket.

'You know why, my pretty one.' He pinched my chin. 'It was what I always called your mother. Mary her name was to everyone else, but Maidie she was to me. And you are just like her. Even prettier, maybe.'

'But she had the gift, didn't she? Granny said so. The second sight. She was far seeing.'

'Oh, that.' He shook his head. 'You shouldn't mind your granny, Maidie. She speaks sharply, and who wouldn't, with the troubles life has brought her? She loves you in her heart.'

I shook my head and looked away from him, down into the red caves the fire had made in the burning peats.

'Anyway, be thankful that your mother didn't pass the gift on to you. It's not a comfortable thing, to foresee the future and know beforehand the manner of a person's death.'

Granny came back then, a heavy bucket in each hand, and Tam set about fetching down the beakers and pouring out the whisky, a good long slug for the two of them and a little drop for me. Then he put his hand inside his shirt, and with a flourish he pulled out a duck, holding it up by its webbed feet so that its bright feathered head hung down, its eyes dead and glazed.

'Will you look at this. A king's feast, that's what we'll have tonight. You'll want to save the feathers, Elspeth. Where shall I pluck the wee fellow?'

Oh, it was good, that night. The duck's feathers flew and the pot simmered and the whisky sank in the bottle. And Tam, as he always did, started on the old stories. They were stories of the sea, put into his head by the whale. He told my favourite, the one about the seal who shed her skin and became a beautiful woman, and married a fisherman. Her children were as pretty as she was, and she loved them, I suppose, but one night she found her old sealskin and put it on, and a longing for the sea overcame her. Back she went under the waves, a seal once more, and her children never saw her again.

Like I never saw my mam again, I thought.

Tam went on to tell tales of mermaids and sea horses and a monster that lived in a loch along with the hero who killed it. But what with the purring of Sheba on my lap, and the good food in my stomach, and the peat smoke in my eyes, and the whisky in my head, and the tiredness in my arms and legs, I couldn't stay awake.

'No, no, Elspeth.' I heard Tam say. 'It was Canola who invented the harp. She heard the wind blow through the sinews that clung to the ribs of a rotting dead whale, and it gave her the idea.'

Whales again, I thought. I was so sleepy I almost fell off my stool. Tam saw me nod, and laughed.

'Away to your bed, Maidie, and dream sweetly all night long.'

Chapter Two

I think I did have happy dreams that night, but they floated away like wisps of mist, and I couldn't remember what they were. My sleep wasn't long anyway, because before dawn there came a battering on the door, startling me awake so suddenly that I shot up out of the straw like a hunted hare.

'Elspeth! You're to come quickly! My Jeanie's got her pains!'

It was Mr Macbean, and I knew what he wanted. Granny was a famed midwife, and if his wife's time had come he'd need her to bring the baby safely into the world.

It was pitch dark in the house so I kicked at the peats. A little flame flared up, giving enough light for me to see Granny lying dead asleep on the floor, her empty beaker of whisky by her hand. Tam had gone.

'Wait a minute, Mr Macbean,' I called out. 'I'll wake her up.'

'Is that you, Maggie?' the voice outside the door was hoarse with anxiety. 'Get her up quick, for the Lord's sake. Jeanie's pains are bad.'

Granny's snores were as loud as the snorts of Mr Macbean's bull in a rage, and I had to shake and shake her before she'd stir. When she did wake, she only pushed me off and tried to roll over.

'No, Granny! You must get up. Mr Macbean's here, and the baby's on its way.'

She opened one eye and glared at me, and even by the dying flame I could see that the drink was still on her. My heart sank.

'Get up, Granny. You have to.'

The hammering on the door started again.

Granny lurched to her feet, took a deep swallow of water from the pail of water and splashed her face.

'My shawl, Maggie,' she croaked, and staggered to the door.

She was in no fit state, I could see that. I fetched my own shawl, still damp from yesterday, and followed her outside. She'd need me to bring her safe home.

Mr Macbean was the one man in Scalpsie Bay rich enough to own a horse, and he had ridden it to our cottage. There was only a faint glimmer of light outside from the quarter-moon, but he could see how far gone Granny was.

'Look at the state of her. Drunk,' he said with disgust. 'Tonight of all nights.'

Without waiting for a word from Granny, he picked her up and heaved her on to the horse, then set off at a smart run up the lane, with me trotting along behind.

The cold night air, the jolting ride and the water she'd drunk seemed to sober Granny up, because she was looking sharper when we reached the Macbean farm. It was the biggest holding for miles around, standing proud in its own land. Mrs Macbean's serving

13

girl, Annie, was standing outside the farmhouse door, twisting her apron round in her hands.

'Oh, it's you, Maggie,' she said, pursing her mouth in the irritating way she put on whenever she saw me. 'I thought it was a wild animal creeping up like that.'

There was a hiss from Granny, who had heard her, and Annie shrivelled up like a leaf held to a flame. I couldn't help grinning. Annie was only a servant but she gave herself more airs than the Lady of Keames Castle herself.

Mr Macbean had plucked Granny off the horse and she was already at the farmhouse door.

'Where is she?' Granny demanded, and I heard with relief that her voice was firm and clear.

Mr Macbean led the way into the farm kitchen and beyond it to the inner room. There was a lamp burning in there, and looking in I saw a proper bedstead, with sheets of linen and all, and a ceiling hiding the rafters, and a chest of carved wood. I was so impressed I barely noticed Mrs Macbean, who was lying with her back arched and her face red and wet with sweat.

Then Granny said, 'Where's that Annie girl? Fetch water, can't you? And the rest of you, give a body room to breathe.'

By that time, the three older Macbean children were crowding round the door beside me, along with the manservant and Mr Macbean himself, but Granny shut the door in our faces, and we were left standing in the kitchen.

I don't remember how long we waited, listening to

the poor woman crying out in pain, but I do remember the faces of the little Macbeans, their eyes round with fear, huddling close together. I liked to be with children. I didn't often get the chance. I felt sorry for them anyway, so I knelt beside them and said, 'Your mammie's going to be fine, you'll see. While we're waiting, why don't I tell you a story?'

They nodded, and the smallest one, Robbie, put his thumb in his mouth.

'A while ago, not far from here,' I began, 'there was a seal who came out of the sea and took off her skin and turned herself into a beautiful—'

Mr Macbean came in from stabling the horse.

'No more of that,' he said roughly. 'If it's stories you want, read them true ones from the Good Book. I won't have their heads filled with fairies and magic and the works of the Devil.'

He took a Bible down from a shelf and put it into my hands. It was so heavy I had to rest it on my knees. I'd never seen such a big Bible outside the kirk before. Granny couldn't read and there were no books in our house.

'Open it,' Mr Macbean said unpleasantly. 'Read a story.'

'I – I can't read,' I said, lifting it back up to him.

'No, Maggie, you can't, but it's time you learned. You should study the Scripture and follow the path of righteousness before that grandmother of yours leads you to Hell and destruction.'

I didn't know what to say. Little Robbie had crept

close and laid his head down on my lap. I knelt there, stroking his hair and staring up at Mr Macbean.

'Well,' he said, in a kinder tone, 'you're a good lass, Maggie, after all. Mind now, that you don't take on the infection of wickedness from Elspeth. She—'

Then came the sounds from the next room we had been waiting for – a final loud cry from Mrs Macbean and a thin wail from the new baby. Mr Macbean's face cracked open in a great smile and I saw a glimpse of something in him that could be good and loving. I'm glad I did, because later all that came from him to us was hatred and cruelty.

The door of the next room opened and Granny came out with the new baby in her arms. The children jumped up and ran to look, but she kicked out at them to shoo them away.

'Elspeth,' came a weak voice from the bed behind her, 'you're a good soul, whatever they say, and you've saved us both. I can never thank you . . .'

'The basket,' Granny said. 'The bread and cheese. It won't work without them.'

She was looking at Annie, who was standing sulkily by the corner shelf – jealous, I think, of the way the children had taken to me. Annie picked up the basket beside her, putting into it a loaf and a round cheese from the shelf. Impatiently, Granny grabbed it from her, planted the baby on top of the food, and stamping across to the hearth in the middle of the room, she began to swing the basket round and round on the iron hook from which the cauldron usually hung. She was singing something under her breath. The peat fire had died down and the only light came from a small flame guttering in the oil lamp by the door. It cast Granny's shadow so monstrously on the wall behind her that even I was frightened.

Mr Macbean darted forward.

'Stop that! How dare you? I won't have devilish practices, not in my house!'

Granny stopped muttering, and jerked the basket to a standstill. The baby inside it set up a wail again. I could see that Granny was tired, and her head was aching, and the anger that always simmered inside her was ready to break out. Her eyes, red from the drink and lack of sleep, narrowed, and she thrust the basket into Mr Macbean's hands.

'Take him, then. It was a favour I was doing you, to protect him from evil. You'd best christen him quickly, for by the look of him he'll not be here long.'

Mr Macbean put the basket gently down on the ground and bent to lift his son out of it. As he held him close to his chest, the three other children clustered round him. They looked afraid.

'John, what are you doing? Bring him back to me!' came Mrs Macbean's weak voice from the next room. 'Elspeth, are you still there?'

Granny, ignoring her, picked up her shawl, and flung it over her wild grey hair.

'I wish you joy of him, while he lives,' she spat out, and without a glance at me flung out of the house into the cold night.

It wasn't until we had stumbled halfway home, and the moon, coming suddenly out from behind the clouds, shone a sliver of light over the water of Scalpsie Bay, that I remembered the end of the seal story and was glad after all that Mr Macbean had stopped me from finishing it. The seal mother goes away and never comes back. It would have been a hard thing for wee Robbie to hear just then.

Perhaps it was the Devil that put the story into my head, to torment those poor children, I thought with a shudder. And to be on the safe side, I chanted to myself, 'Deliver us from evil, deliver us from evil,' all the way home.

Dawn was on its way by then, and a grey wet dawn it was too. It didn't break, as the saying goes, but slithered up upon the land and sea in a misty, ghostly way.

I was ahead of Granny as we reached the cottage, and I jumped with fright because the door of Blackie's byre swung slowly open. Then Tam stumbled out. He was covered in wisps of straw and clots of dried dung stuck to his hair. Granny burst into a cackle of laughter.

'Old fool! Too blootered to find your way home, were you? You never slept the night in the byre with the cow?'

Tam mumbled something then turned away, fumbling with his breeches to relieve himself. He was doing it too close to the house for my liking.

I went inside quickly. I was afraid that other feelings for Tam would push their way in and spoil the love I felt for him. I didn't want to see weakness and silliness and the blur of drink in his eyes. I didn't want to feel pity or contempt.

The fire was nearly out and it took a while to coax it back to life. The floor needed sweeping, Blackie needed milking, and the porridge had to be cooked. Granny, who had shooed Tam away from our door with a shake of her broom as if he was a stray dog, kept me at it all morning.

The lane running along the head of Scalpsie Bay goes directly past our cottage and anyone coming or going to the Macbean farm has to pass right by us. It annoyed Mr Macbean, as I knew well, to see the good land of our small field and kail-yard, which took a bite out of his big farm. He was envious of the stream running so close to the cottage, and the treasures of the beach being ours for the first taking. He'd long wanted to gobble our place up and take it into his own holding.

Later that morning he rode by with a sack of oatmeal as payment for Granny's services, and his eyes wandered possessively past me towards the cottage. I flushed with annoyance at the sneer in his voice when he spoke. 'When was it you last put fresh turf on your roof? You must be flooded through those holes every time it rains.'

'It's dry enough,' I said stiffly.

He pretended to look sympathetic.

'It's too much for you though, this place, isn't it, Maggie? An old woman and a young girl! I wonder you don't give it up and move somewhere more fitting.

Elspeth could find a place in Rothesay, couldn't she? And you could go to be a serving girl like our Annie.'

I had to bite my lip to stop my anger bursting out, but I wasn't like Granny. I could always hold it in. I stared back at him coolly and said, 'I hope the baby's well, and Mrs Macbean. Have you chosen a name for him? When is the christening to be?'

He looked embarrassed.

'The christening will be soon enough. We'll see. He's to be named Ebenezer.'

He mounted his horse and rode off.

'Ebenezer!' snorted Granny, who had come out of the cottage in time to see Mr Macbean disappear over the rise towards Rothesay. 'What kind of fool name is that? Not that the child will bear it for long. The mark of death is on him.'

Chapter Three

The gossips of Scalpsie Bay had been right. The whale stank as it rotted. Foulness hung in the air and even the seagulls, which had feasted on the flesh at first, would not tear at the carcass any more.

The other news was that a new minister had come to the church at Kingarth. His name was Mr Robertson.

'A busybody, by the look of him,' Granny said sourly, watching the man's lean, black-coated figure stride energetically up the lane towards Macbean's. 'He'll be after us to go to the kirk every week, so he can insult us from his pulpit. They're all the same. Crows in black suits.'

I watched for the minister coming back so that I could take a peep at him. There were hardly ever strangers in Scalpsie Bay, and a new face was always a wonder. I hid behind the hedge and looked through a gap. Just as he came into view, a swan flew overhead. The minister took off his round, broad-brimmed black hat and looked up at it, letting me get a good view of him.

Mr Robertson was a young man, lean and pale. His hair fell in thin, fair wisps to his shoulders. His skin was pink, not reddened or tanned by the wind and sun, as everyone else's was in Scalpsie Bay. He looked clean all over. There were no smears on his face or hands, and no specks on the black cloth of his coat.

I had thought that all ministers were like the last one had been – red-faced, old, stout and angry. I thought they would all have a loud, booming voice and a frowning face. I was so surprised at the sight of this earnest, nervous-looking young man that I craned forward clumsily and set the hawthorn twigs rattling. He picked the sound up at once, and came right up to the hedge, then bent down and stared through it, so that his eyes and mine were no more than a foot's length apart.

He started with surprise when he saw me and straightened up. I had to stand up too, and face him, though I was so embarrassed I wanted only to bolt into the cottage. He settled his hat back on his head and pulled at the two white bands that fell from his collar over his black-clad chest. He was trying to look dignified, I could tell.

'You'll be Maggie Blair,' he said. 'And yours is a face I've yet to see in the kirk on the Sabbath Day.'

He was trying to sound severe, but spoilt the effect by giving a gigantic sneeze which made his pale eyes water.

'H-how did you know my name?' I stammered.

'I know the name of every soul in my parish.' He wiped his nose on a snowy kerchief which he folded carefully and tucked inside his sleeve. His earnest eyes rested on me again. 'And I'm discovering things about some of them that sadden me. You live here with your grandmother, Mistress Elspeth Wylie, isn't that so?'

I nodded warily. In my experience, mention of Granny usually involved severe disapproval.

'When was the last time that Mistress Elspeth brought you to the kirk, Maggie, to hear the word of the Lord?'

I looked down. In truth, it had been more than a year since Granny and I had tramped the four miles to the kirk and back again. Once the old minister's coughing had started, he had been like a fire damped down. He'd lost the strength to chase after his lost flock, and Granny was certainly not going to go to him of her own accord. Luckily, I thought of a way to change the subject.

'When's the baby to be christened, Mr Robertson?' I asked.

He looked harassed.

'What baby would that be? There's one by every hearth hereabouts.'

There was only one baby in my world.

'Ebenezer Macbean,' I said.

Mr Robertson raised his thin eyebrows.

'Tomorrow! Didn't you know? The whole parish seems to have been summoned to the . . .'

He broke off, his eyes fixed on something behind me. I turned to see Granny appear at the cottage door. She was holding a bucket of water. I knew she'd seen the minister, but she slung its dirty contents in our direction anyway, making him jump backwards. Then she set it down and marched towards me, her arms crossed on her chest. I couldn't look at her. I was ashamed of her dirty clothes, wild hair and blackened teeth. Beside the minister, so neat and scrubbed, she looked like a straw man set up in the fields to scare birds.

'Who's this keeping the girl from her work?' she demanded, pretending not to know Mr Robertson. 'Oh, it's you, Minister.'

'And good morning to you, Mistress Elspeth,' said Mr Robertson gravely. I glanced at him sharply, but he looked more alarmed than mocking. He coughed awkwardly. 'I'm glad of the chance to speak with you. I've been at my parish three months already and I haven't seen you or your granddaughter on one Sabbath Day.'

Granny's bare, hard-soled feet were planted firmly apart on the rough ground, but now she bent one knee and slapped a beefy hand down on to her hip.

'Pain in my joints,' she said. 'Ill health. A recurring fever. I'd never be able to walk such a distance.'

Mr Robertson pursed his lips.

'Oh now, I saw you in Rothesay not one week ago, and it's a full two miles further to walk.'

'I know that fine, Minister.' Granny's head was thrown back and she was staring down her nose at him. 'Crawled all the way, didn't I, on my hands and knees. The pain – you can't imagine.'

Knowing how fast Granny strode along the lanes, covering the miles at a steady trot, I had to stifle a giggle.

A pink flush of irritation was colouring Mr Robertson's cheeks.

'Mistress Elspeth, I have to remind you that it is your duty, both by earthly and heavenly law, to attend divine service at your parish kirk on the Lord's Day. If you fail to do so, you will incur a fine. Do you understand?'

Granny pretended to cringe in fear.

'A fine!' she whined. 'Oh sir, don't take from a poor old widow woman the little she has and leave her destitute!'

Mr Robertson held up his hands, as if defeated, and began to back away.

'Hear the psalmist's words, Mistress Elspeth, and if you won't hear me, hear him.' And he began to intone, in a surprisingly strong voice, *Enter His gates and courts with praise, to thank Him go ye thither . . .'* but before he could finish a gust of wind snatched off his hat and sent it rolling down the lane. He ran after it, with Granny's mocking laughter following him.

'The wind heard you, Mr Minister, blowing the empty air out of your mouth and it couldn't help joining in!' she said, a little too loudly.

Then, turning back towards the cottage she let out a shriek. Blackie had wandered in from her pasture and was tearing at the shaggy thatch and turf that hung low off the cottage roof.

'You Devil's bit! You creature of Satan!' she screeched, beating Blackie away from the roof with her fists. The wind must have carried her words along the lane because I saw the minister stop in his tracks with shock, then bend over and hurry on, one hand clamping his hat to his head.

*

Annie appeared that afternoon. She came tripping down from the farm, her shawl pinned under her chin just loosely enough to let the curls escape from it to frame her face. I suppose she thought it pretty that way. I thought her plain silly. She carried a basket on her arm and I guessed she was on her way to ask for contributions from the neighbouring farms for the christening feast.

The christening feast. It occurred to me, as I saw Annie, how odd it was that no news of it had come to us. I remembered too that in the past few days Mr Macbean had spurred his horse to go faster as he passed our cottage. The truth hit me as sharp as a blow.

We've not been invited. I'll not get the chance to hold baby Ebenezer. Everyone else is to go, but not Granny and me.

I was desperate not to believe it. I put up a hand to smooth back my hair, made myself smile and called out, 'Hello, Annie. Where are you away to? How's the baby, anyway?'

She raised her eyebrows when she saw me, in the sneering way she had.

'Eb-en-e-zer's just fine.' She separated out the sounds to make the long name seem even grander. 'And I'm fetching eggs from the folks at Ambrismore for the christening.'

My fingers curled tightly into my palms.

'The christening, eh? When's that to be?'

'Tomorrow of course. *Everyone* knows—'

She pretended she had made a mistake and clapped her hand over her mouth but above her twitching fingers her eyes were dark with malice.

'We couldn't have come anyway,' I said, as carelessly as I could. 'Granny's not well.'

I couldn't help looking down towards the beach where Granny was bent over, vigorously pulling something out of a clump of seaweed. Luckily, Annie didn't notice.

An idea hit me.

'I've three eggs to spare. I'll give them to you if you like. For the christening.'

Three eggs. They were a treasure to us. They'd be enough, surely, to buy us an invitation.

Annie nodded without answering and I opened the little gate into our yard for her. She was right behind me as I went into the cottage, and turning round I caught a curiously greedy expression on her face.

She thinks it'll be all dirty and messy in here, I thought with disgust, *and she wants to spread stories about us*.

I was glad that I'd swept the floor that morning, and washed the table, and arranged the dishes neatly on the shelf.

'I see you're not fussy about spiders then,' she said at last, pointing triumphantly at the tangle of webs in the corner where the roof beam came down to meet the stone wall.

'Annie, you'd never clear away the spiders' webs?' I was genuinely shocked. 'Not when there's a baby in the house?'

'And why wouldn't I? Dirty, creepy things.'

I was amazed at her ignorance.

'Don't you know that they're lucky? Don't you know that the spiders spun their webs around the Baby Jesus to keep him hidden from the soldiers?'

She looked confused for a moment, then frowned suspiciously.

'Did you read that in the Bible? Oh, I forgot. You can't read, can you?'

'No but it'll be there.' I spoke with a confidence I didn't feel. 'It must be. Lucky spiders? *Everyone* knows.'

Her eyes were sweeping the cottage again. They rested disdainfully on Sheba, who was staring at her unblinkingly, lashing her tail from side to side.

'Get me those eggs, Maggie. I've to get on or Mrs Macbean will be after me.'

I was regretting my offer now, but there was no going back on it. I went to the corner of the room by the chest, where it was quite dark, and put my hand into the crock where I'd placed the eggs that morning. I could feel them, round and smooth, under my fingers. Three eggs! And all for nothing. Annie wouldn't even tell Mrs Macbean that I'd given them. There'd be no invitation, however many eggs I handed over.

'Oh,' I said, trying to sound surprised, and hoping that the darkness of the corner would hide my lying blush. 'There's only one here, after all.'

As I turned, with the egg in my hand, I saw Annie

move quickly away from beside the shelf where she'd been standing. She was settling her shawl again, tight under her chin.

'I'll be off then,' she said, putting the egg in the basket, and without a word of thanks, without even looking at me, she scuttled out of the cottage as if the Devil was after her.

Something woke me in the middle of the night. I don't know what it was, but I knew at once that I was alone. Granny had gone.

She had taken the news of the christening more quietly than I'd expected, though I saw the flesh round her mouth whiten as she clamped her lips tightly together. When she had finally spoken, she'd sounded more contemptuous than angry.

'They'd not have dared in your grandad's day. Mucky midden-crawlers! My man once cleared a room of the likes of them with one swing of his axe.' Then, to my surprise, she noticed the tears drying on my cheeks and put a hand on my shoulder. 'Don't think of them, Maggie. There's better company to be had than cold-hearted psalm singers like Macbean.'

Better company! Her words came back to me as I lay with my eyes open, looking up into the pitch-dark cottage room.

Tam, I thought. *She'll have gone to Tam.*

I sat up, woken properly by a surge of fury.

They don't want us at Macbean's, and she didn't even ask me to come to Tam's. Well, I'm going anyway.

29

I went to the door and looked out. The night was mild for December, the moon full and shining dully through thin low cloud. There was no rain in the air, and enough light to see my way to Tam's old shack.

I was going back inside to fetch my shawl when I heard from some way off the heart-lifting, spirit-dancing skirl of the pipes. The sound wasn't coming from Tam's tumbledown hovel under the hillside, but from up near Loch Quien, the little loch which lies half a mile or so between the hills behind the beach. I was running up the lane, called by the music, before I knew what I was doing.

The piping stopped on a half-note and its enchantment vanished in a second. Thicker cloud had crossed the sky, shutting out the moon's thin light. I shivered.

This is daft. I must go home.

As I turned, a flicker caught my eye. A fire was burning up on the knoll at Ambrisbeg, halfway along the edge of the loch.

That's where they'll be.

It was a hard business finding my way up there in the dark, working round thickets of gorse, squelching through bog and stumbling against stones. I ended up in a dip with the firelight out of sight, and I'd have given up and gone home if the piping hadn't started again. I could hear voices too – whoops and shrieks of laughter. I was closer than I thought.

Something held me back from running into the circle of firelight to join the revelry. I suppose it was the thought of Granny's certain rage. At any rate, I wanted to stay hidden and watch. I knelt behind a boulder and peeped over it, almost sure the tree above me would shelter me from view.

They had lit a fire in the centre of a circle of stones and by its light I could see eight or ten people. Apart from Granny and Tam there were a couple of soldiers back from the wars who spent the winters lying in barns or ditches, begging for food, and Daft Effie from the Butts, whom the farm boys teased, and Peter the serving man from Ardnahoe. I suppose there were two or three more whom I didn't recognize.

A cloth had been laid on the ground and there were some oatcakes on it, and bones stripped of meat. Tam's black bottle lay on its side, empty, along with two others. Tam had taken the mouthpiece of his bagpipe away from his lips and now he let the air out of the bag so that it wailed like a dying animal, making everyone lurch about with laughter. Then he put it to his mouth again, and as his fingers flew to a fast jig, they shook themselves like dogs at the sound of the hunting horn and danced, arms flying, legs leaping, plaids and shawls unravelling, hair wild, eyes lit up with joy, and my feet itched too and my fingers tapped out the rhythm on the boulder.

I had to join them, I had to get up and dance, and I was starting to my feet when I caught a movement away to the side. Peering into the dark, I saw the oval paleness of a face. Someone else was standing there, watching from the shadows.

I sank back down again, not knowing what to do. Tam's fingers were racing over his chanter and the dancing was faster than ever. I saw Granny stoop and pick up a wisp of straw. She flung it in the air. It caught a leaping spark from the fire and flared into flame, rising up like a living thing into the air.

'Fly, fairies, fly!' yelled Granny. 'By horse and hattock, go, go!'

The wisp burned out and disappeared. The music stopped. I looked back into the shadows. The face had gone. I wasn't sure, now, that I'd seen anything there at all.

It was as if Tam's piping had held the revellers' wits together, because as soon as it stopped they seemed to fall apart and began stumbling about, laughing stupidly and clinging to each other, groping for the empty bottles and holding them to their lips in the hopes of squeezing out a few last drops.

They're just old drunks after all, I thought, and I was weary, as if I'd run a long way. I wanted my bed. I turned to slip away, and as I felt my way back down the hill from Ambrisbeg to the cottage, I heard Granny's cracked voice rise in a hideous song.

'Tinkletum, tankletum,' she was singing.

The words seemed to follow me, gaining in volume, becoming harsher and more threatening.

'Tinkletum, tankletum, *tinkletum*, *tankletum*, TIN-KLETUM, TANKLETUM!'

The words were still drumming in my ears, making me shiver with more than the cold, as I lay down on the straw in the cottage and pulled my plaid up over my ears.

Chapter Four

When I woke next morning, Granny wasn't there. I scrambled to my feet, afraid that something was wrong. Perhaps she'd never returned from the wild night at Ambrisbeg. Or maybe she'd gone off with her vagabond friends, leaving me and Sheba all alone. Or, worst of all, unearthly beings – fairies or the Devil himself – could have snatched her away to their own dark world.

But then I heard her voice coming from Blackie's stall behind the thin partition. Her words were too indistinct for me to make out, but the venom in them made me shudder. She was in the foulest mood, and I would need to watch my step.

A moment later she marched into the cottage, hanks of grey hair lying matted over her face, eyes bloodshot, hands crooked like claws.

'So, Mistress Lazy, you're awake at last. Sneaking off in the night, were you, you dirty girl? Going to meet some man or other? You get yourself a baby before time and I'll flay you till you scream for mercy. Don't think I'll take your brat in. The pair of you will be out of this house begging for every crust you eat.'

I felt my face flush scarlet.

'I've never gone out to meet . . . I don't even know any—'

'Any what?' She thrust her face right into mine and I had to stop myself recoiling from her rotten breath. 'You were out spying then, weren't you? Creeping about. Following me.'

My hands were clasped so tightly together behind my back that my knuckles cracked.

'Following you where, Granny?' I was looking as innocent as I could. 'Did you go out? I slept all night. I was tired from – from cutting all those peats yesterday.'

She stared at me a moment longer, her red eyes unblinking, then turned away.

'Get down to the beach. The tide's well out by now. Pick up what you can find.'

Scavenging along the soft wet sand, where the weakened edges of the waves rolled like curls of white hair up to my feet, was my favourite part of the day. Usually Granny spoilt it by coming with me, and it was a treat to be alone except for Sheba, who was picking her way along beside me, patting at clumps of seaweed to make the little crabs jump out.

The whale was stinking worse than ever, so I worked as far away from it as I could, walking backwards and forwards along the beach, my eyes down, looking for anything that might be useful. Pieces of driftwood were the most precious things. They made fine burning if they were not big enough for other uses. Sometimes they were tangled and half hidden in hanks of brown seaweed. Lengths of rope and pieces of netting might drift ashore, and even bottles. Once I'd found a whole one, corked and still full of wine.

After half an hour my apron, bunched up in one hand, held a few whelks and a good-sized length of wood, whitened and smoothed by the sea. I was about to make one last sweep before heading reluctantly back to the cottage, when I heard voices and laughter in the distance. I looked up and saw a crowd of people walking down from the upper glen.

The christening party, I thought. *They're on their way to Macbean's.*

The sight of thirty or more people in our narrow lane was so rare, and the times when we saw strangers were so few, that I was desperate to watch them go by. I took off fast, sprinting up the beach, over Blackie's field, and in through the gap in the straggly thorn fence to arrive panting just as the procession came within a bowshot of our gate.

Mr Robertson the minister was walking out in front, striding awkwardly on his long black legs, with Mr Macbean strutting along beside him, quite shiny with pride and satisfaction. Mrs Macbean came next, riding on the horse, with Ebenezer bundled in her arms. The other children trudged along behind, little Robbie dragging on his sister's hand. They must have gone out very early, slipping past our cottage while I was still asleep. It was a long walk to the church at Kingarth, and the children were tired.

Behind them came a crowd of guests, the men in their good coats and tall hats, the women in stuff gowns

36

with brightly coloured best plaids. I knew most of them by sight. They came from the town of Kingarth as well as from the farms around Scalpsie. Mr Macbean was the big man. No one would want to offend him by turning down his invitation. In any case, there would be good food and drink at the farm – sides of beef, and red wine, and wheat bread, and even custards.

I'd wanted to watch the procession without being seen. I'd meant to hide behind the hedge and peer through the gap in it, but I saw, with a lurch of my heart, that Granny was standing outside the gate, half blocking the lane. Her arms were crossed on her chest and the scowl on her face would have turned a whole bucketful of Blackie's milk sour.

I ran to the hedge and crouched down. Now I could only see the back of Granny's head, but the faces of all our neighbours and the good folk of Kingarth were in full view, and on them I read scorn and a kind of glee, as if they were glad to see the humiliation of the old woman they had despised for years. Even Mrs Macbean, who had been so grateful when Ebenezer was born, was looking away as if something had caught her eye up on the hill, while Annie beside her was grinning with open delight.

I felt a rush of anger at the lot of them, all dressed up in the good clothes we had never had, all so pleased with themselves, all salivating over the feast they were about to enjoy, and before I knew it I had stood up and run out to stand beside my grandmother and face them.

Mr Robertson had stopped. He said awkwardly,

'Now, now, Mistress Elspeth. Will you stand aside and let the good people pass?'

Granny took no notice of him. She lifted her arm and pointed her forefinger at the bundle in Mrs Macbean's arms.

'I brought that child into this world.' The finger rose up to jab at Mrs Macbean's face. 'And I saved your life. This is the thanks I get for it. Feast as much as you like. You'll be sorry for it.'

Everyone had stopped now. They were crowding forward to enjoy the spectacle. I tugged at Granny's arm.

'Come away, Granny. Let's go in.'

She shook me off. I could tell from the tension in her that the brewing storm was going to break. Nothing would stop her now.

Mrs Macbean had gone pale. She was clutching Ebenezer closely to her chest. He set up a thin wail, which cut me to the heart. Mr Macbean strode forwards, his full, fleshy face red with anger.

'Are you threatening me, you old witch?' The word 'witch' drew a shocked hiss from the crowd. 'Are you calling the powers of darkness down upon my son?'

People looked at each other uneasily. Parents took hold of their children's hands. Some shuffled backwards.

'The powers of darkness?' Granny laughed mirthlessly. 'I've no need to call to the Devil. He'll come to his own – to you, you tight-fisted, preaching hypocrite!

I wish ill to you, do you hear? Ill to you! Sickness and pain and death!'

'Let her alone, John!' Mrs Macbean called out feebly.

Mr Macbean ignored her.

'Did you hear that, Mr Robertson?' he said over his shoulder. He stepped forward and raised his hand. I thought he was about to strike Granny, but instead he shook his fist in her face. 'As the Lord is my witness, if any harm comes to me or mine, you'll pay for it, Elspeth Wylie. You . . . you . . .'

He spluttered to a stop as Mr Robertson took his elbow.

'Move aside, man. I'll deal with this.' He turned to the crowd and called out, 'Go on up to the farm, all of you. This matter is for me to settle. Mrs Macbean, get that child into the house. Run ahead, little ones. That's right.'

Reluctantly, the crowd moved on, glancing backwards as they went, not wishing to miss a thing. Mr Robertson waited until they had all filed past, then turned back to Granny. 'Be careful what you say, Mistress Elspeth. Those who call upon unearthly powers, who consort with the Evil One—'

Granny interrupted him by spitting on the ground, narrowly missing his boot. Mr Robertson stepped back, nervous as a colt.

'Evil has come to me all my life, Mister Minister,' she snarled. 'I've had no need to go out and seek it.'

I watched Mr Robertson's pale eyes blink rapidly as he tried to think of a response.

'And I'll thank you to remember,' he went on at last, attempting to appear dignified, 'that threats and insults and slanderous talk are within my power to punish. More of this and I'll have you dressed in sackcloth and sitting on the chair of repentance before my pulpit in the sight of the whole congregation.'

He was no match for Granny, however solemn he tried to be, and he knew it. He was like a dog yapping at an enraged bull. It made matters worse for him when he stumbled as he turned away and trod heavily in a puddle, splashing mud up the sides of his boots. I might have laughed if I hadn't heard Granny draw in her breath to deliver a final blast to the crowd's retreating backs. 'The fires of Hell light on you all, do you hear, and firstly on you, John Macbean. May you boil forever in the Devil's cauldron!'

Mr Robertson faltered, almost tripping himself up, then scuttled after the others, who were hurrying away towards Macbean's farm.

'So we're barred from the feasting, Maggie, and all the meat and wine,' Granny said, seeming to notice me for the first time. 'But we'll laugh last, you'll see.'

She seemed almost pleased with herself, but I felt weak, trembling still from the humiliation of it all, anxious for Ebenezer's sake and filled with a new dread I couldn't explain.

For the rest of the day, as I went about my work, I found myself looking about at the familiar sights of home with new eyes. The old cottage with its rotting roof, the kail-yard with its raggedy rows of cabbages, the stream running over the pale stones of its bed, Blackie's field, the beach and the sea and the mountains of Arran beyond, all seemed strange and distant, as if I had parted from them long ago, and had returned only as a visitor for the briefest time.

She'll make Ebenezer die, I know she will, a voice kept repeating inside my head as I drove Blackie back from the field towards the byre when darkness was beginning to fall. *And if he does die, they'll blame her for it. They'll blame you, too.*

I had a strange fancy that I could see hostile faces everywhere I looked: evil, grinning mouths leering up at me from the water in the stream, glittering eyes peeping down from the tree, hands with long white fingers reaching out to clutch me from the hedge. I could hear angry whispers, too, hissing at me in the wind.

You must leave. You must go away, the voice in my head said. *They'll hate you here forever, even if Ebenezer lives.*

The idea of leaving the only home I had ever known frightened me so much that I stopped dead, and Blackie, who had been walking behind me, nearly bumped into me, and gave a reproachful moo. I had never been further from Scalpsie Bay than the towns of Kingarth and Rothesay. The Isle of Bute was my whole world. Beyond it were strange realms peopled by fearsome creatures, the monsters and giants and goblins that filled Tam's stories.

I pushed the thought aside and walked on. Where

could I go, if I left the cottage at Scalpsie Bay? Who would take me in? I had no relatives on the Isle. My father had come from a place called Kilmacolm, over on the mainland. A brother of his, my Uncle Blair, lived there still, as far as I knew – on a farm called Ladymuir.

I had sometimes dreamed of being spirited away from Granny to live with my Uncle Blair. I had a picture of him in my head that was as real as the black bulk of the cow plodding along beside me. My uncle would be a big man like my father, with a deep voice, slow in speech. He wouldn't get drunk or shout at people. He wouldn't pinch and slap children. He wouldn't go about with dirty clothes half hanging off him. He would be orderly and respectable and liked by everyone. His family would eat well and often, and they would have fresh linen and a new, clean plaid to wear when the old one fell into holes. And Uncle Blair would have a wife. She would be a sweet-faced woman with a soft voice, like – but here my imagination always failed me.

My best memory of my father was of him swinging me up in his arms when I was a little girl. He would do it every time he came home from a trip. I'd scream with fear and joy and clutch at the silver buckle he always wore on his belt. It was his drover's buckle, which had gone with him wherever he'd roamed with the cattle. It had been his surety, he said, his treasure, something he could sell if trouble came to him.

The buckle was mine now. It had been taken from my father's body before they buried him, and given to me. I kept it tucked away behind the salt box on the shelf, and often I'd reach up and touch it, as if it was a good-luck charm.

Trouble was coming to me, I was certain of it. And the buckle would be my surety, as it had been my father's.

I hurried over the last bit of field, tugging Blackie's halter to make her walk faster, and as soon as she was safe in her stall I went into the cottage and pulled out the salt box, wanting to hold the buckle and feel its reassuring metal in my palm.

The shelf was bare. The buckle had gone.

I felt along the shelf, sure that I would find it. But I didn't.

Granny's moved it, I thought. *She must have put it somewhere safer.*

Then an awful suspicion came to me. What if Granny had taken the buckle and sold it? What if it was my buckle which had paid for the food and drink for the riotous night before?

I dropped the idea at once. Granny was hard, she was always angry and often cruel, but she was never underhand. A strain of honesty ran through her like a thread of gold through a dirty cloth. She might rant and curse and say the harshest things, she might strike out with her fists and send me out to do the hardest work, but she could never lie and she would never steal.

I stood there, frowning, as I tried to remember when I'd last seen the buckle. It had been only the previous morning. The salt box had been moved a little way along the shelf to make room for one of Tam's black bottles, and the silver of the buckle had gleamed out at me from among the cobwebs.

The cobwebs. Annie. She had talked about the cobwebs. She had been standing beside the shelf when I was feeling for the eggs in the crock. I saw again in my mind's eye how suddenly she'd moved away from the shelf, and how her hand had hidden itself in her shawl. And why had she run so fast out of the cottage, as if she was being chased?

I knew then, as surely as I knew my own name, that Annie was a thief, and that she had stolen my buckle.

'What's all this? Why are you standing there like a gate post when there's work to be done?'

Granny's voice at the door startled me.

'My buckle. It's gone. Annie must have stolen it,' I blurted out.

'That girl of Macbean's? What was she doing here?'

I wished then that I'd held my tongue, because I had to tell Granny that I'd given Annie an egg. To my surprise, she only smiled triumphantly.

'So the girl's a thief? I'm not surprised. We'll have them on that. I'll get you yet, Macbean! My granddaughter's silver buckle – her dowry from her father – stolen by your servant?'

Why did I break out crying? Why did such a feeling of desolation sweep over me? I'd learned a long time ago that tears were no route to Granny's heart. She would be more likely to stop them with a slap than a kiss. I stumbled to the door, careless of the cold December drizzle and the darkness which had now fallen, wanting only to go into Blackie's byre and lay my head down on her rough warm neck and cry there.

But Granny barred my way.

'Aye, girl, you may well cry.' The rough sympathy in her voice was so unexpected that I was shocked to silence. 'The world's a cruel place, but there's no need to burden the poor dumb cow with your troubles. Sit down by me.'

She set her three-legged stool by the fire, sat down and drew her skirts up over her knees so that she could warm her legs. I fetched my stool and sat down too.

'They'll be going past on tiptoe soon on their way home from Macbean's, stuffed full of the meat and wine that by rights we should have enjoyed too. But we're to take no notice of them. I've had my say.' She laughed, the sound rasping in her throat. 'I've given them something to think about. Did you see them run up the lane, the dafties? Each one as terrified as a hare when she smells the fox. As for that fool of a prating minister . . .'

She lapsed into silence, staring into the fire, and her face was full of a fierce joy as she relived her triumph.

'But I've something to say to you, Maggie.'

She pointed up to the whisky bottle on the shelf. I fetched it down for her, glad to see that it was nearly empty. She took a long pull at it, shook it to check that nothing was left, and set it down regretfully.

'Crying on a cow's neck is no way to fight your battles. You've got to take the war to the enemy. Make them fear you. If Macbean hadn't been afraid of me, he would have got me out of this cottage long ago. Just because you're a girl, and you'll be alone in the world when I'm gone, you're not without power.'

Her eyes, reddened with peat smoke and whisky, stared into mine. A chill hand closed round my heart.

'Granny, you wouldn't – not Ebenezer! You wouldn't hurt—'

Her heavy brows snapped together, then she threw her head back and laughed.

'Hurt that miserable little scrap? He'll need no help from me to find his way out of the world. Maggie, what are you thinking? That those precious fools are right? That I'm a witch? The Devil's servant? With the power of life and death?'

It was what I had been fearing, in my heart of hearts.

'No,' I lied, 'but when you said, out there in the lane, that evil had come to you all your life—'

'And so it has. I was a farmer's daughter, from Ettrick. Two good plaid cloths I had and a plate of meat once a week, summer and winter. Sickness took my parents. Your grandfather brought me here and fished the herring from Scalpsie Bay. Much good did he do me, for the sea took him as it took your father. He left me with this miserable cottage and no more money than a pauper.'

'But you had my mother.'

'Mary. Yes.'

She seldom spoke of my mother, except when she wanted to compare me unfavourably with her. I held my breath, willing her to go on. She only heaved a sigh.

'Your father came and took her. She died. He died.

46

And here we are, you and me. Evil came to me, you see? All my life. Sorrow and death and evil. One after another.'

I'm not an evil, I thought rebelliously.

She read my mind, as she often seemed to do, and jabbed a dirty finger towards me.

'You, Maggie, are no evil, but the hope of my life. And I wish good on you. Only good. But you're weak. If they harm you and insult you, you cry and run away. You must turn. Show them you're not afraid. You must be angry, Maggie.'

Much good anger does you, I thought. *Everyone fears and hates you. Even I'm scared of you, most of the time.*

Aloud I said, 'So you think I should go up to Macbean's and shout at them all and make Annie give me back my buckle?'

She gave me a shrewd look.

'Is that a dig at me? I suppose I've earned it. And it's what I would do, right now, if there'd been more in this whisky bottle to give me the courage. But we'll bide our time on the buckle. The moment for it will come. We'll get our own back on them all. Fear's a great weapon, Maggie, and when you're poor and alone it's the only one you have.'

Chapter Five

Ebenezer Macbean lived for another six weeks. All that time I watched the comings and goings from the Macbean farm with dread, but as the weeks passed and nothing happened, I began to feel hopeful that Granny had been wrong, and that he would live after all.

Granny and I were out in the kail-yard, binding sticks into the hedge to stop Blackie from breaking through. It was a wintry February day, the sky as grey as the heaving sea. Granny looked up to watch a skein of geese fly overhead.

'*Wild geese, wild geese, going to the hill,*' she muttered.

The weather it will spill, I finished automatically in my head.

I looked in the direction they were flying, as I always did, to see if there were rainclouds in the sky, and caught sight of a woman, her head uncovered, her hair flying wild, running down the lane towards us. Granny had seen her too.

'Here she comes, with trouble on her, but I won't pity her, for she'll bring that trouble to us, you'll see.'

Jeanie Macbean's rage and grief were almost choking her as she reached our gate. She clung to it, her hand to her side, trying to get her breath.

'You wicked – you vile – murderous – *witch*!' she gasped. 'You killed him. You killed my Ebenezer!'

'Now, Jeanie,' Granny said, with unusual mildness. 'You know that isn't true. I would never harm a child. Come inside. Sit down for a while.'

'I – wouldn't cross – your threshold – to save my life!' panted Mrs Macbean. 'Why, Elspeth? Why did you do it? It was because of the christening, John said, because you weren't invited. I wanted you to come! I told him! He said you weren't to be asked, because of the respectable folk of Kingarth. But to kill the wee man just for that! To take his life!'

She began to sob, unable to go on, hitting at the gate with her fists.

'Jeanie,' Granny said, sounding almost pleading, 'will you listen to me? It was I who brought that child into the world. Why would I harm him? I tried to charm away the evil from him at your hearth, but your man wouldn't let me. There was a sickness on him from the start – the blue on his lips and in his face. I've seen it before. I knew what it meant. I didn't say it to threaten you, but to warn you, Jeanie. That was all.'

It was the nearest thing to an apology that I'd ever heard Granny make, and I breathed a sigh of relief, sure that it would convince Mrs Macbean. She wanted to believe Granny, I could see it in her face, but then came a man's shout from up the lane. Mr Macbean was running towards us, his face dark with rage.

'Get away from her, Jeanie! Don't go near her! The witch'll kill you too!'

49

I was learning more about Granny that day than I'd ever learned in my whole life, and now I saw, for the first time ever, that she was afraid. It set up an answering fear in me, turning my insides to water.

Say something soft, I silently urged her. *Say you're sorry that Ebenezer died. Tell him what you told her. Tell him you didn't harm him.*

But Granny took a deep breath, and scowled. She would follow her own rule, I could see, and try to make her enemies fear her.

The look she turned on Macbean was as hard as a blow and cold enough to freeze the man's liver. He shuddered under her stare, turned pale and put his arm round his wife's waist.

'Come home, Jeanie, before she puts the evil eye on you too. She's of the Devil, and it's the minister who'll deal with her.'

'You see, Maggie?' Granny said triumphantly as we watched Mr Macbean support his wife's tottering steps up the hill. 'I made them fear us. Now they'll leave us alone.'

But they won't, I thought. *They won't.*

Chapter Six

They came for us in May, when the late primroses were still making yellow splashes on the banks. The first I knew of the trouble to come was the sight of Tam hurrying down the lane on his stick-like legs, his tattered coat flapping around him.

'Where's Elspeth?' he gasped, trying to catch his breath.

'Here she comes now.' I nodded towards the distant figure of Granny, who was walking back from the shore, carrying the finds of the morning bunched up in her apron. 'Why? What's the matter?'

Tam grasped my arm.

'Get away, Maidie! Run! Now!'

I gaped at him.

'Run? Why?'

'They're on their way here! To arrest her!'

My hand flew to my mouth.

'Arrest who? For what?'

'Elspeth!' He was dancing in an agony of impatience from one foot to the other. 'For being a witch!'

'Granny's not a witch! You know that! Everyone knows it. All this fuss is coming from Macbean because he wants our cottage. We'll explain and they'll let her go.'

'No! You don't understand! Rothesay's in a panic.

The talk's all of witches and the Devil and wildness. I'm telling you, they're looking for women to burn! There's no help for Elspeth. And you'll be next. You will, I know it.'

I clutched at the doorpost.

'Tam! What am I going to do?'

'Do? I'm telling you! Run!' His almost hairless brows rose till they disappeared beneath his bonnet. 'You must leave here. Now! This minute!'

'I – I can't! Granny—'

'Maidie, your granny's a dead woman, or as good as. They'll never let her go. They've been wanting this for a long time. There'll be a hanging at the Gallowgate, and a burning afterwards, and they'll do the same to you if you give them the chance.'

'Me? They'd burn me? But I'm not a witch!'

'I know that! You're wasting time!' He snatched off his bonnet in exasperation, then clapped it back on to his head. At any other moment I'd have laughed at the way he looked, with it dangling down over one eye. 'I knew this would happen! How often have I said to her, "Don't speak so sharp to everyone. Don't give those preachers and praters and black-beetle Presbyterians the chance!" But she would never listen, and now she's done for.'

I was slowly catching up with what he was saying.

'They're going to hang Granny? And burn her?'

'Yes. Yes! I told you! And you too! Maidie, you must get off the island.'

'Where to? Where can I go?'

He looked behind me into the cottage, as though he would find the answer written on the cottage wall.

'I don't know. Come with me. We'll be vagabonds together.'

'I can't leave Blackie. And there's Sheba.'

'The cat'll fend for herself. We'll get word to the farmer at Ambrismore. He'll take the cow. Come on now. They'll be here any minute!'

I backed away from him.

'Tam, I can't. How can I just run away and leave Granny to fight this on her own? Everyone knows I'm not a witch. They wouldn't hurt me.'

I was sure I was right. Granny, I could see, might be in danger, but I couldn't imagine how anyone could accuse me. I knew, too, in my heart of hearts, that I would be a fool to trust myself to Tam. He would run away and leave me at the first sign of danger.

And I was right about that, because a moment later, when figures appeared on the crest of the hill above, and Tam saw them hurrying down the track towards us, he turned and sprinted up the narrow path past Loch Quien to disappear among the trees.

My knees had turned to water at the sight of the approaching crowd. My confidence vanished and I wished I'd run when I'd had the chance. It was too late now.

Granny arrived up from the shore. She hadn't noticed the crowd coming ever closer down the path. She pushed past me into the cottage, tipped out the contents of her apron on to the table, and dusted the sand off her hands. I found my voice at last.

'Granny! Tam was here! He said – they're – it's—' was all I could say.

'What the matter with you?' She scowled at me. 'You've gone white. You're not falling into another fit, are you?'

She heard the sound of voices then and came back to the cottage door, shading her eyes to look up the road.

'They'll be on the way to Macbean's for something or other,' she said, but I heard uncertainty in her voice.

'No, Granny! They're coming here! To arrest you – to arrest us! Tam said.'

They were close now. I could see Mr Robertson in front, carrying a Bible, and Mr Macbean beside him, slapping at his thigh eagerly with his riding whip. But what scared me most was the sight of two soldiers, sheriff's men from Rothesay, and a raggle-taggle crowd of loons and loafers, who had thought it worth the five-mile walk to see an old woman dragged from her home.

We could do nothing but wait, and watch them come.

They crowded into our little room, filling it entirely. I saw them look round avidly, though goodness knows what they expected to see – instruments of some kind to make magic, herbs drying for potions – the Devil himself, perhaps, with his fiery eyes.

'Mistress Elspeth,' Mr Robertson said, with the utmost solemnity, 'you are to come with us to Rothesay, to answer charges of malefice, casting spells and using witchcraft, and you will be tried by a court assembled for the purpose.'

Granny swayed, and I was afraid she would fall. I think she saw at that moment that the greatest battle of her life was about to begin.

Mr Robertson paused and cast a sideways look at Mr Macbean.

'If you are free of guilt, as you may well be, you have nothing to fear. The court will find out the truth.'

'And if you take me away,' said Granny, recovering herself at once, 'who is to care for my granddaughter? And my cow?'

'Surely Maggie's old enough to look after herself?' Mr Robertson looked at me, his face suddenly anxious. 'You have turned sixteen, Maggie, have you not?'

'And I'll make sure that the cow and the land are properly cared for,' Mr Macbean broke in, too eagerly. 'Leave that to me.'

'Now there's a surprise!' one of the hangers-on called out from by the door. 'It's not your place yet, Macbean!'

Most of them laughed, but Mr Macbean scowled.

I was seized with panic.

'You can't take her! She's done nothing! She never hurt Ebenezer, or anyone else. Leave her alone! Take your hands off her!'

One of the soldiers had already grasped Granny by the arms and I could see that he was going to drag her out of the cottage. I threw myself at him, trying to beat him away.

'Ouch! Little viper,' he panted. 'Shouldn't we arrest

her too, Mr Robertson? She'll have taken the evil from the old woman.'

'Go on then! Why don't you?' I yelled at him, suddenly reckless with anger.

'Stop that, Maggie!'

Granny put all the fear and anger she was feeling into the command. I automatically obeyed her.

'Let me go!' she said, turning such a glare on the soldier holding her that he dropped her arm and stepped back in a hurry, knocking her stool over in his panic.

'I'll come with you, Mr Robertson. You don't have to use violence on me.' She wiped the touch of the man off her, and in spite of her dirty, ragged dress and the roughness of her uncombed hair, she looked as magnificent as a queen conferring a favour.

The crowd began to back out of the cottage, thinking that there was no more to be seen inside. I could see Mr Macbean looking round, assessing the place. He seemed disappointed at the sight of the daylight coming through the holes in the roof, and the beams so powdery with rot that they barely held it up.

'That's right,' Granny spat at him. 'Take a good look. You've wanted it long enough. But you'll not enjoy it, John Macbean. I'll see to that.'

Before anyone could stop her, she had pushed him aside and was kneeling down on the hearthstone.

'All the witchcraft I ever had, I leave it on this hearth,' she intoned, staring boldly up at him. 'If I never return, the vile toad and the cold snail will be the only creatures here. And if anyone takes this place from me

56

and my granddaughter, he will be cursed, and his cattle will die, and his children—'

'Granny, stop it!' I cried, the picture of little Robbie coming suddenly to me. 'Don't say those things!'

Scarlet with rage, Mr Macbean lifted his hand to strike her, but Mr Robertson caught it and pulled it down.

'Out of her own mouth she has condemned herself,' he said, shaking his head.

Another man rushed in and gave her a violent blow across the face, before Mr Robertson could stop him.

'That's for last summer, witch!' he roared. 'It's for the storm you called up that flattened my crops and left us with nothing for the winter. There's never natural hail in June. It was a Devil's strike. You brought it on us.'

'That storm swept my brother's boat away – four men drowned and all the fishing gear was lost!' burst out another man, elbowing the first aside.

Then came a voice that I knew too well.

'I saw her making magic with my own eyes,' Annie was squealing excitedly. 'She said something foreign, and the ashes from her hearth flew up the cauldron chain and then – and then there was a noise.'

'What sort of noise?' someone said, above the general intake of breath.

'A – a horrible sort of a voice,' said Annie.

It was too much. I couldn't bear to listen any longer.

'She's a liar!' I shouted, startling everyone. 'Don't listen to her! She's a liar and a thief! She stole my father's silver buckle!'

57

Annie went pale and stepped back, but she recovered almost at once.

'Maggie's a witch too!' she shrieked. 'She learned it all from the old one. There was a witches' sabbath at Ambrisbeg. *She* was there. I—'

Mr Macbean turned on her.

'Hold your tongue,' he said furiously. 'This is not the time or the place. If you've something to say you'll be called as a witness. Get back to Scalpsie and your mistress.'

Annie stared back at him with a boldness that surprised me, and made no move to go. Mr Macbean hesitated, but Mr Robertson said worriedly, 'If this young person has evidence of a material nature she must come with us and give it before the court. A witches' sabbath! I had no inkling that things had gone this far. The matter must be investigated. Superstition and hearsay must be separated from fact. I will remind you all –' he nodded gravely at the crowd which was swelling all the time as people from Rothesay ran up the hill to watch and listen – 'that the only grounds for the conviction of witchcraft is consorting with the Evil One. I must warn you against heeding mere gossip and slander.'

Annie was nodding earnestly at the minister's words, an expression of the most sickly humility on her face.

'Oh, Mr Robertson,' she said sweetly. 'I wouldn't slander anyone, but that girl is tainted with evil like her grandmother, and there are things – I can testify—'

'Stop it, Annie,' interrupted Mr Macbean. 'Don't

bother the minister now.' He turned to Mr Robertson. 'But the girl is right. The witch's granddaughter should be examined too. We can lock them up together tonight and let them both answer to the court in the morning.'

'Let them burn together! Let them rot in hell together!' shouted the man whose brother had drowned.

I saw too late what a fool I'd been, and as one of the sheriff's men caught hold of my arms, gripping them with painful strength, I was flooded with such fear that I thought I would faint. The man shoved me towards Granny, who staggered under the impact so that we had to clutch each other to save ourselves from falling into the fire.

'Look at them, bound with the Devil's pact!' some-one shouted, while others jeered and some began to jostle us and hit out with their fists. The sheriff's men, at a command from Mr Robertson, put a stop to that, or I really believe that we would have been murdered on the spot.

'Little fool!' Granny hissed in my ear. 'Why didn't you hold your tongue? Now you're in trouble. Don't let them see you're afraid. Do you want them to tear you to pieces?'

She was led out first, and as she emerged into the bright light outside the cottage, a kind of howl went up, the sound that dogs make when they scent their prey. I sensed a movement behind me, and looking round saw an old woman scooping oatmeal from our barrel into the linen bag lying on the table.

The insolence of such a barefaced theft enraged me. I opened my mouth to shout at her, but she frowned at me to be quiet and thrust the bag into my hands.

'Hide it quick, under your apron,' she said. 'You'll be needing this. They'll not feed you in the prison.'

This small act of kindness shook me almost more than the terror and anger of the past half-hour. Tears started into my eyes.

'Th-thank you,' I stammered.

Her face hardened.

'Don't thank me. Tell your grandmother what I've done. She'll curse everyone that's come here. Tell her Christian Kirkwood did this, and she'll keep me out of it.'

I had no time to reply. They were coming in for me. I snatched up my plaid and wrapped it round my head and I let them take me.

And so we left the old cottage, with all the tattle-mongers and wonderseekers of the island jeering and capering around us, and set off up the long road to Rothesay. I stuck close to Granny's side. She had tossed her hair back and the weal on her face where she'd been hit showed up as a scarlet slash. She marched with her usual deliberate stride, planting her feet down one after the other with force, as if she was stamping on the earth to punish it. Her mouth was set tight, and her eyes gave nothing away.

The people following us had fallen into a sullen silence, whispering to each other, passing poison back and forth between themselves.

All around us lay the quiet fields of Bute, green and lush, speckled with gold and blue flowers, and the sea curling in quietly on to the beach.

Then I saw a lapwing strutting through grass, and it began to cry, as it always did, '*Bewitched! Bewitched!*'

'Oh hold your noise, you dratted bird,' I hissed at it. 'There's no bewitching here!'

Chapter Seven

There were only twenty or thirty houses in Rothesay, clustered along the stream above the blackened, ruined walls of the castle, and there can't have been more than a hundred or so people baying like hounds around us, although it seemed like a vast multitude. The door of the grim little tollbooth was unlocked at last and we were bundled up the steep steps to the iron-bound door. I turned for a last fearful look at the faces of the people below us, grinning with hatred, before the door clanged shut. I saw Annie standing on the edge of the crowd, deep in conversation with Mr Macbean. There was something about the way she stood too close to him – looking up into his eyes with her head on one side – that seemed odd to me. But just as my glance fell on them he bent his head and said something with a fierce look. She stepped back, her mouth open in shocked surprise. She reached forward and caught his sleeve but he shook her off and turned to go. I saw nothing after that because the door had slammed shut. Granny and I were alone in the cold stone room.

Though it was already May, it was a bitter night, with a near frost. The small barred window was set high in the wall, and the shutter was hooked back on the outside, where we couldn't reach to close it. The wind blasting through the open space set my teeth chattering. Our bellies were empty too. No food was brought to us, and without water I couldn't even stir up a cold porridge with my oatmeal.

'You're a fool,' Granny said. 'Why didn't you run when you saw them coming? You could have saved yourself.'

'They'd have come after me. Where could I have run to?' I spoke sharply, but I don't think she heard me. She was listening to the din outside, the crowd in an ugly mood, whistling and calling, and the gaoler, Master Donald Brown the locksmith, trying to keep them at bay.

'There's sixpence for you, Donnie my man,' someone yelled out, 'if you'll open the door and give us a peep at the witches.'

'Get away to your houses and stop bothering us,' Mr Brown growled in reply. 'You'll get your fill of their evil faces in the morning.'

'What does he mean, in the morning? Where? What are they going to do with us?' I whispered to Granny.

'You think anyone's told me?' She gave a bitter laugh. 'Listen to them, the dregs of the island. If my father could see this day . . .'

She turned away and began a kind of mumbling, her jaw working. She'd been doing it often recently, and I didn't like it. She looked old, and a little mad, talking to herself like that.

We heard the outer door creak open then clang shut.

The bolt shot across and there was a cough which told us that Mr Brown had withdrawn to his little sanctum outside our cell. The noise from outside slowly died away.

'For the love of Christ, Donnie Brown,' Granny suddenly called out, 'will you not give us a blanket to cover us, or a crust of bread and a drink of water?'

Slow footsteps approached the door.

'A blanket you want now? With a swansdown pillow and linen sheets, I suppose? And a supper of roasted venison? My wife's cousin was on that ship that sank in the storm you magicked from the Devil. Get him to feed and warm you. You won't get anything from me.'

'She never called up a storm!' I burst out, banging on the door with my fists.

Granny dragged me away.

'Save your breath. He'll not listen. He's closed his mind against us. You'll only make things worse.'

'Worse? *Worse?* How can things be worse than this?'

'Ha! You really want to know? Just wait, miss, and you'll find out.'

She had been prowling round the cell and now she sank down into the far corner from the door.

'The draught's not so bad here. Settle down, for the Lord's sake. Let me think. There's things, maybe . . .'

Her head fell back against the cold damp stone wall, her eyes rolled up and her lips began to move. I knew she was pulling from her memory spells and enchantments, blessings on us and curses on others, looking to her old knowledge to save us.

It would have been a natural thing for two people, facing a long night in a cold place, to sit close together and gain a little human comfort from each other's bodily warmth, but Granny had repelled my childish affection so often in the past that I stood hesitating. At last she snapped out, 'Oh stop dithering, Maggie, and sit here beside me. Wind your plaid round both our shoulders, and I'll lay mine across our knees. Be quiet and don't fiddle about. Go to sleep. Fetch the Lord Christ back again, why don't you? The Second Coming's about all that'll save us now.'

Her sarcasm sounded like blasphemy to me, and I shivered with more than the cold.

I must have slept through a little of that long, weary night, in spite of the chill of the hard stone and the gale blowing through the open window – enough, anyway, to dream. Wild nightmares pursued me, and I woke several times with a start of horror, though the dreams fled before I could recall them.

Dawn came at last. The rising sun sent a little warmth into us. It sent no breakfast, though. There had been nowhere, not even a bucket, in which to relieve ourselves, and the place stank already.

There was a strange absence of noise from outside: no cottage doors opening, no water splashing, no footsteps or greetings as people went off to work.

'What do you expect?' sniffed Granny, when I expressed surprise. 'Today's the Sabbath. They'll all be getting themselves cleaned up to go to the kirk. They'll be spending the day droning out psalms and feeling pleased with themselves and having their holy ears filled with lies about us.'

She had only just stopped speaking when I heard quick footsteps on the outer steps of the tollbooth and someone rapped on the massive iron-bound door.

'Open up, man! You can't still be sleeping!'

'It sounds like Mr Robertson,' I said fearfully.

'Are they ready?' Mr Robertson was saying. 'Have they breakfasted?'

The great door swung open. We heard Donald Brown mutter something inaudible.

'Is that you, Mister Minister?' Granny called out. 'We've not had so much as a crust of bread or a drink of water since you had us put away. So much for your Christian charity.'

The bolts of our cell rasped back and Mr Robertson, as clean and pink as ever, appeared. He was frowning and seemed about to say something severe in answer to Granny's impertinence, but then his nose wrinkled at the smell and he looked with surprise at the window.

'How did you open the shutter?'

'We did not. The man never closed it,' Granny informed him stiffly. 'The cold wind had nothing to check it.'

Mr Robertson's long, thin frame twisted round and he disappeared out of the cell.

'Common decency . . .' we heard him say, '. . . will not countenance undue . . . some bread at least . . .'

We heard his quick retreat and a few moments later

Mr Brown appeared. He planted a loaf of bread and a pitcher of water just inside the door, and kicked a wooden bucket viciously towards Granny before slamming the door shut again.

I was so hungry and thirsty that I could have eaten three times the amount of bread and drunk the whole pitcher of water, but Granny made me keep some of it back.

'Wash yourself,' she commanded. 'No, not like that. I'll do it.'

She dipped the corner of my plaid in the last of the water and scrubbed painfully at my face.

'Now do mine.'

'What for?' I asked, when I'd done my best on her wrinkled red-veined cheeks. I was puzzled. She'd never made me wash before.

'They'll be taking us out today, I know it,' Granny said. 'We won't give them extra reasons for despising us. Here. Take off your cap.'

I undid the strings that tied my little white cap under my chin and let her run her sharp nails through my hair by way of a comb, trying not to cry out as she tugged painfully at the knots.

Before I had finished tying the strings again, and had the chance to do something to tame Granny's wild hair, Mr Robertson's light footsteps were running back up the tollbooth steps.

'Bring them out, Donald. The sheriff's men will keep the crowd off them. I want them in the kirk before the people start arriving.'

You can be beaten and starved and locked up in a cold damp cell, but worse than any of these things is to be shamed in public, in front of people who know you. That's what they did to Granny and me on that Sabbath morning in Rothesay.

We were hurried the short distance up the hill to the church of St Mary, the Virgin mother of Jesus. The Virgin was a kindly woman, so Tam had always told me. I believe he held to her more than to the Lord Jesus, but that was papist thinking, I knew, and so it must be sinful. Anyway, there was no help for Granny and me from the Virgin Mary, nor from anyone else.

The kirk was new, the ground all around it still strewn with the masons' offcuts, and the sheriff's man was holding me so tightly against himself I couldn't look down to see where I was going. I stubbed my toe painfully and cried out, and he took the excuse to hold me closer. He was a dirty-minded man.

Granny was in front of me. By the time I came up to her they had already ripped off her outer dress so that she was standing shivering in her shift. They had the dress of sackcloth ready, a horrible brown shapeless thing, stained with the filthy things people had thrown at the last person they had shamed.

I couldn't help struggling and crying out when it was my turn, but a look from Granny stopped me. It was nearly eight o'clock, time for the service to begin. The church bell was jangling in the steeple and people were hurrying up the hill – more eager to see us, I'm sure, than to hear Mr Robertson's sermon.

There was nothing in their faces but hatred and cruelty and malice as we stood there at the church door, tied to the post, and the good people of Rothesay jeered and leered at us, jostling each other to get a good look.

The first gobbet of spit hit me on the shoulder. The second caught me on the cheek. Someone shouted, 'Devil's whore! You lay with him, didn't you? Enjoyed it, too!'

A hand plucked at my sackcloth robe, then another.

Mr Robertson came hurrying out of the kirk.

'Get them inside,' he said sharply to the sheriff's men. 'They shouldn't be tied up here but sitting before the pulpit on the stools of repentance.'

He even took a kerchief from his pocket and handed it to me once my hands were free.

'Wipe your face, Maggie. Compose yourself. You are entering the House of the Lord. Pray for forgiveness. The Lord is gracious and merciful. Cast yourself upon Him. If you have not consorted with Satan you have nothing to fear.'

I heard Granny mutter, 'Hypocrite,' but I didn't think it was that simple. I couldn't understand Mr Robertson. He'd come with the others to arrest us, but he seemed to be trying to protect us too.

The repentance stools were right at the front of the church, under the pulpit. We were shoved down on to them and had to sit there facing the congregation, who could stare at us as much as they pleased throughout the four long hours of the service. I knew what they were thinking. I'd not been to our parish church at Kingarth more than a few times a year, but once or twice I'd seen some poor soul sitting on the repentance stool, in the hideous sackcloth robe, and I'd spent the entire service enjoying my feelings of righteous indignation, despising the poor woman who was being punished for slander, or the red-faced man who'd been riotous and drunk.

There was a great rustling and creaking of stiff Sunday boots and a clatter of wood on stone as the people opened their folding stools and set them down on the flagstones, then settled themselves, ready to work their way through the psalms and prayers, waiting eagerly for the sermon.

Most of them had never heard Mr Robertson preach before. The minister of Rothesay, Mr Stewart, who was away on the mainland, was a hot preacher. He loved to denounce sinners and proclaim humiliating punishments. Mr Robertson was standing in for him. I could see in the faces in front of me how curious the congregation was, and how they were looking forward to some thunderous ranting from the pulpit. It was Granny and me they hoped to see condemned. They were longing for it.

It was cold in the church, and the sackcloth robes were thin, but I was so nervous that sweat trickled down my back.

All too soon, Mr Robertson mounted the steps to the pulpit, high above our heads. The congregation had been singing the psalm lustily, and now they coughed to clear their throats, gazing up at him.

'I have been commanded by the presbytery,' began Mr Robertson in a solemn voice, 'to preach to you today on the subject of witchcraft. My text –' he ran a bony finger down the page of the Bible open in front of him – 'comes from the Book of Deuteronomy, chapter eighteen.' He found the place, cleared his throat, looked up and paused, making sure that all eyes were fixed on him.

'*There shall not be found any among you,*' he read, '*that shall use divination, or is an enchanter, or a witch.*'

A satisfied hiss went from row to row, and though I didn't dare look up, I knew that heads were nodding. '*Or is a charmer, or a consulter of familiar spirits.*'

The silence that followed was uneasy and glancing up at the faces for a moment I saw that some were no longer meeting the minister's searching eyes.

'*All that do these things,*' he went on, stabbing at the book with his finger, '*are an abomination unto the Lord, and the Lord thy God doth drive them out before thee.*'

He closed the Bible and looked up.

'Now,' he went on, dropping his reading voice and speaking more naturally, 'there are those among you who have accused Elspeth Wylie and Maggie Blair of using vile sorcery and witchcraft. But I am punishing them today for the true faults that are proven against them: that they have failed to keep the Sabbath, that they have not come to church at the set times, and that, in the case of Elspeth Wylie, she has used slanderous

71

language and stirred up anger among her neighbours. It is for these sins that they sit before you today in a state of repentance, and if they will confess their sins before the Lord and their neighbours, they will be forgiven in the sight of man and the sight of God. As for the other charge, they will be brought tomorrow morning before a proper court assembled for the purpose, and until that judgement has been given, these women are not to be molested. Let everything be done decently, and in order.'

The thought of standing before a court made me shudder, but I was comforted by Mr Robertson's words. He seemed determined that we should be treated fairly, and at the very least, protected from the crowd. I twisted my head round and stared up at him gratefully. Granny, I could tell, was just as surprised. She was blinking rapidly and a grim little smile creased her cheeks.

'At this point, I shall announce the following punishments,' Mr Robertson went on, pulling a sheet of paper from his pocket. 'Alison Garlie has been found guilty of drunkenness and accusing her neighbour of eating the lice off her head . . .' He paused for the laughter to die down. 'She is to stand on the pillar for the next four Sundays. Andrew MacLoy was seen ploughing his field on the Sabbath Day. He has admitted his fault and will be fined forty shillings. Robert . . .'

A murmur had begun as he had started on his weekly list of dull misdemeanours, and it was growing louder. There was a crash at the back of the church. Mr

72

Macbean had sprung to his feet, knocking over his stool.

'Exodus, chapter twenty-two, verse eighteen,' he roared, shaking his fist at the minister. *'Thou shalt not suffer a witch to live.* Do your duty, Mr Robertson, and clear these evil women out from among us.'

To interrupt the minister while he spoke from the pulpit was such a rare and shocking thing that a shudder of delicious horror swept the congregation. They had all turned to stare at Mr Macbean, but now their heads swivelled round again to see what the minister would do.

'To clear out evil,' Mr Robertson said, fixing Mr Macbean with such a stare that the man fumbled for his stool, righted it and sat down again. 'Yes, indeed. I have another text to preach to you today.'

He laid his palm down on his Bible, quoting from memory: 'From the twenty-third chapter of the Gospel of Matthew: *Woe unto you, hypocrites! For you devour widows' houses, and for a pretence make long prayer.'*

An inarticulate objection came from the back of the church but Mr Robertson ignored it.

'I have heard,' he said, his pink face flushed, 'of heathenish devices and old superstitions practised by many on this island. Oatcakes and milk left outside for the fairies and other such uncanny beings. Charms being told over sick cattle. Wicked and fruitless attempts to cure sickness by the use of herbs and ointments. Spells being cast to find a missing shilling or suchlike. Things no Christian soul should tamper with.'

73

'He's got them there,' Granny muttered beside me. 'The old ways are still alive. The things I could tell!'

'Leviticus, chapter nineteen,' Mr Robertson went on. '*Ye shall not use enchantment*! If these two women are found to be guilty of such sins, of which I have some doubts, they will of course be punished. But I say to you, all of you, look first into your own hearts and see to your own behaviour. Let him that is without sin cast the first stone!'

I didn't hear the rest of Mr Robertson's sermon. It went on for long enough. The half-hour glass ran out of sand and was turned twice before he'd finished.

Mr Robertson's words had obviously had an effect, because nobody tried to harm us as we were taken back to the tollbooth. Heads were bent and eyes were cast down as the people hurried by. I heard some disappointed mutterings though. Mr Robertson, it was clear, had not come up to Mr Stewart's thrilling standards.

The market cross of Rothesay stands outside the tollbooth, and it was here that everyone gathered to gossip after the service. Mr Robertson's sermon had impressed one man at least. Our gaoler, Donald Brown, looked at us with more doubt than disgust when he opened up the tollbooth to let us in.

'I'm not saying that I think you're innocent, Elspeth Wylie,' he said. 'You're a crabby old hag with a mean tongue in your head and a wicked heart in your chest. But whether you've lain with the Devil or not is not for me to say. The girl looks as frightened as a mouse. I'll not think ill of her till I have to. I'll do as Mr Robertson says and give you the benefit of the doubt till I hear the evidence in the court tomorrow.'

He seemed to have surprised himself with this long speech and added, 'So, I'll let you have a couple of stools to sit on and if you give me a penny I'll bring you some porridge.'

Granny had been listening with her arms crossed on her chest and the usual deep frown scoring her forehead. I longed for her to smile and show some gratitude and meekness, but it was like wishing for a rose to bloom in February.

'And where would I get a penny?' was all she said.

'I've got some oatmeal in my bundle,' I put in. I was smiling for the two of us until my cheeks cracked. 'If I give you a cupful you could get porridge made for us, Mr Brown.'

He took the oatmeal with a grunt, and came back a moment later with two stools. Granny sat down on hers, leaned against the wall and closed her eyes, but I set mine beneath the window and found that if I stood on tiptoe I could see the people below.

There was no sign of Mr Robertson, but Mr Macbean and Annie were standing with the folk of Rothesay clustered round the pair of them, their heads leaning forward as they listened.

After a moment or two, one of them looked up towards the tollbooth and I ducked out of sight. When I looked back again the first drops of a shower of rain were pattering down, and the group was breaking up.

Annie and Mr Macbean were hurrying towards the toll-booth. They stopped to shelter under the eaves, right below our window.

'Now, Annie, if you want to please me you'll speak up and say what you've said before, slowly and clearly,' said Mr Macbean. 'The court will like your evidence. They'll want to hear it. No one will say anything unkind to you.'

'Well, I don't know.'

They were too close below the window for me to see them, but I could hear doubt in Annie's voice.

'There's things I'm not sure of,' she went on. 'I – I might have been mistaken. It's like Mr Robertson said just now. To give false witness is a terrible sin.'

'Your witness isn't false, girl.' Mr Macbean's voice was hardening. 'You heard what you heard and saw what you saw. You couldn't have made up such details, or imagined such wickedness. You have a plain duty, in the sight of God, to—'

'If only I was sure! It seemed – at the time – so – and when I thought about it, it was like a story in my head. But now . . . Ouch!'

She broke off, and as clear as if I'd seen it I knew that Mr Macbean had grasped her arm in a bruising grip.

'You know my hopes for you. For both of us, Annie. You do as I wish, and speak up, and I'll do all I've promised. But if you let me down you'll be on your own. I'll deny it all. You'll get no help from me.'

I heard his footsteps retreat and a moment later I was

looking down on his tall hat as he strode away towards the inn. Below the window Annie was quietly snivelling.

'Annie!' I called out, standing on the stool as tall as I could, though stretch as I might she was still out of sight. 'Annie, it's me! Maggie!'

The crying stopped and I could tell that she was listening.

'Don't say what's not true, Annie. All that about the ashes up the chain, it's lies. You know it is. You'll burn in Hell for lies. I'm not a witch, Annie. You know I'm not. You can keep the buckle if you tell them the truth.'

I stopped, listening hard, my heart beating fast. There was a long silence, and I knew that Annie was biting her fingers.

'I'll not stand here listening to you!' she shouted at last. 'You're wicked! You're evil!' And then she was off, and I watched her running after her loathsome master, as if she was afraid that I would call the Devil down on her, which to be honest I would have done willingly, if I'd had any inkling how.

Chapter Eight

The second night in the tollbooth was bad, but not nearly as bad as the first. For one thing Mr Brown closed the shutter, and although it was cold we were spared the howling gale. He even gave us a blanket, a coarse thing smelling of horses and full of fleas, but it kept out some of the chill. We had porridge in our bellies too. Best of all was the hope that Mr Robertson would soften the feelings against us and make sure that the court judged us fairly.

The knock came on the door when dawn had barely broken. I woke to the sound of the bolts scraping as Mr Brown drew them back. I expected Mr Robertson's light step, but instead of the tap of his leather-soled shoes I heard the clang of iron-tipped boots and spurs ringing on the stone floor. The door swung open and the sheriff's men came in.

'Come on, you idle hag. The court's waiting,' one of them said, hauling Granny to her feet.

We were outside in the square a few moments later, our stomachs empty and our hair dishevelled.

'Where's Mr Robertson?' Granny asked.

One of the men laughed.

'You'll not be seeing him today. Word has come from Paisley. The court's to be held by the elders of Rothesay. Your precious Mr Robertson's been sent back to

Kingarth, where he belongs. The man's soft in the head when it comes to you. They'll get the right verdict here. They'll see that justice is done.'

That's when I knew, in my deepest heart, that there was to be no justice for Granny and me, and that we had been condemned even before a word was spoken in the court. My knees felt like water and my tongue stuck to the roof of my mouth. It was all I could do to walk the short distance to the Session House without falling to the ground.

Oh, they were a dour and solemn lot, those elders, sitting around a long table, their beefy hands laid out on the boards. They had been talking quietly, grey heads bent close to each other, but they fell into a chilling silence as we came in. I was so afraid that I could barely stand for shaking. Even so, I noticed that one or two of them looked at us with more doubt than disgust, and I took from that a little spark of courage, hoping that a few of their minds had still to be made up.

The grand chair at the head of the table was empty. The man beside it stood up and cleared his throat.

'Sir James Stewart, the Sheriff, is absent on state duty, and I am empowered to open this court and to pass judgement,' he pronounced. 'A very serious charge has been brought against these women. They are said to be witches, users of malefice or witchcraft, and consorters with the Evil One.' He looked down at the paper in front of him. 'It is claimed that they have brought about, through their curses, the death of the boy

Ebenezer Macbean, that they raised a storm which destroyed crops and sank a fishing boat, with the loss of four lives, and that . . .' He picked the paper up, read the words slowly, shook his head with disgust and went on, 'that they took part in a witches' sabbath where they did lewdly give themselves in lust to the Devil and did mate with him.'

I glanced sideways at Granny. The sinews of her neck were taut, standing out like strings, and her jaws were clamped together. I knew her temper was rising and that the result would be disastrous. I tried to take her hand but she shook me off. She was staring boldly at our accuser.

'I know you, Duncan Lamont.' Her voice was loaded with contempt. 'You're in the pocket of that greedy miser John Macbean. He's filled your head with his lies. He wants my cottage and my field – that's what this is all about. What did he promise you to bring this false charge against us?'

'Granny, stop it! Granny, don't!' I whispered, clutching at her sleeve. It was too late. A flush was rising in Mr Lamont's cheeks.

'Hold your tongue, Elspeth Wylie,' he said furiously. He turned to the clerk who was scratching away with his quill on a long roll of paper beside him. 'Note down what the accused has said. Add the charge of slander to her other crimes. Now let the first witness come forward.'

It was then that I saw, sitting in shadow under the window, our accusers. Mr Macbean was there of course, leaning forward, his elbows on his knees. He was turning his broad-brimmed hat round and round in his hands. Annie was beside him, her eyes darting nervously round the court. But what made my heart sink even further was the sight of Mr McKirdy from Ambrisbeg, and Mr Wilson from Ambrismore, and four or five others from Scalpsie, who had been shouted at and cursed by Granny many times in the past. They were staring at her with cold triumph in their eyes.

'John Macbean, the first witness,' called Mr Lamont.

Mr Macbean stepped forward to the table, almost tripping over in his eagerness.

'The witch Elspeth Wylie laid a sickness on my son the night that he was born by placing him in a basket and swinging him round the hearth,' he began. He was staring at a point in the wall behind Mr Lamont's head and spoke as if he was reciting a text he'd learned. 'She cursed the child at his christening in the hearing of many people present.' I saw the row of witnesses nodding in agreement. 'Ebenezer died from her cursing.'

I was reliving that terrible morning, remembering how Granny's anger had seared the very air around her, how Mrs Macbean had cowered on the horse over the baby in her arms, and how the party of guests had stared at Granny with horror in their eyes. Without meaning to, I stepped away from Granny. I had feared her then too. I had thought she meant to harm Ebenezer.

The witnesses were called one by one. Granny had put a spell on a cow and stopped its milk, they said. She had laid an enchantment on a field so that nothing would grow in it. She had brought sickness to a farmer and his wife and made their goat miscarry its kids. None of it was true. Granny had done none of these things, but I could see that our neighbours were sincere. They believed in her guilt. And Granny had brought it on herself. She had wanted to make herself powerful. She had tried to make them fear her. She had succeeded too well.

At last came the call I was dreading.

'Let the servant girl Annie step forward,' Mr Lamont said.

Annie had had time to compose herself. She no longer looked like a scared little rabbit. She put on the innocent, sickly smile that I knew too well. It signalled that a string of lies was about to tumble out of her pretty, false mouth.

'Maggie's just as much in it too,' she said, daring to look at me as if she was sorry for what she had to say. 'She called up a whale to lie on the beach at Scalpsie Bay. It was an evil spirit. I saw her talking with it.'

I wanted to shout out, 'She's lying! It's not true!' but I was paralysed with the shock of it.

It was a surprise to the court too. They were looking at me with narrowed, suspicious eyes.

'And I heard her and the old woman talk,' Annie went on, not daring to look at me now. She put her head charmingly on one side as if she was trying to remember. 'They said they would dig up the body of Ebenezer Macbean and make a pie of his head and feet and hands.'

'No!' I shouted, over the horrified buzz of talk. 'That's a horrible thing to say! I would never think of such a thing! I love babies!'

'Be quiet, girl,' Mr Lamont rapped out. 'What else do you have to say, Annie?'

She hesitated. I could tell by the way she was bunching handfuls of skirt in her fists that the lies she was about to tell frightened even her. She looked back at Mr Macbean almost pleadingly. He frowned back and nodded sharply.

'Go on, girl.'

'There was a – a witches' sabbath at Ambrisbeg. I saw them all, those two and others, dancing, and there was music, and then – the Devil came.'

'Ha, the Devil! What were you doing, miss, running round at Ambrisbeg in the middle of the night?' Granny scoffed.

It was the question everyone had wanted to ask. They leaned forward to look at Annie more closely.

'I had lost something precious,' Annie said. 'A silver buckle.'

I was so startled by her cheek that I stepped forward with my fists clenched in the air. The sheriff's man pulled me back.

'I didn't dare tell my mistress,' Annie went on, 'in case she was angry with me for being careless. I waited till everyone at Scalpsie Farm was asleep, then I went out to look for it. The moon was up and I thought it would shine on the path. I'd lost it on the way home

83

from Ambrisbeg where I'd gone to ask for eggs for Ebenezer's christening.'

I couldn't stand it any longer.

'She's lying about the buckle! It was my buckle, from my father! She stole it from behind our salt box!' My voice was half strangled with outrage.

Annie ignored me.

'I heard music and a piper and I went to look.' She pointed at Granny. 'That woman there, Mistress Wylie, she was dancing and she had no clothes on.'

'Ha ha! That would have been a sight! It would have frightened more than the Devil!' Granny's spontaneous laughter actually produced a smile from one or two of the judges.

'It didn't frighten the Devil,' Annie said sweetly. 'I saw him there.' She was staring at the wall now, like Mr Macbean had done earlier.

'What was he like, the Devil?' Mr Lamont said, with the curiosity everyone was feeling. 'Come, Annie. Don't be afraid. Speak up.'

'He was a big tall man, dark, with grey clothes on. He – he took Mistress Wylie in his arms, and she cried out, *By horse and hattock*, or something, and then she threw a magic substance on the fire and up flew a stick and she and the Devil flew on it into the air and then they . . .' She stopped and looked round, blushing as if she was too pure to say more. 'Well – he climbed on her and used her like – like a bull uses a cow.'

'What?' I said. '*What?*'

It was so silly I couldn't believe my ears. And I

thought that no one else would believe it either. But then, to my dismay, Mr Wilson, the farmer from Ambrisbeg, stood up.

'It's true, there was a witches' sabbath, or some such,' he said, scratching unhappily at his stubbly chin. 'I heard unearthly music, and when I went to my door to look, I saw sparks fly up, and it looked as if there were fairy people dancing in the air.'

He sat down again, his knees cracking, and nodded twice, as if he knew he had done his painful duty.

'Thank you, Mr Wilson,' Mr Lamont said gravely. 'And did you hear any words spoken? *Horse and hattock*, or such like?'

'The woman was calling out *Tinkletum, tankletum*,' Mr Wilson said. 'She sang it loud, over and over. I heard that clear enough.'

'I see. Spelling words, I suppose. And did you see the Devil? Did you witness sexual congress between him and this woman?'

'No. I—'

'But I did!' I hadn't noticed Mr Wilson's sharp-nosed, meek little wife, whom Granny had bullied and delighted in mocking year after year. She had sprung to her feet, and I could tell from the shine in her eyes and the quiver in her voice that her years of humiliation had boiled up within her and were spewing out at last in a triumphant blast of revenge.

'The girl's right! The Devil himself was there! I saw the two of them as they left their wicked sabbath. Elspeth and the Evil One. Conjoined. His eyes red like fire. There was a – a wailing, like the souls of the damned screaming from Hell.'

'Who's going to listen to this rubbish?' shot back Granny. 'The woman heard the sound of the air coming out of the bagpipes. You all know what a din it makes.'

She spoke bravely but I could see that the Wilsons' evidence had rattled her more than the rest of it.

'And what have you to say, Mistress Wylie, to the charges brought against you?' Mr Lamont said, giving her a turn to answer at last.

If only Granny had been able to control her anger! If only she had learned to speak calmly and show respect, and tell clearly what was truth and what was lies. But her one refuge was anger, and her only weapon was to create fear. She stood with her feet wide apart, her head thrown back, and ranted and denounced and denied and scoffed, insulting the judges one by one. 'I call upon the fires of Hell to fall on all in this room!' she shouted at last. 'May the Devil's burning brands scorch your flesh till it falls from your bones, and may you boil in the cauldron of his rage for ever and ever!'

She stopped suddenly and her eyes widened. She crossed her arms on her chest and bowed her head. I think she knew that she'd gone too far. She was defeated, and had brought her destruction on herself.

Mr Lamont raised a hand and said into the breathless silence, 'Elspeth Wylie, out of your own mouth you have condemned yourself. You are judged to be a witch and to have used malefice against your neighbours. You will be taken to the shore and strangled upon the gallows tomorrow at two o'clock in the afternoon. And your body will be tied to a stake and burned as an example to all those who might be tempted to follow in your path of wickedness.'

People can say what they like about my grandmother, but no one could doubt her courage. She did not show by so much as a blink that she was afraid. But I could smell the fear on her. I could sense her inner trembling.

Aloud she said, in a quieter, more natural voice, 'I expected no less than this from such a court of hypocrites. I'm no witch, and most of you know it. Fine judges you are. But tomorrow I'll be standing in front of God my maker, the Judge of all the earth. If I lied now my soul would be damned to Hell. So here's the whole truth. I've spouted off curses at the lot of you. I've used charms and spells like everyone else, and I've made medicines with healing herbs. Half of you have had the benefit. I've been treating your rheumatics and bringing your babies into the world for years. Yes, and I've met my friends out in the night for a bit of music and whisky and a dance or two, to cheer us all up when the rest of you have cast us out. But as for the Devil, I've never met the man, nor do I want to. Having sex with him? Pure nonsense, and you know it. You're no better than murderers and your souls will be damned to Hell for it, especially yours, Miss pretty-little-innocent Annie, you wicked liar. When the demons come for you, to take you down to the everlasting fires—'

I looked across at Annie. She was biting her lip so hard her teeth might have gone right through it.

'That will do,' Mr Lamont began to say, but Granny shot out at him, 'I haven't finished yet. It's my right to speak. You can't take that from me.'

She paused, then put a heavy hand on my shoulder and drew me unwillingly to her side. She'd dropped her harsh tone and now sounded almost pleading.

'Whatever you think of me, you must believe that my granddaughter is innocent of any wrong whatsoever. She hasn't cursed anyone, or attended any party in the night, or done anything against a single person. Leave her alone, for the Lord Jesus Christ's sake.'

And my heart lurched as Mr Lamont said, 'Yes, yes, now we come to the case of the girl Maggie Blair. I must ask the court what evidence is brought against her. Mr Macbean, will you speak?'

The man had been grinning delightedly at the sentence cast on Granny, but he made himself look solemn as he stood up again.

'It's well known that a witch's child is a witch too. This girl looks pure and innocent, but she is infected by her grandmother. When she summoned the whale to die on the shore, she was taken in a trance, and there she communed with the Evil One. There are many witnesses.' He looked along the row of our Scalpsie neighbours and marked the nodding heads.

'Please,' I said, daring to interrupt, 'it wasn't the Devil I saw that day but it was – I thought I saw the

Lord Jesus, coming down from Heaven in a cloud of glory to judge the living and the dead. And I was afraid. I . . . fainted.'

I knew at once that I'd made a mistake.

'And why would an innocent girl fear the Lord Jesus?' Mr Lamont said sternly. 'Surely your soul should have rejoiced, and you should have cried aloud with joy and run to meet Him with praises on your lips? But you were afraid. What other reason could there be, but that you had sold your soul to the Devil and feared the Divine Judgement?'

I didn't know what to say. I stood in silence, twisting my hands together. The Divine Judgement *was* what I had feared. I had not been sure of my salvation.

'What other accusations are brought against this girl?' the hateful voice of Mr Lamont went on.

Annie stood up, propelled forward by a sharp dig in the back from Mr Macbean. Her confidence seemed to have deserted her. She couldn't bring herself to act the sweet innocent now. She looked desperately round at Mr Macbean, who frowned and shook his head.

'Maggie was at the witches' sabbath too,' she gabbled. 'She – I saw her. She took off all her clothes and danced around a stone.'

'Annie, how can you say that?' I called out. 'You know it's not true! Why are you doing this?'

She glanced up at me, then away, and in that moment I saw terror and misery in her face, and something almost like regret. But Mr Lamont was speaking.

'Maggie Blair, you are condemned as a witch, along

with your grandmother. You will be taken with her to the shore and strangled from the gallows, and your body will be tied to a stake and burned so that . . .'

But I didn't hear the rest. I had fainted dead away.

Chapter Nine

O nce I had come to myself again, and we were back in our cold, cheerless cell, I was attacked with such a fit of trembling that I could hardly stand upright. Then I understood properly that I was going to die.

Pictures kept rising in my mind of all the things that I would never see and feel again. They were small, silly things that I didn't know I'd loved: the yellow irises flowering in the bogs by Loch Quien; Sheba twisting round to lick her back; the geese coming back in the springtime to nest in Scalpsie Bay; the warmth of the summer sun on my face; and then the winter again, with the door closed against the cold night and Tam telling stories by the fire.

How can it all go on without me being there? I thought. *How will Blackie and the cottage and the sea exist if I'm not there?*

Worst of all, I thought of the man I'd always secretly dreamed of, who I would now never meet, and the baby I would never carry about in my arms.

The sweetness of living pierced me and a deep, choking sob came up from the depths of my lungs. It was as if I'd been punched in the stomach. I had to gasp for air.

A stinging slap from Granny shocked me to silence.

'Stop snivelling. What good does it do? You're not dead yet. It's not over till it's over.'

'It'll be over tomorrow! We'll be dead tomorrow!'

I wanted to slap her back, to claw and bite her, to tell her that this was all her fault with her endless quarrelling, but my old fear of her held me back, even then.

'We'll be dead, eh? That's what *they* say.'

Her eyes were darting about the cell as if there was a door she might yet notice that would lead us out to freedom. 'That court was a sham. There was no person of authority to condemn us. And all the evidence was malicious lies, as half of them knew.'

My heart pounded in a sudden wild flight of hope.

'What do you mean, Granny? They might still put a stop to it?'

'It's possible.' She began to march about, her heavy bare feet slapping down on the stone floor. 'The Sheriff, he won't like things being done behind his back. And that minister man, when he hears about this, he'll be for saving you, anyway. To condemn a girl like that! For nothing! On the say-so of that wicked little thief!'

'Mr Robertson!' I cried, clutching at the thought. 'Yes! He'll find a way. He tried to help us before!'

Shouts came from outside. I could hear the clop of horses' hoofs, and laughter. I picked up my stool and set it below the window.

'Leave it, Maggie. Don't show your face, for God's sake,' Granny said, and I think she was sorry that she'd hit me, because she spoke quite gently.

But I had to see what was happening. I climbed on to the stool and peered out.

'There's four – no, five, packhorses with loads of wood,' I told Granny.

'For the burning,' she muttered.

I don't think she meant me to hear, but I had.

'For burning us?'

The thought was so terrible that I had to hold on with both hands to the bars to stop myself falling off the stool. My eyes were fixed on the bundles of wood. I could imagine them flaring up into flames, hear the crackling, smell the smoke.

'Will it hurt?'

'What?'

'The burning.'

'Are you out of your wits? We'll – I'll – be dead by then. They'll have made sure of that on the gallows.'

'The hanging then. Will that hurt?'

'How should I know?' Oddly, I found her exasperation almost comforting. It was familiar, anyway. 'I've never been hanged before, so I've no way of telling. If I had, I'd tell you all about it.'

She was smiling grimly.

A voice came, louder and clearer than the rest. A man dressed in black with the white collar bands of a minister had stepped up on to the bottom of the market cross and was holding up his hands for silence. I peered at him, but I was sure I had never seen him before.

'Good people of Rothesay!' he began. 'We are called here today, in the sight of God, to prepare ourselves with prayer and fasting to cleanse our community of the evil of witchcraft, which has so grievously flourished in our midst.'

The other voices had fallen silent. The children were being hushed and people were setting out their folding stools, settling themselves to listen to the preacher. I didn't dare stay at the window any longer. I was afraid he might point, and they would all turn and stare at me.

I could still hear him clearly though.

'I say to you all, beware! The Devil prowls among you like a roaring lion, seeking whom he may devour. He tempts you with the lusts of flesh, with greed, and envy and adultery. These two women –' I shrank as I imagined heads turning to stare up at our window – 'these wicked women have sold their souls to Satan, and tomorrow we shall send them to an eternity of Hell with their evil master.'

'Wait! Stop this!'

A familiar voice had cut the preacher off in mid-flow.

'Mr Robertson! Granny, it's Mr Robertson!' I cried. 'You were right! He's come to save us!'

'What's going on here?' Mr Robertson sounded out of breath. I had to know what was happening. I hopped up on to the stool and peered out cautiously, keeping my head as low as possible. This time, Granny brought her stool over and joined me.

Mr Robertson was holding his horse by its bridle. His face was flushed and he was talking angrily to the other minister. They were too far away for us to pick out their words, and the crowd was buzzing with talk now too.

At last, Mr Robertson turned his back on the other man and held up his hand.

'Things are going too fast here. I'm not satisfied that the court set up to try Elspeth Wylie and her grand-daughter was a proper one. They haven't confessed! To condemn without a confession is absolutely against the law. And where is the proof brought against them? The testimony of a hysterical girl!'

I was looking for Annie as he spoke, but couldn't see her sly, deceitful face in the crowd.

'Well said, Mister Minister,' Granny said under her breath. 'I'm sorry I insulted you, after all.'

The other minister came forward and laid a soothing hand on Mr Robertson's sleeve.

'My dear brother in Christ! Your compassion does you credit. But think of the danger of allowing the witches to live, even for another day! When I heard that there was going to be a witch trial here in Rothesay, I knew that the Lord intended me to be here, even before the minister of Rothesay, Mr Stewart, asked me to come and represent him. My own congregation in Inverkip, over the water on the mainland, have discovered and executed six witches. Six! You see how widespread this evil has become.'

'Aye, we've heard about you!' someone shouted. '*In Inverkip, the witches skip!*'

'They skip no longer,' the minister said with horrible

95

joviality. 'They've gone where, God willing, the witches of Rothesay will go tomorrow.'

'That's right! Hang them! Burn them!' people started shouting.

Mr Robertson tried to speak again, but his horse, which he had had no time to tether, was excited by the noise and began to kick out and whinny. By the time he had calmed it, the crowd had turned away from him and was running across the short space that separated the market cross from the tollbooth.

'Hang them! Burn them!'

Granny pulled me down from the window and for a long moment held me in her old arms.

'He's lost them. He might have done it, but he's lost them.'

We could hear feet running up the outer steps, then a deafening hammering came on the outer door. I thought that at any moment they would come bursting through and kill us with their bare hands. I clung to Granny with all my strength and she actually let me bury my face in her side.

'The door will hold. It's got to hold,' she was muttering. Aloud she shouted, 'Donnie Brown, don't let them in! They'll tear us to pieces!'

'I know my work, witch,' Mr Brown growled from the far side of our cell door. 'Don't worry. I'll keep you safe for your hanging in the morning.'

Then from the outside came different shouts, the sound of horses, the thwack of cudgels on flesh and indignant shouts of protest.

'Get away from that door!'

'It's the sheriff's man,' I said to Granny. 'That's his voice.'

'Get back, all of you!' someone else shouted. 'Clear the square!'

'Yes,' came the fluting, odious voice of the strange preacher. 'Come to the kirk. The cleansing of Rothesay must be performed with prayer and the singing of psalms and the preaching of the Word. Follow me!'

The steps receded. An uneasy silence fell over the market square. All I could hear now was the scream of a gull as it swept on its white wings above the little town's smoking chimneys.

'That was our chance and it's gone,' I said, hoping that Granny would contradict me, but she didn't.

The afternoon crawled past. Granny said very little. She looked suddenly old and tired. Her cheeks had sunk in, and her face had paled to a sickly grey. She sat slumped on her stool, her head leaning back against the damp stone wall. I couldn't keep still. I would sit for a moment, then horror would come over me and I would jump up and pace the cell talking to myself, then try to sit, and get up again. Granny let me be.

The townsfolk came back hours later, when darkness had already fallen. We heard them singing as they marched down the hill from the church. The sheriff's men were ready for them though, and hurried them past the tollbooth. We heard no more from them than a few hoots and catcalls, and a couple of frightening thuds as stones were hurled against the wall below our window.

'Will you close the shutter, Donnie Brown?' Granny called out at last, as the evening wind got up.

'You get no more service from me, witch!' he called back. 'I heard them condemn you this morning. You can freeze for all I care, like my wife's cousin froze in the cold water when you drowned him. You'll be hot enough in Hell tomorrow.'

'Then we won't get supper either,' Granny said grimly. The minutes dragged by.

And then, when I had stopped my restless pacing and was sitting hunched over with my arms wrapped round my body for warmth, came the last sound in the world that I was expecting. It was a dear, familiar voice. A cheerful, friendly voice. Tam's voice. He was singing, right under our window, the very song he'd sung to me ever since I could remember:

> Fy, *let us all to the bridal,*
> *For there will be lilting there,*
> *For Jock's to be married to Maggie,*
> *The lass with the golden hair.*

'Tam!' I called out. 'Oh, Granny, did you hear that? It's Tam!'

She jerked upright and though it was now too dark to see, I knew that a grin had spread over her face.

'Tam, you old—' she began.

'Shh!' Tam whispered urgently. 'Don't talk to me.'

'Who's out there? What is it now?' Mr Brown sounded as if he'd been woken out of a deep sleep. We could hear his steps drag as he went to the outer door, and saw the chink of light move below our cell door as he walked past it with his lantern, the ring of keys clinking in his belt as he moved.

'Donnie, is that you?' came Tam's cheerful voice. 'You know me. I'm Tam the piper.'

'Go away, Tam the ruddy piper,' Mr Brown said crossly. 'You've no call to come here. If you want to see the witches you'll have to wait till morning and watch them swing along with everyone else.'

'The who? Oh, you mean those women?' Tam did a wonderful impression of a man innocently surprised. 'What would I want with them? It's you I've come to see. There's a wee job I've been wanting to ask you to do for me.'

'A job? What nonsense are you on about now?'

'A lock, of course. I've a chest from my father's day. A beautiful thing. Carved on both sides. Brass bound. I need a proper lock made for it.'

'Who are you fooling, Tam?' snorted Mr Brown. 'You think I don't know that you've no money to pay for locks? You're in debt over your ears. By rights you should be locked up in here, along with the witches.'

Tam's laugh was a marvel of cheerful amusement.

'That's where you're wrong, Donnie my man. I've been piping so busily my lips are bleeding raw. Weddings, processions – on and on. I'm a clear man. No more debt. And I've got a picture in my head of just the lock I want. What's more, I've a fine bottle of whisky here. We could share a drop or two, maybe, while I tell you what's in my mind.'

'The cunning old devil,' Granny said, her eyes glinting in the dark.

'I'm on duty here,' Mr Brown said, after a doubtful pause. 'There'll be a terrible song and dance if they catch me away from my post.'

'I wouldn't take you away from your post!' Tam sounded shocked at the very idea. 'Just let me in, and you can lock the door behind us, and I'll show you my plan and take a tot or two.'

'Tam, Tam, you know I can't do that.'

'Suit yourself, Donnie. No doubt you've too much work on already. Don't worry about it. I'll have a word with that new man, the locksmith in Kingarth. Peter Thomson. He's getting good business now, I hear. No hard feelings. I'll just raise a toast to you before I go.'

He clinked the bottle, and we heard the whisky gurgle in the neck of it.

'Goodnight, Donnie!' he called out, and started to move slowly away.

My heart had leaped with hope at the arrival of Tam, and now it was sinking deeper and deeper with every one of his retreating steps. And then came the familiar rasping noise as the bolts on the outer door scraped back, and we heard Mr Brown whisper hoarsely, 'Come back here, man, and bring the bottle with you. It's cold enough in this tomb to freeze the blood in my veins.'

'Ha!' said Granny softly. 'Well done, Tam. Now we'll see what's what.'

Tam was already running up the outer stair to the door, which Mr Brown had opened a crack. He paused on the way up and pushed our shutter to, cutting out the worst of the freezing wind.

I'd always hated watching Tam and Granny drinking themselves to silliness, but the sound of Mr Brown going under the whisky was the sweetest I'd ever heard. Tam was clever. He didn't rush things. We couldn't catch all the words as they sat outside our cell and talked, but we could tell he was talking first about the lock for his mythical chest, and then Mr Brown started on about his wife's cousin drowning, and Tam was murmuring sympathetically.

Granny and I sat in the dark, hugging ourselves, laughing at every new stage of Mr Brown's drunkenness.

'Let's hope Tam has the sense to stay off the stuff himself, that's all,' Granny kept saying.

At last, Mr Brown got to roaring and singing, and we sat terrified in case someone heard him and came to see what was going on, but luckily the tavern nearby was full of people come in from all over the Isle of Bute to see the execution in the morning, and they were making such a din that Mr Brown's rants were drowned out.

At last, after a couple of hours, he quietened down to indistinct mumblings, and then there was a thud as something heavy hit the floor.

'That's him out cold,' Granny said with satisfaction,

'and I wish him joy of the head he'll have in the morning.'

There came a jingle of keys and a rattle and scrape at our lock and at last the cell door swung open.

For one second, behind the figure that stood in the doorway, I saw a flutter, almost like wings. It was probably just a trick of the shadows cast by the lantern which Tam was holding up high, but I thought for an instant there was an angel standing there. Then I saw Tam's dirty blue bonnet, and his gap-toothed mouth as he cackled, 'Come on, you two. Let's get away from here.'

He was swaying and flushed, but he was sober enough.

'Tam, you – you . . . !'

I couldn't say another thing, but threw myself at him and hugged him till he panted for breath.

'That's enough of that,' Granny snapped behind me. 'Get going while you've got the chance.'

'Yes, come on!' I was out of the cell already, struggling to draw back the heavy bolts on the big outer door. Tam came up behind me, stepping over the snoring body of Mr Brown.

The bolts were back, and I was turning the great door handle with both hands, when Granny called out, 'Take care, Maggie. Don't open it till I've checked if there's anyone outside.'

I could hear her stool clatter on the floor as she set it below the window and the rustle as she climbed up on it.

'Good. No one's about. Get going now, the pair of you.'

I had the door half open before her words had sunk in. I shut the door again.

'What do you mean, "the pair of you"?'

'I'm not coming with you,' Granny said, glaring at me. 'Get out of here. Hurry.'

'What?' I couldn't believe my ears. 'Granny, you've got to! They'll kill you in the morning. You've got to escape. This is our only chance!'

She was standing in the obstinate stance I knew too well, her mouth set in a grim line, her arms folded on her chest, her feet planted wide apart as if she was conquering the very ground she stood on.

'It's *your* only chance, Maggie. How can we both get away? There'll be a hue and cry all over the island. They'll not leave one stone unturned. Where could we hide? Who would help us? But if you cut your hair, and Tam gets you some breeks in place of your skirts, you could maybe get off the island on a fishing boat, or – or—'

'Get away with you, you old fool,' said Tam, tugging at her arm. 'Do you think I've gone to all the trouble of pouring good whisky down that idiot Donnie's throat for nothing?'

'Not for nothing! For Maggie!'

She had seized his arm in turn, and was shaking him.

'Listen, Tam. I'm right. You know I am. Maggie can get away. You can think of how to do it. It's me they really hate. I'm the one they want. And you know what?

103

I don't care any more. I'm an old woman. My hips hurt. It's a quick death on the gallows. I'm not afraid of dying. Heaven or Hell, God will judge me. And I'll have the satisfaction of knowing they've all damned themselves for condemning me. All I want – *all* I want – is for Maggie to live! Do you hear me? Maggie must live!'

Outside, there was a burst of noise from the tavern as someone opened the door. It died away as the door was closed again.

'For God's sake, Tam, will you get her away from here before it's too late!'

She let go of Tam, who stood nursing his bruised arm, an aggrieved look on his face.

'You were always an awkward old cuss, Elspeth Wylie,' he said, sounding like a sulky child. 'I thought you'd be grateful.'

'Oh, Tam!' Her anger dropped off her like a cloak. 'If you only knew! And I'd be even more grateful if you'd just get going and take her to safety.'

I'm ashamed to say that I was so desperate to get out of that awful tollbooth that I didn't try to make Granny change her mind. In any case, I knew, in my heart of hearts, that she was right. Tam knew it too.

'I'll not see you again then, this side of death,' he said, tears in his voice.

She ignored him, and fixed me with an urgent look.

'Go to Kilmacolm, Maggie. Go to your Uncle Blair. Your father's brother – who else should care for you?'

'I don't know how to get there!' I could hear my

voice rising in a wail. 'I don't know where it is! How am I going to manage on my own?'

'Stop all that *I can't, I don't*,' she snapped. 'Feebleness, Maggie. Your great fault. Learn to master it. Anyway, I've shown you often enough. You know the peak of Misty Law you can see from Rothesay Bay, over on the mainland to the east. Kilmacolm's just over there on the other side of it. Now get going. Get *on*!'

'Oh, Granny!'

I ran to her and hugged her. I couldn't help myself. Granny had never been one for love and affection, and I'd hardly ever dared do such a thing before. As usual, she pushed me away. And then I felt her hand on my head. It was trembling. And she said, 'I've not done much for you, Maggie, but I'll give you all I've got. My blessing.' And she shut her eyes and intoned, in the voice she used for spells, '*I will put an enchantment on the eye, from the bosom of Peter and Paul. The one best enchantment under the sun that will come from Heaven to earth.*' Then, in her ordinary voice, she said, 'Is that bread and cheese that drunken fool's lying on top of? Give it to me before you go. The sides of my stomach are sticking together here.'

Chapter Ten

We were out of the tollbooth only just in time. The tavern door opened as we reached the bottom of the steps and people began lurching out into the half-light of the summer night.

'Oh look at that now, oh we're in trouble!' Tam said, and I could see he was about to panic and have us both caught.

Act. Don't be feeble! I heard Granny say in my head, so I gave Tam a shove in the back and said, 'Go on. Join them. I'll be all right. Just act drunk like the rest of them.'

He didn't need telling. The fresh air had turned the whisky in him and he was half out of his head anyway. Obediently, he staggered off to join the crowd.

I whisked myself round the corner into a dark back lane, and then I began to run, the ground flying away beneath my feet. Like an animal freed from a trap, I went the only way I knew – home, to Scalpsie Bay.

I halted at last and bent over, gasping for breath, nursing a stitch in my side. I was desperately hungry and tired to my bones, but fear is a marvellous spur. It was past ten o'clock now, and the short darkness of May had fallen at last. I'd have six or seven hours till the sun rose again. There was no sound of pursuit – no shouts or running feet or pounding horses' hoofs.

I set off again at a fast walk, listening out for any strange sounds. Once, a barking dog nearby made me jump half out of my skin, and I realized I was close to the farm at Kerrycrusach, but no door opened. I stole past on tiptoe, and the dog soon quietened down.

There was no moon that night, but a faint greyness still lingered on the western horizon and when I came at last to the old cottage I could see enough to find the door and open it. I sensed at once that Blackie had gone. Her byre was silent and empty. She would have been in pain at being left so long without milking, but I'd hoped foolishly to find her here. I'd been longing for a deep drink of warm, frothy milk.

Those thieving Macbeans will have taken her, I thought, and rage nearly choked me. I felt Granny inside me at that moment.

'Sheba!' I whispered. 'Are you there?'

But there was no answering miaow, and no warm black shape came out of the darkness to greet me.

I knew I couldn't stay in the cottage. To be there at all was dangerous, even in the middle of the night. One of our neighbours might easily come, under cover of darkness, to help himself to whatever he could find. I needed to get going quickly.

The ashes on the hearth were cold, of course, so there was no glow from the fire to see by. I had to feel my way round with my hands.

To my amazement, the oatmeal barrel was still half full. The feel of the soft grain under my fingers cheered me like a kind word. There were even the oatcakes that

I'd made the day before yesterday (a lifetime ago) still sitting on the table.

Granny's curse at the hearth, I thought, smiling to myself in the dark. *It's keeping them away. She knew it would.*

I grabbed the oatcakes and crammed them into my mouth, then went to the pitcher and took a deep draught of water. My hand brushed against the jug beside it and I heard the slosh of liquid. Milk! I had poured some into it on Saturday from Blackie's bucket. I raised the jug to my lips and drank the half-soured milk down in a long, satisfying gulp.

The food worked on me better than any enchantment could have done. It gave me courage and cleared my head. I sat at the table, looked out through the doorway into the starry night, and thought.

Where could I go? What could I do?

The Isle of Bute is less than one day's ride long from tip to tip, and three hours of walking across the middle. Every man and woman on it would know in the morning that I'd escaped, and they'd all be after me. There was no one who would want to help me, except for Tam, but he'd done what he could, and though I loved him, I knew he was too foolish to be relied on.

I have to get to the mainland, I told myself. *I have to get across the water.*

There are boats of all kinds that come and go from Bute, carrying men out to fish, taking goods and people from island to island, and over to the mainland, but there wasn't one, I knew, who would have the courage to take me, a convicted witch, on board. My heart failed at the thought of trying to slip on to one of them unseen. But it was the only thing I could do.

There came a clatter of stones outside. Something was moving close to the cottage. I froze with fright and my hair rose on my scalp. For a long moment I sat motionless, then I heard a splash and let out my breath. It was only an animal, after all – an otter most probably, fishing in the stream. It felt like a warning. I couldn't stay in the cottage any longer. I had to get away.

Dress like a boy, Granny had said.

Our knife lay on the table. I took off my cap and sawed at my long mouse-brown hair. It fell in hanks on to the floor.

They'll find it. They'll know what I've done.

I groped around and picked up what I could, swept the whole area, then carried the hair in my apron out to the kail-yard. I grubbed a hole with my hands, dropped it in and covered the place with earth.

I was thinking fast and well. I felt my way to the worm-eaten chest in the corner of the cottage, opened it and groped among the few things inside. My father's linen shirt, his leather belt and his long trousers still lay in it. Granny had never sold them.

A drowned man comes back for his own, she'd always said.

Quickly, I took off my own clothes and put my father's on. They were far, far too big for me. I picked up the knife and sawed away at the trouser legs till they fell only to my ankles, then tied the belt tight round my waist to keep them up. I rolled up the sleeves of the shirt and wrapped my plaid around and over it all to keep everything in place. Then I laid the blanket from my bed on the ground, put my own gown on it, along with a supply of oatmeal tied into a cloth, and bound it all into a bundle. I tied it to the end of the stick Granny had always used to urge Blackie on her way, and I was ready.

I knew where to go. There were caves above Scalpsie Bay, a mile or so from the cottage. People were afraid to go there. Lights had been seen in the night, they said, and strange sounds. Unearthly beings were thought to live there, fairies and kelpies who were best not disturbed. Granny had said that the fairies only used one cave, the biggest one, and they were friendly enough as long as you left them alone. As for the others, the only beings who went there were strictly earthly, herself and Tam and their vagabond friends, and the music the good folk heard was only Tam's pipes and the party's drunken singing. At any rate, I wasn't afraid of the fairies. It was people of flesh and blood who were after me.

I stepped out of the cottage and closed the door behind me. I needed to hurry – I had to reach the caves before the early May dawn coloured the sky and people began to stir. I couldn't think about tomorrow, or the day after. The first thing was to save my skin today.

To reach the caves I had to edge round the side of the bay and strike up the lower slope to the cliffs above. The caves were tucked in up there, under the overhanging rock. It wasn't easy to find my way in the dark, but the edges of the waves rolling in on to the sand of the bay gave off a faint white glow, and by it I could at least judge my distance from the sea.

I was heading for the smallest cave. Cows and sheep wandered into the large ones for shelter sometimes, and I had no wish to be disturbed by a farm dog looking for them. In any case, the smallest cave looked out over the bay, and I'd be able to keep watch and see if anyone approached.

By the time I found the little cave I was so tired that I didn't care any more whether I was safe or not, as long as I could lie down and sleep. I unwrapped my bundle, lay down and pulled the blanket round me. I must have fallen asleep at once.

I don't remember most of the dreams that came to me that night, though I know they were troubled and fearful. But the last one I can't ever forget. I dreamed that I was standing on the ramparts of Rothesay castle, and I knew that I could fly. I was powerful and filled with evil. My lips drew back from my teeth in a Devil's grin, and my eyes grew wide, green and slit-pupilled like a cat's. I knew that if I leaped from the ramparts and flew over the heads of the people staring up at me below, I'd become a true witch, a daughter of Satan. I didn't want to. I clung to the parapet behind me. But then I fell, and opened my arms to save myself, and the air bore me up and I was flying.

'No,' I called out. 'I'm not a witch! I want to be good! Let me come down!'

I woke up crying, my blanket twisted round me. The sun had risen hours ago. I sat up, filled with the dread of my dream. The horrors of yesterday came back to me at once, and I shivered at the danger I was in. I sat up and looked out between the bushes that grew in front of the cave.

Scalpsie Bay lay calm and peaceful in the morning light. The oystercatchers, with the cross of Christ painted on their backs, were wheeling in the air above the shore. Smoke drifted up through the turf roofs of the farmhouses, making them look like steaming loaves of fresh bread. Above the slow *sh-sh* of the sea I heard a woman calling to a child. Life was going on round Scalpsie Bay and it was as if a hole had opened, and I'd dropped right through it, and it had closed over my head.

I didn't dare make a fire to cook my oats into porridge and I was hungry again. I looked longingly down at our cottage. It seemed forlorn, even on this bright morning.

And then I saw that people were moving along the lane in ones and twos, a steady stream, going towards Rothesay.

They're going to see Granny die. They're going to gloat.

At that moment, I wished my dream had ended differently, that I'd let myself become a witch and could call the powers of Hell down upon them.

But not to little children, I thought. *Not to babies. And*

112

*not to their mammies and daddies either, or they would be left
alone.*

I had to admit, too, that I would have followed the
crowd if things had been different. I would have walked
to Rothesay out of sheer curiosity to see the hanging
and burning of a witch.

I could choose to hate and curse and make people
fear me as Granny had done, or I could go another way.
I'd made my choice already, in my dream.

I saw Tam coming late in the afternoon, when the sun
was halfway across the sky to its sinking place behind
the mountains of Arran. His bonnet bobbed like a bluebell above the bracken. He was half running on bent
legs, looking over his shoulder.

I waited till he was close enough to hear me.

'Tam! I'm here! Up here!'

He bolted up the slope and dived down behind the
bush where I was hiding.

'Maidie, I've found you! I was afraid those fools
would be back from Rothesay and catch me hunting for
you. Look at you, girl! A proper boy already.'

I shook his arm.

'Granny! Is she . . . ?'

He looked away.

'Best not to think about all that.'

'Tam, you've got to tell me! Did they—'

'Yes. If you must know, she's gone.' His pale, red-
rimmed eyes filled with tears. 'Hanged and burned,

down on the shore, with all of them loons hooting like donkeys.'

'Did she say anything?'

He laughed, but it choked on a sob.

'*Did* she? Oh yes! Told everyone who'd listen that the Devil had come flying into the tollbooth in the night, and broke down the door and snatched you away, so there was no point in looking for you on this island, or anywhere else on the earth. Looking after you, you see, even at the very end.'

Oh, Granny! I thought, seeing her, stern and defiant in her last hour, as magnificent as a queen.

'She wouldn't let them drag her to the gallows but she walked to them freely, and the hangman, the butcher from Kingarth, Dicky Greig, he says to her, "Don't curse me, Mistress, for what I have to do," and she shoots back to him, "I'm done with cursing, you silly wee man," and she couldn't resist adding, "but when you get home ask your wife where she was last Wednesday night." And that was funny, Maidie, because everyone knows what Sally Greig's been up to with the apprentice, except for Dickie, so the whole crowd cracked out laughing. Then poor old Elspeth, she looked up at the rope that was going to hang her, and her legs gave a bit at the knees and she went pale, but she wouldn't let anyone touch her and just shook herself and walked up the step to it. That Inverkip fool of a minister had been preaching and praying himself hoarse all morning, and he set up a psalm-singing, and Mr Robertson wasn't liking it at all. He was shaking his head and staring at the other fellow with his face all shut up like a clamp. Then he goes up to Elspeth and says kindly and gently, "Shall I pray with you, Mistress Elspeth? Your judgement is upon you and an hour from now you will be standing before the Throne of Grace to answer for your sins." And Elspeth snaps at him, "Thank you, Mister Minister, but I'll pray for myself," and she cries out, "Lord Jesus, I'm no witch, but I'm a sinful old woman and I pray you to forgive me!" and then she adds, "And your mother, the good Virgin, can put in a word for me too." Well, they all took that to be sheer blasphemous papistry, Maidie, as well she knew, and it maddened the Inverkip fellow, and he shouted, "Do your duty, Mr Greig! Let's hear no more from this whore of Satan!" And you know what, I do believe that's why she brought in the Virgin Mary, just for a last poke in the man's eye, and because she wanted to get the business over.'

I couldn't speak for a minute. At last I said, 'Do you think it hurt her, when Mr Greig did it?'

'I don't think so. All over in a minute.' He patted me kindly. 'The crowd went quiet when it was done, then that fool starts up again, preaching, and calling for the fire to be stoked up, but I caught sight of Donnie Brown being taken off by the sheriff's men. I was afraid he'd blether about me and get me taken up too. With luck, he'll stick to Elspeth's story about the Devil flying away with you, but he's an old blabbermouth, and I won't trust him to keep quiet. I need to keep out of the way of things, Maidie, till the fuss has died down.'

The bark of a dog below made us both shrink back into the little cave. We peered out cautiously, but couldn't see anyone.

'You must get going,' Tam said, 'before all those fools have had enough of fires and burning, and come back home.'

'Go where? Tam, I've been racking my brains! How can I get away? No one will take me in a boat. There's not a single person . . .'

His face had broken open into a big, sloppy grin.

'Ah but there is, Maidie, and I've been so clever I hardly know myself. It's all fixed. You're to swim with the cattle across the narrows to Colintraive on the mainland.'

I stared at him in horror.

'Swim? I can't swim! You know I can't! I'll drown!'

He ignored me.

'I saw that fellow in Rothesay – Archie Lithgow, the head drover. You don't know the man, but he comes here every year to round up the cattle and walk them down to the markets in Glasgow. He knew your daddy. He worked with him. Good friends they were. Well, the idea popped into my head as soon as I saw him walking along the high street of Rothesay. "Hello, Mr Lithgow," say I. "And have you come to witness the execution of the witch?" He gave me such a look, as if I was a louse he'd found in his hair, but I was very glad to see it. "What a lot of nonsense!" he said. "I've known Elspeth Wylie for years. She's a foul-mouthed old cuss of a woman, but she's no more a witch than I am. And neither's her granddaughter. I'm just glad that poor Danny Blair isn't alive to see this day. I don't know how the girl escaped from the tollbooth, but if I could help her now I would." You see, Maidie? Wasn't I just the brilliant one? "Ah but you *can* help her, Mr Lithgow," I says straight out. And I tell him how I got the better of Donnie Brown, and he claps me on the shoulder, and bursts out laughing, and says if you'll just get yourself up to the muster place at Rhubodach he'll see you across to the mainland and take you down as far as Dumbarton. "Once you've crossed the Clyde, it's only five miles or so down to Kilmacolm," he says. "She can walk it easy in an hour or two."'

I was staring at him with horror.

'Tam, I can't! I told you, I can't swim! I'll drown like my father did.'

'Oh, you don't need to worry about that,' he said airily. 'The men go over in a boat. You'll be all nice and dry and carried across like the little queen you are.'

I should have felt grateful but I felt hollow inside at the thought of leaving my island, my only known world, however dangerous it was for me now.

'Well then,' I said, trying to sound brave, 'I suppose I'd better go.'

He looked as disappointed as a child.

'And here was I, thinking you'd be pleased. Here was I, expecting a hug and kiss, at least.'

I couldn't help smiling, and leaned forward to kiss his pitted cheek.

'I'm just scared, Tam. I'm truly grateful. For everything.'

'Then get along with you,' he said, getting cautiously to his feet. 'It's a good fifteen miles up to the muster place.' He squinted up at the sun. 'Four or five hours at a steady pace. Keep to the west and work your way up the coast to the northern tip of the island. You'll see three little islands out in the channel there. The cattle will be down by the shore. There's a bit of a cliff, like this one here. Hide up there in the overhang. Don't show yourself to the drovers yet, because there'll be farmers coming and going, bringing up their cows for the crossing. It's to be first thing in the morning, when the tide is low. I'll come and find you there tonight. Listen out for my whistle, and whistle back.'

'Aren't you going to come up there with me?' I said shakily. 'Please, Tam.'

He looked away from me, his eyes suddenly shifty.

'I can't, darling. There's things I have to do. But I'll see you tonight, I promise.'

'You didn't bring me anything to eat, Tam, did you?' I said plaintively. 'I'm starving.'

He clapped both hands to his bonnet.

'Now here's an old fool,' he said, watching my face fall even further. Then he grinned, and like a conjuror, whipped off his bonnet and pulled out a hunk of bread with a lump of hard cheese stuck into it.

'I stole it from the inn, didn't I,' he said, with simple pride. 'It's real wheat bread, Maidie, like the high-ups

118

eat. Hey, don't gobble it down so fast. You'll choke yourself.'

Until that day I'd never been further away from Scalpsie Bay than Rothesay, which is strange when I think how far I've travelled since then. In any case, after half an hour of half-running, half-walking I was out of my own known world.

At first I was so scared of being recognized and caught that I darted like a hunted animal from one place of shelter to another, making rushes across the open to duck down behind a wall, or drop behind a clump of gorse. But then, just as I was leaping out from under a tree to make a dash across a headland, I ran slap into a farmer, walking silently along with his dog at his heels.

'Watch out, lad. Going like that, you'll knock a body over,' he said, in a friendly enough voice. 'Where are you running off to?'

I was too terrified to speak, and stood poised, ready to bolt again.

'Where are you from?' he said, looking at me more closely. 'I've not seen you before.'

I managed to point vaguely ahead along the coast and mumbled something, in as gruff a voice as I could manage, about being lost.

His face cleared.

'Oh, you'll be Macallister's new boy from Straad. No need to look as if the Devil was after you. Macallister's a good man. He'll not give you a beating for losing your way. Just follow the lane up here, and cut across the top. It'll take you down to Straad.'

I didn't dare try to speak again, but smiled my thanks and went off at a trot, not too fast, in case he became suspicious.

The best thing was that my disguise had worked. It would be more dangerous for me to skulk about like a fugitive. I could walk boldly along in the open like anyone else.

Fifteen miles is a long way to walk on nothing but a piece of bread and a bite of cheese, and by the time I'd reached the northern tip of the island my feet were sore, my bundle hung heavily on my shoulder and my head was spinning with hunger and tiredness. I was beginning to think I would never get there, never see those little islands and find the drovers, and I couldn't help but go slower and slower, weighed down with hopelessness. Then, suddenly, I heard the blessed sound of cattle lowing. It came from over the hill ahead. I ran up it with a burst of fresh energy, then slowed down as I reached the crest, and went on cautiously, keeping my head low, afraid of being seen.

The coast is rocky at the northern tip of Bute, where the channel of water flowing down from the sea loch beyond divides around it. There's a good expanse of flat land below the rocky outcrop. I crouched down under a tree and looked down on to it.

A hundred or more red, curly-backed cattle were milling about on the expanse of grass and bog reed, shaking their long-horned heads, restless, not settling yet to graze. Beyond them, across the water, were the three little islands. The channels of water between them were no more than a bowshot in length, but they looked terrifyingly wide to me.

Across on the other side, the hills of Cowal rose steeply from the water's edge, dark and forbidding. I felt a dreadful ache of loss, for the cottage by the bay, and the beach beyond the field, and the endless change of light on the sea and in the sky, and Blackie, and Sheba, and Granny herself. And I sat down and put my head on my knees, and cried. I don't know how long I cried for, but you can't go on forever, especially when there's no one nearby to comfort you, and in the end the attack of tears stopped.

Mr Lithgow knew my father, I told myself sternly. *He'll look after me. And he knows I'm innocent too. He'll want to help me.*

The midges were out now that the wind had dropped and the evening was coming down. They were in my hair and all over my bare legs and arms, biting. Girls' clothes protect you. Your cap, to start with, covers your ears, and your skirts go down to your ankles. But boys' clothes leave you more exposed, as I was finding out. I needed to find a better place to hide and watch – where Tam had told me to go, under the overhang. Then I could untie my bundle and wrap my gown round the bits of me that my father's shirt and belted plaid didn't cover.

I was about to scramble down the rocky wall to the

shelter below when I heard a voice, and peering round the tree I saw a man standing in the doorway of a little stone bothy that I'd not noticed before. He had his thumbs stuck in the belt that was holding his thick plaid in place, and he was looking over the cattle as if he was counting them.

Even from this distance, I could see that he was a solid sort of person, reassuringly big and strong-looking.

That's got to be him: Mr Lithgow, I thought, and I felt better. I felt as if I'd made a friend of him, even before we'd met.

I nearly fell the last bit of the way down the rocks, and landed heavily on a boulder, but luckily it was covered in thick moss, and I did no more than bruise myself. I felt my way along under the overhanging rocks, and found a cleft with a good soft floor to it. It was damp and very full of midges, but it was a good place to hide and I decided to stay there, covering myself from the little biters as best I could. I could see well from here too, and was unlikely to be seen. The sun was setting behind the hills and my cleft was in deep shade.

Now I could see another man. He was down by a stream that ran near to the little house, squatting to collect water in a leather bag. He had a dog with him. That worried me. If the dog got wind of me, I'd be found out at once. But the man stood up and whistled to the dog, who trotted obediently at his heels back to the little house. They both disappeared inside.

Without my knowing it, my fingers had been picking at the thick moss covering the boulder on which I was sitting. There was already quite a pile of it at my feet.

Make the best of things, Granny's voice said in my head. *Don't fuss.*

Granny! Was she in Heaven now, or had St Peter turned her away from the pearly gates and sent her down into the spitting fires of Hell? He'd have to have been a sharp man to see the good in her. But there was no telling with salvation, I knew that much. God had decided at the beginning of time who was to be saved and who was damned, I'd heard the old minister say, so I supposed there wasn't much you could do about it.

The midges were on me now, in clouds. I opened my bundle, took out my girl's clothes and put them on. They felt comfortingly familiar after the strange freedom of my legs in the trousers. My cap was on a moment later, so that was my head protected.

I gathered up the moss I'd collected. It was damp, but it made a soft place to lie on. I needed to get some sleep. I was tired to the bones, as I had been the day before, and tomorrow would be worse. I lay down, wrapped my plaid around the rest of me, and was asleep a moment later.

A clatter of stones and a gasp of surprise woke me up. It was growing light already. I sat up, not knowing where I was, then everything came back to me. A jag of fear made me scramble to my feet and crouch, ready to run.

'Don't – don't hurt me! Please!' came a girl's voice.

I knew it at once.

'Annie!' I was up and snarling like a springing cat, claws out, reaching for her face to hit and scratch it. 'Thief! Liar!'

'No, Maggie, please, you don't know, you . . .' she babbled, her hands over her face.

I hit out at her with a great blow and she fell backwards, on to a soft boggy patch, luckily for her. Before I could attack again, she had curled up like a little animal and started to cry loudly.

'Shut up, you little fool. They'll hear you. Or is that your plan – to get me caught again? If you do, I'll kill you.'

'No!' she cried, much too loudly. I looked over my shoulder in the direction of the drovers' bothy, but it was still too dark to see that far.

'Will you shut *up*?' I hissed at her, but she'd won the first battle. I'd lost the wish to hit her again. She disgusted me so much I didn't want to soil myself by touching her.

'Maggie, I'm really, really sorry. You don't know – I never thought things would go so far. It was Mr Macbean who made me say all that, about the ashes up the chain, and flying, and – taking your clothes off and everything. I didn't want to at all! I . . .'

I wanted to lift my foot and stamp on her, like you would on a nasty insect, but then I remembered the look on her face when she'd spoken against me, the second time. She had been frightened, and even sorry, I had to admit.

'Just let me tell you. You'll understand, I know you will.' Her wheedling voice made my skin creep. 'You can kill me afterwards if you want to. I wouldn't blame you. I wouldn't even mind very much.'

'Very good, Annie. You think you can get round me, like you get round everyone else. Keep trying. You won't succeed.'

'No, *please*, Maggie!' She was half sobbing. 'Listen! I'm going to have a baby! It was Mr Macbean. He – came to me. Often, in the night.'

I was so astonished that I sank down on to a boulder. I wanted to burst out laughing, but kept it in for fear of the noise.

'The old goat! The old hypocrite!'

'Yes,' said Annie eagerly, seeing her advantage. 'He's so awful, Maggie – you've no idea, and really hard and stern. And he promises things, and he preaches and prays, and all the time . . .'

She was coming closer to me and I was afraid she was going to touch me. I moved back hastily. I didn't want to laugh any more. The harm this girl had done was rising up in me and anger was threatening to choke me again.

'He promised me things. Mrs Macbean was ill, before Ebenezer was born, and he said she was sure to die, he knew the signs on her, and she'd never live through the birth, and he'd marry me, and I'd never have to go hungry, and I'd have a nice new plaid and gown every year. If I didn't do what he wanted, he said he'd send me home. I would have died first! You don't know my daddy, Maggie. He's a drinker. He beats me. There's never enough to eat at home. I never had anything pretty to wear till I started working at Scalpsie.'

She started crying again.

'Stop snivelling,' I snapped, knowing as soon as I'd spoken that I sounded just like Granny. She made an effort and drew in a shuddering breath.

'And then – that night, you remember, you were there! Mrs Macbean started having Ebenezer, and I saw that he didn't want her to die at all, because he rode down quickly to fetch your granny, even though he hated her, because he knew she'd be able to get the baby out. And then afterwards he made such a fuss of Mrs Macbean, calling her "my dear" and "my darling", and he was in a good mood, so I told him I was going to have a baby too, and he turned on me, and said I was nothing but a sinful slut, and it was all my fault for leading him into temptation, and he'd send me off back to my father if I didn't do what he told me. And then he said that it wouldn't be difficult, and if I did it he'd look after me and the baby, and give me everything I wanted.'

'So you told all those lies,' I said harshly. 'You sent my grandmother to be hanged and burned and you tried to have me murdered too, just to save yourself from going home.'

'But I never thought it would happen!' she said desperately, managing this time to seize my arm, though I shook her off at once. 'I never thought they'd kill her! I didn't know they'd take any notice of a story of mine.

Anyway, it wasn't all lies. I saw them all up at Ambrisbeg, dancing and carrying on. The Devil might have been there. It looked as if he might have been.'

'And what were you doing out in the middle of the night at Ambrisbeg?'

She hung her head.

'We used to meet outside, near the loch. That's where he . . . I heard the music and I went to look. I was curious.'

I heard her smug little voice again, in my head.

'Maggie took off all her clothes,' I quoted, *'and danced around a stone.'*

'Oh, Maggie, I wish, I *wish* I hadn't said it, because now I've committed another terrible sin, and the Lord Jesus will never forgive me, and it didn't even do any good because Mr Macbean broke every promise he'd ever made, and said I would disgrace his good name, and he'd deny he'd touched me, and I was to go back to my father without a penny in my pocket. And then I had to watch everything, what they did to your Granny. It was so horrible. I thought I was going to be sick. I felt like a murderess.'

'That's what you are,' I spat at her. 'A thief, a liar and a murderess. Not many people can manage all that.'

'At least I won't be a thief any more,' she said, and the sigh she let out was the sincerest sound I'd ever heard from her. She fumbled inside her bodice and I saw a faint gleam of silver in her hand.

'Your buckle.' She handed it to me. 'I only took it because I was frightened. If I went home to my father he'd beat me half to death. I thought – if I only had a bit of money, I could manage on my own till the baby's born, and then I'd see. I'd try and find . . .'

I'd stopped listening to her. I'd suddenly realized the answer to the question that had been bothering me.

'Tam sent you, didn't he? That's how you knew where to find me. You cried all over him, and told him all this, and he's so soft he was sorry for you and said he'd help you.'

She sniffed, and I could tell that she was peering at me, trying to see my face in the growing dawn light.

'Yes, he did. He said he'd fix it with Mr Lithgow. He said I could get across to the mainland with the cattle.'

'Oh, he did, did he?'

I was enraged all over again, furious with Tam for saddling me with Annie, and jealous too. Tam was mine, my only friend. I didn't want to share him with anyone, especially not Annie.

A whistle sounded behind us and we both jerked our heads up.

'Tam!' we said together.

He slithered down the rocks and collapsed on to the mossy bed I'd made for myself.

'I'm too old for running round the country in the middle of the night,' he groaned, massaging his calves. 'If you girls aren't grateful to old Tam, then I'll die a disappointed man. Now let's get you down to the bothy. Those drovers will have the fire lit and porridge cooking on it, or they're not the men I think they are.'

Chapter Eleven

T am was right. The smell of birch smoke wafted towards us as we approached the bothy, and we could hear the men moving about inside. I had slipped off my girls' clothes and belted my father's plaid round me again, fixing the buckle in place with a defiant look at Annie. She had hardly been able to stop herself laughing at the way I looked, but she caught my eye and dropped her gaze. I strode ahead with my new-found boy's freedom, while Annie tripped daintily across the expanse of grass and bog reed, holding her skirt up to keep it out of the mud.

Tam kept looking over his shoulder.

'Will you hurry up now, Annie,' he kept saying. 'There might be other men along any minute with their cows.'

It was dark inside the windowless bothy and it took me a moment to make out the two men. The younger one was stirring a pot over the fire. The older one stood quietly, studying Annie.

'You don't take after your father,' he said, looking her up and down with a frown. She had tilted her head charmingly to one side and was smiling up at him.

'You've got the wrong lassie, Archie,' Tam said, pushing me forwards. 'This is Maggie.'

I felt Mr Lithgow's eyes on me and knew that a blush

was rising in my cheeks. I didn't like to think how I must look, with my boy's plaid, and my legs showing bare beneath my knees. But the leathery skin crinkled into a smile round his eyes.

'You're a boy now? Good. Much better. And you're not afraid of a long journey, and the rain, and sleeping in the open? Wading through rivers?'

'A bit, but I'll do my best.'

'Good,' he said again.

He nodded to the other man, who handed me a wooden bowl filled with porridge, and a horn spoon.

I moved away into the shadows, ashamed to let them see how eagerly I was gobbling down the food. The light from the open door fell on Mr Lithgow's face. He was frowning at Annie.

'Oh, Mr Lithgow,' she said, before he could speak, 'I'm so grateful to you for taking me. I'll be ever so helpful. I can cook and wash your clothes and – and . . .' Her eyes fell on the black-and-white collie dog lying silently by the fire, looking up at her with his snout resting on his forepaws. 'And look after the dogs,' she finished lamely.

'That's what you can do, is it?' Mr Lithgow said. 'Well, there's no call for finicky clothes-washing on a drove. The rain and the river crossings see to that. Peter Boag here cooks up the porridge. And if you were to interfere with the dogs you'd be away on your own, out of my drove, out of my way.'

Annie's lips tightened in disappointment, but just

then a call came from outside. Mr Lithgow's face darkened.

'I thought we had the full complement,' he muttered. 'Here's a chancer wanting a last-minute bargain price.'

He stepped out of the bothy.

'Glad I caught you, Archie,' came a voice that laid a hand of ice on me. I stood frozen, the last spoonful of porridge suspended in mid-air. 'I've three prime animals here for the market at Dumbarton. What price must I give you for taking them?'

It was Mr Lamont, the man who had sent my granny to her death, and condemned me to the gallows too.

Annie had clapped her hand over her mouth. Tam pursed his lips in a silent whistle and melted back into a dark corner of the bothy. Peter Boag, his face impassive, stood up and walked outside to join Mr Lithgow.

'What'll I do? He'll find me!' whispered Annie loudly.

'Will you shut *up*!' I mouthed at her.

The men outside were bargaining. They came to an agreement, sealed with a slap of a handshake, and then we heard the squelch and suck of mud as Mr Lamont's three cows crossed a patch of bog to join the rest of the herd, which was grazing peacefully by the water's edge.

'When are you off?' Mr Lamont was asking pleasantly.

'Soon,' said Mr Lithgow. 'The tide is low at eight. The ferryman will be rowing up now. He'll be here shortly.'

'I'll just wait and watch the crossing,' Mr Lamont

131

said. 'A fine sight, I'm sure, and one I've never witnessed.'

I held my breath during the silence that followed.

'You can watch all you like,' Mr Lithgow said at last, 'but not from here, if you please. The dogs are fussed by strangers when they're working. If you'll kindly retire to the far edge of the stance, beyond that stone wall, you'll see all you want to.'

'Oh, very well.'

Mr Lamont sounded offended, but there was too much authority in the head drover's voice to be contradicted. His footsteps died away.

Mr Lithgow came back into the bothy, ducking his head under the low doorway.

'This is bad. I take it the man knows you two girls?'

'Oh, not well, not well,' Tam babbled. 'He's seen them. He'll never recognize them. Why would he?'

'He'll know us,' I said firmly. 'He took evidence from Annie at the trial, and I stood right in front of him as he condemned me to death. He'd know me anywhere.'

Mr Lithgow went to the door and looked out, deep in thought, while Peter Boag quietly packed away the empty bowls and spoons in a saddlebag.

'I'll not take you,' he said to Annie at last. 'You'd best stay here in the bothy till the coast is clear, and find someone else to take you to the mainland.'

'Oh, but Mr Lithgow—' began Annie.

'But you, Maggie,' he said, ignoring her, 'by hook or by crook we'll have to get you away. Can you swim?'

I shook my head.

'You can't come over in the boat.' Mr Lithgow's hand was working round the smooth top of his staff as he spoke. 'Lamont'll have too much time to watch you and puzzle out who you are. You'll go over in the water with Samson.'

'S-Samson?' I managed to stammer.

'The pony. You'll hold on to his mane and bridle. He's a strong swimmer. He'll take you across. Kick out your legs to help him. You'll keep on the far side of him. Mr Lamont will see there's a boy with the pony, but he won't think anything of it.'

'Oh, Mr Lithgow,' Annie said pleadingly. 'Couldn't you take me in the boat? I'm not like Maggie. They're not after me the way they're after her.'

'You should have the decency to put Maggie's safety first, after the harm you've done,' Mr Lithgow said with brutal force. 'You'll do as you're told and stay in the bothy out of sight. See to it, Tam.'

'Oh aye,' came Tam's voice out of the corner. 'Leave it to me, Archie. You can trust me for that.'

I couldn't see him, but I knew there'd be a hunted, hurt look on his face, like a child whose cleverness has been mocked by an adult.

'Archie, are you there?' came a shout from the water's edge, and then a splash and a clatter of wood on wood as oars were being pulled back into a boat.

'The boatman's here,' said Mr Lithgow. 'Peter, we must get on. Listen carefully, Maggie. Peter and I will get the cows into the water. Stay inside till you hear me shout, "Danny". That's what you'll be called on the drove, after your father. When you hear it, come out of the bothy, nice and normal, no hurry, unhitch Samson and lead him into the water. He knows what to do. Stay on the left side of him and keep your head down. But don't look as if you're trying to hide. Once you're in the water, whatever you do, don't panic and drag on Samson's neck, or you'll pull his head under and he'll shake you off. Just hold to the mane and the bridle and let yourself be pulled along. We'll take your bundle and your plaid with us in the boat.'

He held out his hand, and, blushing, I undid my belt and handed him the thick woollen plaid, ashamed of standing before them in my father's shirt and trousers. He took it without seeming to notice anything strange, and went out, then I heard him whistle, and the dog leaped up and ran out after him.

'Tam!' I was shaking from head to foot. 'I can't do it! I can't swim across like that. I'll drown.'

He came out of his corner and hugged me.

'You'll be fine, Maidie. Archie Lithgow's the man for this. He knows what's what. You do like he says. He'll watch out for you. A lovely little bath, that's all it'll be, with the horse. No bother. I'd do it myself without a thought.'

I had to smile at that.

'No you wouldn't, Tam. You'd be in a panic if you were me, you know you would.'

'Aye, but then I'm not you, am I? You've got your granny in you, and your daddy too. And if you don't do it, you know what'll happen to you.'

I'd almost forgotten, in my rage with Annie and my terror of the crossing, the fate that awaited me if I was taken back to Rothesay, and I took a deep breath, summoning my courage.

Outside, we could hear splashes as the cows launched themselves into the water. Mr Lithgow was shouting encouragement and whistling to the dogs.

I dared to look out through the door. Most of the cattle were in the water already, swimming strongly, their red, horned heads bobbing swiftly above the eddying currents of the kyle, the fast-flowing channel of water that separated Bute from the mainland. Mr Lithgow was in the boat, being rowed across to the island. Peter Boag, with one of the dogs, was chivvying the last reluctant cows to take the plunge. I had a moment's dread, mixed almost with relief, that I was to be left behind.

'Danny! Bring Samson!' came Mr Lithgow's voice loud and clear from across the water. His shout echoed from the hills on the far side.

'Goodbye, Tam.' I gave the old man one last hug. 'You've saved my life twice now. I won't ever, ever forget it.'

'Get on with you, Maidie.' His voice shook.

'Goodbye, Maggie,' said Annie, and in the quick glance I gave her I saw the old malice sparkle in her eyes.

I went outside, not daring to look at the wall over to my right, and fumbled with Samson's bridle, my fingers all thumbs.

'Danny, come on, will you!' Mr Lithgow called again.

And then I was running beside the trotting pony, down across the lush grass of Bute to the little strip of pale sand, and my bare feet were crunching on the litter of white shells, and then there was the water, ice cold, making me gasp with the shock of it, and I was hanging on to Samson's bridle as he pulled me in, and the touch of land fell away beneath my feet, the last touch of my island, and I was struggling, choking and gasping as the water closed over my head.

It was only the thought of the gallows and the fire waiting for me in Rothesay that stopped me giving up the attempt to cross that fast-flowing channel of freezing water. Without the fear of what was behind me, I'd have thrashed my way back to the shore of Bute. But the thought came to me that if I had to die, I would rather it was by my own action than through the cruelty of others.

I managed to keep my head out of the water until we were more than halfway across. Then my fingers, which were stiff and numb with cold, slipped from the pony's wet mane. I was under the water at once, and only frantic kicks brought my head up again. Luckily, Samson's bridle was wrapped round my other wrist. I was dragging too hard on him, and he was starting to struggle in the water. For a moment I panicked, terrified that he would shake himself free of me, but from somewhere outside myself came a feeling of calm and strength.

Taking a deep breath, I hauled on the bridle and drew myself close enough to catch Samson's mane again. A few moments later his hoofs rattled against the rocky shore of the little island, and he was off at once, scrambling out of the water. I managed to release his bridle just in time to prevent myself being dragged on my knees across the stones. I had done it. I had felt my father's presence with me in the water, giving me the strength to survive. The thought was comforting, but disturbing too, and I put it away from me.

The cattle were already on the far side of the tiny wooded island, plunging without hesitation into the second channel. I stood for a moment, shaking uncontrollably with the cold.

'Danny!' Mr Lithgow called.

I looked round, thinking for a strange, unnerving moment that he had seen my father and was calling to him, but then I remembered my new name, and I staggered stiffly across the rough ground, streams of water running off my shirt.

'You can get in the boat this time,' Mr Lithgow said. 'Lamont won't see you clearly from this distance. Here, take your plaid.'

I dared to glance back. Mr Lamont seemed to have lost interest in the crossing of the cattle. His stocky figure could be seen walking back along the coastal path towards Rothesay. I looked across at the bothy. There was no sign of Annie, but Tam was standing in the doorway, shading his eyes from the rising sun as he peered in my direction. I dared to raise my hand for a brief moment. I didn't wait to see an answering wave, but scrambled into the little boat, keeping my head turned away from the boatman. A few minutes later I was standing with the others on the shore of Cowal, and the boatman, who seemed to have noticed nothing strange about me, was already pushing an oar against the rocks to set himself afloat for the journey back to Rothesay.

I hadn't had a chance until that moment to give any thought to the journey ahead, or the men I would be travelling with, but now I felt self-conscious and unsure of what was expected of me. Mr Lithgow and Peter Boag had quietly loaded their sack of oatmeal along with my bundle on to Samson's back, and they were sending the dogs with shrill whistles of command to fetch back the straying cows.

I watched them, unobserved. They were both stocky, bearded men, their hair shaggy, wearing their bulky plaids belted round their waists like Highland men. I could see how strongly muscled their legs were, and how the soles of their bare feet were as hard as leather. Mr Lithgow was taller than Peter Boag. He was a great bull of a man. They worked quietly, their voices low, their whistles sure, their movements calm and slow to reassure the cattle. Neither of them looked as if they ever spoke much, or gave away their thoughts.

At least the sun was shining. I wrung as much water out of my shirt as I could, hoping it would soon dry off. My dull brown hair, always fine and wispy and now cropped close to my head, was drying already.

Mr Lithgow spoke to me at last.

'We'll stay here for an hour or so. Give the beasts time to rest and recover.'

We sat together, the three of us, on a low stone wall that edged the grazing place, while the cattle, their red backs steaming in the cold air, stood up to their hocks in the boggy green grass. The dogs lay quietly under a nearby tree, their tongues out, watching Mr Lithgow and waiting for their orders.

At last, after a long silence, Mr Lithgow cleared his throat.

'So old Tam got you away then, Maggie. I thought he was nothing but a daft old drunkard, but he turned out cleverer than all those ministers and elders and sheriff's men.'

'I'd like to have seen Donnie Brown's face when he woke up in the morning and found you gone,' Peter Boag put in, as if he'd been waiting for permission to speak.

A rumble of laughter rose from Mr Lithgow's chest and erupted in a guffaw.

'From what I heard, old Elspeth put it about that it was the Devil himself who got you out, flying away with you over the rooftops.' Out of the corner of my eye, I saw Peter shiver and draw his plaid round himself.

'Did you see him – the Devil?' he said leaning forwards. 'What did he look like?'

I stared at him, shocked.

'No, Mr Boag. Of course I didn't! I'm not – it was all lies. Everything they said about me and Granny was lies!'

'Well, about you, but I heard that your grandmother, she could—'

'That's enough, Peter, you loon,' Mr Lithgow broke in. 'You're as bad as the rest of those superstitious fools. I told you, I knew Elspeth Wylie. Danny Blair was her son-in-law, and he was the best drover in the west of Scotland. A great man. "If you have to have a mother-in-law, Archie," he said to me once, "don't pick one like Elspeth Wylie. She's a cantankerous, sour, bitter old body, with a liking for stirring up mischief wherever she goes. But her heart's in the right place, when it comes down to it." Danny would have sniffed out anything wrong in her. He was a shrewd man. And this is his daughter, Peter – don't you forget it. His flesh and blood. So mind your tongue before you throw around talk of witches and sorcery and the like.'

Peter Boag dropped his eyes, but I could tell he wasn't convinced. Mr Lithgow was frowning as he thought of something else.

'That Annie girl,' he said to me. 'What made her do such a terrible thing to you both? The lies she told! What made her hate you?'

I told him about Mr Macbean, and how he'd forced Annie to give evidence, and the baby she was expecting. They stared at me, shocked.

'Such wickedness,' Mr Lithgow said at last. 'I can hardly believe it. I know Macbean's a mean man, slow to settle his debts, but he's an elder of the kirk! To commit adultery in his own house, with his own servant! And to condemn a woman and girl to death for the sake of a

140

wee tumbledown cottage and a field! The Lord will punish the lot of them, Maggie. God is not mocked.'

He stood up and the dogs were at his heels at once, their ears cocked, waiting.

'You go ahead at the front, Peter,' Mr Lithgow said. 'Follow the track along the water's edge. I'll take the rear. Maggie, you'll walk with me. Watch the way we do it. Steadiness and quietness on the drove – that's how it should be. Nothing loud or sudden to alarm the cattle. We're not likely to pass anyone between now and our resting place tonight, but if we do, just leave all the talking to me.'

It was quiet and peaceful walking along the water's edge, behind the strolling cattle headed by Peter Boag, who was leading Samson. I went alongside Mr Lithgow, who didn't seem inclined to speak. His eyes were constantly on the beasts, watching all the time to see if a frisky calf or an obstinate cow took it into their heads to stray. When one did, his lips rounded in a whistle and one of the dogs slipped off, a silent black shadow, to bring the straggler back.

As he walked, he knitted a stocking which fell in a long curve from his needles. The ball of wool was tucked inside his plaid. The clicking rhythm soothed me even more, and I fell into a kind of mindless trance, while the terror and strain of the past dreadful days began to leach away.

After an hour or two, the track began to lead uphill and as we gently climbed I could look back and see the

Isle of Bute lying there, between the kyles. But after the first quick glance I didn't want to look again.

The morning had been sunny, but wisps of mist were curling over the heights above us and soon we were walking through a strange white world. The dogs were busier than ever, and Mr Lithgow put away his knitting and walked briskly from side to side, calling out to Peter Boag ahead, peering into the mist to look for wanderers. Once or twice a gap opened in the cloud, and I saw great sweeps of moorland stretching up and away, and frowning crags above us, and huge slabs of wet grey rock. I had never known that such a desolate place existed.

What if the Devil comes on us here? I thought. *What if he comes roaring down from the mountain tops with his eyes like burning coals, and makes me be a witch and fly on a stick, and then drags me with him down to Hell?*

'No! I won't go!' I must have said out loud, because Mr Lithgow, who was walking beside me again, looked down at me curiously.

'What's that you said?'

'Nothing,' I mumbled. But then there came a terrible wailing cry, piercing and despairing, from the crag that loomed up ahead of us. It was a damned soul, I was sure of it, and I said, all in a rush, 'I'm scared of the Devil, Mr Lithgow. What if he comes here and tries to make me his servant because I wouldn't be a witch?'

He didn't laugh.

'Oh, my lass,' was all he said. 'You've a head full of fancies.'

'But that shriek! It sounded like a soul in torment!'

He did smile then.

'You must have heard an eagle before! That was him, calling to his missus.'

'Oh.' I only half believed him. 'But—'

'It's not devils or dead souls or anything unearthly that worries me on the drove.' He had turned and was scanning the ridge above us, which had momentarily appeared through the mist. 'It's men of flesh and blood. Highlanders. They don't often come raiding this far south, but if they caught us here we'd be as good as dead.'

He touched his belt, and for the first time I noticed the dagger that was stuck in it.

I caught my breath.

'Are they up there? Are they coming?'

I looked up towards the ridge too, but the mist had closed in again.

'No, no. The country's peaceful just now. We'll be safe enough if that dozy lad Peter Boag doesn't lead us all over a cliff.'

The thought of savage clansmen screaming down on us from the north, their swords whirling round their heads, should have made me shiver, but in a strange way I was comforted. They had driven out the idea of Satan and his legions of demons, which were far, far more frightening.

A little later, the mist thinned and turned golden, with the sun shining through it, and the whole world was bathed in glory. The vapour cleared quickly and I looked out, astonished, at the vast new world we'd entered. Hillsides with white ribbons of water streaming down them swooped low into the valleys. Rocks in tumbled piles towered over us. I had never been anywhere like this before. There was nowhere so wild and solitary on the Isle of Bute.

When the last traces of mist had melted away, Mr Lithgow brought out his knitting again and resumed his careful watching of the cows' swaying rumps as they plodded on in front of us.

There was something else I knew I had to say.

'Granny wasn't a witch, Mr Lithgow – not an evil one – but she knew about bringing babies safe into the world, and what was unlucky, like the swifts and the swallows, and things like charming to find lost things, and how to protect from the fairies.' *And curses*, I thought, but kept to myself. *She knew plenty of those.*

'She knew all that, did she?'

It wasn't easy to tell what he was thinking, because the hair falling down over his forehead and the beard curling thickly round his mouth hid much of his face. His voice, though, sounded friendly enough.

'And she knew about healing too, if you had a bad stomach or a headache.'

'Did her cures work?'

'Oh yes! Well, I think so.'

It had never occurred to me that Granny's healing charms might not work. I had just assumed they did.

'But the church people thought all that was wicked,'

I persisted. 'And what I want to know, Mr Lithgow, is do you think Granny has gone to Hell? Is she going to burn in the pit of fire forever?'

He didn't answer straight away, and glancing up at him I saw a frown divide his brows.

'Well now,' he said at last. 'There's a question. You should ask a minister, an educated man.' I said nothing, waiting for him to go on. 'They talk of Hell, the preachers. And if it's in the Bible I suppose it must be right. But look around you. Creation. Flowers. Birds. The sun.' He coughed, as if embarrassed. 'If God could make all this, why would He bother to make a Hell?'

He was looking down at something, and following his gaze I saw a blue butterfly settle with a flutter of its wings on one of the tiny yellow flowers that shone like jewels among the bright green grass. Then he whistled to the dogs, unnecessarily I thought, and speeded up as if he wanted to get away from me.

I didn't mind. I knew I hadn't angered him. He just didn't like talking about such things.

What did he mean? I thought. *Does he really not believe in Hell?* The idea that Hell might not be there after all was so daring that I stopped walking and stood, stuck to the ground. Then I caught in my nostrils a sudden strong honey scent of heather, which the warmth of the sun was bringing out, and I threw my head back to sniff at it luxuriously.

Why would God make Hell, when He can make all this? I repeated to myself, but I was afraid that the thought was wrong, and I put it away from me as I hurried to catch Mr Lithgow up.

It was the faint whiff of peat smoke which told us we were near our evening's rest. We came round the shoulder of a hill and could look down on the roof of a small house lying by a loch. Peter Boag had already led the cattle through a gap in a dry stone wall, and he was lifting our bundles from Samson's back.

The sun was still quite high in the sky, and we hadn't been walking for more than five or six hours. I'd expected to cover a greater distance in a day, so I was surprised when Mr Lithgow said, 'Here we are. The day's over.'

A woman had come out of the cottage. She didn't seem alarmed to see the great herd of cows already grazing in her field.

'The drove always stops here,' said Mr Lithgow, seeing my surprise. 'She'll cook our food for us. We sleep out in the open, along with the beasts.' He coughed, embarrassed. 'You could ask for her to let you sleep inside, Maggie, but—'

'No, I'll stay outside with you,' I said, seeing the woman look curiously towards me. 'I want to keep out of her way.'

'Good. That's best.' He sounded relieved. 'News seems to travel through the air, even in a lonely place like this. Everyone'll know soon enough that a witch girl has escaped from Rothesay. The hunt will be on for you all over the country. I'll tell her you're my sister's son, coming on the drove to learn the way of it, but that you're shy and don't like to deal with strangers. Now stay here while I go and beat some sense into Peter's head, or he'll blab out what shouldn't be said.'

I was scared at the thought of the night to come. At Scalpsie Bay we knew the places where fairies and elves lived, and where ghosts might walk, and it was easy to avoid them. But to sleep outside, in an unknown place, unwitting and unprotected, seemed foolish and risky to me. Granny would have known how to keep uncanny beings at bay, but I had never learned that kind of thing from her.

I put up my hand to brush away the persistent midges, and my fingers touched the silver buckle on my belt. I clasped it tightly. Silver protected people, I knew, against the spirit powers. Perhaps my buckle would be powerful enough to protect me.

I was worrying about this, sitting on a convenient boulder in the corner of the field, when Peter brought my supper out to me. He and Mr Lithgow had eaten their porridge, cheese and oatcakes inside with the woman. He stood beside me, leaning on his staff and looking down at me as I ate. At last he cleared his throat and said, 'You could help me if you had a mind to.'

I swallowed a crumb of cheese.

'How?'

'It's my ear. It's been aching this whole week past. The pain is like a hammer banging away in my head. You can make it better, I know you can. She must have taught you something. You must know what to do. Look –' he fumbled in the pouch at his belt – 'here's a penny for you if you get the pain off me.'

I shook my head.

'I don't know anything about healing, Mr Boag. I'm sorry. I'd help you if I could.'

He glanced swiftly back towards the cottage, but no one was visible.

'I wouldn't tell anyone. Just between you and me. Please! The pain's killing me.'

I heard Granny's voice in my head. There was a thing she would chant sometimes, when she was tying a thread around a sick baby's body, or burning oak leaves on a fire:

> *God teach me to pray*
> *To put this ill away*
> *Out of flesh, blood and bone . . .*

I couldn't remember the whole thing, and anyway, the words would have done no good without the thread, or some such magical thing. I shook my head.

'I'm sorry. I really don't know anything.'

But he had seen me hesitate. He was about to speak again when Mr Lithgow called to him from the cottage door.

The evening was a long one as I sat alone in the corner of the field, idly watching the cows as the voices of the others rose and fell inside the cottage. When the sun finally set, the two men came out, their faces flushed with whisky. Mr Lithgow was already yawning mightily and unbuckling his belt, ready to wrap his plaid more comfortably round himself for the night. He inspected the ground near where I was sitting, kicked away some crusts of dried dung and lay down on his back, his hands crossed on his chest. Peter Boag, grimacing with the pain in his ear, gave me a sour look before he too lay down and closed his eyes. Within minutes, their heavy breathing told me that they were asleep.

Tired though I was, it was a long time before I could shut my eyes. I lay looking up at the darkening sky, watching it turn from deep blue to black as the sunset glow faded. The stars appeared as if they were pinpricks in a cloth at first, then they blazed more and more brightly.

How will I find my way to Ladymuir? I thought. *And if I get there, will my uncle want me? What if I'm caught and taken back to Bute?*

An eerie scream from some way off made me jump and I pulled my plaid over my head, shivering with fright. The noise came again. I relaxed. It was only a hare after all, caught in the teeth of a fox. I poked my head out, smiling at my own silliness. It was reassuring to hear the snores of the men and the quiet slurping as the cows chewed their cud nearby. I turned over on to my side, wriggling to find a comfortable position.

Suddenly, the words of Granny's healing chant came back to me, and I whispered them as I fell asleep:

149

God teach me to pray
To put this ill away,
Out of flesh, blood and bone,
Into the earth and cold stone,
And never to come again,
In God's name.

Chapter Twelve

I slept so deeply that night that it took a prod from Peter Boag's stick to wake me. The sun had been up for hours, and I saw that I had slept long after the other two had risen. Peter was holding a bowl of porridge out to me, and smiling from ear to ear.

'Little miracle worker, you are,' he said. 'I knew it. You needn't have pretended. I wouldn't have let on. Here's your penny. You've more than earned it.'

I must have looked like a halfwit, staring up at him, bemused and still half asleep.

'My earache,' he said, as if I must know what he meant. 'It's gone. Look!'

He bent his head and I saw that a trickle of thick yellow pus was dribbling from his ear.

'The evil humour's coming out, you see? You've purged it.'

'No!' I lurched to my feet and grabbed at my plaid, which had fallen away so that too much of me was open to view. 'I never did anything! I don't know—'

'Oh, lassie, don't bother. Your secret's safe. I told you I'll not tell anyone, and I mean it.'

He thrust the penny into my reluctant hand and turned away before I could stop him.

Well, I thought, as I tied it into my father's shirt-tail, and took up the spoon to eat my breakfast, *a penny is a penny, when all's said and done, and after all, I did say the charm right through before I went to sleep.*

I should have felt glad, I suppose, that Peter Boag's ear no longer hurt him, but in fact I was dismayed. I wanted no strange powers, good or evil. I wanted only to be ordinary, a plain girl, living safe and respectable in a proper family. And a wife one day. And a mother.

We were lucky, on those long, slow days of the drove, because the weather was kind to us. A few sharp showers came tumbling out of sullen clouds which swept as fast as racing horses across the hilltops, but most of the time the sun shone, turning the lochs as blue as cut-out pieces from the sky, and making the heather on the hillsides glow in purple splendour.

I was soon used to splashing through the streams, and even wading across fast-flowing rivers, but I was glad that I never had to swim in deep water again. The further we moved from the Isle of Bute, the less I feared discovery, so I was not afraid to be recognized as we were rowed by ferrymen across the lochs and greater rivers, looking back at the cows who bobbed along after the boat, their noses stretched up out of the water. I was grateful, from the bottom of my heart, that I wasn't struggling along with them.

We seemed to have been on the drove for months, and I had become used to the pace and rhythm of it, but in fact only a week had gone by when Mr Lithgow said, 'Well, Maggie, we'll be in Dumbarton tomorrow, and you'll have to make your own way from there.'

I'd known it was coming, of course, but still my heart sank at the thought. Mr Lithgow must have been watching my face, because he said, 'No need to look like that. It's just a wee sail across the Clyde from Dumbarton, and no more than ten miles south to Ladymuir. You can walk it in a morning, easily.'

I knew Granny would have thought me feeble, but I couldn't help saying, 'How will I find my way, Mr Lithgow? And what if I'm stopped for being a vagabond?'

'I've thought of that.' He lifted his spare knitting needle to poke through his matted beard and scratch at his chin. 'You'll show them your buckle, and you'll tell the ferryman and anyone else who asks that you're the drover Archie Lithgow's young cousin, and you're taking a message down to Mr Blair about the cattle he wants to sell. You've taken colour in your cheeks and legs this past week. You look more like a boy now than any girl I've ever seen. There'll be no need to hide and fear questions along the way. The ferryman will point you on the path to Kilmacolm, and once you're there at the crossroads you'll ask the way to Lochwinnoch. Ladymuir's along that way. You'll find it easily enough.'

'Have you been there yourself, Mr Lithgow?'

'I have. Many years ago. With your father.'

It was the first time he'd told me of it. Questions bubbled up inside me. I had to pause and choose them carefully. I knew Mr Lithgow wouldn't like to be asked too many.

'Did you ever meet my Uncle Blair?' I said at last. 'What kind of a man is he?'

As soon as I'd said it, I knew it was the kind of question he would find hard to answer. He chewed at his moustache as he thought about it.

'He's a tall enough fellow.'

I waited hopefully.

'A good farmer, I'm told. A respectable man. An elder of the church.'

'Oh.'

This was daunting news. What would an elder of the church think of me, a condemned witch, running around the country dressed as a boy?

'He's a man of the Covenant, so I've heard. A very staunch one.'

'A what?'

'A Covenanter.'

I'd never heard the word before. I didn't like to show my ignorance, but luckily he went on.

'You'll not have heard much about the Covenanters, Maggie?'

'No.'

'You will soon. The whole countryside in these parts, and down round Kilmacolm, is buzzing with the struggle.'

'What struggle?'

He scratched at his ear this time, as if he didn't know where to begin.

'You'll have heard of the King, Charles Stuart?'

I nodded warily, though I hardly ever had.

'He sits in England with the crown on his head and thinks he can tell us up here what's right and what's wrong. What business is it of his to tell us here in Scotland how to say our prayers?'

He sounded bitter.

'Are you a Covenanter then, Mr Lithgow?'

'Me? I can't read or write. A drover like me goes around the country here and there. Who's going to ask me what I think about how the Church should be governed, and whether the King's bishops should be the men to do it? No one's asked me to sign a Covenant, and call myself a Covenanter. There's right on their side, I suppose. The King wants his own way, but if it isn't God's way, then he shouldn't have it.'

'What's the King's way?' I asked, even more confused. 'What's God's way?'

But Mr Lithgow had come to the end of his patience with my questions, and, as he always did when he wanted a conversation to end, he whistled to the dogs to round up imaginary stragglers.

We came into Dumbarton late that afternoon. I could hear the noise of the place a good mile before we reached the town, which lay on the shores of the Clyde. There was a din of shouting men and lowing cattle, the clatter of hoofs on wooden ramps and all the hammering and banging of tradespeople at work. There must have been thirty or forty houses in Dumbarton, and more than a thousand people congregated in the open there. I had never seen such a big town, or thought that so many people could be gathered together in one place. I felt nervous, and stayed as close to Mr Lithgow as I could.

We had spent the night at a drovers' stance only a mile or so from the town, so it was still early in the day. I could tell by the frown drawing Mr Lithgow's bushy brows together that he was preoccupied with the business ahead. As he led his cattle into the sales area, his eyes darted about, looking critically at the state of other herds and comparing them to his own.

Down on the shore, wide, flat-bottomed boats were drawn up out of the current of the swift-flowing estuary. Cows were being driven up the ramps on to the boats, bellowing with nerves. The corners of Mr Lithgow's eyes crinkled in a quick smile of recognition as he stared at the boatmen.

'Here, Peter, watch the herd,' he said suddenly, and hurried down to talk to one of the men who was standing by the mast of his boat, untying the reefs of the sail. The boat was already laden with cattle, and the other boatmen were ready at the oars.

Mr Lithgow turned and beckoned to me.

'That's you away then,' said Peter Boag.

I was already hurrying towards the boat and didn't take in what he meant.

'Mr Gillies is ready to take you across, Ma— Danny,' Mr Lithgow said. 'Hurry and fetch your bundle.'

I raced back to Peter Boag. He had already taken my things off Samson's back, and he put the bundle in my arms.

'Good luck you. You're a one, you are. I'll come and find you if the other ear goes.'

I was so shaken by the suddenness of this parting that I didn't know what to say. I looked around to see that the boat was already pulling away from the shore. I sprinted back to it and had to run through the shallows, splashing wildly, before I could scramble on board. The wind had caught at the sail and the oarsmen were already at work.

I looked back at Mr Lithgow. There had been no time to say goodbye to him or to thank him for his part in saving my life. He hadn't even waved at me, but was walking back to his cows.

I'm just a bit of finished business to him, I thought. *He's done with me now.*

A dreadful loneliness swept over me. For the first time I was truly alone. Granny had given me, in her own strange way, into Tam's care, and he had passed me to Mr Lithgow. There was no one I could turn to now. I had grown used, in the days of the drove, to the quiet, thoughtful men and the slowly moving cows. I hadn't had to think of what road to take, or what to eat, or where to rest at night. But now, as I looked out at the mile-wide sweep of the mighty Clyde, I knew that everything was up to me.

Kilmacolm, I said to myself, my knuckles whitening as I gripped the wooden side of the boat. *Ladymuir. Uncle Blair.*

The words were like one of Granny's spells, full of mystery and magic. They held all my hopes.

*

It was already well after midday when I stepped ashore on the far side. The crossing had taken a long time, with contrary winds, and I was afraid that I wouldn't find my way to Ladymuir until after everyone was in bed.

I fumbled for my shirt-tail and untied the penny, but when I offered it to Mr Gillies he shook his head.

'Keep your penny, lad. Archie Lithgow paid me. He told me to put you on the track for Kilmacolm. You've to take the path east along the bank here, to that small stand of trees you can see in the distance. Turn along the path there and follow it up and over the hill. It winds around a bit, but follow on and you'll come to Kilmacolm. You'll see it below you in the hollow. The crossroads is beyond the kirk. Turn south, down to the right. You'll see the peak of Misty Law up ahead. I don't know the farm you're looking for, but that's the way to Lochwinnoch.'

He was off at once, calling to one of the boat lads to tie up more securely before disembarking the cattle. There was no reason for me to linger, and I took a deep breath and started walking fast along the water's edge towards the rowan trees, warmed by the thought of Mr Lithgow's care for me, even after we had parted. I should have known better than to expect fine words from him at parting. I should have known that wouldn't be his way.

I came to Ladymuir late in the evening. My feet were sore from fast walking, my arms ached from the weight of my bundle and my stomach was growling with hunger. Worst of all, my heart was hammering with shyness and fear.

What if they turn me away? I kept asking myself. *Where will I go?*

I'd met few people along the way, but it had been easy enough to find Kilmacolm and the path leading from there to Lochwinnoch. There were clusters of farm hamlets squatting in the folds of the hills all around, and I might have walked right past the track leading to Ladymuir if I hadn't luckily met with a pedlar, who pointed it out to me with a grudging flick of his head.

This is it, I told myself. *I'm here. Now for it.*

If I hadn't been so tired and hungry, I think I'd have stood for hours there in that narrow, muddy lane, plucking up the courage to step up the few hundred yards to the cluster of long stone buildings under the shade of several tall ash trees, but it was already late in the long summer evening, and I knew that if I didn't screw my courage up and knock at the farm door, the family would be away in their beds and I'd have to spend the night supperless in the open.

I looked up and down the lane and scanned the bare hilltops. No one seemed to be about. Quickly, I untied my bundle and shook out my old gown. It would be best to start off on an honest foot, to show myself to my uncle and aunt as the person I really was. A few minutes later, I was a girl again. The strings of my cap were tied under my chin, hiding my short boyish hair, and my father's clothes were wrapped up in my bundle. I arranged his plaid round me like a woman's shawl, taking comfort from the smell of cows and heather it had acquired, then I took a deep breath and marched up the track towards the farm.

The first living creatures I saw were the dogs. Two black-and-white collies which had been lying at the farmhouse door stood up as I approached and came towards me. Trained to silence, they didn't bark, but one bared his teeth and growled. I stood still and let them sniff me. They seemed reassured by the smell of the cows on me, and let me pass.

The farm buildings were set round three sides of a square. The dwelling house was big, bigger than Macbean's farm at Scalpsie. There was even a chimney at one end of it, and two windows, one on each side of the door, their wooden shutters already closed. I hesitated. The door was forbiddingly shut, and I didn't dare to knock. Then I heard the sound of quiet singing. Two or three men's voices rumbled low, with a couple of women warbling above. It was the first time I had ever heard the evening psalm and its sweetness gave me courage:

> *I will both lay me down in peace*
> *And quiet sleep will take;*
> *Because Thou only me to dwell*
> *In safety, Lord, dost make.*

When the singing stopped, there was a confused murmur of 'Goodnight, goodnight,' and then the latch of the door was lifted and two men came out. They started with surprise when they saw me, hovering shyly by the barn.

'Master!' one of them called back into the house. 'There's a lass out here.'

I knew at once that the man who came to the door was my Uncle Blair, and I'll never forget that first sight of him. He was indeed a tall man, as Mr Lithgow had said, and he had to bend his head right down under the low lintel of the door as he stepped outside. His fine fair hair fell to his shoulders, and his face was clean-looking, like Mr Robertson's. It wasn't a drinker's face, I could tell. He stood with one hand on the door frame, peering out at me in the faint evening light.

'Who's there?' he called out. 'Why, it *is* a lass.'

It was his voice that undid me. It unlocked a memory from long ago, of another big man, who had swung me up in his arms. I felt tears prick my eyelids and had to swallow hard.

'I'm Maggie Blair,' I said. 'I'm your brother Danny's daughter.'

A woman appeared at his shoulder. I could barely see her, standing in the shadows.

'Is it beggars again, Hugh? Take care. There may be others hiding behind her.'

He didn't answer her, but stepped out of the house and came to look at me more closely. I was nearly full grown already, but he towered over me.

'I believe you are,' he said. 'I believe you really are

Danny's wee girl. What brings you here so late? Surely you haven't come alone?'

There was such kindness in his voice that I found it hard to control my tears again, but the woman's voice, fretful and suspicious, set me on my guard again.

'Who is it, Hugh? Be careful. What does she want?'

A boy, older than me, had appeared at the door now, and a girl peeped round from behind him.

'It's my brother Danny's daughter, Isobel,' he said, with blessed certainty. 'She looks half dead too. Come away in, lassie. Have you eaten your supper? Get her some broth, and an oatcake. Now then – Maggie, is it? – there's no need for that.'

I had been overcome at last with tears of relief and joy.

'Thank you,' was all I could manage to gasp out. 'Oh, please – thank you.'

It felt like a dream to enter that clean, well-ordered room, to be given a bowl of broth, to have my bundle taken from me and set down on the floor. I felt so shy of the ring of faces staring at me, and so overwhelmed by tiredness and tears, that I could hardly bring out a word in answer to my uncle's questions.

'Let the girl sleep,' he said at last. 'We'll hear all about it in the morning.' He nodded at the girl standing by the dresser. She was about my age and size. 'Grizel, you'll make room in your bed for Maggie.'

He had already slid open one of the wooden doors that lined the wall to show a bed in the cupboard behind it. The room quickly emptied. The two men and the boy went outside again, and I heard their steps retreat

162

towards the barn. The girl, Grizel, had reached into the bed and brought out a linen shift. I stared as she took off her woollen gown and underskirt, and slipped the shift over her head. I'd never known anyone have special clothes for the night before. Uncertainly, I unwrapped my bundle and took out my father's shirt, ashamed to see, in the last faint glimmer of light through the window, how grimed and stiff with dirt it was.

Grizel hopped up on to the bed and I started to climb in after her. A sleepy mumbling from the recess startled me.

'It's only the little ones,' Grizel said, picking up a child and shifting it aside. I couldn't tell from her voice if she was well-disposed to me or not.

Tomorrow, I thought, my limbs so heavy with tiredness that I could hardly find the strength to turn over on to my side. *I'll worry about that tomorrow.*

Grizel leaned across me to slide the door across, and we were enclosed in dense, stuffy darkness. Through the mists of sleep engulfing me, I heard my uncle and aunt settle themselves in the box bed beside ours, and the murmur of their voices.

'How do you know,' I thought I heard her say, 'that she's not been sent to spy on us?' but the words made no sense to me. I heard my uncle's answer, calm and reassuring, and then all was blotted out in sleep.

A rapping on the door startled me awake. I jerked upright, not knowing where I was. The door opened. A glow of morning light shone in, making me blink.

Ladymuir, I whispered to myself. *I'm at Ladymuir. I'm safe.*

Grizel was already climbing over me. Two wriggling little figures scrambled after her. They stood staring back into the bed, astonished at the sight of a stranger there.

'That's Martha,' Grizel said, pointing to the bigger of the two girls, whose solemn blue eyes were round with wonder.

'And she's Nanny.'

The smaller one, hearing her name, shrank behind her sister.

'You'd best get your clothes on quick,' Grizel said, 'before the others come in for their breakfast.'

I jumped out of bed and fumbled to put my clothes on, screwing up my father's shirt to hide its filth and bundling it back into the bed.

'Mistress won't like that,' Grizel said reprovingly, picking it up to fold it neatly. 'You'd best wash it anyway. Look at the state it's in!'

I saw disgust in her face, but I had taken courage from the word 'mistress'. Grizel was a servant, not a daughter of the family. I needn't be too afraid of her.

The room, which had been empty, was suddenly full of people.

'Blow up the fire, Grizel,' Aunt Blair was saying. 'Get the porridge on.' She turned to the boy. 'Ritchie, fetch in water. What's the matter with everyone this morning? You're all half asleep.'

She didn't look at me or greet me, and my heart sank.

I didn't know what to do or how to occupy myself. I stood in the corner like a great fool, with everyone bustling round me. Then I saw that little Nanny was struggling to set her cap on her head, so I knelt down beside her, tucked her long fair locks behind her ears, and tied the strings under her chin.

Uncle Blair came in from outside, ducking his head under the lintel.

'Good, Maggie, good. Making yourself useful already.' He shot a quick glance at his wife, but she was stirring the pot suspended over the fire and didn't turn round. He turned to smile at me again, but a faint frown wrinkled his forehead. 'You'll be wanting to wash your face and hands. Grizel will show you the well.'

A fiery blush rushed up my cheeks. There'd been no thought of washing on the drove. My fingernails were long and black, my hair a matted mess, and my face no doubt streaked with dirt. I must have looked like a common vagabond, as out of place in this orderly room as a blowfly on a butter dish.

Like everything else at Ladymuir, the well was neatly built. Stone slabs had been laid around it to keep the mud at bay. The handle turned easily, and the bucket rose on a sturdy new rope. I did my best with my face and hands, and scrubbed at the worst stains on my bodice, which still bore the marks of the green slime from the walls of the Rothesay tollbooth, but I was sure I looked a fright as I went back to the house.

Breakfast had already been laid. There was a white linen cloth on the trestle table, and bowls and spoons laid out on it for each person. It seemed very grand to me. Granny and I had eaten from one bowl on bare wood, and we had never owned more than two spoons altogether.

The two serving men came in, and all took their places on the benches. I hung back, not sure if I was expected to sit too. The bowls were still empty. Was I meant to serve out the porridge?

'Sit down, Maggie,' Uncle Blair said. 'We can't begin till grace is said.' He waited gravely till I was seated, then everyone bent their heads and he began to pray. I looked round the table. All eyes were shut, all hands clasped, except for little Martha's. She was peeking at me over the rim of her bowl. When she caught my eye, she shut hers quickly and looked down.

I didn't hear a word of the long prayer. I was studying the faces round the table. Uncle Blair and Aunt Blair, one at each end, were clear enough. The little girls were surely their daughters, and Grizel was the servant. But was the boy Ritchie a son of the house, or a serving man like the others who had slept in the barn? He was older than me, seventeen or eighteen I reckoned. He had Uncle Blair's clear, wide forehead and fine pale hair, but he was shorter, more like Aunt Blair in build, stocky rather than lean. By the time the grace came at last to an end I was sure of it. Ritchie was a son of the house, a Blair like me. A cousin. I only hoped he would be my friend.

Grizel served out the porridge and as soon as we had all eaten, the two men went outside to their work. Aunt

Blair stood up to clear the bowls, but Uncle Blair said, 'Sit down, Isobel. Now, Maggie, you know you're welcome here, but perhaps you will tell us what brings you here, on your own, a young lass like you, with no one to accompany you?'

It was the moment I'd been dreading. Aunt Blair sat down again at once, and I could see avid curiosity along with disapproval in her face. Ritchie was staring at me with a measuring look, as if he had encountered an interesting new insect, and Grizel's mouth was half open, like a child waiting to hear a story. The little girls leaned their arms on the table and cupped their chins in their hands, their eyes fixed on me.

I took a deep breath.

'You know that my mother died when I was born, and my father was drowned on the drove years ago,' I began.

'We heard that, to our sorrow, yes,' said Uncle Blair. '*The Lord giveth, and the Lord taketh away.*'

'Up till now, I was living – I lived – I was with my granny,' I faltered. I didn't know how to go on. I'd spun story after story in my head in preparation for this explanation, not wanting to see the horror I pictured on the faces of people who didn't know me when they heard about the trial, and Granny's burning, and the strange wildness of my flight with the drovers, but looking at Uncle Blair's honest, kind face I knew that I couldn't lie to him.

I started slowly with the birth of Ebenezer Macbean, and Annie stealing my buckle, and Granny's party at

Ambrisbeg, and the curse at the christening, and then it all tumbled out – the trial, and the false witnesses, and the meanness of Donnie Brown, and Tam's clever rescue, and Granny's horrible death, and my flight to Rhubodach, and Annie's revelation, and my swim with the cattle (I shuddered again as I remembered that) and the kindness of Mr Lithgow, and my solitary walk to Ladymuir.

They listened, silent and rapt, to every word, even the little girls. Every now and then, Uncle Blair made a comment.

'Such wickedness!' he'd say. Or 'Superstitious non-sense!' or 'Danny's buckle, aye, I mind when he first bought it at Paisley fair,' or 'Archie Lithgow, a good man indeed.'

But it was my aunt's face I chiefly watched. I saw fear, horror and disgust give way to pity, and even a kind of admiration, and I finished more hopefully than I'd started.

A collective sigh went round the table when at last the story was over. Uncle Blair said, 'Well, Maggie, you've lived through more in your short life than many do in long ones. You did well to come home to us. You'll stay with us, and be a part of our family. The Devil has been after you, body and soul, to snare you in his cunning traps, but with prayer and God's good grace you'll stay free of him. Now you must submit to your aunt's authority and be a good help to her.'

The words sounded judgemental but his tone was kind, and the smile he gave me lit up his eyes with warmth as he went outside to his work. Aunt Blair had been smoothing the linen cloth on the table with her hands.

'I never heard such a story in my life,' she said, standing up and crossing to the fire. 'And here we are in the middle of the morning and not a pot stirred or a floor swept.' She spoke complainingly, but to my relief patted me on the shoulder. 'But you're a good girl, Maggie, I'm sure, if your uncle says so, and you'll do your best.'

She put a hand into the small of her back, and as she turned I saw the bulge at her waist and realized that she was expecting a baby. She saw where my eyes were fixed.

'So you've noticed. Another mouth to feed soon enough.' She sighed, but brightened at once. 'Now then, what are we going to do about these old clothes of yours, and that stinking plaid? Grizel, go to the linen press and fetch out my old brown gown. It'll do for Maggie just now. It's a fine drying day for once. Take out the soap too. You two girls can get on down to the burn and do a big wash. There's a mountain of clothes in this house to be seen to.'

Chapter Thirteen

I felt as fresh as a posy of daisies in the clothes my aunt gave me to wear, though they had been put away, she told me, as too old and worn for her to use. The petticoat was linen of a good strong weave, with no more than two or three rips in it, and although the sleeves of the gown were frayed and it was much too big for me, the woollen cloth it had been cut from was the finest and softest I had ever touched.

'Th-thank you, Aunt,' I stammered, as I stood dressed in front of her.

She looked at me with sudden interest, as if seeing me for the first time. I could tell that she was pleased with her generosity.

'We'll get you a new cap,' she said, retying the strings of my old one under my chin. 'This old thing's stained and torn past using. Your uncle wouldn't like to say this, Maggie, because he disapproves of vanity, so we don't talk of such things when he's around, but you're a pretty girl, I must say. When we get you a new gown from the weaver we'll make sure it's blue to match your eyes.'

'Are my eyes blue?' I was surprised. 'I'd always thought they were brown, like Granny's.'

Aunt Blair laughed.

'Poor child! You've never seen a mirror, I suppose? Grizel, fetch the glass down from the shelf.'

She watched with pleasure as I took my first real look at myself, twisting and turning my head to see as much of my face as I could. I'd caught glimpses of myself from time to time in the still waters of the loch at Scalpsie, but it was brown and peaty, and my reflection was always dim. Something had always disturbed the water, shattering even that faint image into fragments.

I am pretty, I thought, trying out a smile.

'That's enough, dear,' said Aunt Blair, hearing a step outside. She took the glass quickly from my hand. 'Grizel, put this away.'

Uncle Blair came in.

'The girls are just away to the burn to wash the clothes,' Aunt Blair said, going a little pink.

'That's good. Very good,' said Uncle Blair, not listening.

He sat down heavily at the table.

'What is it, Hugh?' Aunt Blair said, touching his hand.

He glanced up at her, and I was pierced by the sweetness of the look they exchanged. I wasn't used to seeing love. It made me feel oddly happy and lonely at the same time.

'It's that man Irving. He's after me for a fine. A heavy one. He'll ruin me if he can.'

'The new minister?'

'Minister?' Anger sparked in my uncle's face. 'He's no true minister. An ignorant false prophet, put in our kirk to preach over us and lead us astray in the path of worldliness. He's no man of God. A jumped-up servant of Charles Stuart, who calls himself the King. And if—'

Aunt Blair shook her head at him, as if in warning.

'Oh aye, girls, off you go,' Uncle Blair said.

Grizel had picked up a pile of linen and was making for the door. I bundled together my own dirty clothes, and my father's shirt and plaid, and followed her outside. She crossed to the other side of the courtyard and dropped her armful of clothes into a tub that was lying inside the storeroom. She picked up one handle, and nodded at me, in the curt way that seemed natural to her, to take the other.

'Who's Mr Irving?' I asked, as we staggered together over the few hundred yards to the little stream that ran past the back of the farm.

She looked sideways at me, and I could tell that she hadn't decided if she liked me or not.

'He's the new minister, put into the kirk in Kilmacolm,' she said unwillingly, 'after the old one was chased off by the King's men. Turned out of his manse, he was.'

'Oh. Is that why my uncle doesn't like Mr Irving?'

'Yes. Master holds to the Covenant.' She saw a question in my face and hurried on. 'Mr Alexander was a good minister and everyone hereabouts liked him. The people had chosen him themselves. They won't have anything to do with Mr Irving.'

'What happened to Mr Alexander?'

'I don't know. Look, this is the best place for wash-ing. It's muddy up there.'

She does know, but she won't say, I thought. *There are secrets here.*

I didn't have time to wonder any more, because Grizel was already working on the clothes, sloshing water from the burn into the tub with the pitcher she had carried in her spare hand. When the clothes were well covered, she knelt by the tub and began to rub at them with the soap.

I watched, fascinated. We'd never had soap at Scalp-sie Bay. In fact, we'd never gone in for much washing of linen at all.

I took my place on the other side of the tub, lifted a shift, groped for the soap and tried to copy her, but the slippery cake dropped out of my hands into the water.

'Watch out,' she said, fishing the soap out. 'Mistress will scold if much of it's melted off.'

I bit my lip. I hadn't known that soap melted in water. She was looking at me curiously.

'You haven't lived on a big farm like this, then? Over there, in Bute, don't they have soap and that?'

'Not that I've seen,' I said shortly.

She had stood up and was hitching her skirts high, exposing her pale legs. She tucked the folds of cloth into her girdle, and, to my amazement, she stepped right into the tub and began to trample the washing with her feet, humming as she went. Her little triumph over the soap seemed to have cheered her and she grinned at me.

'Come on in and give us a hand – or a foot.'

I had to smile back.

'I will if you like.'

I hoisted up my own skirts and clambered into the tub. The cold water came up over my ankles. There wasn't much room for the two of us, so we had to stand close with our hands on each other's shoulders, making our legs go at the same time. Grizel suddenly threw her head back and began to sing.

'*The gypsies came to Lord Cassilis' gate . . .*' and before she'd finished the first line, I burst out laughing and joined in: '*And sang in the garden shady . . .*'

Together we chorused, '*They sang so sweet and so complete, That well they pleased the lady.*'

'How does it go on?' she asked, breaking off. 'Do you know any more? All the story of it?'

In answer, I rollicked through the long list of verses, which Tam had sung to me hundreds of times, and as we splashed and pranced in that tub of washing, my spirits rose with the cheerfulness of it, and her face shone with friendliness.

'If they're not clean now, they never will be,' she said at last, staring down into the murky water. 'We'd best get on with the rinsing.'

I didn't mind, now, admitting how useless I was with the washing. I was happy to let Grizel show me how to do it. I felt that we'd made friends.

I was still humming the tune of Lord Cassilis's song as we spread the linen on the gorse bushes to dry.

'Better not sing that while Master's around,' she warned me. 'It's worldly. He'd give us a frown for that.'

Grizel's words puzzled me. What was wrong with the old song? But I didn't have time to wonder for long. As soon as we were back at the house, there was water to fetch and floors to sweep and butter to churn.

'Maggie,' Aunt Blair said, 'help Martha with her reading, will you, dear? She can't manage the long words.'

And I had to answer, 'I'm sorry, Aunt. I can't read.'

'Oh! Then fetch down the spare distaff and spin. You can look over Martha's shoulder and learn while you work.'

'I've never spun either, Aunt,' I mumbled with a burning face.

She gave up expecting me to know anything useful at all in the end, and though I was desperate to learn, she didn't seem able to teach me. I watched helplessly while she sorted feathers for stuffing a pillow, or skimmed the cream off the milk and set to work at the butter churn, or cut down an old linen sheet to make a dress for the new baby, gently sighing and saying as she worked, 'Now, Maggie, there must be *something* you can do. The Devil has work for idle hands, you know.'

It was Grizel who came to my rescue.

'Here, Maggie, you turn the grindstone and I'll pour in the oats,' she said, and I sat eagerly at the quern, turning the heavy handle till my arms ached. Grizel taught me how to shake out the springy heather and smooth the sheets back over it in the box beds every

175

morning. She showed me where the hens were likely to lay their eggs in the barn, and how to spin a decent thread without making lumps or breaking it. When I tried to thank her, she would smack my shoulder playfully with her beefy hand.

'It's the help I'm glad of. There's more work on this farm than's right for only one maid. And mistress is so particular! Clean shirts and shifts for the whole lot of them every month! And the fuss she makes with the cooking! Go on, tell me again about how you had to swim across that raging torrent with the horse trying to kick your brains out.'

She had never been more than ten miles away from Kilmacolm in her life, and she could never hear enough of my adventures, which, I must admit, I coloured up a little for her. I think she looked on me as a rare creature, like a bird with strange bright feathers that's flown in from far away.

For the first few months at Ladymuir, I watched and learned and worked without a moment's rest, and I'd drop into bed at night dead with exhaustion, my arms aching and my hands red and sore with work. I was hardly able to keep my eyes open during Uncle Blair's long evening prayers round the kitchen table.

There was one thing that puzzled me though. For all my uncle and aunt's deep religious faith, their constant Bible readings and psalm singing, they never walked the few miles into Kilmacolm on Sundays to go to church. The Sabbath Day was strictly kept. We did no work at all, beyond what was strictly necessary, such as milking the cows or feeding the hens. Family worship lasted for up to four hours, with Uncle Blair reading to us from the Bible and praying, and all of us singing psalms.

One blustery October Saturday, when rowan leaves were drifting down from the trees like golden rain, the routine suddenly changed. There was a great fuss of preparation in the kitchen. Aunt Blair scraped at Uncle's chin with her scissors to get off his week's beard. The men's coats and our women's gowns were brushed down and the stains worked at with dabs of soap. Aunt produced shoes from her chest, and held a pair against my foot.

'These will do,' she said. 'Try them on, Maggie.'

I'd never worn a pair of shoes before and they felt stiff and cramping round my toes, but I was proud too, and stammered out my thanks. Aunt Blair, even though she tried to be a good plain Puritan, always softened when it came to matters of dress.

'Don't mind if they pinch a little, dearie. You'll carry them till we're nearly there and put them on before we arrive.'

'How far is the church?' I asked.

'Well . . .'

She shot a look at my uncle. He had been sitting at the table filing a metal link for his plough, but he put it down and patted the bench beside him, inviting me to sit.

'You can forget about that haunt of evil men that calls itself a church,' he said gravely. 'While you're

177

under my roof you'll have nothing to do with that dunghill of royal wickedness, and neither will any of my household. Now listen, while I tell you what's happening here in Kilmacolm.'

'Hugh . . .' began Aunt Blair, but he silenced her with a nod.

'No, Isobel. Maggie's one of us now. She's a good girl. We've all seen how hard she's tried to do her best in this family these last months. She's my brother Danny's daughter. She'd not betray us, not even for silver or gold, I know it.'

I was warmed all through by his words and felt a rush of love for him.

'I'd never betray you, Uncle. But how could I, anyway?'

'Very easily.' Aunt Blair had picked up her sewing again. 'One word to the minister . . .'

Uncle Blair ignored her.

'Maggie, you'll have heard of the Covenant,' he said. 'Do you know what it means?'

'Not really,' I admitted.

'Then it's time you did.' He paused, as if gathering his thoughts. 'King Charles Stuart, of evil fame, and his wicked father and grandfather before him, puffed themselves up with pride and arrogance. They took it into their heads that it is the right of the King, and not the right of the Lord our God, to be rulers over our Presbyterian Church in Scotland.'

I was frowning, trying to understand. I could imagine the King, all swollen with pride so that he was monstrously fat, and I supposed he'd be wearing a silver coat and have a golden crown on his head, like the fairy king in one of Tam's stories. And his wicked eyes would be red like glowing embers.

I nearly missed the next part of Uncle's explanation.

'We are a chosen few,' he was saying earnestly, 'a sacred remnant. The Lord has called us to stand firm for the difficult right against the easy wrong. If we give way, Maggie, and bow our necks humbly to this King, the bishops he wishes to set over us will force us to obey them. They'll tell us how to pray and what to preach. They'll try to make us think that what the King wants, God wants. They'll take away our freedom and make us servants while they loll fatly in their luxury and gluttony.'

His words rolled richly round and over themselves, as if he was preaching a sermon himself.

'But if we're not going to the kirk tomorrow, Uncle,' I dared to ask at last, 'why have we been brushing our clothes and fetching out the shoes?'

'Ah, Maggie!' He smiled, with a look that was almost mischievous, like a boy planning to raid a neighbour's apple tree. 'That's the nub of the matter. Mr Irving, the King's chosen minister, will preach to an empty kirk tomorrow morning, as he has done to his own rage and fury these many weeks past. But we'll be up early, and away across the moss into the hills, with all of the true Presbyterian brothers. Our good old minister, Mr Alexander, who was thrown out of his kirk and his

179

manse by the King's men, will lead us in our prayers, and preach to us from the Good Book.'

'But it's a great secret, Maggie,' Aunt Blair said, holding up her forefinger. 'To meet for prayer in the open is against the law—'

'Against the *King's* law, not against God's,' interrupted Uncle Blair.

'Yes, Hugh, but let me tell her. Maggie, if we're caught by the troops, or if someone betrays us, they will put us in prison. They'll take everything from us in fines. They could even hang us from the gallows! Hugh . . .' Her voice had risen with anxiety and she stopped, looking pleadingly at her husband.

'Now, my dear,' Uncle Blair said, 'you know fine that the Lord is the rock of our strength.'

'I know, Hugh, but the children—'

'If we're to be cast out like criminals or outlaws, or even slain, it will be in the Lord's holy name. We'll be martyrs, Isobel, don't forget. The Lord will take each one of us by the hand and lead us into glory, and say to us, "Well done, my good and faithful servant."'

I could hardly bear to look at my poor aunt, who had put down her sewing and was twisting her apron in her hands. Martha and Nanny, feeling the tension, had crept close to her and were folding her skirts round themselves. Grizel, who had been stirring the stew for tomorrow's dinner in the cauldron over the fire, was standing with the spoon in mid-air, as if mesmerized by Uncle Blair's stirring words. I hadn't noticed Ritchie come in through the door behind me, but now he broke in eagerly, 'Will we go armed into the hills, Father? If you take the musket, can I carry the sword?'

Uncle Blair tried to frown at him, but I could see that he shared Ritchie's excitement.

'Aye, son. We've no choice. If the forces of evil—'

'You mean the King's Black Cuffs! Armed to the teeth and with fast horses,' Aunt Blair interrupted, her usual mild fretfulness giving way to bitterness.

'Yes, my dear. Charles Stuart's cavalry. If they come after us, we'll have no choice but to defend ourselves in the Lord's name. You'd best look at the powder horn, Ritchie, and see if it's dry. I'll check the musket balls. I've sharpened the sword. It'll do for the Lord's purposes.'

Aunt Blair threw up her hands as if she despaired of both of them.

'I'm away to my bed,' she said. 'We'll be up before dawn. Ritchie, get off now to the barn. Grizel, cover the fire. Stop pulling Nanny's hair, Martha, and get into your nightshift.'

A few minutes later, Grizel, the little girls and I were enclosed within our stuffy cupboard bed, but tired as I was, it was a long time before I could sleep. I had thought I had left danger behind when I'd fled from the Isle of Bute, but I seemed to have leaped from the cauldron into the fire. In Rothesay they'd wanted to string me up for being in league with the Devil, but here in Kilmacolm you could be hanged for trying to be too close to God. My stomach churned with terror at the thought of fleeing once again, pursued by a cruel enemy.

Why can't I just be ordinary? I wanted to cry out loud. *Why does all this happen to me?*

I was afraid that the thought was sinful, and I tried to pray, but the words of my prayer seemed to rise no further than the roof of the box bed. Nanny rolled over, muttering in her sleep. I put my arms round her and held her close, taking comfort from her childish peacefulness.

We got up and dressed by candlelight, and Aunt was just buttering some oatcakes for a hasty breakfast when a loud rapping came at the door.

'Lord have mercy!' she cried out, dropping the oatcake she'd been holding, which fell, butter-side down, on the table. 'It's the soldiers! Hugh, hide yourself!'

But Uncle Blair was calmly opening the door. He stepped outside and we heard men's voices raised first in greeting, then in discussion. He came back in a few minutes later, shaking his head.

'Isobel, you'll not be coming out today after all. The troops are out. They were seen last night riding out from Paisley, and now they're fanning out, scouring the hills.'

A smile of pure relief lit my aunt's face.

'It's the Lord's will, Hugh. We must accept it. We'll have a quiet Sabbath here at home.'

'Aye, you will, my dear. You and the girls. Ritchie and I—'

'You'll not go out there, Hugh! Please! What if—'

She had caught his arm but he gently took her hand away and held it in both of his own.

'Isobel, don't tempt me away from the path of right-eousness! If Mr Alexander has the courage to preach up there in the hills, who am I to let him down? There'll be others – all our good neighbours. Barbour from Bar-naigh is here just now. He's going with all his sons. And Laird of Newton. The Flemings from Whinnerton. Do you want Blair of Ladymuir to be the only one to skulk at home in cowardice?'

'No.' She was biting her lip. 'But Hugh—'

'Aye, aye, we'll take care. We'll set a watch around the meeting place. This is our country. We know every stone and hollow. We can melt away like snow in April if they come upon us, while they blunder about on their English horses, getting mired in our bogs.'

He was trying to make her smile, but she shook her head at him.

'Look after your son, Hugh.'

He was at the door already, but he turned back.

'Give me your blessing, Isobel. I won't go without that.'

'Well, yes, you have it; you know you have.'

She held her hand out and he pressed it, and then he was gone. I looked out of the door and saw Ritchie, his face ablaze with excitement, with his father's long sword dangling from his belt. Two other farmers, solid men, nodded at Uncle Blair as he joined them, then the little group of them set out at a brisk walk along the track that led up into the hills behind the farm, two with muskets over their shoulders and all with their Sunday hats neatly brushed on their heads. The dogs, who had been lying by the barn door, got up and followed them, silent black shadows hugging the ground.

I was looking forward to that long, quiet Sunday, when all work was forbidden and my tired arms and legs could rest. I would have time, I thought, to look at the autumn colours around the farm, and play with the little girls. I would have enjoyed it, too, if it hadn't been for my aunt's dreadful anxiety, which was as catching as a bad cold. Since she couldn't work without sin, she couldn't even occupy her hands with her needle or her distaff. The oatmeal had all been ground the day before, the stew prepared and the oatcakes baked. She had nothing to do but sit at the table, or walk backwards and forwards to the door, looking up the track in the hope of seeing the menfolk come back.

While her back was turned, Martha climbed up on to a stool.

'What are you doing, silly child?' said Aunt, noticing her at last.

Martha was unused to hearing such a sharp note in her mother's voice. Her chin wobbled, and tears filled her eyes.

'I'm going to preach a sermon, Mammy,' she whispered, 'to tell Nanny to be good.'

Grizel and I couldn't help laughing, and even Aunt Blair smiled.

'Out of the mouths of babes,' she sighed. 'You're

right, darling. We must hold a service of our own. Fetch down the Bible, Grizel. Martha, since you're learning to read so well, you'll be the one to read to us.'

Martha, pink with pride, went to stand by her mother, following Aunt Blair's finger as it ran along the line of words. I marvelled at Martha's confident high voice, reading out all but the hardest words.

'*There be three things which are too wonderful for me,*' she intoned. '*Yea, four which I know not. The way of an eagle in the air . . .*'

'What's a neagle?' Nanny interrupted.

'A big bird, dear,' said Aunt Blair. 'Go on, Martha.'

'*The way of a serpent upon a rock; the way of a ship in the midst of the sea; and the way of a man with a maid.*' She looked up, puzzled. 'What does that mean, Mammy, "the way of a man with a maid"?'

Grizel sniggered, and I couldn't help giggling myself. Aunt Blair snapped the Bible shut.

'You'll know soon enough. There, I knew I wouldn't get it right. Your father would have chosen a better chapter. What's that you're saying, Nanny?'

Nanny had been muttering in the secret language she shared with Martha. Now she wriggled, and hid her head under her apron.

'She means *I to the hills will lift mine eyes,*' translated Martha. 'It's the psalm, Mammy.'

'I know it's the psalm,' Aunt Blair said, unable to hide her exasperation. 'Well then, we'd better sing it,' and in a quavering voice she began:

I to the hills will lift mine eyes,
From whence doth come mine aid.
My safety cometh from the Lord,
Who heaven and earth hath made.

As I sang I too looked out through the door, longing for the sight of the brown coats and tall hats coming down to us from above.

They appeared at last, long after the sun was beginning to sink. Grizel saw them first.

'It's them, mistress,' she called out, 'but it looks like the master's lost his hat.'

Aunt Blair was off the bench where she'd been sitting and was running up the track, her shawl blowing out behind her, before the rest of us had moved. I saw her stumble, and Uncle Blair catch hold of her, and Ritchie take her other arm. They almost carried her between them back to the house. I didn't know which to look at first, my aunt's deathly pale face or the blood pouring down my uncle's forehead.

'It's nothing! Nothing!' he said irritably, as the little girls set up a wail, and Grizel and I stood gaping at him. 'A tiny nick in the skin, that's all. The real damage is to my hat, which the musket ball blew clean away. A good hat it was too.'

'We shook them off, Mother, just as Father said we would,' Ritchie burst out exultantly. 'Seven troopers, mounted, and a captain, but they were floundering around in the bog and they couldn't come near us! The

186

others got Mr Alexander away. He's hiding at Whin-nerton.'

'It was a grand sermon he preached, Ritchie, that's the main thing,' his father said with a frown.

A gasp from Aunt Blair made him turn round.

'What is it, Isobel? Oh, my dear, you're not – it's not—'

'It is,' she panted. 'The pains have come. Help me inside, Hugh. Ritchie, get away to Barnaigh. Fetch Mistress Barbour to come and help me. Ahh! Hurry, now!'

Chapter Fourteen

The birth of my little cousin Andrew was quite, quite different from that of Ebenezer Macbean. There were no wild clouds racing across the moonlit sky, no drunken Granny to curse and stumble, no furious rages on the one hand, or plaintive, weak cries on the other. And of course, there were no mumbled charms round the fire. My aunt, so particular in all her ways, had everything ready.

Ritchie must have run all the way to fetch Mistress Barbour from Barnaigh, because she was back almost at once. She was a round-faced woman, sober and clean. I took the little girls into the rarely used best room, wrapped them in a plaid and sang them to sleep. Grizel, unconcerned, was already snoring in a corner. Then I opened the shutter at the little window and leaned out.

It was a calm evening. The sun had set, but a late glow of red blushed across the sky, casting glory on the land. From the barn nearby I could hear the cows chewing their cud, and a snuffling sound as my uncle's horse blew the dust out of his nostrils. From the next room came Mistress Barbour's quiet, encouraging voice, and the occasional groan from my aunt.

Why am I not happy? I thought. *Why am I so restless? Why do I still feel like a stranger here?*

Baby Andrew's first cry was more like a bellow than

the weak mewing which was all that Ebenezer had managed. I heard the outer door squeak open as Uncle Blair, who must have been waiting outside, hurried in to see his new son. I wanted to go myself, but I thought: *They won't want me in there. I'm not really one of them.*

Uncle Blair was praying now. I could hear the familiar rise and fall of his special worship voice. Then there was a splashing of water, Mistress Barbour's voice crooning, and the baby's shocked scream.

For the first time since I'd been at Ladymuir, I felt a pang of regret for Granny. But the very thought of her brought a prickling to my scalp at the memory of her cruelty and her violent rages.

It's better here. I'm better here, I thought, pulling in the shutter to close off the starlit darkness which had now blotted out the splendour of the evening sky.

I lay down on the floor beside the little girls, tired out. I didn't miss the closed-in bed, the loose nightgown, the springy heather, the smooth linen sheet and the soft pillow. It was almost a relief to lie as I always had done, on the hard floor, in my day clothes, with my head resting on my arm. I slept better that night, I think, than I had done for a long time.

When I woke I was alone. Voices and the clatter of pots were coming from the next room. I jumped up, smoothed my dress and hair and opened the door.

'Maggie!' cried Martha, running forward to take my hand. 'I've a wee brother! He's all red. Come and see!'

She began to drag me across the room. Uncle Blair was bending over the fire in the chimney place, coaxing heat from the peats. Ritchie was coming in from the yard outside, pink with effort, two heavy pails of water in his hands. Grizel was measuring meal ready for baking oatcakes. Nanny was curled up beside Aunt Blair in the opened cupboard bed, sucking her thumb and stroking her mother's arm. I felt a rush of love for them and a painful longing to be loved in turn, but they seemed far away from me, and out of reach, although the room was so small.

I stood beside the bed looking down at my new baby cousin's crumpled face. He was already neatly dressed in a little gown with tucks along the front. His eyes were shut but his mouth was working in and out as if he wanted to suck.

'He's beautiful,' I said politely. 'A lovely baby.'

But I was thinking of Ebenezer, whom I'd only glimpsed a couple of times but who had tugged at my heart and filled me with pity. This sturdy, noisy baby would never take his place.

Aunt Blair was plucking fretfully at the sheet.

'Maggie, be a good girl and bring a fresh sheet for my bed. And my new cap, dear, and knitted shawl. There'll be visitors coming and going all day.' She looked over my shoulder at Grizel. 'Fetch in the special cheese, and mind you sweep the floor well. Off you go now, Nanny, and let Martha tidy you up. I'll not have the good folks see us all in a mess.'

She shut her eyes and let her head fall back, and I saw how pale she was, and how tired.

*

Visitors did indeed come throughout the long day: other farmers from the lands nearby, my uncle's own few tenants from the cottages near the lane, and even some townsfolk from Kilmacolm. Aunt Blair's orders became shrill as she grew ever more weary.

Grizel had been right. There was too much work for one girl at Ladymuir, and with Aunt Blair slow to recover from the birth, she and I were busy now from morning till night. Aunt lay in her cupboard bed, the doors thrown open, and issued her commands, while Grizel and I ran about, trying to satisfy her.

Martha had become attached to me, and she followed me like a shadow, towing Nanny in her wake. I didn't mind.

'Listen to me reading, Maggie,' Martha would say. 'I'm really good at it now.'

'Lift not your soul up unto vanity,' Uncle Blair would say reproachfully if he heard her, but his fond proud look would belie his words, and Martha took no notice of him. She laid the great Bible on the table, and began to read wherever the pages fell open.

'And – it – came – to – pass – in – those – days . . .' she would intone, underlining the words with her little finger. I would frown down at the page too, trying to make sense of the black marks that scrawled like insects across the page.

'Look, Maggie. That's a *p*, and that's a *b*.'

Her blue eyes stared earnestly up at me.

She was a good teacher, that little Martha. I was soon

picking out the letters myself, and then the words, and my reading wasn't far behind hers.

It was well into December before Aunt Blair was able to drag herself out of bed, and ploughing was long since finished in the strip fields below the house. Grizel and I worked till our fingers were red and raw, and when Sundays came I revelled in the rest, finding it hard to stay awake during my uncle's hour-long prayers. He and Ritchie went twice more out on to the moors for secret meetings with the old minister, Mr Alexander, but there were no more skirmishes with the King's troops.

'When will Andrew be christened, Aunt?' I said one morning, watching Aunt Blair listlessly put the baby to her breast.

I wished I hadn't spoken then, because a frown of worry creased her forehead.

'Oh, I don't know! Don't ask me, please!'

Luckily her eye fell on my apron, soiled from carrying peats in for the fire.

'Look at you, Maggie! What if someone should come to call?'

That very afternoon, a visitor did come. He announced himself with a loud rapping on the door and opened the latch without being invited in. I'd never seen Mr Irving, the minister of Kilmacolm, before, but I knew who it was from the style of his black coat, his tall hat and the two white bands that fell from his collar.

'Good day, Mistress,' he said frostily to Aunt Blair. 'Rumour has spoken right, I see. There's a new child born to this house. And why have you not brought him to the kirk to be christened?'

Aunt Blair, unprepared for this assault, lifted Andrew up to her shoulder and began to pat his back.

'Because, Mr Irving,' said Uncle Blair, who had come into the house behind the minister, making him jump at the sound of his voice, 'my wife is still not yet recovered from the birth, and the walk to Kilmacolm is too far for her.'

'You have a horse, man!' said Mr Irving. 'Take her on your horse!'

Uncle Blair didn't deign to answer, but moved to the fireplace and stood in front of it, his arms crossed. Ritchie had appeared too. He took up his place in front of his mother, as if he was protecting her.

There was tense silence.

'You are in breach of the law, Mr Blair!' Mr Irving burst out. 'You have not attended the kirk for many weeks past, as you are duty bound to do.'

'My duty, sir, is to the Lord my God, and Him only do I serve,' Uncle Blair said magnificently. He was the second member of my family whom I had witnessed seeing off a minister, and I must admit he was more effective than Granny had been.

Mr Irving paused, but then with a wave of his arm he swept my uncle's words aside.

'You consort with traitors!' Colour was rising in his pale cheeks. 'You and the other renegades in this benighted parish. You have been seen out on the moss!

Taking part in unlawful worship! With the criminal Alexander!'

'Mr Alexander isn't a criminal!' Ritchie said hotly. 'He's our real minister. You're just a—'

Uncle Blair silenced him with a look while Mr Irving wagged a furious finger at him.

'You are leading your own children – your son – into the ways of wickedness! I'm warning you, Hugh Blair, that if you do not bring this child to be christened according to the rites laid down by our lawful bishops—'

It was too much for Uncle Blair.

'Bishops?' he thundered. 'Rascals set over us by a treacherous king! How dare you, Mr Irving? How *dare* you threaten me with your bishops! I am a Presbyterian, do you hear? I'll have nothing to do with bishops!'

'Hugh, please Hugh, don't!' Aunt Blair's voice was no more than a bleat but it pulled my uncle up short. Mr Irving was smiling with horrid satisfaction.

'Ha! Aha! You have spoken treason, Hugh Blair. You leave me with no choice. No choice! If this child is not in the kirk next Sabbath Day, I myself shall ride to Paisley and report you to the captain of the King's troop. The fine will make you think. I assure you, you are not going to like the fine. One whole year's income from a farm such as this, I would think. We'll see then what you have to say. We'll hear you talk so rudely then about our gracious King Charles, and his chosen bishops.'

Grizel and I heard voices from my uncle and aunt's bed until late that night. She was pleading with him, I could

194

tell. He was urging her to be defiant. It was hard to know next morning which of them had won the argument. Uncle Blair went out to his work on the farm with his normal calm demeanour, but Aunt Blair sang the morning psalm with more than her usual warmth: *'Thy loving kindness to show forth, When shines the morning light . . .'* she carolled, while Grizel and I exchanged puzzled looks.

Saturday evening brought a positive frenzy of clothes brushing and linen smoothing.

'So we are going to the kirk tomorrow morning?' I asked Ritchie, who seemed to spend all his time out on the farm with the men, and was making a rare appearance in the kitchen. He was usually shy with me, blushing when our eyes met, but this time he nodded eagerly and his smile was mischievous.

'Yes. So is everyone in the parish. You'll see how it will be.'

He wouldn't say more, but relapsed into his usual bashful silence.

It was a long walk into Kilmacolm, but I didn't mind. I liked seeing new views and new faces. The morning was cold, with ice crackling on the puddles and frost riming every blade of grass. Many families were streaming into the village from the small farms all around. I noticed how few men there were, and how many women, each of whom seemed to have a baby in her arms, while older children staggered along with their toddler brothers and sisters in their arms.

The bell was ringing as the kirk tower came into

view. There was already a crowd round the door, and though no one would have been indecent enough to call out noisily or laugh out loud on the Sabbath Day, there was an atmosphere of mirth, with nods and winks between the women.

Everyone was wearing shoes, and looked fine in their Sunday best. I had carried my shoes until we were almost at the church, and only remembered to put them on when Nanny whined for me to pick her up and I needed both my hands. The shoes pinched my feet but I was pleased to be seen in them. I even enjoyed the clatter they made on the kirk's stone floor.

Uncle Blair had brought folding stools for him and my aunt, and he set them up right in front of the pulpit. Ritchie stayed standing by the door with the other young men. Glancing back at them I had the oddest feeling that they were forming some kind of guard, though none of them seemed to be armed. Grizel and I sat down on the floor and Martha climbed into my lap at once, annoying Nanny who tried to push her away. I could see a storm was brewing between them, and I looked to my aunt for help, but she was rocking Andrew, who hadn't been fed for hours and was grizzling fretfully.

A bustle at the door made everyone look round. Mr Irving, the minister, was clearly used to his church being empty on a Sunday, and he had halted in astonishment at the sight of people jammed in from wall to wall. A smile of triumph split his gaunt face and he stalked up to the pulpit.

'You have repented of your sins!' he boomed. 'Repented, I say! Your necks, stiffened in treason, have come at last to bow beneath the . . .' He seemed to lose the thread of what he was saying, as Nanny, infuriated by Martha, swiped at her, unluckily hitting her in the eye, so that Martha howled with pain and rage.

Mr Irving glared at me, making me tremble with embarrassment.

'Control these children of Beelzebub or remove them from this place,' he snapped. I began to scramble to my feet, but Uncle Blair shook his head at me.

'Stay where you are, Maggie. Never mind the children,' and to my astonishment he winked at me, his face alight with amusement, before turning to look up innocently again at the minister, who was now struggling to pull a long roll of paper from the pocket of his coat. In his haste, he tore it, and as he tried to hold the pieces together I could see that he was becoming nervous.

Martha and Nanny were brawling now in an all-out, hair-pulling, nail-scratching fight, and baby Andrew, hungry and tired, was drawing in a shuddering breath as he built up to a full scream. I was red-faced with shame for them all, but then I realized that the same little scenes were going on all around the church. Small children, unrestrained for once by their parents, and inspired by the rowdiness of Martha and Nanny, were quarrelling and crying and running about, while not a single baby appeared to have been fed that morning, and they were all screaming in protest. Mr Irving succeeded at last in holding up his paper. He stood, a stiff black pillar of a man, and began to read.

'For non-attendance at the kirk, Barbour of Barnaigh is fined twenty pounds. Fleming of Whinnerton . . .'

The noise was now so terrible that I couldn't hear him, close as I was, and I only knew that he was still speaking by the way his lips were moving. A flame-red flush of rage was spreading up his neck into his cheeks and his eyes looked as if they would pop out.

Suddenly he threw down his paper and slammed his fists down on the edge of the pulpit, making a bang so loud that even the hungriest babies were startled into a moment's silence.

'Quiet, I say! I will have quiet! I will have silence in the House of the Lord!'

But the babies were already screaming again, as if the moment's pause had increased their strength. Mr Irving took out a large handkerchief and mopped his forehead.

'Mr Blair,' he said, leaning right down from the pulpit and shouting in my uncle's face, 'for decency's sake, sir, these people all respect you. Do something! This riot is blasphemous. The Devil is among us!'

'Of course, Mr Irving, for decency's sake,' said my uncle, nodding enthusiastically, and he stood up, turned his back to the minister and put up his hands to call for silence.

'Neighbours! Friends!' he bawled. 'Jesus said, *Let the little children come unto me*, and I say, teach them to do what's right, for decency's sake!'

Behind his back, Mr Irving was nodding, but I could

see what he could not. There was a broad, encouraging grin on my uncle's face, and he was winking again, at one grinning mother after another.

'Well, Mr Irving, carry on with your duty,' he said, turning back to face the minister, then settling himself down on his stool again. 'But you'll never get far with that list of yours. Best to proceed to a psalm, don't you think? The singing will quieten the little ones, for sure.'

Without waiting for the minister's permission he began to sing, in his rich bass voice, '*All people that on earth do dwell, Sing to the Lord with cheerful voice . . .*'

The women began to sing with him, as loudly as they could, but they sang all in a different key, out of time and out of tune, their voices cracking with the effort, keeping their faces straight with difficulty as the noise in the little church, bouncing back off the stone walls, grew so terrible that I had to clap my hands over my ears.

Mr Irving's face had gone from red to white.

'Enough, I say! You generation of vipers! Enough!'

'But the psalm, Mr Irving, you cannot stop us from singing the psalm,' bellowed my uncle.

For a long moment, Mr Irving stared at him, scarcely able to control the shaking that convulsed him. Then he stumbled down from his pulpit and, pushing through the throng of women and children, fled to the door. Ritchie and the other young men, standing solidly together, bowed low as he approached, so low, in fact, that they blocked his way. He hit out at them with his hat and fists, and then he was through them and gone, his long black legs carrying him at a gallop back to the safety of his manse.

'Martha! Nanny! Stop that at once!' Aunt Blair shouted, glaring at the little girls as she jiggled the now hysterical Andrew up and down against her shoulder. 'I've never been so ashamed in my life!'

But Uncle Blair had picked up his daughters and, sitting with one on each broad knee, he kissed their tears and rage away.

'The Lord spoke out of the mouths of babes, Isobel,' he said. 'Take the poor wee man outside and feed him, before he cries himself into a fit.'

The church was emptying fast. Outside, there was a most un-Sabbath-like atmosphere of festival as the excited children were allowed, for once, to run around the churchyard. The women, settling themselves on gravestones, unbuttoned their gowns to feed their squalling babies and the men, their laughter now over, talked in small urgent groups.

'Did you see the minister's face, Father?' Ritchie said eagerly, as we set off down the long lane towards home. 'Stop lurching about like that, Nanny.'

He shifted Nanny, who was riding on his shoulders. Nanny had not forgotten her quarrel with her sister and was leaning sideways to pinch Martha, who was sitting behind her mother on the horse.

'Of course I did.' Uncle Blair allowed himself a crack of laughter, but then his tender conscience made him say, 'It was a terrible thing to see, though, a man so humiliated. I almost felt sorry for him, instrument of the Evil One though he is.'

'Sorry!' retorted Aunt Blair. 'You'll be sorry when the Black Cuffs come and force you to pay the fine. A year's income! It means ruin for us, Hugh.'

'Where's your faith, woman?' Uncle Blair said peaceably. 'The Lord will provide. Look, Ritchie! There! A hawk! It's going to dive!'

He caught Ritchie's arm and they stood still to watch the great bird fold its wings and plunge to the earth, to rise a moment later with a baby hare in its talons.

But I was watching my uncle and my cousin, and not the bird.

My father and I would have loved each other like that, I thought.

'Did you hear any news there in the churchyard, Father?' Ritchie asked in a low voice as we plodded on.

'About what, son?'

'The man. The preacher. Mr Renwick.'

The name meant nothing to me, and knowing that I wasn't meant to hear, I hurried on.

The early morning had been bright, but a bank of black cloud was building in the west, promising a storm. We could see rain fall in drifting curtains across the hills, coming ever nearer to us. Aunt Blair dug into the pony with her heels and it broke into a reluctant trot, while the rest of us quickened our pace.

The rain struck as we branched off the lane on to the track for Ladymuir, and Grizel and I began to run, holding our plaids over our heads so that we could hardly see where we were going.

Puddles had already formed in the farmyard, and I was splashing through them, shoes in hand, when a well-known voice behind me called out, 'Maidie, Maidie, don't run past your old friends!'

I whipped round and saw two figures standing in the shelter of the barn. Tam was holding his blue bonnet in his hands, his weak mouth open in a toothless smile, his eyes wet and pleading like a dog who is afraid of being kicked. And beside him, her head tilted to one side and a sweetly innocent smile curving her pretty mouth, stood Annie.

Chapter Fifteen

I was so shocked at the sight of Annie and Tam that I thought they were evil spirits come to torment me and drag me back to Bute and the gallows. I even looked past and behind them, half expecting to see Mr Macbean and Donnie Brown and even Granny herself. But then Tam said, 'You're surprised, Maidie, and I don't wonder, for I'm amazed to be here myself,' and Annie rushed forward and put her arms out as if she was my long-lost best friend and wanted to hug me.

I stepped back, out of her way. The thought of being touched by her made my flesh creep.

'Who are your friends, Maggie?' Uncle Blair said pleasantly. 'They must be in dire need if they have been forced to travel and break the Sabbath Day.'

Before I could say a word, Annie broke in, 'Oh yes, please, sir, we would never have committed such a sin, only . . .'

She faltered, looking at Tam. I knew she was casting about for a reason that would please my famously Puritan uncle. I could see that already she was trying to worm herself into his good graces, and my heart sank even further when I saw that he was smiling at her.

'Well, well,' he said. 'No doubt your reasons are good,' and he waited, his eyebrows raised, expecting her to speak. When she didn't, he looked enquiringly at me.

'That's Tam,' I said unwillingly. 'The piper from Bute. And she's Annie, who – who . . .'

Uncle Blair's brows had snapped together, while Aunt Blair drew in a shocked breath and pulled Martha and Nanny close.

'You are the young woman who gave false witness at my niece's trial?' Uncle Blair said sternly. 'Who tried to send her to the scaffold? Who lay with a man in adultery?'

Annie burst into tears.

'Oh sir, oh please, it was all a dreadful misunderstanding. I never meant – I honestly believed—'

Aunt Blair stepped forward.

'Where's the child?' she demanded. 'The baby you bore in sin? What's happened to the baby?'

Annie looked from her to my uncle, her face a perfect study of innocent bewilderment.

'What child? I don't have a child! How could I, when I'm not yet married, and I'm – I'm a virgin?' She turned to me, shaking her head sorrowfully. 'Oh, Maggie, what have you been telling them? I knew you never liked me, but I would never have thought you'd tell such lies.'

I could hardly believe my ears.

'Tam!' I burst out. 'Tell them! How can you stand there and listen to this! Tam!'

But Tam was shuffling uneasily from one foot to another.

'Well now, Maidie, I wouldn't want to . . . Girls' quarrels, you know. Is there any chance, mistress, that you might give us a little water to drink – and just a crumb to eat? It's been an awful long road to walk.'

I don't believe that anyone, not even the greatest rascal in Scotland, could appeal to my uncle's kindness and hospitality and be turned away. Though he looked grave, he invited Tam and Annie into the house and made Grizel set extra places for them at the table, while I was speechless, struck dumb by Annie's impudence.

Tam could hardly wait until the long grace had been said, but fell on the cheese and oatcakes with such ravenous hunger that I thought he would choke, and though I could tell he was disappointed that the jug held water and not whisky, his smile to my uncle was one of simple gratitude.

'I knew little Maidie's good folks would not turn away a starving man,' he said, 'for starving I am, and so's this girl here, or we would have been, but for your kindness.'

No one answered. Tam became aware of the disapproving silence at last. He seemed to shrivel into himself, but Annie, who had eaten with modest delicacy, shooting glances round the table as she assessed one person after another, heaved a great sigh, laid down her spoon and said, 'Now I know that what everyone says hereabouts is true. You are godly people, full of Christian charity for the hungry and homeless. Anyone but you would have thrown a wretched sinner like me out to starve up there on the moss. Oh sir – mistress –' she clasped her hands and looked beseechingly, first at my uncle, then at my aunt – 'if you only knew how sorry I am for the wrong I did to Maggie! How deeply I repent! I've struggled with the evil in my heart, and I've undertaken this long journey, full of perils, only so that I could cast myself on the floor and beg her to forgive me.'

She was acting her part so well, with brimming eyes and little catches in her voice, that even I might have believed her if she hadn't lied so blatantly about her baby. Her words made me feel as if I'd been smeared with dirt. I put my hand into the pocket of my apron to feel my father's buckle, afraid that she might somehow have stolen it again already. The touch of it brought back the terrible memory of the trial, and Granny's defiance, and the desperate nights in the tollbooth.

'Uncle,' I protested, 'don't listen to her. Please!'

But it was too late. I could see that he was touched by the sight of a beautiful sinner repenting, a straying lamb returning to the fold.

'Maggie,' he said with his usual gentleness, 'this child has done you a terrible wrong, but if her repentance is real, the Lord has already forgiven her, and you must find it in your heart to forgive her too.'

I thought I would choke.

'Aunt, please, you don't know her! She's—'

But my aunt was impressed, I could see, by Annie's prettiness, by the curls escaping from her cap and the dimples in her soft pink cheeks. Annie had now turned her swimming blue eyes on me.

'You must believe me, Maggie! I know now that what I said was – well, not quite true. But I honestly believed it. I really did think Mistress Elspeth had evil powers, and had consorted with the Devil. When I remember how she swung the baby round the hearth, and cursed him before he died . . .' She shuddered artistically, and stole a look at Aunt Blair. I could see that this shaft had found its mark. 'And what I saw, that night at Ambris-beg—'

'Where you had gone to meet your lover!' I interrupted furiously.

The smile she turned on me was full of understanding sorrow.

'I don't blame you, Maggie, for making up such lies. But it's not true. You know that. I admit that I was . . . I have been a creature of sin. It wasn't earthly lusts that drove me to that place that night. It was the Devil himself, luring me, calling me to the witches' sabbath. I was even – I admit it freely! – tempted to offer myself to the service of the Evil One! I was willing to let myself be seduced by him!'

'There was no witches' sabbath,' I said hotly. 'Granny wasn't a witch. You know that. Be careful what lies you tell.'

My anger had been growing like a surging wave, gathering to break in violent spray on rock. I could feel wildness in me. I wanted to make Annie fear me. I wanted to threaten her with Granny's haunting from beyond the grave, to terrify her with incantations and hints of enchantments, but I pulled myself up. I'd seen where the use of that kind of power led. It was no way out for me.

'How can you know that there was no witches' sabbath,' Annie was asking me in a tone of deadly innocence, 'unless you were there yourself?'

'Because I was there! I told you all that before. I didn't take part. I watched. I heard music from our cottage, and saw Granny go out. I followed her, because I was – I was angry at always being left alone. All I saw were some poor old people, the lonely ones of the isle, who had lit a fire to warm themselves and were drinking a drop too much, and dancing and singing for comfort and friendship. Ask Tam! He was there! You tell them, Tam. Did the Devil come to you all that night?'

All eyes turned to Tam, who was caught in the act of putting his hand out to take the last morsel of cheese from the platter. He withdrew it hurriedly.

'No, no, of course not. The evil gentleman himself? I never saw. But then, the whisky, you know. How can I remember who was there and who was not?'

He subsided with a cough.

I saw that Annie was satisfied. She'd planted seeds of doubt in the family's minds. They had believed my story entirely, and had been sure that both Granny and I had been victims. Now they were not so certain. Annie cleverly pushed her advantage. She clasped her hands and looked at me pleadingly.

'The Lord has shown me that I was too . . . too sure in the evidence I gave about that night. The light was bad, it was cloudy, and the Devil was in my heart. I thought I saw – but I should have said at the trial that I couldn't be certain! I didn't understand, Maggie. I didn't know what they were planning to do to Mistress Elspeth and you. If I had, I'd have lied. I'd have *perjured* myself to save you!'

She saw at once that she'd made a mistake as Uncle Blair, who had been leaning forward, drew back and frowned. Annie bit her lip, aware that the spell she had so artfully woven had been broken.

Uncle Blair said doubtfully, 'And so you left the Isle of Bute, and the protection of your master's house, and undertook this long and dangerous journey for the sole purpose of asking Maggie to forgive you?'

I couldn't tell from his voice whether he approved or not. Neither could Annie.

'It was Tam,' she said at last. '"You'll never rest easy, Annie," he told me, "and the Lord will never accept your repentance, if you don't go in person and throw yourself on the mercy of the girl you have wronged." Isn't that so, Tam?'

Tam jerked in his seat, and I was sure she'd kicked him under the table.

'Eh? Oh, aye. Yes. That's right.' He was nodding, but licking his lips nervously at the same time. I saw then that she had acquired some kind of hold on him, and that he was terrified of her.

All eyes now turned to me. Uncle Blair leaned across the table and picked up my hand.

'My dear, the Lord said, *If thy brother repent, thou shalt forgive him.* Annie has repented, Maggie. Will you forgive her?'

It was too much. My heart was pounding. I was panting as if I'd run up a mountain. I leaped to my feet, knocking over a stool.

'Can't you see, all of you? Don't you understand? She's a liar! A cheat! A thief! She ran away from Bute because she was afraid of being punished for adultery. She must have got rid of the baby she was carrying. She's come here because she's desperate and she knows you're good and kind, and you'll take her in and look after her, but she'll destroy you, like she destroyed my granny and tried to destroy me. Don't listen to her! I'm begging you! Don't!'

It was no good. Uncle Blair was shaking his head sadly at me, and Aunt Blair had leaned down over Andrew's cradle, turning her back on me. Blinded by my tears, I stumbled to the door and ran outside into the driving rain.

It was Ritchie who found me much later. I had thrown myself down against a bale of hay in the barn and had gone from storming tears, through fist-clenching rages and wild schemes of revenge, to the quiet misery of despair. Since I'd come to Ladymuir I'd found a healing calm, and though I hadn't been truly happy, I'd been accepted by a kindly family. Now I felt as if a malignant hand was reaching out to drag me back to the terrors and violence of the past.

I couldn't speak to Ritchie, who was standing diffidently in front of me, embarrassed by my distress.

'Are you all right, Maggie?' he said at last.

'No. Of course I'm not all right. I don't know what to do.'

He squatted down beside me. He had been so shy with me up till now that I hardly knew how to speak to him.

'She's a one, that Annie,' he said.

I picked up a wisp of straw and knotted it round my fingers.

'She's the best liar I've ever met, anyway,' he went on.

My eyes flew up to meet his. A sprout of hope took root.

'You mean she didn't fool you?'

'I saw her kick the old man. To make him back up her story. She scares him. Why would he be afraid of her if she was a good person? That kick was vicious. Has she some kind of hold on him, do you think?'

I threw the straw aside and sat up.

'It could be lots of things. Tam – he's kind and I love him, but he's weak and easily scared. He's always in trouble. She'd only have to threaten him with the law over a debt or something and he'd not be able to stand up to her.'

He cleared his throat.

'It wasn't just the kick. When you told us your story, it came out different. It was hard for you to tell. I thought you were brave, the way you decided not to hide things from us. That girl was all smooth and clever. Everything about her felt wrong to me.'

I wanted to throw my arms round his neck and kiss

211

him, but if I had, he'd have bolted out of the barn and up on to the moor like a startled deer.

'Ritchie, you've no idea! Just to know that you believe me!'

'I do, Maggie, and I always will.'

There was a quiet steadiness in his voice that warmed me through. I looked at my shy cousin, with his square Blair features and direct blue eyes, as if I was seeing him for the first time.

'But she's convinced my father,' he went on. He saw the distress in my face and said quickly, 'No, not that. It's not that he doubts you. But he believes in the girl's repentance. You know what he's like, Maggie. He's thrilled to see a sinner return to the Lord and seek forgiveness in such a – such a dramatic way, like a story in the Bible.'

'He'll never make me say I forgive her!' I said fiercely. 'How can I, when she's not a bit sorry for anything she's done and hasn't confessed to the half of it? She tried to murder us, Ritchie, Granny and me. And what's she done with her baby?'

'There'll be time enough to find out,' Ritchie said, standing up and turning to look out of the barn towards the house. 'My father's said she may stay with us while he finds her work on a farm near here.'

'He'll be sorry,' I snorted. 'He might as well take in a poisonous snake.'

Across the courtyard, the door of the house opened.

'Ritchie, are you there?' called Martha. 'Mam says

you're to come in for the evening worship. Where's Maggie?'

Ritchie put out his work-hardened hand to pull me to my feet.

'We'd best go inside. Put a brave face on it, Maggie. You know my father. Once he has an idea in his head, there's no use trying to shift him. If he's decided to trust that girl he won't be swayed.'

I tried, in the short distance from the barn to the house, to pick the wisps of hay off my gown and smooth back my hair, knowing how much my aunt disliked untidiness. But when I saw the family, sitting round the cleared table, with the Bible already open in front of my uncle, I knew I'd wasted my efforts. Annie had used the time well. She was sitting in the privileged position beside Aunt Blair, rocking Andrew in her arms, while Nanny leaned against her side, sucking her thumb contentedly. Tam had retreated to a stool by the fire and looked up at me with his eyes full of misery and apology. Grizel stood beside him, frowning, her arms crossed on her chest. She gave me a grim little nod, as if to tell me that she, for one, hadn't fallen under Annie's spell. Martha still hovered by the door.

Uncle Blair looked at me gravely as I slipped into my usual place on the bench, with my back to the wall.

'Come here, you dear little thing,' Annie cooed to Martha, 'and sit by me.'

But Martha scrambled on to the bench beside me, cramming herself against me and flinching from Annie's

213

outstretched hand. Uncle Blair frowned, not liking a display of feeling at prayer time.

'From the Gospel according to Luke,' he said, and began to read. '*What man of you, having an hundred sheep, if he lose one of them, doth not leave the ninety and nine in the wilderness, and go after that which is lost, until he find it? And when he hath found it, he layeth it on his shoulders, rejoicing. I say unto you, that likewise joy shall be in heaven over one sinner that repenteth, more than over ninety and nine just persons, which need no repentance.*'

He looked across at Annie who, with Andrew's rosy face nestled in her arms, and Nanny, now twisting one of Annie's curls round her finger, made a picture of sweet goodness that curdled the blood in my veins.

'The angels in heaven tonight are rejoicing over your repentance, Annie,' he said with a happy smile, 'as we too rejoice. And we will pray for our dear Maggie, that the Lord will work in her heart and bring her to forgive the wrongs that you have done her.'

When the long, long prayers were over at last, it was time for bed.

'Grizel, you will sleep in the other room,' Aunt Blair said. 'Annie will share the box bed with Maggie.'

I said nothing, but I pulled Grizel back as she went into the other room.

'Go back to our bed,' I whispered to her. 'I'd rather share a ditch with a mad dog than sleep in the same bed as her.'

Grizel grinned at me.

'Don't blame you either.'

214

'Where are you going, Maggie?' Aunt Blair called out as I opened the door to the next room.

I managed to smile meekly.

'Annie will sleep better without me beside her,' I said. 'I'm an awful one for wriggling in bed.'

She gave me a sharp look, but said only, 'Well, dear, take a blanket from the press, and a pillow too.'

I didn't even try to sleep. I lay on my back, looking into the rafters with unseeing eyes, my mind seething with anger and anxiety.

Tam stole into the room so quietly that I didn't know he was there until he laid his hand on my arm, making me start up in fright.

'Shh, Maidie, it's only me,' he whispered. 'I've come to say goodbye.'

'What do you mean, goodbye?' I hissed back at him. 'Tam, why have you done this to me? Why did you bring her here?'

The pale light of a full moon was seeping into the room round the ill-fitting shutter, and in its dim glow I could see him look back anxiously towards the door.

'Be careful. She'll hear.' His fingers were trembling. 'I'd swear she can hear through walls of stone. Oh, Maidie, she made me bring her here! I didn't want to – not at all! After you'd escaped, I knew I had to get off the island too. I wanted to go to Glasgow, where a piper can always pick up a groat or two. But she latched on to me. She forced me to bring her along.'

'Forced you!' I said sarcastically. 'How could a girl force a grown man like you?'

'You don't know what she's like.' He was shuddering all over now. 'She was a sweet wee thing at first, all soft and kind. She took me in. And it was true, she couldn't travel alone without a man to help her. I was sorry for her, with the baby coming and all. But when we got to Glasgow, she . . . she—'

'She got rid of it, didn't she, Tam?'

'Yes! There was an old woman who used some herbs and did what she was paid to do – you'd not want to know more of that, Maggie. And after that, Annie turned on me and said if I didn't do what she asked she'd say I'd caused her to abort her child, with witchcraft. She'd got your Granny hanged and she'd do the same to me.'

'But why did she want to come here? What does she want with me?'

'She didn't have anywhere else to go. You're the only person she knows on the mainland. She knew that your uncle was a well set-up man. Respected. What can a girl do, alone in the world? She reckons she can worm her way in here and make them like her, so they'll speak for her to a respectable family. She wants a good position as a servant, and then she'll try to catch herself a husband. She'll be after that cousin of yours, I can tell you.' He covered his face with his hands. 'I wish I was a better man, my darling! I wish I was a braver one! I wish I hadn't brought this trouble on you!'

I could never stay angry with Tam for long. I put out my arms and hugged his poor, thin, trembling old body.

'Where will you go, Tam?'

'Eh? I don't know. Anywhere. Everywhere. Edinburgh, maybe.'

'But where are your pipes? Have you lost them?'

He grinned.

'I hid them in a haystack down by the lane. Your uncle's not the man to appreciate my music, so I thought.'

'God bless you then, Tam,' I whispered. 'I'll never forget how you saved me from the gallows.'

But I was speaking to an empty room. He had already slipped away.

Tam's disappearance hardly made a stir the next morning.

'Where's old Tam?' Uncle Blair said, looking round vaguely as we took our places round the table for morning prayers. 'Did he slip away in the night like the wee shadow he is?'

Annie pursed her lips.

'He's not a very – very *good* person, I'm afraid.'

I had to clamp my mouth shut to stop myself from flying out at her, and in doing so I bit my tongue, which hurt so much that I couldn't have spoken anyway.

'I'm sorry he's gone,' Uncle Blair said. 'I would have liked to express my gratitude in due form. He was wonderfully brave to rescue our dear Maggie as he did from the Rothesay tollbooth, even though he had to tell untruths to achieve it. And he was clever too to send her off the island with that good man Archie Lithgow.'

I could see that Annie didn't like that. I saw her eyes

217

shift from side to side as she tried to think of a dart to prick me, but fortunately Uncle Blair had already opened the Bible and had begun to read.

There was a stir at the door as we finished our breakfast and Mr Barbour, our stout, red-faced neighbour came in. My uncle jumped up from the table with unusual eagerness, almost upsetting his bowl.

'What is it, Stephen? Has he come?'

'Has who come?' asked Aunt Blair, bewildered.

'Mr Renwick! It's Mr Renwick, isn't it?' Ritchie said eagerly. 'Is he in Kilmacolm already?'

She frowned at him.

'Mind your tongue, Ritchie. Maggie, Grizel, get along to the barn and look for eggs. Take Annie and show her where the hens like to lay. Go on!'

She almost shooed us out of the kitchen.

Annie lingered by the door, pretending that she'd dropped something and was looking for it, but I saw that she was only trying to eavesdrop. I dragged her away.

'Ouch! Don't hold my arm so tight. You're hurting me,' she complained.

I let go reluctantly. I was longing to get her away from the house, so that at last, out of earshot of the family, I could pour out my fury. Grizel looked from me to Annie and back again.

'Never mind the eggs. I'll gather them in,' she said with one of her jerky nods, and went into the barn.

Annie dodged my arm, trying to follow her.

'No, you don't,' I said. 'You're coming with me.'

She hesitated, then shrugged, and followed with sur-
prising meekness as I led her down to the kail-yard, out
of sight and out of hearing of the house.

'Maggie, listen,' she began, as soon as we reached the
rows of sprouting cabbages.

'No. You listen to me.' I knew her poisoned, clever
tongue. She'd got round me cleverly, the night we'd
met on the shore of Bute, with her tears and her
entreaties. I was determined to speak first before she
could play her tricks on me again. She had the sense, I
could see, not to try to make me pity her.

'You're a thief!' I said hoarsely, my throat thick with
fury. 'A hypocrite! A lying, sneaky snake!'

She was standing with her hands on her hips, mocking me, and her insolence outraged me so much that
rage clotted up my words, and I could say no more but
only stammer and choke on my tears.

'Well,' she said at last, as I spluttered to silence, 'I can
see that I've made you cross, Maggie, but—'

'Cross? *Cross?*'

'But,' she went on smoothly, 'what else could I do?
Where else could I go? I didn't know anyone, and I
need a new home as much as you do. You must admit,
it's very nice here, in spite of all the praying and
preachifying. Your aunt's a good housewife, I could see
that at once. Linen, dishes, everything of the best. You
ought to be grateful to me. Did you really want to live
in that hovel in Scalpsie Bay with that old witch for the
rest of your life?'

The urge to batter the smile from her face was so

219

strong that I turned and pummelled the trunk of the rowan tree that stood at the corner of the kail-yard.

'I'm not going away, you know, just because of you,' her hateful voice went on. 'They like me, I can tell. I'll stay as long as I want to. And if you try to turn them against me, I'll do the same to you, and I'll win, you know I will.'

Suddenly I was more frightened than angry. She was right. She could turn my uncle and aunt against me easily. She had already begun.

'Why do you hate me so much, Annie? What have I ever done to you?'

She opened her eyes in genuine surprise.

'I don't hate you. Why should I? I don't hate anyone, except for old man Macbean. But you've got what I want, and I want to have it too.'

'I haven't got anything. What do you mean?'

'You have, Maggie. You've got a family, and food every day, and a decent gown to wear. And there's all that money waiting for you when you go back to Bute.'

It was my turn to stare in surprise at her.

'What money? What are you talking about?'

She laughed.

'Don't tell me you don't know! The money Mr Macbean and the Laird of Keames owed your father. For the drove. I saw the letter.'

'Letter?'

'In Macbean's strongbox. It said . . .' She stopped. 'You really don't know, do you?' Her calculating mind was casting around now for an advantage. I could see that she regretted telling me so much.

'You can't stop there.' I was too eager in my curiosity, I knew, but I couldn't hold back. 'What did the letter say?'

'Oh, I don't remember. Some old thing. It meant nothing to me.' She had the upper hand again, and she knew it. 'I might tell you, if I think of it. But you'd better watch out, Maggie. You'll be sorry if you try to turn your uncle and aunt against me. I'll make you really, really sorry.'

I shivered at the cool menace in her voice. But as she followed me back up the path to the barn, I realized that Annie was using Granny's weapon, trying to exercise power through fear. In the end it hadn't worked for Granny. I took comfort from the hope that it wouldn't work for Annie, either.

When we went back into the house at last with a few eggs held in our aprons, I was surprised to see that Mr Barbour was still there, and my uncle and Ritchie had not yet gone out to their work. My aunt looked pale and agitated, and Martha and Nanny, sensing the tension in the room, were staring round-eyed from one adult to another. Only Ritchie showed no sign of anxiety. He was sitting with his father's sword across his knee, carefully polishing the shining blade. His mouth was set in a determined line, but excitement danced in his eyes.

'Is this all your household, Hugh?' said Mr Barbour, looking round at us all.

'There are the two serving men. They're sound. True servants of the Lord and His Covenant.'

'You know what a word of betrayal will cost us, and the price that is set on James Renwick's head?'

Uncle Blair nodded impatiently.

'Aye, man, of course I do. But what choice do we have? *Be thou faithful unto death, saith the Lord, and I will give thee a crown of life.*'

'Amen,' said Mr Barbour and Ritchie together.

Uncle Blair glanced up and saw the puzzlement on our three faces.

'Look at you innocents,' he said with the gleam of a smile. 'There's no help for it now. The truth must be revealed to you of what is to come to this house. And you will delight in it, as I do, for a great servant of the Lord is trusting us with his precious presence. James Renwick himself, a saint touched by the Holy Spirit, has promised to preach on our own moss, and when he comes he will be staying here with us in this very house. Oh!' He slapped himself on the chest, stood up and walked around, so deep was his excitement. 'This is the Lord's doing, and it is marvellous in our eyes!' He stopped walking, and his voice dropped to a deep, thrilling tone, as if he was delivering a sermon. 'Our poor Scotland has been overrun by wicked men, worldly men and the bishops who are their tools. And it is up to us, the faithful few, the godly remnant, to struggle for the pure and holy way, for . . .' He stopped and looked up. 'What's that? Horses outside in the yard? Ritchie, see who it is.'

Ritchie dropped the sword with a clatter and sprang to the door.

'Black Cuffs, Father!' he called over his shoulder. 'All mounted! Seven or eight of them. With an officer at their head!'

Chapter Sixteen

S even men riding seven horses may not sound like a great crowd, but when we all poured out of the house and saw them filling the yard it seemed as if a whole regiment had come upon us. Their coats were as scarlet as spilt blood, their cuffs as black as beetles, and the eyes under their broad-brimmed hats were hostile and intent, like cats on the hunt for rats. They didn't try to rein in their horses, but let them mill about nervously, and the clatter of hoofs and jingle of bit and bridle was as threatening as drums of war.

'Where's the man Blair?' said one. He was the officer, I could tell, from the silk sheen of his sash and the silver brocade that trimmed his hat.

'I'm Hugh Blair,' said Uncle Blair, gently detaching Nanny, who had been clinging to his knee. 'And by what name may I call you?'

'Dundas, Lieutenant of His Majesty's dragoons, though that's no business of yours.'

The man was handsome, I suppose, in a cold way, with his long, high-bridged nose and piercing eyes. I had never seen such magnificence of dress before, such rows of polished buttons, or such richness of lace edging on the cravat that foamed in a white cascade from his neck.

'He's come for the fine, Hugh, for non-attendance at

the kirk,' I heard Aunt Blair whisper. 'Just give him the money.'

The lieutenant hadn't heard her. He was nodding at two of his men. They leaped down from their horses and drew their swords. As the blades hissed from the scabbards, my stomach clenched with fright, and I found I was clutching at Grizel's arm for support. But the men went into the barn opposite the house and a minute later we flinched at the bang as they kicked open the door of the storeroom.

'What are they doing in there? What do they want?' Aunt Blair cried out, thrusting Andrew into my arms and starting forward. Uncle Blair held her back.

'Keep calm, Isobel. Trust in the Lord, who is our strength and shield.'

'Spew forth Scripture as much as you like, Covenanter,' Lieutenant Dundas said with a sneer. 'But listen to me.' He put his hand inside his coat and pulled out a piece of paper. 'I have a warning for you – and for everyone here. If you don't heed it, you will be sorry. As sorry as it is possible to be.' He paused, looking round to check that all eyes were on him. 'It concerns the traitor, the rebel, the bringer of terror, the so-called preacher, James Renwick.'

A grunt of anger came from Mr Barbour and I saw that his face was reddening. The lieutenant noticed it too.

'Who's this? Another damned Covenanting Presbyterian, I suppose.'

'Stephen Barbour of Barnaigh,' Mr Barbour said stiffly. 'What do you want with James Renwick?'

'I shall be delighted to tell you.' The lieutenant held up the paper, but I was watching, rigid with horror, as the two men who had gone into my aunt's storeroom appeared again, kicking in front of them one of her precious cheeses. They aimed for the stinking dungheap in the corner of the yard, and crowed with triumph as the cheese sank into the filth.

The other troopers were guffawing in approval.

'. . . The vagabond Renwick,' Lieutenant Dundas was reading, 'a pretended preacher . . . cast off obedience . . . the most damnable rascal . . .'

Aunt Blair was holding her hand to her mouth, stifling whimpers of distress, as the men approached the well. They were unbuttoning themselves, winking back over the shoulders at their whooping comrades. Lieutenant Dundas smiled with satisfaction when he heard the faint splash of his men's urine hitting the pure water of our well, and waited until they had buttoned their breeches. Then he raised a hand to silence his soldiers and began to read again.

'The words of our gracious Sovereign Charles, King of Scotland: *We command and charge all our subjects that none of them presume to provide the said Mr James Renwick, rebel, with meat, drink, house, or anything useful to him; or to communicate with him by word or letter or message in any way whatsoever, under pain of being guilty of the same crimes, and being pursued to the terror of themselves and others—*'

226

'Crimes! What crimes?' burst out Mr Barbour. 'How dare you sit there, man, on your high horse, and cast judgement on a true servant of the Lord, who—'

'Arrest that man,' Lieutenant Dundas said shortly.

'What is this persecution? Sir, let him go!' said Uncle Blair, stepping forward and putting a hand out to fend off the soldiers, who had leaped eagerly on Mr Barbour and were tying his arms behind his back with stout cords.

Everything happened so quickly that I hardly knew where to look. The lieutenant ripped out his sword and slashed it across my uncle's face. Ritchie yelled in rage and ran at him but was pulled up short as the point of the sword quivered against his chest.

'Hugh! What have they done to you? Hugh!' my aunt was crying, kneeling on the muddy ground beside my fallen uncle.

'You've been warned, Blair,' Lieutenant Dundas said, as his dragoons flung Mr Barbour on to the back of a horse, behind one of the mounted men. He bent down and snapped his fingers in my uncle's bleeding face. 'I wouldn't give *that* for your life if you're found consorting with the man Renwick. The same goes for this rude puppy of yours.'

He put his heels to his horse, turning its head to ride out of the yard, but the horse, excited by the noise and confusion, trampled backwards and reared. In the few moments that it took to bring it under control, I caught sight of Annie. She was standing apart from the rest of us, and was gazing at the lieutenant with sickening admiration in her eyes. He seemed to notice her for the first time, and I saw the long look he gave her. She showed him her dimples in a flirtatious smile, then quickly turned her head away, afraid of being noticed.

A moment later, the dragoons had ridden out of the Ladymuir yard, with poor Mr Barbour lying helplessly over the horse's rear as if he was no more than a sack of oatmeal.

Shocked into silence, we stood motionless. Ritchie broke the spell.

'I spit on them. I *spit* on them!' he shouted. 'Father, are you badly hurt?'

Uncle Blair was already on his feet, fending off Aunt Blair, who was clinging to him and crying.

'It's just a scratch. On my cheek.' He was trying to sound calm but I could see that he was shaking. He let Aunt Blair have her way at last, and she led him into the house.

'I'll take the horse,' Ritchie called in through the doorway after them. 'I'll ride to Barnaigh. Mistress Barbour needs to know.'

He didn't wait for an answer but ran to the stable, and a minute later was clattering out of the yard on the farm's stocky little horse.

I was still holding Andrew, who had begun to grizzle, and it took all my efforts at rocking and crooning to calm him again. When I looked up, I saw that Annie was still staring at the distant scarlet riders.

'Don't even *think* of it,' I hissed at her. 'If you betray this family, I'll . . . I'll . . .'

She raised her eyebrows mockingly.

'You'll do what exactly, Maggie? Do tell me. I long to know.'

'I really – think – I – would – kill – you,' I said slowly, and was instantly frightened at the realization that I meant it.

She shrugged, a little impressed by my anger, in spite of herself.

'What makes you think I plan to betray anyone?'

I opened my mouth to list her many past lies and treacheries, but she said hastily, 'Oh, save yourself the trouble,' and went into the house.

Half an hour later Ritchie returned, leading the horse, which Mistress Barbour was riding. Her plain face was puffy with crying, but her mouth was set in a determined line. She let Ritchie help her dismount, then marched forcefully into the kitchen, pushing the door open with a shove of her strong arm. I followed her. Andrew was crying properly now, and needed his mother.

I could see at a glance that Uncle Blair's wound, though it stretched from his temple to his chin and was bleeding freely, wasn't very deep. When he saw Mistress Barbour, he took the cloth which Aunt Blair had been dabbing over his cheek and held it to the wound, then jumped up to greet her.

'Dorcas, I wouldn't have had this happen to your good man for anything.'

'This is no more than we've been expecting, Mr

Blair. It's the Lord's will. He works in a mysterious way, but His saints will receive a crown of victory at the last.'

She spoke the Biblical phrases in an ordinary voice, as if she was talking of a rain shower, or a day at the market.

There was nothing heroic in the appearance of Dorcas Barbour. She was short, stout, red-faced and plain, straightforward and rock-like in her conviction. I felt a pang of envy. She knew with complete certainty that the cause of the Covenanters was right. She had no doubt that the King's desire to make himself the head of the church in Scotland, and rule it through his bishops, was worth resisting with everything she had. She was ready to give her husband to the struggle. I felt sure, looking at her standing there, with her work-reddened hands clasped at her thick waist, that she was ready to die for it herself.

I was used to my uncle's passionate Presbyterianism, but I sensed that his enthusiasm was made less harsh by the sweetness of his temper and the softness of his love for his family. There was nothing soft about Mistress Barbour.

I don't feel like she does about anything, I thought. *I wish I did. I don't care enough about anything to die for it.*

'Where have they taken Stephen? Did they say?' Mistress Barbour was demanding.

'Oh, Dorcas, my dear, you must be so desperately worried!' Aunt Blair was clutching Andrew to her shoulder, rubbing his back as if in solidarity. Uncle Blair was frowning.

'They didn't say. But it will be to Paisley first. The tollbooth in Glasgow tomorrow, I suppose.'

'Did they talk of a penalty? A fine? A trial? Or were they – would it be a – a summary execution?'

In spite of her strength, her voice wavered.

'I can tell you nothing more. I wish I could. But they have nothing on him, you know. He wasn't caught attending a meeting of worship in the hills. He wasn't in the company of a wanted preacher. All he did was protest against the persecution of Mr Renwick and try to defend the man's good name.'

Mistress Barbour had recovered herself, and nodded briskly.

'Thank you, Mr Blair. That's a comfort. Now I've a favour to ask.'

'Oh, anything!' cried Aunt Blair. 'We'll have the children over, cook their food, take care of the cattle—'

'Lend me your horse,' interrupted Mistress Barbour. 'My old pony's gone lame. I'll ride to Paisley and look out the officer. Lieutenant Dundas was his name, Ritchie said. Isn't that so? I have money put by in case of such a day. The King's servants are crooks to a man. They'll sell him back to me for a price.'

'Let me go instead!' said Ritchie, his face flushing with eagerness. I could see that he was still filled with rage at his helplessness in the face of the dragoons and was desperate for action.

'I wouldn't hear of it.' Mistress Barbour shook her head, forestalling Aunt Blair's anxious objection. 'If the case needed a young man, I'd send my own David, but he's a hothead too and would only get into worse trouble than his father. Anyway, you're forgetting this wicked law forbidding travel without a pass. A young man is sure to attract attention, but no one will notice an old woman on a nag. And if I'm stopped and questioned, I'll remind them of my midwife's skills and state that I'm summoned to assist a poor soul in trouble, which will be no lie at all, for Stephen's in worse trouble than he's ever been. In spite of your kind words, Mr Blair, I really fear that they may have already shot him without a trial. He wouldn't be the first to be murdered in such a way.'

'Not your Stephen! Oh, Dorcas, no!' said Aunt Blair with a shudder. Mistress Barbour frowned, not liking this display of feeling, and without another word Uncle Blair and Ritchie went out to the yard and brought the horse up to the door.

'That's a brave woman,' Uncle Blair said, coming back to the kitchen, as the clop of the old horse's hooves died away. 'If anyone can face down the enemy, it's Dorcas Barbour.'

'Hugh! Sit down. Your wound's still bleeding,' commanded Aunt Blair, looking a little put out.

Ritchie went to the fire and gave the burning peats a savage kick, sending sparks flying.

'Is she right, Father? Do you think Mr Barbour's been executed already?'

Uncle Blair let out a groan.

'It's possible. Look what happened to William Lyle, and Patrick Holm. Taken up at an open-air meeting, drummed out by a couple of soldiers into their own fields and shot. You saw the arrogance, the cruelty of that man – that officer.'

'Fouling our well! And ruining our cheese!' cried Aunt Blair.

'It's worse than that, Mother,' said Ritchie. 'They've slit every meal sack with their daggers. The store room's awash with oats.'

Aunt Blair started up with a cry of horror, planted Andrew in the nearest pair of arms, which happened to be Annie's, and rushed outside.

'Father, we must *do* something! We can't just let Mr Barbour go like that! We must go into Paisley, whatever the risk, speak to—'

'That's foolishness, Ritchie. What good would it do to be arrested ourselves? There's only one thing we can do, and it's the most important thing of all.'

'What's that?'

'We must pray. Without ceasing.'

I saw the effort that it cost Ritchie to say, 'Yes, Father, of course.' But then he brightened. 'And the more that pray the better. I'll run over to Newton and tell the John Lairds.'

He dashed off, and my own feet itched as I watched him go. I was still shaking with anger at the soldiers' contempt for us, and fear at the threats of Lieutenant Dundas.

I wish I was a boy. At least there's something he can do, I thought enviously.

'Grizel, take two buckets to the burn and fill them

with water,' came Aunt Blair's voice from the door. 'The well will be unusable for weeks. Annie, put that child in his cradle. Martha, rock him to sleep. Maggie, fetch out the needles and yarn. You and Annie can get down all the bowls from the shelf and come to the barn to salvage the meal.'

I had never heard such a hard edge to her voice. Though I didn't realize it until later, Lieutenant Dundas had achieved what all Uncle Blair's preaching had been unable quite to do. He had roused a passion for the cause in Aunt Blair. She had become a rebel in her heart.

The winter days slipped past, and Mr Renwick didn't come. Uncle Blair, who had expected his arrival hourly, stopped looking up eagerly every time a knock came at the door.

I was relieved. I liked the quiet rhythm of life at Ladymuir and had no wish for more turmoil and danger. I set myself to learn all that I could, and by the time the buds were swelling on the ash tree by the entrance to the yard I could read the Bible quite well, except for the long difficult names, and I could write a little too. I could spin a decent thread, churn butter, make a posset and sew a straight seam.

Annie had the sense to keep clear of me most of the time. Bit by bit, she had wormed her way into the heart of the family. For my aunt, she could do no wrong, and Nanny followed her around like a devoted lamb. Martha and Grizel staunchly refused to be charmed by her, and Ritchie, on whom she never ceased to work her wiles, ignored her and spoke curtly to her whenever he had to speak at all. I was grateful to him for that.

Mr Renwick arrived one ordinary afternoon, when a clammy, cold mist hung over the hills. He slipped into the house as quietly as a whisper, following Dandy Fleming, who had brought him by lonely mountain paths across the hills from Whinnerton. I was alone in the kitchen, minding Andrew and turning the oatcakes on the griddle over the fire, while Aunt Blair, Grizel and Annie were busy in the store room.

I knew Dandy by sight. He had been one of the young men who had stood with Ritchie by the kirk door, hindering Mr Alexander's escape.

'Are you Maggie?' he asked me. 'Is your uncle at home?'

'He'll be out with the sheep,' I said. I had barely noticed the other young man, standing quietly by the door, and I turned back to my oatcakes. 'He'll be in soon with the men for their dinner, if you care to wait.'

Dandy came up close to me.

'I've brought Mr Renwick,' he said in my ear. 'Is there anyone here who shouldn't be told?'

I whipped round and peered forward to see the face of the man standing in the shadow by the door. Then he stepped into the middle of the room and I saw how slim he was, how short, and how very young.

'Are you really Mr Renwick?' I said disbelievingly.

He laughed.

'I am indeed. "The boy Renwick," my enemies call

me, "that the nation is so troubled with." Or, if you prefer, "the seditious vagabond".'

His voice was surprisingly deep and musical and I felt a little shock at the sound of it, as if I'd touched something hot.

'But you're so young,' I blurted out, then blushed scarlet with embarrassment.

He smiled and moved further into the room, so that he was now staring down into the cradle at Andrew, who was peacefully asleep.

'There are none too small, too young or insignificant to become true servants of the Lord Jesus Christ, whose service is perfect freedom. Are you the Lord's servant, young woman?'

There was something irresistible in his face and voice, something so confident and thrilling that I felt a trembling inside me.

'I – I don't know,' I stammered. 'I'm Maggie.'

And then, as I stood, staring foolishly, Aunt Blair burst into the kitchen and I could turn my burning face back to the fire where the oatcakes had begun to smoke and singe on the griddle.

Chapter Seventeen

The arrival of Mr Renwick put my aunt into such a spin that we three girls could only stare at her, bewildered, as one order contradicted another. Her mind seemed split between anxiety to show this honoured guest her warmest hospitality, anguish that her wrecked storehouse had so little to offer, and fear that the troopers might return.

'Grizel, go and look for eggs. No, fetch more water from the burn. Maggie, what have you done to the oat-cakes! Look, all of them burned. Go and bring cheese – no, milk, no – Annie! Run into the parlour and bring the silver spoon from the press. It's on the top shelf.'

In the end, I copied Grizel, who stolidly worked at one task after another, ignoring my aunt's distracted orders.

Uncle Blair came in at last, bending his head under the low lintel of the door. He snatched off his bonnet at the sight of Mr Renwick and grasped the preacher's slim hand in both his great ones.

'So the Lord has brought you safely to us! The whole country is on fire with your preaching. You will work a wonderful work among us.'

Mr Renwick managed to remove his hand before it was entirely crushed.

'Praise the Lord indeed that I am here at all, brother.

Without his aid I would have been caught long ago. The Father of Lies has whipped up such hatred against us that it's only by God's providence that I reached Ladymuir today. They're pursuing me everywhere, on horse and on foot. The escapes that I've had – the runs over moors, climbing from windows, hiding in gullies—'

'You'll tell us everything,' Uncle Blair interrupted enthusiastically, 'but my dear brother, I must ask you first, are you strong enough to preach tomorrow? There's a place on my land, not far from here, wonderfully hidden from any who don't know it. It's a hollow, by a stream, and any noise of voices would be muffled from afar by a waterfall. I do believe that God has made it especially for our purpose. If you are able – there are hundreds of the good souls around Kilmacolm who long to hear you. Can you do it? If so, I'll send word out to the faithful, with the time and place—' He broke off, as Mr Renwick's slight body shook with a racking cough. 'But you're not well! The strain of it would surely be too much for you.'

Mr Renwick's cough went on so long that Uncle Blair looked more and more anxious, while my aunt came and fluttered round him with a beaker of water and a kerchief.

'Hugh, don't ask it of him. You can see Mr Renwick's not well. He needs to rest.'

Mr Renwick took the water and sipped, dabbed his mouth with the kerchief, and smiled. I had been whisking the crumbs off the table and his smile sent my heart into a flutter.

'Don't be anxious on my account, sister,' he said. 'My poor body is a weak and feeble vessel, but the Lord fills it with strength as the need arises.'

'Amen,' said Uncle Blair reverently.

'But that's an awful cough,' Aunt Blair said doubtfully.

'Well now,' Uncle Blair said with a change of tone, 'you women will be busy, I'm sure, preparing a good dinner for us, and you'll be wanting the kitchen to yourselves. It's a fine morning. Mr Renwick and I will send the men off to gather the brothers and sisters in Christ for a field meeting tomorrow, and then he and I will sit out on the stone seat by the door. We'll be able to watch from there if the Black Cuffs are busy in the hills.'

'The Black Cuffs?' said Aunt Blair, flushing with anger. 'If any of them go near my store again . . . But they'll not return today, surely.'

'They're swarming like the hornets of Satan across the whole of our poor Scotland,' said Mr Renwick cheerfully.

'Yes, yes, but don't fret, Isobel,' my uncle said hastily. 'Trust only in the Lord and all our ways will be safe.'

My aunt's hospitable instincts quickly swept all other thoughts from her mind, and for the rest of that long afternoon we were set to chop up onions, pluck hens, stir pots, cut slices of salt beef, smooth the linen tablecloth with hot stones, and shake out the heather of the girls' bed for Mr Renwick to sleep in (which made

239

Annie pout at the thought of the night she'd have to spend beside me on the parlour floor). The domestic tasks were so normal, and we were so conscious of the fame of our visitor, that I forgot for long quarter-hours at a time the danger that surrounded us. Then the memory of Lieutenant Dundas and his threatening henchmen would come back to me, and my heart would give a thump of fright. The fear died down quickly. Mr Renwick cast about himself a ring of brightness, a wall of light and faith and confidence which felt stronger than the ramparts of the stoutest castle.

Every now and then, I would make an excuse to cross the yard on an errand to the storehouse. I lingered as long as I could to catch snatches of Mr Renwick's voice. He was always the one who was talking, and Uncle Blair sat speechless beside him, his hands resting on his knees, his face turned towards his guest with an expression of complete absorption.

'. . . and so the meeting was a blessed one, brother, with hundreds of faithful souls bearing witness to the Lord. We posted our men, fully armed, round the whole congregation. We knew that our enemies were scouring the hills for us, but they stuck together in one troop, too afraid of our muskets to risk going in ones and twos. We saw them coming over the hilltop, and they saw us too, but at the very last minute . . .'

'Maggie!' my aunt's voice came from the kitchen. 'Where's the girl gone? Hurry up with that butter!'

The next time I managed to sneak outside Mr Renwick was saying, '. . . after that, our men went to meet

240

them, and there was some musket fire. Two of theirs met their deaths, but, praise the Lord! we got off without a scratch, and . . .'

But I heard a clatter from the kitchen, and wouldn't dare to anger my aunt by waiting to hear more.

The feast we had prepared was ready at last. My uncle gave up his stool at the head of the table to Mr Renwick, who was then persuaded to say grace. His prayer lasted for at least a quarter of an hour, and although I sensed that my aunt was growing restless with the fear that her dinner was spoiling, I could have gone on listening to Mr Renwick's beautiful, fluid voice for hours. Afterwards, though, I couldn't remember a word of what he'd said.

In spite of my aunt's efforts, Mr Renwick ate very little, and coughed frequently between mouthfuls. The talk between the men was all of politics. I felt my dinner curdle in my stomach as Mr Renwick described the new laws brought in against those who refused to renounce the Covenant, and who would not swear loyalty to the King.

'You mean that you can be sentenced and hanged just for attending a prayer meeting in the hills?' Ritchie demanded, his cheeks burning with indignation.

'Yes, young man. Satanic laws whispered into the ears of earthly princes by the Prince of Darkness himself,' Mr Renwick replied.

Uncle Blair shook his head sorrowfully.

'And how many of our men are dangling from the gallows at Paisley Cross?'

'Many. Too many. But their murderers will not go unpunished, for "*God is a man of war*,"' Mr Renwick answered, the softness of his look contradicting the violence of his words.

From time to time as the meal progressed, I glanced at Annie and saw that she was using all her tricks on Mr Renwick, trying to catch his eye, then dimpling and lowering her own. I saw too, with triumphant satisfaction, that he was taking no more notice of her than if she'd been one of the soot-blackened cauldrons hanging on the hooks by the fire. I wouldn't have demeaned myself by behaving like Annie, but I had to admit a little disappointment that Mr Renwick took not the slightest notice of me either.

When the bowls and platters had been cleared away, Uncle Blair said, 'If you're not too tired, brother, after your wearisome trials and travels, can we prevail upon you to read us a word from the Good Book?'

'Certainly,' said Mr Renwick.

He took the Bible from Uncle Blair's hands, and after he'd opened it began to read a psalm, but quite soon lifted his eyes from the page and recited the chapter without reading.

Does he know the whole Bible by heart? I thought incredulously.

He closed the book at last and laid his hand on the cover.

'Brothers and sisters, the sun has long gone down, and tomorrow will be a hard and busy day. Perhaps now is the time to sleep.'

'Oh, sir,' said Uncle Blair. 'Before we go to bed, we – Mrs Blair and I – have a request to make. As you know, there's no true minister now in Kilmacolm, and we've had no chance to bring our new child to the Lord for baptism. There are so many like us! You'll see them come tomorrow, babies and little children, streaming across the hills to our meeting place above Ladymuir. Will you christen Andrew, sir? Andrew and the others?'

Mr Renwick gave that smile again and I had to look away.

'Of course, dear brother.' He stifled a yawn. 'But now . . .'

'Aye, time to prepare for bed.' Uncle Blair placed a hearty hand on Mr Renwick's slim shoulder and the preacher seemed to buckle under its weight.

At that moment, one of the serving men, who had gone out to his bed in the byre, put his head back round the door.

'Black Cuffs in the lane, Mr Blair! And on the moss behind!'

'Lord have mercy upon us!' cried Aunt Blair, jumping up from the table. 'Hugh! What are we to do? What if they come here and find Mr Renwick?'

'Dear sir, come with me if you please,' said Uncle Blair, ignoring my aunt.

He thrust open the door into the little parlour next to the kitchen, and the rest of us, crowding in through the door, saw him draw out a ladder from behind the press.

'Stand back! Give me some room!'

I could tell he from the irritation in his voice, which I had never heard before, that he was alarmed. He poked the ladder at the ceiling, and pushed back a trap-door between the beams.

'Quick, Isobel. A sheet! Blankets! A bolster!' he said, disappearing up into the loft space.

Muffled noises came from overhead, then his face appeared again.

'Come on up, Mr Renwick. You'll be comfortable here, though it's not warm, I'm afraid. I slept in this loft myself when I was a lad. There's straw to lie on. They'll not find you, however hard they search the house. What are the rest of you gawping at like a row of silly sheep? Get away to your beds. If the enemy comes he must find us peacefully sleeping, with nothing suspicious about us. That's right, Mr Renwick. Mind the third step. It's a little shaky. When I've gone down, draw the ladder up after me and set the hatch back tight.'

'So you'll be able to sleep in your own bed after all,' I said over my shoulder, to the place where Annie had been a moment before. But she was no longer there.

It had been a long and tiring day, but in spite of my weary limbs I couldn't get to sleep. The thought of Lieutenant Dundas and his vile troopers creeping about outside, searching every fold of the hills and stand of gorse for Mr Renwick, made me tremble with fear. Now that the enemy were so close, I no longer felt secure behind the wall of brightness I'd sensed before. Mr Renwick seemed no more than a sliver of light against great darkness, a being too otherworldly in his courage and beauty for the earthly brutality of soldiers.

If they come for him, I'll fight them myself with my bare hands, I thought fiercely. What was that he said? '*God is a man of war!*'

The phrase pleased me, and I repeated it to myself while sleep began to come.

And then suddenly I was wide awake again.

Annie, I thought. *Annie. She's up to something.*

I went over the events of the past hour carefully in my mind. After Mr Renwick had gone to his bed in the loft, it had taken the rest of us a good three quarters of an hour to clear away the last of the meal, damp the fire down for the night and work through the usual chores, while Ritchie had kept watch, coming back frequently to report on the Black Cuffs' lantern lights bobbing as they searched the hills. Annie had reappeared only as we were putting on our nightshifts. Her forehead had been beaded with sweat and her cheeks were flushed as if she'd been running.

'Oh, Mistress Blair, I'm sorry I've taken so long. You know how I hate to be behind when there's work to be done. I went to check that Maggie had shut the chickens in, and found the gate open, and they were all out in the yard! That little black hen ran away as usual. It took me ages to catch her.'

'But I shut the gate to the coop!' I had protested indignantly. 'I always do!'

My aunt had frowned at me, and smiled indulgently at Annie.

'What a good thing you checked, dear. Get to bed now. We've a long day tomorrow.'

Annie can't have been chasing the little black hen, I thought. *That was the one we ate for supper. I plucked it myself. Why did she lie? Where did she go?*

The answer came at once. I threw off my blanket and sat bolt upright.

She went to betray Mr Renwick to the Black Cuffs.

The thought was so monstrous that I pushed it aside.

Not even Annie would do such a thing. And if she had, they'd have been here already to arrest him. Anyway, what would she have to gain? They'd probably arrest her too, just for living in a house with Covenanters.

Slowly I lay down again. Then I heard the outer door of the other room creak open. My heart began to pound.

They're here, they're creeping into the house. In a minute they'll be in this room!

I knew then that I wouldn't be brave enough to fight, even for Mr Renwick. I'd hide away and cower in some corner.

I waited, trembling, but nothing happened. No one came.

It was Uncle Blair, going out to relieve himself, I told myself.

A moment later, I was asleep.

I slept badly, disturbed by fears of a raid by the troopers, and by Mr Renwick's coughing overhead. I woke to the sound of many voices in the yard.

By the time I had got up and tidied away my bedding, there were at least thirty people congregated outside the farmhouse. Some were neighbours from nearby farms whom I recognized, but others must have come from much further away. They would have been walking through the night to reach Ladymuir in time to hear the famous preacher.

A few had brought their little farm ponies, but most had come on foot, and many of the women carried babies in their arms, as Uncle Blair had predicted.

'I was in such a state, Jeanie,' I heard one woman say to another, 'about the risk, bringing the children and all, what with the troops all over the place, but Isaac's going to be two years old in a week's time, and this is our only chance to have him properly christened by a true man of God.'

'My Matthew felt the same,' the other woman said. 'He was all for staying at home. But I was sure, you know, that there'll be a blessing on us today. "Where's your faith, man?" I asked him. *Cast all your burdens upon the Lord, for He careth for you.* He had no answer to that.'

In the entrance to the yard, Ritchie was standing with other farmers' sons, and I recognized Davie Barbour, Dandy Fleming and Mungo Laird. They were enthusiastically comparing their swords, daggers and muskets.

'You'll see what to do when we get to the hollow,' I heard Ritchie tell them, crossing his arms and frowning, like a master giving orders. 'I went out to check the best lookout places yesterday. The bracken's not up yet, more's the pity, so we won't have much cover, but—'

'We can lie down in the heather,' interrupted Dandy. 'And not wear our blue bonnets. They won't be able to pick us out from a distance.'

'Just what I was going to say,' said Ritchie frostily.

Mungo was scratching at a crop of spots on his chin, made itchy by the new growth of beard pushing through the skin.

'We kept watch last night from the moss at Newton,' he said. 'The troops withdrew off the hills late. We didn't see where they went though.'

'They're quartered miles away, at Sorn,' said Ritchie impatiently. 'If you'd all just listen I'll tell you. The point is that they can't have gone back that far last night, so they must have stayed close by. That means that we won't know which direction they'll come from, if they come at all.'

'They'll come.' Davie Barbour was squinting experimentally down the barrel of his musket. 'They know Mr Renwick's around here somewhere. They came as close as anything yesterday.'

'You brought him to Ladymuir, didn't you, Dandy?' asked Mungo. 'What's he like?'

'You'll be amazed. Just a wee slip of a fellow. But when he starts to speak his words go all the way through you. I can't explain. You'll see.'

So Mr Renwick has the same effect on everyone, I thought, and I was oddly disappointed. I didn't know why.

Uncle Blair came out into the yard then.

'Ritchie, and you lads, get all the people out of here now and off to the meeting place,' he said. 'The sooner they're hidden up there in the hollow, the better. Come back and lead the others as they arrive, then get into your lookout posts and keep yourselves hidden. You all have dry powder? And a good supply of musket balls? God willing we won't need to use them, but if the attack comes, then fight bravely. The enemy's hearts are filled with the strength of their wickedness, but if God be for us, who can stand against us?'

His words fired up a flame of courage in me, so that I blurted out, 'Uncle, I'll stand guard and fight with the lads, if you have a spare musket.'

He laughed, which made me flush with shame.

'Fighting's man's work, Maggie. But your courage does you credit. Go in now, and help your aunt.'

'She's a right one, that Maggie,' I heard Ritchie say as I went back into the house, and Davie Barbour laughed and said, 'Ritchie Blair, I do believe you're sweet on her. Look at you, blushing like a girl.'

In the kitchen, my aunt was flustered, trying to pre-pare a huge breakfast for Mr Renwick of which, I was sure, he would eat only a few mouthfuls.

'There you are, Maggie,' she said crossly. 'Disap-pearing again, just when you're needed. Help Nanny to dress, and mind Andrew. Annie dear, watch the oat-cakes. I daren't let Maggie take charge of them and burn them again today.'

I bit my lip and bent over Nanny.

Why does she dislike me so much? I asked myself. *She never took to me, not even before Annie came.*

Mr Renwick appeared in the kitchen soon after. He was heavy-eyed, and pale. Aunt Blair hovered round him, pressing on him bowls of porridge, eggs, fresh buttered oatcakes and cream. He ate no more than a few morsels, as I'd predicted, and those I was sure were only for politeness' sake.

'It's as I thought,' said Uncle Blair, coming in from the yard. 'The people of God are assembling fearlessly under the very eyes of the enemy. Dozens of saints are here already, and more are moving this way across the hills. Did you sleep well, Mr Renwick? It'll be a hard day's work for you, I fear. Have you given the man a good breakfast, Isobel?'

'He won't do more than nibble at it!' my aunt complained.

'Come, sir, come. You must eat to keep up your strength,' Uncle Blair said earnestly.

Mr Renwick turned on him his glorious smile.

'You know the promise we've been given, Brother Blair. *They that wait upon the Lord shall renew their strength; they shall mount up with wings as eagles; they shall run and not be weary; they shall walk and not faint.* It is prayer, you see, that will give me strength, and not this excellent breakfast.'

I was standing by the table, watching and listening, and I couldn't bear to see how little he had eaten. I spread an oatcake thickly with butter and honey.

'Please, Mr Renwick,' I said, offering it to him.

'Well, well.' He was looking directly at me so that I thought for a minute I would sink to the floor. 'If you wish it so much.' And he took the oatcake, to my intense delight, and ate it all.

'Shall we go now, brother, and begin the Lord's work?' he said, when the last crumb had gone.

'Ritchie will come and tell us when they're all assembled,' said Uncle Blair, going to the door and looking out. 'See there, up on the hills, more are coming. The young men are posting themselves all around on vantage points, watching for the troops. They'll come and fetch us when the time is right.'

'Then I'll go aside into the other room and pray, to prepare myself,' said Mr Renwick.

Everything seemed duller – the light dimmer, the colours more grey – when he had left the room.

'Girls, take the children now and get on up to the meeting place,' said Uncle Blair. 'Grizel, you know where to go. Watch out all the time for Black Cuffs. If you see them coming, call to warn the others, then creep home down the gully where you'll be hidden.'

Aunt Blair gave a little bleat of anxiety. 'Don't take Andrew and Nanny. Just Martha. I'll bring the little ones with me,' and she snatched Nanny's hand out of mine as if she was afraid she was about to lose her forever.

It was a relief to get away from the tense mood inside the house. The morning was fine and fair, the sun not long risen, and everything bright and gleaming after rain. Heavy droplets clogged the heather and sparkled

251

on the new green grass. I took a deep breath and felt my anxious heart lift. Surely nothing bad could happen on such a beautiful spring morning, out here on this ordinary, familiar hillside?

In all my time at Ladymuir I had never been to the place where the meeting was to be held. Grizel led the way to the stream, which I knew well enough, but instead of jumping over it, as I had expected, she turned along the bank and followed a little path which led up round the curve of the hillside. Below, the stream ran along the bed of a deep gully.

It was easy to see that many people had just passed that way. The print of feet was fresh in the mud, and the wet grass along the edges of the path was beaten down. I looked up to the hilltop above to where a young man was standing, scanning the horizon, his gun on his shoulder. Then ahead, as we rounded a spur of hillside, I saw a slow-moving family walking wearily along, the small children's sleeping heads nodding over their parents' shoulders.

A quarter of an hour later, we came round the last curve of the stream and, though I was expecting it, I was still astonished at the sight of hundreds of people, men and women, the old and the very young, milling about on a high flat bank above the fast-running stream. Opposite us, spouting down the black rocks, was a waterfall, rushing and foaming white. The pounding of the water as it fell into the pool below was so loud that it muffled the buzz of the people's excited voices. It was a perfect place to hide a crowd of people, out of sight of anyone looking across even from the highest vantage point of the hills above.

Above the flat space was a slope dotted with mossy rocks. Some people were already settled on these, as if they were sitting on their own stools in their own kirk, while others stood about, talking eagerly and looking down the burn as they waited for Mr Renwick to appear.

'Is there news of Stephen Barbour?' I heard someone ask.

'He's been taken to Glasgow, to the tollbooth. There's to be a full trial.'

'A trial! There's many who don't even get that. Muir of Rashiefield was taken up last week, told to renounce the Covenant and swear loyalty to the King, and when he refused he was shot dead, right there in his own field.'

Looking up, I could see the young men now posted about on each side of the gully. Ritchie himself stood on the highest point. He was signalling to Mungo to get into the right position. High above them, dark against the blue sky, a buzzard wheeled on tilted wings. On the far side of the narrow gully rose a steep hillside, covered with trees.

In the same quiet way that he had appeared in the farm kitchen, Mr Renwick slipped into the crowd milling about the hollow so unobtrusively that at first no one realized he was there. People had arranged themselves in groups. Some were already praying together, their heads bowed. Mothers were calling sharp warnings to their children, who, unused to being with so many people at once, were running around excitedly. Silence washed in on a slow wave as people realized that the preacher had arrived. Uncle Blair signalled with a sweep of his arm, and everyone began to settle themselves against the hollow side of the hill, and on the flat ground below, laying their thick plaids down on the wet grass before they sat, then turning their faces up eagerly to listen.

Uncle Blair and Mr Renwick stood with their backs to the waterfall cascading down behind them.

'Dear friends, dear neighbours,' began Uncle Blair, 'you have come – we are here – the honour of welcoming you to Ladymuir – the danger we face today . . .'

He was unable to go on. For a moment I thought he was tongue-tied by nervousness at addressing such a large crowd, but when he turned to Mr Renwick and signalled to him to carry on I saw that he was moved beyond bearing with emotion, and my own eyes pricked with tears in response.

Mr Renwick stood silent for a long moment, his head bowed in prayer, then he raised it and swept the expectant crowd with a long, penetrating look, as if assuring himself that all eyes were upon him. Only then did he begin to speak, and his voice, thrilling and deep, penetrated to the edge of the crowd even through the sound of the water, and made the goose pimples rise on my arms.

'Those that choose Christ make the right choice, yes, and a noble choice, for if Christ is theirs, all is theirs.

His glory is theirs, and He will be a hiding place to them in the days of trouble.'

He took a small Bible from the pocket of his coat, opened it, and read, '*For Thou hast been a strength to the poor, a strength to the needy in his distress, a refuge from the storm, a shadow from the heat, when the blast of the terrible one is a storm against the wall.*'

'Amen!' several voices called back in response.

A strength to the needy in his distress, I thought. *A shadow from the heat.*

Was that true for me? Was it Christ who had rescued me from the gallows and the fire? Or just Tam?

It was Tam, I thought. *It must have been.*

I knew that I wasn't pure enough – I had never been good or faithful enough – to deserve that Christ himself would make such an effort to rescue me. I could believe much more easily in Tam's love, and his delight in making mischief.

While my mind had wandered Mr Renwick had been been turning the pages of his Bible, and now he was tapping it with his forefinger.

'Oh, brothers and sisters!' he cried. 'Listen to the love-thoughts, bound here in this book in a bundle of precious promises! Every one of them drops like honey from the honeycomb! See how Christ shows His love to us.' And he read out, '*He brought me to the banqueting house, and His banner over me was love, and He fed me with apples, and comforted me with wine.*'

My chest tightened with longing as he spoke.

Nobody has ever loved me like that. But does Jesus? Is it really true?

'And what does He want from you in return?' I could hardly bear to look at Mr Renwick now. I felt as if his words were burning me, singeing my soul. 'Jesus wants to have your heart, and all that you have and are. If He calls for your eyes, give them to Him! If He calls for your ears, give them to Him! If He calls for your heart – oh, brothers and sisters, give! Give!'

'I do! I give everything!' I whispered, and my heart seemed to bound in my chest. 'I give—'

'Maggie!' said my aunt, pulling on my sleeve. 'Where's Martha?'

I looked round. I could see Nanny with a knot of other little girls. They had crept away to the side of the congregation and were playing quietly with sticks of wood wrapped in little cloths, cradling them like babies. But Martha wasn't there.

'I don't know, Aunt. I thought she was with you.'

Annie, sitting right behind us, leaned forward and whispered, 'I'll go and look for her, Mistress Blair.'

'Oh, thank you, dear.' Aunt Blair nodded gratefully. 'She can't have wandered far.'

I turned back to Mr Renwick, ready to sink back under the spell of his sermon, but as Annie stepped over my outstretched legs I looked up and saw a glint of fierce purpose in her eyes. She was suppressing a smile of triumph, as if she'd been waiting for something and it had happened as she'd hoped.

A jag of fear shot through me.

256

'Stay here, Annie. I'll go,' I said catching hold of her skirt.

She shook me off without looking at me or answering, and was already slipping away to the edge of the crowd where the path led out of the hollow.

'No!' I called out, too loudly, making heads around me turn. 'Come back, Annie!'

'Be quiet!' Aunt Blair hissed at me furiously. 'You're making a spectacle of yourself.'

Annie had halted and was looking down at the stream, where some of the little boys were squatting on the bank, floating sticks on to the water and watching them spin away down the current. She turned to shake her head at Aunt Blair, as if to say that Martha wasn't there. I knew she was only making a pretence of looking. I began to get up to run after her.

'These are Gospel days,' Mr Renwick was calling out, 'when the high places shall be forsaken, and the cities left desolate, and the towers shall be dens for the wild beasts, until the Spirit of God is poured on us from on high!'

Aunt Blair grabbed at my foot and pulled me down again.

'For goodness' sake, Maggie! This jealousy of yours is too much. I thought even your heart would be softened by Mr Renwick.'

I stared at her.

'Oh, Aunt, I'm not jealous of Annie! I'm afraid of her! She's up to something, I know she is. Last night, when she was gone for so long, I'm sure she was meeting the soldiers. I'm so scared – I'm afraid she's running off now to betray us!'

'Don't be ridiculous, girl! This is pure ill-nature. No more fuss, please. People are looking at us.'

I subsided unwillingly.

Perhaps she's right, I thought. *Perhaps I'm just jealous and suspicious.* I looked up, and caught sight of Ritchie, who was sitting with his back to the hollow, his musket across his knees.

'We are a Church and a people in an extremity of trouble,' Mr Renwick was crying out, 'but the sureness of our Covenant sets our feet upon iron ground! We will not turn aside, neither to the right hand nor to the left!'

At least Ritchie and the boys are keeping watch, I thought, my anxiety lessening. *They'll see the Black Cuffs from miles away. They'll see if Annie's meeting up with them. There'll be plenty of warning for us all to get away, if we have to.*

Mr Renwick's tone had changed, and his voice had dropped to a new and terrible pitch. There was no sign of the cough that had racked his chest all through the night.

'Oh, hard-hearted people! Remember that God is a great and a terrible God. A God of revenge on those who sin! Think on this – there is a day coming where you will all be called before His judgement seat, and the question will be asked of each one of you, "O man! O woman! Why did you do such things against Me?" And on that day, how will you answer? Have you failed to

258

keep faith with God and His Covenant? Then He will be revenged! Have you made peace with His enemies? God will be revenged! He will say to you, "Depart from Me, you who are cursed," and He will cast you into everlasting fire!'

Here it came again, that terrible threat of Hell and fire. For a fleeting moment I remembered Mr Lithgow on the mountainside, gazing down at the perfection of a bluebell.

'If He could make all this, why would He bother to make a Hell?' he had said.

I had nearly believed him. I shuddered at the sin I had nearly fallen into. Mr Renwick knew the truth. I would give my heart and my eyes and my ears and all that I had to Jesus, and stay faithful and true forever, and I would be saved from the fires of Hell.

'Who is on the Lord's side?' Mr Renwick's voice was cracking with the effort to be heard by those furthest away, above the noise of the waterfall. 'Who? There are but two sides, the camp of the Lord and the camp of the enemy. He who is not with us is against us!'

And then came the sounds that I had dreaded – shouts of 'Black Cuffs!' from the boys above, and the crackle of musket shot, which made the whole crowd flinch and cower.

Chapter Eighteen

For a moment there was mayhem as everyone jumped to their feet, shouting and milling about, not knowing which way to run. Then Mr Renwick, his voice calm and unhurried, called out, 'Don't be afraid, brothers and sisters! Who shall separate us from the love of Christ? Shall persecution, or peril, or sword? Nay, in all these things we are more than conquerors . . .'

'Aye, well, but there are women and bairns here,' a man close to me muttered. He called up to the guards above, 'How close are they, lads? How many?'

Before an answer could come, I saw the flash of a red coat in the trees on the far side of the gully, a mere stone's throw away, and then came another terrifying crack as the soldier, steadying himself against a tree, took aim with his musket and fired.

He would have hit Mr Renwick without a doubt if the preacher hadn't at that moment bent down to pick up his fallen Bible. The man hid behind the tree to reload his musket. Dandy Fleming, from his high vantage point, had a good sight of him and fired. I saw that the ball had hit its mark, because the soldier toppled forward and, slowly gaining speed, rolled down the slope to splash face down and motionless in the stream below.

'Well done, Dandy! You've killed the scunner!' one of the lads was shouting, but then I noticed nothing more, for the panic all around me swept me up in a great whirl of terror. I wanted to hit out at everyone in front of me and scratch and claw my way out of that narrow place, and I would have lost control completely if Aunt Blair hadn't screeched in my ear, 'Take Nanny! Get her home! Go the other way, up the gully and over the top. Martha! Where's Martha?'

I saw at once that she was right, because everyone was trying to rush down by the lower way and they were caught in the bottleneck of the narrow little valley. Now that I had a clear idea of what to do, I felt steadier. I picked up Nanny, who was crying hysterically, and hugging her to my chest, ran low to the ground like a hare, then up the slope, ignoring the gorse thorns that tore at my gown and my skin.

'It's all right, Nanny. Be quiet, darling,' I kept saying. 'We're going home.'

We were up on the level ground a few moments later, from where I could see right across the hillside. Aunt Blair had been right. The twenty or so red-coated soldiers, who had fanned out across the moor, were leaping down towards the lower end of the gully, from which people were running as fast as they could get away. I could see Ritchie and the other young men forming a kind of guard, their muskets to their shoulders, but I didn't wait to watch.

'You've got to be quiet now, Nanny,' I said sternly. 'If you don't stop screaming the nasty men will catch us.'

She gulped and hiccuped, terrified, and her arms tightened so hard round my neck I was afraid I would choke, but at least she was quiet.

Ducking and weaving from hollow to bush, around boulders and through bog, we reached the farm at last. In the distance I could hear shouts and screams and the occasional crack of a gun. Though the soldiers might burst into the farm at any moment, I felt safe in the calm enclosing walls of Ladymuir.

'Here we are, Nanny. Good girl. There you go,' I said, peeling the little girl's arms from my aching neck and setting her down in the yard.

'Where's Mammy?' she whimpered. 'I want my mammy!'

'Well now, look! Here she comes.'

Aunt Blair was indeed running into the yard with Andrew in her arms and Grizel behind her.

'Oh, Nanny! Safe! Thank goodness! But where's Martha? And Annie?' She was at the entrance to the yard again, looking wildly round. 'Oh! Annie's down there! But who's that with her? *What?* It can't be!'

I looked over her shoulder down the track that led from Ladymuir to the lane. There was a tree on the corner to which a horse was tethered. Annie was standing with her back to it, deep in what was obviously a willing embrace with Lieutenant Dundas. As we watched with open mouths he pulled away from her, patted her on the bottom, then cupped his hands for her foot and threw her up on to his horse's saddle. She bent down for a last kiss before he smacked the horse's rump, and Annie, her cap ribbons flying, her skirt billowing out around her, trotted away and disappeared down the lane into the hollow at the bottom of the hill.

Aunt Blair staggered as if she'd been struck.

'Oh!' was all she could say. 'Oh! I can't believe it! It can't be true!'

I couldn't help the smile of grim, justified triumph that I knew had lifted my mouth. Unfortunately, Aunt Blair saw it.

'How can you smile like that, Maggie? You can say *I told you so*, and I wish now I'd listened to you, but it was a bad day for us all when you brought that wicked treacherous girl to Ladymuir.'

Her injustice stung me.

'Aunt! I didn't bring her! I never wanted—'

'Oh never mind all that now! Where's Martha? And Ritchie? And Hugh? I'm out of my mind with worry.'

'I'll go and look for Martha,' I said, swallowing angry tears. 'She must have hidden somewhere close by.'

I no longer cared about the danger swirling around the hillsides. I wanted only to take my hurt away from Ladymuir. I wanted too to prove my courage and my worth to Aunt Blair.

I stumbled blindly out into the open, not caring where I went and not even bothering to hide myself, running directly up the hill in full view of anyone who might be looking. Furious words hammered round in my head.

She's so unfair! It wasn't my fault. I tried to tell her. Why didn't she listen? And Annie! How could she be so wicked?

When I had nearly reached the top, I stopped for a moment to catch my breath. I felt calmer now, and the horror of the battle on the hilltops came back to me. I was suddenly terribly afraid again. At any moment I might be shot at, or captured and taken away.

I looked around. From where I stood I couldn't see the lower exit to the gully, but I could clearly see the lane. People were hurrying back up towards Kilmacolm, carrying their children and looking back over their shoulders. There was no sign of the Black Cuffs.

There aren't enough of them to arrest everyone, I thought, *and our lads will be protecting the people. The soldiers will care most about catching Mr Renwick.*

Shouts came from behind. Turning, I saw two men, one tall and heavy-built, and one as short and slight as a boy, a quarter of a mile away. It was Uncle Blair and Mr Renwick, I was certain. And they were hurrying towards a dip in the moor where I could see three scarlet-coated dragoons lurking, waiting, like pike in the depths of Loch Quien, for their prey to come close enough to snatch.

I wanted to warn Uncle Blair, to scream out to him to turn and run, but I didn't dare risk the soldiers seeing me. In desperation, I tore off my bleached linen petticoat and stood like a mad woman waving it over my head.

Uncle Blair saw it. He grasped Mr Renwick's arm to halt him. I pointed to the hollow and mimed a soldier peering down a musket barrel. Uncle Blair seemed to understand, because he spun Mr Renwick round and together they stumbled away towards the hillside behind. The soldiers were out of their hollow and after them as keenly as dogs let off their leashes. One of them turned, realizing that Uncle Blair must have received a signal, but I had dropped down to the ground and was almost sure he hadn't seen me. I lay there panting as if I'd run a race, dreading the thud of the soldiers' boots coming towards me, but nothing happened and at last I dared to lift my head and look.

The soldiers were fanning out, running away from me, some peeling away to the left and some to the right. I could see that they were trying to surround the hill to cut off Uncle Blair and Mr Renwick.

I've got to warn them! They won't see what's happening! I thought, and I gathered my skirt up above my knees and raced towards the hill.

There were no more than six or seven dragoons, and they were spread quite far apart. Their scarlet coats made them easy to see against the greens and browns of the heather-clad hill. Ducking behind gorse bushes and keeping low to the ground, I was soon halfway up the slope. I stopped, a stitch stabbing my side, to draw breath.

And then I saw them. Uncle Blair and Mr Renwick were only a short way ahead, moving fast along the path that would take them round the shoulder of the hill. On the far side lay the slope that led across the moors northwards, towards the banks of the Clyde.

'Uncle!' I called out recklessly, though I was too

scared and too short of breath to shout loudly. Luckily he heard, and turned round.

'Maggie! What are you doing out here? Get back home! Don't you realize how dangerous this is?'

'Uncle, listen! They're surrounding the whole hillside. I saw them! If you go on this path they'll be waiting on the far side.'

Mr Renwick came towards Uncle Blair.

'What was that? What did the lassie say?'

His eyes were alight with the excitement of it all, but a groan broke from Uncle Blair, who was pale with anxiety. I understood, suddenly, that he had risked everything – his farm, his family and even his life – for the cause, and that he had done it knowingly, because he thought it was right. And I loved him for it.

'O Lord, save us!' he was muttering. 'O God, help us!'

'Have courage, brother,' said Mr Renwick cheerfully. 'Is there no hollow or dip where we can lie and hide? Surely there's some small place . . .'

'Up there! Two men, and a girl! One of them's Renwick!' came a shout from below.

There was nowhere to go but on up the hill, even though I knew the noose was tightening around us.

'There's still a chance. We might slip through their cordon on the far side,' panted Mr Renwick. 'We must pray that the Lord hides us for long enough from their eyes!'

We were nearly at the top of the hill. It was crowned with a high cairn of stones. I looked over my shoulder.

There would be no safe way down for any of us now. Lieutenant Dundas's men were closing in. We were trapped on this windy peak.

'Ha!' Uncle Blair exclaimed suddenly. 'Praise the Lord! He has shown me a hiding place! Get up the cairn, Mr Renwick, quick! Climb the stones! There's a hollow inside it that Danny and I made when we were boys. No one will think to look for you there.'

'But you—' began Mr Renwick.

'It's you they want. It's your life that must be preserved to carry the word. Be quick! Hide!'

Mr Renwick was already clambering up the pile of stones, and he whisked himself down inside as fast as a startled lizard shoots across a stone.

'Now, Maggie, we must face this out,' said Uncle Blair. 'We can't run from them. Sit here by me, my dear, and wait for them peacefully. I wish your father could have seen you today. He would have burst with pride. They'll take me, Maggie. You know that. My life then will be the Lord's to do with as He sees fit. I'll not have the chance to say goodbye to them all at home. Comfort your aunt, Maggie dear. Help her with the little ones. I know that it's not always been easy for you but . . .' He picked up my hand and pressed it. 'And try to forgive Annie, who has meant no harm, I'm sure.'

It was Annie who betrayed you, Uncle, I wanted to protest, but the Black Cuffs were so close now that I could hear the buckles jingle on their scabbards and I didn't want to distress him further.

'There are heavy fines to pay,' Uncle Blair went on

urgently, his thoughts running ahead. 'There's silver put by in the strongbox. Not enough, but some. Tell Ritchie to apply for more to the Laird of Duchal if he has to, but only if things grow desperate. And tell him that the infield must be the first to harvest, when the oats are ripe. Tell him—'

'Uncle! You'll be back before harvest time, wherever they take you!' My voice was dry with dread.

'I don't think so, Maggie.'

He stood up and stepped forwards with a calm face to meet the first of the dragoons to reach the summit, who had drawn his sword and was pointing it directly at Uncle Blair's chest.

'Put your weapon away, man. There's no need for violence. But let the lassie go. She's a child. She wished only to see me safe.'

Three other soldiers had arrived now. They grabbed Uncle Blair by the arms, but took no more notice of me than if I'd been a stray sheep.

'Go on, Maggie,' Uncle Blair said over his shoulder. 'Go back home.'

One of the men had taken Uncle Blair by the front of his coat and was shaking him in a terrier's grip.

'Renwick! The preacher! Where is he? What have you done with him?'

'You'll not find him,' Uncle Blair said, setting his jaw. 'The Lord of hosts is with him. The God of Jacob is his refuge.'

'Refuge? I'll give you refuge!' said the dragoon furiously, smacking Uncle Blair across the face with a swipe of his hand, so that the sword wound on his cheek opened and began to bleed again.

I took a deep breath.

'I saw a short little man, in a brown coat, running that way,' I said, pointing towards the Clyde, 'if that's the one you're looking for.'

I didn't dare look at my uncle. Even at this moment of extreme danger I knew he'd never stoop to such a blatant untruth.

'You're lying.' The tallest dragoon came up and stood so close to me that I could smell onions on his breath. Though my heart was thudding, I managed to stare boldly back at him.

'Why should I lie? The man's nothing to me.'

One of the others snorted with contempt.

'She's another light skirt, like the lieutenant's new fancy piece. Sick and tired of all the preachifying. Women are all sneaks anyway.'

I flushed, but held my tongue. My lie was working. They were looking in the direction I'd pointed, shading their eyes to scan the moorland. I seized my chance and backed away, then began to run down the far side of the hill. I lost my balance almost at once on the steep slope, and slithered down a good stretch of it on my back.

'The devil Renwick's slipped through between us!' I heard one of the soldiers shout to the others. 'Get off after him! We'll take this treasonous Covenanter back to the lieutenant. What? The girl? Let her go, the little Jezebel.'

*

It was a long way back to Ladymuir and I was aching with tiredness before I was halfway there. I could only hobble slowly on sore feet by the end, but when I came within earshot of the house, I heard sounds that made me pick up my skirts and run.

Men were shouting and laughing, and a woman was screaming.

I raced, panting, through the yard entrance to find Black Cuffs swarming. Two were holding Ritchie by the arms, and he was struggling desperately to free himself. Another man had seized Grizel, who, crimson with rage, was trying to beat him off with her fists. Aunt Blair was standing by the door, her face as white as her cap, her hands held out in front of her as if she was warding off the Devil himself.

'No!' she was screaming. 'No!'

And then I saw Lieutenant Dundas. He was standing beside the well and he was holding Andrew over the lip of it by one arm. The poor baby, wriggling and bellowing, was threatening to slip out of his grasp at any moment.

'Where is he? If you want your squealing brat you must tell me where you've hidden the preacher!'

'I know where he is! I'll tell you! Don't drop him!' I shouted.

Lieutenant Dundas spun round.

'Who are you? What do you know?'

'My niece! That's my niece! Maggie, catch Andrew! Don't let him fall!'

'Please, sir, give me the baby,' I said, walking forward

slowly, as if I was approaching a dangerous dog. 'I'll tell you. I know. I saw him. I know where he is.'

'Maggie!' Ritchie called out. 'Mind what you say!'

Lieutenant Dundas almost flung Andrew at me. Aunt Blair darted forward and snatched him out of my arms.

With a final frantic lunge, Ritchie shook off the two soldiers. They made no effort to restrain him again. Everyone was looking at me.

'My uncle's taken,' I said to Aunt Blair. I turned back to Lieutenant Dundas. 'Your men took him, up on the top of Windyhill, by the cairn.' I bit my lip, wishing I hadn't mentioned the cairn, afraid I'd given too much away.

'The Devil can take your damned uncle,' Lieutenant Dundas barked impatiently. 'Where's the traitor Renwick?'

'I'm telling you. They surrounded Windyhill and chased Uncle Blair and Mr Renwick up it. But Mr Renwick slipped between them and I think – I didn't see – perhaps he hid behind some stones or a – a gorse bush. But then he went on northwards, across the moor towards the Clyde. They've gone after him, some of them. The others arrested my uncle. They said they'd bring him back to you. But please, sir, you don't want him. Please, let him—'

Lieutenant Dundas's hand shot out and he gripped me painfully by the throat.

'Are you telling the truth? You'll be sorry if it's a lie.'

I knew I'd be sorry for the sin, but not for the result.

'I'm telling you,' I managed to croak, though he was

half strangling me. 'They nearly caught Mr Renwick on the top of Windyhill, and now they're chasing him north, over the hills.'

That's the truth, after all, I told myself.

'Hugh? They've taken Hugh?' Aunt Blair cried out, as if she'd only just understood. Still clasping Andrew, she sank down on to the stone seat by the door.

Lieutenant Dundas had lost interest in us all.

'There's no more to do here,' he said curtly to his men. 'Watkins, leave that girl alone. There are still hours of light left. Get mounted, all of you. We'll ride up past Kilmacolm and cut the traitor off before he reaches the coast. He'll be trying to get a crossing to Gourock or Dunoon.'

No one spoke as the sound of the horses' hoofs died away down the track, but the silence was broken by Aunt Blair's moaning sobs.

Behind me, Ritchie cleared his throat.

'I'm sorry you betrayed Mr Renwick. That wasn't well done.'

'I didn't betray him.' I blushed at the scorn in his voice. 'He's hiding inside the cairn on the top of Windyhill. I – I told a lie to send the troopers away in the wrong direction. They believed me and chased after him.'

Ritchie managed to smile at this news.

'Well done, Maggie! You mean he's safe?'

'I suppose so, as long as he stays out of sight inside the cairn.'

'I'll go and find him and take him to a good hiding

272

place,' said Ritchie, making for the yard entrance. 'It's what Father would want.'

Aunt Blair started up.

'Ritchie, you will *not*. It's enough that your father's been arrested. There's to be no more running about the countryside today. If you're taken too, who's to keep us going here? Who's to run the farm?'

'Mother . . .'

'No!' I had never heard my aunt speak so forcibly. For once, I agreed with her.

'If you go up there you'll just draw attention to him,' I dared to chip in. 'He's well hidden. He's safer by himself till the troops are called off the hills.'

Ritchie tightened his lips but nodded reluctantly.

'Uncle Blair gave me some messages for you. He said to pay the fines with the silver in the strongbox, and if you really have to, you can ask the Laird of Duchal for a loan. And he said to harvest the infield first when the oats are ripe.'

Aunt Blair let out a cry of despair and Ritchie looked shaken.

'Harvest? But that's months away! Did the soldiers say what they were going to do with him? Did they talk of a trial? Maggie, did you hear anything about – they're not going to execute him?'

I shook my head. 'They didn't say anything. They just said they'd take him to Lieutenant Dundas.'

'That monster!' Aunt Blair was rocking on her seat.

Grizel, who had run into the house dishevelled and

red-faced when the dragoon had at last let her go, came outside again.

'Mistress, you'll not be pleased,' she said reluctantly. 'They've been in and out of everything. It's turmoil in there. The cauldron's overturned and the fire's out and the silver spoon has gone.'

Nanny had been cowering in her mother's skirts and she set up a wail, only daring to raise her voice now that the danger was over. Aunt Blair looked down at her, startled, as if she'd only just realized she was there.

'And where's Martha? Maggie, you went out to find her! Where is she?'

'I'm here, Mammy! Have the nasty men all gone away?'

Martha's little white face appeared, peeping fearfully out round the frame of the kitchen door.

'Martha! Where have you been all this time?'

Martha looked at Aunt Blair doubtfully, not sure whether she was in trouble or not.

'I came home from the preaching,' she said at last. 'I didn't like it. Then Annie came and started looking for things. She was in a big hurry. She turned the heather out of our bed. She only found a groat though, in Grizel's little bag.'

'Ha!' snorted Grizel. 'I knew all along she'd try to steal my wages. I hid them well.'

'And then Annie slapped me, Mammy, and told me to fetch the key to the strongbox.'

Aunt Blair gasped and clapped her hand over her mouth.

'The wickedness of her! I'd never have believed it!'

'The strongbox? We're ruined!' muttered Ritchie.

'I didn't want to give it to her,' Martha said, frowning. 'I don't like Annie. You said I had to like her, but she's not nice, Mammy. Not to me. I found the key before she did and I put it in my pocket and pretended to go on looking for it. And then that man came, the horrible one, and he called her, and said he'd send her off to Sorn Castle with an escort on a horse, and she should wait for him there, and she just snatched up the silver spoon and ran out to him. I was so scared. I hid in your bed.'

'Brave Martha,' Aunt Blair said shakily, holding out her arms, and Martha went into them and was fiercely hugged.

Behind her, Grizel beckoned to me from the kitchen door.

'Might as well make a start,' she said, looking round disgustedly at the wreckage. 'Mistress is going to have a fit and half when she sees all this. She's not going to have it easy now. We'll not see the master back. He's done for, if you want my humble opinion.'

After Lieutenant Dundas and his men had come to Ladymuir the first time, we'd been able to repair much of the damage, scooping up the spilt meal and stitching the torn sacks, rescuing most of the cheeses and generally putting the storeroom back in order. But this time the destruction had been complete. The troopers had stripped the storeroom, carrying off sacks and jars and barrels and trampling what they left into a filthy mess on the floor. Inside the house, they had ripped the linen, tumbled the pots and dishes off the shelves, and smashed whatever would break.

I'd thought, when I saw the ruin of her home, that Aunt Blair would sink into helpless despair. In fact, when she first saw the extent of the disaster, she could do nothing for at least half an hour but sit, crying and trembling, on the bench by the table, on which the remains of the breakfast porridge had been spilt and smeared and made inedible with handfuls of ash from the dead fire.

I crept round her, not wanting to irritate, not knowing where to start. I envied Grizel who, in her usual practical way, was getting on with the work – picking up cooking pots, sweeping ashes and fetching in twigs to try to relight the fire – while the little girls, upset by the horror of the day, squabbled noisily in the corner.

Aunt Blair stopped crying at last. She bent her head and clasped her hands and I saw her lips moving.

She's praying, I thought, and I knew I should be praying too, so I leaned on the broom I was holding, squeezed my eyelids together and said in my heart, *O Lord, deliver us from evil.*

As the familiar phrase formed in my head I remembered the last words I'd said to Jesus. I'd been filled with a rush of overwhelming love, up there by the waterfall, and I'd said, *I give everything! I give!*

I wasn't sure now what I'd meant, or what had happened to me. I only knew that I'd felt something miraculous at the time, and that a glow, like the last pink streaks of a sunset, still lit something inside me.

'Maggie,' said Aunt Blair, startling me.

I opened my eyes. She was sitting upright, and a little colour had returned to her cheeks.

'You saved Andrew from that fiend,' she said. 'I'll not forget that. You were wonderful, dear. So brave.'

She spoke more warmly than she had ever done, though I could tell that her words came from a sense of duty rather than affection. Even so, I blushed with pleasure.

'And she saved Mr Renwick too,' said Ritchie, coming in from outside. 'Mother, I thought they'd driven off the cows, but they only let them loose. I've rounded them up. They're all accounted for.'

'God be praised. There'll be milk then, at least, when they've calved.'

Nanny and Martha heard the word *milk*. They stopped tussling and looked up.

'I'm hungry, Mammy,' said Martha.

'So'm I,' said Nanny.

'That's just too bad,' Aunt Blair said with determined briskness. 'You'll have to get used to it. Maggie, see if you can find any scraps of oatcake left over from this morning and give them to the children, then put the bedding together and get them to bed. Grizel, leave the fire now and clean up the mess on this table. Then we'll have to see if there's anything that can be rescued from the storeroom. We'll have to sift the oats from the mess on the floor grain by grain.'

'Then what are we going to have for supper, mistress?' asked Grizel.

'Supper? *Supper?*' Aunt Blair's self-control, which she had wrapped around herself like a cloak, fell away for a moment. 'Don't you understand, you silly girl? There is no supper. There'll be nothing for breakfast. Your master's gone. The storeroom's empty. The silver will all be taken in fines. We're ruined, Grizel. If we survive until the harvest it will be a miracle.'

And then the cloak closed round her again and she began to give us orders in her old contradictory way, and she fussed and bustled and tutted and grumbled until the house had been restored to some kind of order, the fire was lit, the children had gone whining to bed, and Andrew had been suckled and laid for the night in his cradle.

But when we were in bed and I was sinking into the sleep of complete exhaustion, in spite of the hunger gnawing at me, I heard her weeping softly behind the wooden partition that separated her bed from ours.

Chapter Nineteen

Of all the people at Ladymuir, I think I was best able to cope with the sudden, total poverty in which we had been plunged. I'd lived on the edge of hunger all my life, before I'd come to Kilmacolm. On the many, many days when there had been no food in the cottage at Scalpsie Bay, I'd scavenged for limpets on the rocks by the sea, gathered berries or nuts in the autumn and picked edible leaves and flowers wherever I could find them. But the spring, I knew, was the worst time for famine. Everyone's winter supplies were low, there were no wild fruits to gather, and the crops were a long way from harvest.

I did what I could, stinging my hands raw and red with nettles to make soup, and hunting for birds' eggs on the moss. Aunt Blair wrinkled her nose at my offerings, but used them all the same. She was more grateful for the stream of gifts of oatmeal and barley and even valuable cheeses from those kind farms nearby whose stores had not been raided, and I saw more than ever how greatly Granny had caused us to suffer by her endless quarrelling with our neighbours.

The officers from Paisley came a few days after Uncle Blair had been arrested in order to collect the fine for non-attendance at the kirk. Although we'd been expecting them, we'd hoped somehow that my uncle's arrest would have spared us, and the shock of the sum they demanded was a final blow.

They were decent men, I suppose, not like Lieutenant Dundas's dragoons. They counted out the silver pieces so carefully put by in the strongbox, piled them neatly on the table and gave my aunt a written receipt.

'There's another two pounds owing,' the older man said, almost regretfully. 'Do you not have it, Mistress Blair?'

My aunt's eyes filled with tears. She shook her head.

'You've taken every penny we have. It's all there, in front of you. How am I to feed my children?'

'You should have thought of that before you broke the law,' the other man said, 'What harm would it have done, to sit through a sermon or two? You needn't have listened, after all.' The older one frowned him to silence.

'There's nothing I can do. I'm just carrying out my orders. I'm sorry for your trouble. These are bad times for everyone. There's not a household hereabouts that isn't suffering. The gaols in Paisley and Glasgow are so full of Covenant men – and women, come to that – that they've had to send some of them on to the tollbooth in Edinburgh.'

'What?' Aunt Blair eyes started. 'What about my husband? I was told he was in Glasgow. Is he one of them? Why would they send him all the way to Edinburgh? Oh – I know what this means! They're going to hang him! There'll be a trial and the next thing we know . . . Lord, have mercy on us!'

'Hold on, mistress. I don't know if your husband's one of them. It's no use asking me. I'm just telling you what I heard. Some have been hanged already, but you'd have heard if your husband was one of them. Some are to be kept in Glasgow, and some are sent on to Edinburgh.'

Aunt Blair collapsed on to her stool and looked so dreadful that I thought she would faint. The officers clearly thought so too. They exchanged quick, embarrassed nods, tipped the silver pieces into leather pouches and almost tiptoed to the door.

'We'll not bother you for the rest of the money now,' the older one said, as if conferring a great concession. 'But we'll have to come back for it, mistress. The fine must be paid in full, as you well know.'

At that point Ritchie, who had been out since dawn doing the work of two men on the farm, came into the yard, and the officers scuttled away.

It always seems wonderful to me how fast news travels from one end of Scotland to the other, reaching remote farms and hamlets, spreading out from towns and drifting across the mountains and firths and lochs like thistledown blowing in the wind. By the evening of that day, we were reeling from the news that my uncle had indeed been among the group of prisoners taken to Edinburgh.

'It's because he was with Mr Renwick,' said Dandy Fleming, who had come all the way over from Whinnerton carrying an offering of meal for my aunt, with the kind compliments of his mother. 'Anyone connected with such a great preacher is given special treatment. All the important ones have been taken off to Edinburgh.'

He spoke as if this ought to be a matter of pride.

'Edinburgh!' Aunt Blair repeated faintly.

I'd heard of Edinburgh, of course. I knew that it was a place of power, where lairds and kings and great men of all kinds sat in power and state, sending out cruel decrees to tax and persecute the poor people of Scotland. Tam had been there once, playing his pipes for money. He'd told me stories that I hardly believed about buildings so tall they reached to the sky, and nobles wearing velvet and silk. He'd managed to stay for a month or more, his earnings keeping him fed and constantly drunk, and then he'd been taken up as a vagabond and thrown out of the city.

I shivered at the thought of Uncle Blair being imprisoned in such a strange, dread place. I felt again the kindness of his hand gripping mine as we'd sat so calmly on the top of Windyhill, waiting for the dragoons to come up and take him away, while Mr Renwick lay hiding a few feet away from us inside the hollow cairn. A lump came into my throat as I remembered the affection in his voice.

'What's the news of Mr Renwick?' asked Ritchie. 'He got away all right, didn't he?'

'Aye.' Dandy grinned. 'He skipped across to Dunoon. What a man! There's no danger that stops him. It was a good job you did that day, Maggie.

Ritchie's been boasting of you right and left, how you sent the dragoons off on the wrong track.'

I was unused to praise, and it warmed me through.

It was only later, as I went down to the stream with buckets to fill, that I let rise to the surface a kind of resentment which had begun to grow in my head.

It's all very well for Mr Renwick. He doesn't have a family or a farm to lose. It must be a kind of adventure to him.

And then I remembered how the young preacher had sent me reeling with the glow of his smile, and how his presence had seemed to light the room, and his words had penetrated my heart and quivered there. What was it he'd said? *His banner over me was love, and He fed me with apples, and comforted me with wine.*

Yes, I thought, leaning down to scoop water into my bucket, *oh yes, yes*. And I repeated to myself, *I give. I give!*

Something in the stream caught my eye. A shoe, washed down by the current, was wedged between two stones. I fished it out. It was a woman's shoe, solid and heavy. Its owner must have run out of it in her desperate haste to flee from the dragoons after Mr Renwick's preaching.

The horror of the attack came back to me, and with a spurt of anger I flung the shoe into a clump of gorse on the far side of the stream.

'Why?' I said out loud. 'How can it be against the law to meet out in the hills and sing psalms and read the

Word of God and preach sermons? Whatever is wrong with that?'

I heard Uncle Blair's voice in my ear: *The King and the great men around him desire in their wickedness to remove God from His throne as head of the Kirk, and put themselves in His place. And we must resist them, Maggie, or be traitors to Him, and to Scotland, and to ourselves.*

Could I ever care for the cause as much as Uncle Blair did? Would I give up everything, and even risk death?

I knew the answer.

'No,' I whispered, ashamed of myself. 'No.'

The knowledge frightened me. On the Day of Judgement, when I stood before Almighty God, He would curse me, like Mr Renwick said, and cast me into everlasting fire for failing to keep the faith.

But I would suffer anything for a person I loved, I told myself. *Perhaps that would be enough. I'd be ready to die for someone who really loved me.*

I picked up the two full buckets and began the long trudge back up the slope towards the farm. I saw Ritchie ahead. He was talking to Davie Barbour, and his hand was on Davie's shoulder, as if to comfort him.

Something's happened, I thought, my heart sinking, and I hurried up to the farm.

My aunt's raised voice came out of the kitchen door towards me as I hurried in.

'Dorcas, the poor soul! And the children! Ritchie, if they've done such a thing to Mr Barbour, whatever will they do to your father?'

'They've executed Mr Barbour,' Ritchie told me quietly. 'Hanged him. For being a rebel and a traitor because he refused to take the Test.'

'What test? What's the Test?'

'Don't you know? The oath of allegiance. They make you swear that the King is the head and ruler of the Church, and you have to say, "God save the King." You used to have to pay a fine if you wouldn't say it, but now the penalty is death.'

'You mean they hanged Mr Barbour just because he wouldn't say all that?'

I could hardly believe it.

'And they'll hang your uncle too, you'll see,' Aunt Blair said bitterly.

'Mother, you don't know that.' Ritchie touched her gently on the shoulder. 'Mr Barbour was executed in Glasgow, where they've all gone mad with rage against us. They might not be so severe in Edinburgh.'

She stared at him, misery in her face, and said at last, 'It's not knowing that's the worst. It's the dread of waiting for news.'

Things had been bad at Ladymuir before we'd heard of the death of Mr Barbour, but a grimmer depression descended afterwards. I missed the company of Grizel, who had been sent back to her family to save on wages and food. Her absence meant more work for me, but even though I did my best, and never rested from morning till night, I couldn't please my aunt. She found fault constantly, and her eyes seemed to follow each mouthful that I took at our meagre mealtimes as if she resented the food that her children might have had.

Ritchie rode out early one morning and came back looking pleased with himself. He strode into the kitchen and put a clinking pouch of coins on the table in front of his mother.

'From the Laird of Duchal,' he said proudly. 'I asked him to lend us the money for the rest of the fine, and he gave me a bit more too for Father. You need money when you're a prisoner, he said, if you want to eat enough to keep body and soul together.'

'You borrowed this money from the laird?' Aunt Blair said anxiously. 'Ritchie, how are we ever to pay him back?'

'We will. After the harvest. It's what Father said to do.' I heard a new note of authority in Ritchie's voice. He was the man of the house now, and was taking charge. 'Anyway, the laird's in no hurry. He's a good man of the Covenant himself. He spoke so admiringly of Father. You'd have been proud to hear him, Mother. The real question is, if Father needs this money, how are we to get it to him?'

Aunt Blair shook her head so vigorously that Andrew, who was in her arms, set up a wail.

'No, Ritchie,' she snapped. 'You're not to go to Edinburgh. You'd be arrested before you were well on the road out of Kilmacolm.'

Ritchie nodded.

'I know. But we'll have to do something, Mother. We have to get this money to him somehow.'

I knew at that instant what I had to do, and the thought was so frightening that it made me shiver.

I would go to Edinburgh. I would take the laird's money, and find my uncle, and give it to him. I'd discover if there had been a trial, and if he was in prison or awaiting execution. I'd use any trick to free him. And I'd bring him safely home to Kilmacolm.

I went out into the yard, thinking furiously.

I could be a boy again, like on the drove. No, that wouldn't do. I was too noticeably a young woman now, and anyway, a boy was more likely to be stopped and questioned. I could pretend to be a servant girl, like Grizel, making her way home after losing her position. I could – I could . . .

I was still furiously thinking when I went to bed that night, and I lay for a long time, thinking through one fantastic plan after another, while the little girls slept snuggled close up beside me, snuffling in their dreams.

Weeks went by, turning into months, and all the time we became hungrier and more anxious, and my inner turmoil grew. July came. There was still some time to go before the harvest could be brought in to fill the storeroom again, and I could hardly bear to look at the pinched faces of the children. Aunt Blair wouldn't touch the laird's money.

'It's for your father,' she snapped one day, when she saw Ritchie eye it longingly. 'If we're in need, think what it's like for him.'

I kept out of my aunt's way as much as I could. All the

time I dreamed of how I would travel to Edinburgh, rescue Uncle Blair heroically from his dungeon and bring him back in triumph to Ladymuir, and how everyone would love me for it, and forgive me – even Aunt Blair – for being the cause of Annie's coming, and her betrayal.

Once, after Aunt Blair had scolded me for taking a second oatcake, I almost started off towards Kilmacolm on my own, but I knew I'd never reach Edinburgh. I would have starved to death or been arrested as a vagabond long before I'd walked half the distance.

And then, early one morning, as I was rooting about in the barn, hunting for eggs, someone cleared his throat right behind me. I jumped and spun round.

'Tam! Where have you been? What are you doing here?'

He had the humble, servile look of a dog afraid of a whipping.

'Why, Maidie, I came to see how you were doing. I crept in last night when you were all in bed and slept here with the cows. I came because I heard what happened to your uncle, and – and about Annie.'

'Yes,' I said bitterly, wanting to punish him. 'No thanks to you for all that, Tam. I knew as soon as I saw her that she'd bring trouble here, but not even I thought she could be so wicked.'

'I know, I know.' He saw that I wasn't going to scold him any more. He pushed his hand up under his filthy old bonnet and scratched at his head, looking a little happier, then began to pick a few wisps of straw off the front of his tattered coat.

'You'll be interested to hear, maybe, that that fine soldier of hers has got rid of her already. Less than a week she had, queening it around Sorn Castle. He threw her out in the middle of a rainstorm.'

'Good,' I said vindictively. 'I hope she died of cold.'

He shook his head again, looking solemn at the thought of it.

'Tam!' I stared at him. 'You're not – you *can't* still be sorry for Annie! Not after what she's done! Tam, you haven't brought her here again?'

'No, no!' He shuddered. 'I never want to see the girl again. If I'm lucky, I never will. She found herself another rascal straight away. One of those flouncy military fellows, his red coat all covered over with shiny brass buttons and leather straps and whatnot. He'd got more feathers on his hat and more silver braid on his cravat than that bully Dundas, so I guess Annie thought she'd done well for herself after all.'

A shadow fell at the door and Ritchie came into the barn. His brows twitched together as he recognized Tam.

'You're back, then,' he said drily. 'Alone this time, I hope.'

Tam twisted himself into a knot of writhing humility.

'Oh yes, indeed, young man. I came to tell you how very sorry I am for your trouble. I never knew what that girl would do! If I'd had any idea, I'd have cut my right hand off rather than bring her here.'

He thrust out his scrawny arm as if to prove he was sincere. The sleeve of his coat, worn to strips of rag, fell away from it, and I was shocked to see how thin he was, his bones seemingly held together by nothing more than their casing of skin.

Anger died out of Ritchie's face. I could see he was torn between pity and contempt.

'Well,' he said at last, 'it wasn't your fault, after all, but we're in a bad way here, thanks to that girl.' His eyes brightened as he looked down and saw a little bulge in the pocket of my apron. 'Did you find any eggs, Maggie? The children are crying for their breakfast.'

'Breakfast!' said Tam, a slick of spittle gathering in the corner of his slack old mouth. 'Now there's the finest word I've heard in a long time. My insides are stuck together with hunger.'

I could see that Ritchie was torn between his natural generosity and the knowledge of how little food there was for his family. Generosity won.

'You're welcome to share what we have,' he said at last, as willingly as he could.

But suddenly I had seen what I had to do, and I shook my head at Ritchie.

'We've no time for breakfast. Tam's come to take me away. I'm going to Edinburgh. I'm going to try to see my uncle and help him if I can. I've still got my father's silver buckle. I'll sell it to pay my way. And then I'll find a way to send you news of him.'

Tam's mouth had dropped open, showing his few crooked, blackened teeth.

'Wait now, Maidie. I never came to take you away. It's a bit of rest I'm needing. The road's a hard place for an old man.'

'I can't help that,' I said mercilessly. 'You can't stay here, Tam, anyway. There's no food here. This family's practically starving. You're taking me to Edinburgh.'

He stared at me, aghast.

'Edinburgh! It's an awful distance to Edinburgh. And how are we to live on the road? Walking's a hungry business.'

'We'll find a way,' I said firmly.

Ritchie was biting his lip and frowning at me.

'I can't let you do this, Maggie. It's too dangerous. Travelling without a permit's forbidden. You know that.'

'Then we'll keep out of people's way,' I said impatiently. 'For goodness' sake, Ritchie, I escaped the executioner in Bute and found my way to Ladymuir on my own. Surely I can get myself to Edinburgh! Anyway, you don't know Tam. He's spent a lifetime creeping around Scotland, making himself invisible. He knows how to keep himself out of harm's way. He's so clever. He's always been able to get me out of trouble.'

Tam simpered, looking foolishly pleased. Then his face dropped and he shook his head mournfully.

'It's not what I had in mind, Maidie. A little rest, that's what I'd hoped for. A little time to gather my strength.'

'But I *need* you, Tam!' I cried. 'I can't do this on my own!'

He shook himself and sighed.

'I never could resist you, darling. Not since you were a tiny little thing. What's that buckle of your father's worth, do you think? Would it stretch to a little whisky now and then along the road?'

'Maggie—' began Ritchie.

'It's no good,' I told him. 'My mind's made up. Let's go and tell my aunt.'

I have to admit that Aunt Blair was a good woman. A spark of relief lit her eyes when I told her my decision, but she doused it quickly and tried to persuade me to stay. The danger was too great, she said. She was responsible for me. She'd never forgive herself if I came to harm.

In the end though, when she saw how determined I was, she came round to agreeing.

'When will you go?' she asked.

'Now! Today! Look, the weather's fine for a walk. There's not a cloud in the sky.'

'You'll not go till you've eaten,' she said. 'There's a little cheese left, and those eggs you found, and the last of the oatmeal that Dandy Fleming brought.'

Tam was so pleased at the thought of breakfast that he seemed quite reconciled to the long journey ahead.

'This is fine! This is kind, mistress!' He cracked his dirty knuckles as he looked at the meagre meal laid out on the table.

'It's not what it was,' sighed Aunt Blair.

'Or will be again,' said Ritchie.

Tam stretched out his hand towards the oatcakes, and I nudged him just in time as Aunt Blair said, 'You'll ask a blessing on our food, Ritchie.' And Ritchie, sitting in his father's place, said a mercifully short grace.

I was so tense with excitement and dread that I could hardly eat. Now that the moment had come, I hated the thought of leaving this neat, homely house, and the family who'd treated me so kindly and taught me all I ever knew.

No one said much at the table, and when the last crumb had been eaten Ritchie scraped back his stool and went into the parlour. He came back a moment later carrying his father's old coat and put it into Tam's hands.

'What's this? It's not for me?' said Tam doubtfully.

'Yes, of course, what a good idea, Ritchie,' said Aunt Blair, bustling forward. 'And there's a shirt too, and some breeches that I was going to cut down for dresses for the girls. We can spare them easily. Take him into the other room, do, and get him dressed.'

I hardly recognized Tam when he came back into the kitchen a few minutes later. His old rags, patched, faded and torn, had been part of him for so long that they had seemed like a second skin. My uncle's clothes were far too big for him. They hung loosely on his skinny frame, the coat tails dangling below his knees, the sleeves falling down over his hands. I wasn't sure that I liked the new Tam. He looked even more frail and pathetic than before.

He was so entranced, though, with his new clothes

that I couldn't help smiling. He gazed down at himself, awestruck, fingering the strong woollen weave of the shabby brown coat between his claw-like fingers.

'There's an old bonnet of your father's too,' said Aunt Blair, who seemed to be enjoying the chance to dress even such an unpromising figure as Tam.

But when Ritchie had fetched it, Tam looked at the clean blue bonnet with dismay.

'You're very kind, mistress.' He was clasping his disgusting old headgear tightly to his chest. 'But my old one, you know – like a friend – I wouldn't feel quite right in another. Keep it for your man when he comes home.'

Aunt Blair's smile faded.

'When he comes home,' she repeated bleakly. 'Aye, God willing.'

I had been gathering together my few possessions and had tied them in my old bundle. Martha had been following me about, trying to hold my hand whenever it was free.

'You're not really going away, are you, Maggie?' she said, her chin wobbling.

I bent down and hugged her.

'Yes, sweetheart, but I'll come back, and maybe when I do I'll have your daddy with me.'

Big tears began to roll down her cheeks, and then, in her usual way when she was distressed, she ran off to hide.

We were ready at last. We stood at the door, and I took a deep breath as I looked down the track that led away from Ladymuir, on into the valley below, then away up and over the hills.

'Here,' said Ritchie, who had reappeared from the parlour, 'take this.'

He put two silver pieces into my hand.

'What, Ritchie? You can't!'

'It's the rest of the laird's money. For my father, and for you, if you really need it.' He hesitated, then his face flushed red. 'I *hate* you going off like this. It's a man's work you're doing. It ought to be me!'

'You can't, Ritchie. You have to run the farm and look after your mother.'

'I know. But it's a bitter thing to have to stay. I – I haven't said this to you, Maggie, but you know how much I admire you and – and . . .'

I didn't want to hear any more. I hitched my bundle up on to my shoulder and said quickly, 'Thank you for everything. You're a good cousin and friend, and I'll do my best for your father.'

Aunt Blair put her arms round me and hugged me with what felt like real affection.

'God go with you, Maggie dear, and may His angels watch over you. We'll pray for you and your mission without ceasing.'

And then we were away, and I was hurrying after Tam, who had retrieved his pipes from the barn and was scampering down the track at his usual amazing speed. I turned to look back, after a while, and saw them still standing there, Aunt Blair with Andrew in her arms, waving his little hand, and Nanny jumping up and down at her side, and Ritchie, who had come a little way down the track after us and was standing by the rowan tree, with his hand resting against the trunk as if he needed the support. But Martha hadn't reappeared, and I knew she was hiding in the bed we had shared for so long, curled up in a tight little ball, crying.

Chapter Twenty

It's no more than sixty or seventy miles from Kilma-colm to Edinburgh, so Ritchie told me, and if we'd been able to travel along the highway, with plenty of food to keep us strong and energetic, the journey would have taken three days at the most. But the whole country was in the grip of terror. There was a kind of madness in the air. The soldiers' bright uniforms stood out in splashes of scarlet against the soft greens and browns of the May countryside. They trotted on their jingling horses in bands of six or seven down the muddy lanes, they sang and swore and brawled in the village inns and appeared suddenly out of the remotest farmhouses, where they'd been planted to live with Covenanting families, to harass them and eat up their supplies as punishment for refusing to swear the oath to the King.

I'd told Ritchie no more than the truth when I'd bragged about Tam's cleverness. Even in peaceful times he had avoided the main routes, wary of officials and ministers and lawyers and busybodies, who always seemed to want to arrest him for begging, or drunkenness, or being a vagabond. A lifetime's wandering about the south of Scotland had made him familiar with every burn and sheepfold and stand of trees. He knew which cottage housed an old companion who might be good for a meal in exchange for a tune or two on the pipes. He knew the back doors of every laird's house, which ones had a mean cook or a ferocious dog, and which had a kind housekeeper with a full storeroom. He could sniff his way as if by instinct to the lairs in remote glens and bothies where outcasts met to divide the gains of their thieving, or to roast the meat and fish they had poached, and comfort themselves with whisky.

Tam showed his true colours when we had got no further than the end of the track to Ladymuir, where it met the lane running up to Kilmacolm. I turned to the left, heading for the village.

'No, no, Maidie.' Tam grasped my arm. 'We'll not need to trouble the folk of Kilmacolm with our presence.'

'But the troops aren't there. They're at Sorn. And the lane's easy walking,' I objected.

'Aye, well.' He grinned apologetically. 'There's an awful irritable lady I'm not anxious to run into, and a couple of fellows—'

'Tam,' I said accusingly, 'what did you do?'

'Nothing! But we'll give the place a wide berth, if you don't mind.'

My walk with Archie Lithgow on the drove to Dumbarton had seemed like a great adventure all those months ago, but it had been nothing at all compared to my furtive progress over the hills and through the glens with Tam. I thought almost with longing of the cattle's gentle, ambling pace, the steady, reassuring click of Mr Lithgow's knitting needles and the hearty bowls of porridge morning and night. With Tam, there was haste, and dodging and darting, and very little food. We would scurry over a high empty moor in the morning, ducking down to hide in the ditches of peat cutters if a farmer or a shepherd came by. Then we would creep stealthily past a highland farm, snatching a chicken from the yard as we went, and end the day in a high nook by a lonely crag, sharing our little bit of meat with a band of destitute old soldiers and highwaymen, while Tam entertained them with stories and music in return for some drink and a little of their food.

'Keep your silver pieces and your buckle out of sight,' he warned me. 'The temptation might be too much for these poor fellows.'

I marvelled at how he kept us both alive and fed from day to day, with the help of a little begging, a poached trout or two, and payment for his piping.

'And to think,' he said sometimes, looking down at his new clothes, 'that I could pass for a respectable man now, and walk down the main street of any town raising my bonnet to the ladies like a gentleman.'

I hadn't the heart to point out to him that after only a couple of days of sleeping out in the open, and being drenched in constant showers, and hiding in stands of gorse, my uncle's old clothes were unrecognizably dirty and crumpled and torn.

Seven days after we'd left Ladymuir, we came round the edge of a hillside and stopped to take in the awe-inspiring view. The city of Edinburgh lay along a raised spine that sloped down from the west to the east, where it crouched close to the ground. Along its back rose ranks of tall buildings, so closely crammed together that they seemed to squeeze each other thin. Church spires sprouted above the chimneys, and long gardens fell to the valley below, fenced in by the high wall that enclosed the whole city. At the far, lower end of the spine I could see a palace of such size and magnificence that my mouth fell open.

'Aye,' said Tam, enjoying my wonder. 'You may well gasp, Maidie. That's Holyrood, the King's palace. There's enough jewels and furs and silver and gold in there to feed an army of poor bodies till their bellies burst, but never a bit of it comes to us.'

But now I was looking at the great rock at the top end of the spine. It reared up, as forbidding as a monster's head, and was crowned by a castle whose massive stone walls made me shudder.

'Is that where my uncle is? In the castle?'

'No. They'll not have put the Covenanters in there. The place is buzzing with soldiers like bees in a jar. Your uncle will be in the tollbooth. See that tower halfway down the city? That's it. That's the prison. He'll be in there, for sure.'

My knees felt weak and I sat down on the ground. From the castle at the top to the palace at the bottom, with the bristle of houses in between, the city of Edinburgh seemed to glare at me.

You'll never get in here, its frowning walls seemed to say. *And you'll never get your uncle out. Go away. Go back. Go home.*

But I had no home to go to. I'd come this far. I had to go on.

'How do we get in?' I asked Tam. 'And where will we go once we're inside?'

Tam had sat down beside me, and was pulling from his pocket the singed carcass of a hare, which he had trapped the night before. He tore it into two pieces and handed my share to me. He studied the city as he gnawed on the hare's bones, his eyes half shut in calculation.

'It's not going to be easy, Maidie.'

'I can see that.'

'We can't go through the gates like ordinary folk. Terrible strict they are these days, with all the panic on. It's permits and badges and letters you need before they'll let you in. But I have a trick or two. And I've some old friends who will help us out once we're inside the walls. You'll have to trust me, Maidie.'

I felt a rush of love and gratitude for the wily old man.

'I do, Tam! I always will! You don't know how grateful I am. You always look after me. You always know what to do. I just wish I was rich. I'd give you lots to eat and plenty of whisky, and you'd have a new coat every year, and a bed with a linen sheet like they have at Lady-muir.'

His mouth opened in a hideous grin.

'That's very kind of you, darling. I take that very kindly.' He looked as pleased as if I really did have a comfortable home to offer him. 'When you're settled, if you can find room in your house for poor old Tam, I'll end my days as happy as a king. It won't be long. A pretty girl like you can always find a husband. That cousin of yours, Ritchie Blair, he seems a nice enough young man. A bit serious, perhaps. But he likes you, I could tell.'

He stopped. His sharp ears had caught the sound of footsteps above us and he was already on his feet and creeping quietly into a crevice in the hillside. I followed him. We stood motionless until the lone traveller went past, then settled ourselves comfortably again for the long wait until dusk.

Talking of the future had set a question nagging in my brain. Annie had talked of a letter. Of money owing to me from the Laird of Keames and Mr Macbean.

The seed she had planted in my mind that day had grown like a weed at first. I'd thought and dreamed about having money of my own. I'd asked Annie again several times, but from the way she'd laughed at me I'd decided that the whole thing had been just a malicious invention that she'd made up to torment me.

But if there's any truth in it, I thought, *Tam might know. He's from Bute. He knew my father.*

'Who's the Laird of Keames, Tam?' I asked.

'Mr Bannantyne. Whatever made you think of him?'

'It was something Annie said. Months ago. She said he'd owed my father money. And Mr Macbean did too.'

'Did she now?' Tam had cracked the bone he was chewing and he was sucking out the marrow. 'I wouldn't set any store by that, Maidie. Your father died a long time ago, God rest his soul.'

'She said she'd seen a letter about it. At Macbean's.'

'A letter, eh?' Tam looked impressed.

'What kind of a man is Mr Bannantyne? Do you know him?'

'I wouldn't say I *know* him.' Tam inspected the bone and regretfully threw it away. 'But he's a decent sort of body. He caught me once with a fat trout that I'd . . . rescued . . . from his stream, and he let me off with a cursing. In fact, as lairds go, he's not bad. Not bad at all. Mind you, he doesn't live in Bute most of the time. He's in Edinburgh, so I believe.'

He slapped his greasy hands together as an idea occurred to him.

'A good thing you put me in mind of the gentleman, Maidie. Mr Bannantyne would be just the kind of fellow to help your uncle. He's a laird, even if Keames is only a wee place on a far island. He'll be in with all the big-wigs. Wears a big wig himself, when he's in the city, I'll bet. But he's a Bute man before everything. If he refuses to help one of his own he's a disgrace to his name.'

The prospect of Edinburgh had cast me down so low that I would have seized anything to lift me up, and the idea of a great man taking me under his wing and help-ing me to free my uncle was so attractive that for a long moment I said nothing and allowed myself to day-dream. Then reality struck me down again.

'You're forgetting, Tam, no one from Bute will want to help me. I'm a witch, remember? I've been sentenced to hang and burn. Mr Bannantyne's more likely to have me arrested and sent back.'

Tam waved a careless hand.

'That's all past and gone, darling. All that fuss and panic – it's over. They'll be ashamed of themselves by now – the better half of them, anyway. Plenty of questions were asked after your trial, I can tell you, about how hasty they were to carry out the sentence, and whether it was legal at all. Even those who were sure about Elspeth had their doubts about you, and there was a lot of murmuring against the court and that raving minister from Inverkip. Annie scampering off the way she did will have made them wonder even more. I know how these things are.'

He did too. If ever there was an expert in judging when it was best to lie low, and when it was safe to return to the scene of old troubles, it was Tam.

'Well,' I said doubtfully, 'maybe.'

'You can't run and hide forever, Maidie.'

By the time the sky had darkened Tam had more or less convinced me that seeking out the Laird of Keames was the best way forward. Half a skinny hare doesn't make a whole day's eating for a hungry person, and I was famished and longing for some supper. I would have risked anything for a bowl of steaming porridge, or an oatcake or two with a hunk of good cheese.

'Time to get going,' Tam said suddenly, cocking his ear to listen. Even a mile away from the city we had been able to hear the clamour of sounds that rose from it. Barking dogs, hammerings on metal, shouting voices and the bellowing of cattle had made such a racket that I couldn't imagine how noisy it would be inside the forbidding walls. But now, above it all, came the jangling of bells.

'They'll be shutting the gates soon.' Tam was already hurrying down the hill. 'If we're not quick, Maidie, there'll be another night out in the heather and no supper.'

Even now, I can barely believe how Tam got us past the soldiers who stood, with their halberds and steel helmets, guarding the southern gate of the city. I followed him down a long lane flanked with houses and thickly spattered with fresh cow dung. It hadn't been easy to keep up with him. Tam had the gift of darting through a crowd with the speed of a fish through murky water, and that crowd was a big one. Some people were coming out – leaving the city, I supposed, to go to their homes outside – and others were hurrying in before the gates closed. I could see, as we came to the bottom of the hill, that there was a great hold-up at the narrow gap in the high stone wall. The soldiers were checking everyone in turn, examining the papers waved impatiently under their noses.

'Tam!' I hissed, grabbing at his sleeve. 'What'll we do? We haven't got any papers!'

'Never mind that.' He was as taut as a fiddle string, and his eyes were dancing. 'Stick close to me, darling. Be my little shadow.'

And then, all of a sudden, the peaceful crowd was in turmoil, and Tam was everywhere, pointing, accusing, nudging, whispering, and calling out indignantly, 'A thief! A thief!'

And people were shouting, 'Where? Who's been robbed?'

'I have! Look, he's there! The man in the red cloak. No, the one in the blue hood!'

'Hey! What are you doing? Let go of me! I'm no thief!'

And then there was such brawling and shouting and cursing that the guards began to panic and started trying to shut the heavy gates, pushing them against the mass of bodies.

'Hey, what are you doing, man?'

'Let us in! You can't shut us out.'

'Look, will you? Here's my pass!'

The crowd put their shoulders to the gates and heaved them open, forcing the guards back, and then they surged up the narrow passageway ahead with the force of ale exploding from a shaken bottle.

'Ha ha! An old trick, but it works every time!' chortled Tam, who had raced ahead of everyone else to the top of the steep alleyway, with me at his heels. 'Aren't I the clever one, Maidie?'

'Yes, but won't they come after us?' I was looking fearfully back down towards the gate.

'Not them! They won't dare leave their post. Come on now. Supper and bed is what we're needing.'

If it hadn't been for Tam, I do believe I would have been paralysed with fright on my first sight of Edinburgh as

306

we emerged from the top of that narrow wynd into the broad High Street. Rothesay was the biggest town I'd ever been in, and it had no more than thirty or forty houses, only one or two of which had an upstairs part at all. I could never have imagined that so many people could be together in one place. I almost cricked my neck staring up at the vast height of the buildings, which soared six or even seven storeys high on all sides. I took a step or two, still looking up, but then my feet slipped in the mush of human filth, and the stench of it hit my nostrils. I had to hold my plaid over my nose to stop myself from gagging.

The din was as bad as I'd feared. People shrieked at each other out of the open windows. Barrels rumbled as they were rolled over the cobblestones. Pedlars shouted. Hoofs clattered.

Behind me came a rattle and a barking command.

'Tam! Soldiers! We've got to hide!' I cried out, my knees turning to water at the sight of a troop of red coats.

He seemed unworried, but pulled me into the side of the reeking street.

'They're not on the hunt for us. But it would be best, maybe, to get on. It's a bit too open up here for me. Stay close now, while I find my way. It's down one of these long wynds, I know, but which one?'

I pulled my plaid up round my head and scuttled after Tam, though I couldn't help looking round at the astonishing sights of the city, at chair boxes being carried on poles by two men, with a lady sitting in the little room inside, jewels flashing, silk dress gleaming, or at a pair of gentlemen in wigs of flouncy curls so long they hung down below their shoulders, who were mincing between the piles of filth in high-heeled shoes.

I'd been staring open-mouthed at a man with a big bright-green bird sitting on his shoulder when I came back to myself and realized that Tam was nowhere to be seen. I was about to shout for him when his long arm shot out from the shadows behind me. He tugged at me so hard that I almost lost my balance.

'We'll need to wait out of sight for a moment,' he whispered in my ear. 'There's a couple of fellows coming down the street that I'm not too keen to see.'

He stepped further back down the steep, narrow passageway.

'Why, isn't that a stroke of luck! This is the very place. A little way down here, these steps, the broken door – come on, Maidie! Here we are, at old Virtue's place. Aren't I a clever Tam? There's a welcome waiting, I promise you.'

I tumbled after Tam down a short, steep stair into a cave-like room which was lit only by a single rush flame. From lines stretched across the low ceiling hung a mass of old torn plaids, holed blankets, coats and gowns worn to shreds and rags, in the last stages of rot. Ducking under these, we came to the far end of the room where an old woman was hunched over a cooking pot in the small chimney place.

'Virtue, my sweetheart!' carolled Tam, dancing up to her with his arms outstretched.

She didn't look round, but seemed to recognize him by his voice and went on stirring her broth.

'Oh, so it's you. I thought they'd have hanged you long ago. Where's that groat I lent you last time you came to sponge off a poor old woman?'

'What groat? You're thinking of some other fellow. Would I ever fail to return what I'd borrowed? I thought you'd be pleased to see an old friend, and make a new one. Turn round, Virtue. See who I've brought with me. Look, isn't she a lovely girl? Wouldn't anyone be pleased to give her a bite of supper and a safe place to sleep?'

Mistress Virtue turned at last and I saw her face. I had to stop myself from stepping back in horror. Her skin was as crumpled and snagged and pulled out of shape as one of her own old rags. One eye was white with blindness and the other was hitched up at the edge by an old gash. Her nose was half missing and her only remaining teeth were two or three black stumps.

'A girl?' she said, peering at me. Her voice was unexpectedly clear from such a hideous mouth. 'What's her game? I won't have a light skirt in my house, Tam. You shouldn't have brought her here.'

Tam tutted reproachfully.

'Maggie's no light skirt! Now what's that you're cooking, Virtue, my old darling? It smells like a lifesaver to a starving man.'

He had leaned forward over the pot to snuff up the aromatic steam, which was making my own mouth water so that I had to keep swallowing. Mistress Virtue pushed him away.

'If she's a good girl, what's she doing running round with the likes of you?'

'And why shouldn't she? I've known her since before she was born. She's here to help her uncle who's in prison in the tollbooth.'

'In prison? What's he done? A murderer, is he? A thief? A pimp?'

'Virtue! Virtue! He's a respectable farmer. A man of property. A Presbyterian.'

'Oh. A Covenanter. I suppose he's been running about the hills with one of those preaching mountain men.'

'With James Renwick himself, the silver-tongued terror of the countryside!'

'Humph. You've come too late. The tollbooth was crammed with Covenanters until last week, but there's not one of them left in it now.'

I felt the blood drain from my face.

'Too l-late? What do you mean?' I gasped. 'He's dead, isn't he? They've hanged him already!'

Blackness prickled behind my eyes, and the room began to spin. I sank down on a heap of rags and put my head in my hands.

Chapter Twenty-One

The strange feeling passed before I had fainted completely, but hunger, exhaustion and dread seemed to paralyse me so that I could barely move or speak. I was aware, though, of Tam hovering over me and the beaker of ale he was trying to press into my hand.

'Look at her! Gone as green as pond scum,' observed Mistress Virtue from a distance.

'You would be green if you'd suffered half of what this lassie's borne this past year,' said Tam, with unusual sharpness. 'Drink up, Maidie. You'll be better in a minute.'

I nodded to show that I was all right, and took the beaker from him. He sat down on a bundle, stretched out his legs and began to give Mistress Virtue such a dramatic account of the witch trial in Bute, my escape from the tollbooth, my swim with the cattle, the Covenanters at Ladymuir, the hunting of Mr Renwick and the arrest of my uncle that even I listened fascinated, as if the story he was telling was nothing to do with me, while Mistress Virtue forgot her stew and stood still with the spoon suspended over the pot, her eyes never leaving Tam's face.

When Tam had finished, he turned his back on the old woman and winked at me, and I had to hide a smile.

He knew what he had been doing, and it had worked. Without another word, Mistress Virtue filled two bowls to the brim with her savoury stew.

'Here, girl,' she said, passing one to me, and handing me a hunk of wheaten bread to go with it, 'if I'm to believe half of what this old fool says you deserve a good dinner at least. And there's no need to look so miserable. Your uncle's not swinging from the gallows, as far as I know. The Presbyterians were cleared out of the tollbooth here a week ago and taken up to the north. They're away across the Forth to Angus. Held in Dunnottar Castle, so I believe.'

Tam had been jabbing his bread into his stew and cramming the dripping pieces into his mouth with sighs of blissful contentment, but he started, and stopped chewing.

'Dunnottar? That's terrible! It makes you tremble just to hear the name.' Then he saw my stricken face and said, 'Oh, what am I saying? It was Dunvegan I was thinking of. Or Dunrostan maybe. Dunnottar's a fine place, I'm sure of it, right beside the sea. But why did they shift them away from Edinburgh?'

'Where have you been these past months?' Mistress Virtue asked sarcastically. 'Up with the man on the moon? You must have heard of the invasion?'

'Oh, that! The Earl of Argyll and his little army from Holland. But it was all over weeks ago. The man's head will be stuck up on a pole by now.'

'It is.' She nodded grimly. 'Along with the other fools who followed him. When the big folks heard that Argyll

312

was on his way, they got in such a panic they sent all the rabid Presbyterians out of the city. Marched them north to Dunnottar to get them out of the way.'

'Has anything been heard of them?' I burst out. 'Are they safe?'

'Safe?' jeered Mistress Virtue. 'It depends what you mean by—' I saw Tam shake his head at her. 'How would I know? I've no patience with preachifying and psalm-singing. *Don't do this, don't do that, you're all sinners and you're going to Hell.* I've had enough of the lot of them.'

I knew I should be standing up for Uncle Blair and the cause he cared so much about, but I was too hungry and too tired. Despising myself, I picked up my spoon and began to eat my stew, which had cooled to the point where it no longer burned my mouth. I could think of nothing but my ravenous hunger, and slurped and chewed and scraped round the bowl till every drop was gone. Then, with a full stomach for the first time in months, I lay down on a pile of Mistress Virtue's rags and fell asleep, utterly exhausted.

The clatter of a bottle dropping to the stone floor woke me a couple of hours later. I lay bemused, not knowing where I was, staring with fright at the two enormous black shadows flickering across the ceiling. I turned my head and saw that they were cast by Mistress Virtue and Tam, who were sitting with their heads together by the fire, cups in their hands, and an empty bottle rolling by their feet.

'Where did you get this money from, you old sinner?'

Mistress Virtue was holding a coin up to the light, squinting at it.

'You don't want to know, my dear.'

'Oh, I do, Tam. I do.'

'Well then, it fell from a gentleman's pocket in all the turmoil at the city gate this evening. What could I do? If I hadn't caught it, someone else would have done so. But don't tell the girl. An awful tight conscience she has in these sorts of things. And she's been living with the strictest Presbyterians this past year.'

Mistress Virtue tucked the money away in a hidden pocket. I closed my eyes. I didn't want to know about Tam's crimes.

'Is she one of them fanatics? Does she hold with all their nonsense?'

I listened for Tam's answer.

'My Maidie? No! She's a sensible one. She'd lay down her life for a friend, but not for some minister's rant about the rights and wrongs of who rules the Kirk.'

I bit my lip, half ashamed that what Tam had said was true.

'But you have to wonder at them, when all's said and done,' Tam went on. 'Stubborn! It's not the word for it. They hold to their beliefs unto death. Did you hear about the two women in Wigtown? They wouldn't take the oath, so off they were bundled, down the beach at low water, and tied to stakes. Up comes the water, slowly, slowly, covering their feet, and then their legs, and then their bodies and at last their heads. One was just a young girl. They kept saying to her, "Give in, give in, you silly wee fool," but she wouldn't. She stood there, singing away, till the water filled up her mouth.'

I felt goose pimples rise along the length of my body, and had to cover my own mouth with my plaid to stop myself from crying out. Tam shook his head, sighed, and pulled the cork from a new bottle with practised fingers. 'Crushed bones, lopped ears, turned out of their farms and houses – and all for the sake of a word or two! Fools, the lot of them, if you ask me.'

'Fools and worse,' growled Mistress Virtue. 'They've set the whole nation at each other's throats, and brought the English soldiers in to persecute us. Who are they, to think they're so perfect? They've done their share of executing and ambushing and murder. You know what they shriek when they go in to fight the soldiers? *Jesus and No Quarter!* It doesn't make it any better if you sing psalms while you're drawing blood.'

Tam belched, and Mistress Virtue yawned. They drained their cups and lurched to their feet. I heard them settle themselves in different corners of the cavernous room, and then I turned over and fell back into a deep sleep.

Edinburgh by daylight was less alarming than Edinburgh by night, but I still had to stop myself from clutching at Tam's arm as we stepped up from Mistress Virtue's gloomy cellar into the racket of the crowded High Street. Among the brightly coloured coats and gowns, the immense wigs of the men and the long-curled locks of the ladies, I felt as out of place as a dull brown sparrow in a crowd of squawking jays. The working women carrying pails of milk, or hawking fish and bread, might have been as poor as I had always been, but they looked smarter than me and sharper, fast in their speech and quick in their gestures.

They'll be laughing at me, I thought. *They'll be thinking I look stupid.*

I needn't have worried. In Rothesay or Kilmacolm a stranger was never ignored. Curious eyes would be on them and they would be greeted and questioned by everyone. I pinned a half-smile to my lips and prepared responses to the curious enquiries I was sure would come, but to my surprise no one noticed me at all. Eyes slid past me. People called out to each other over my head. I might have been one of the dogs that lay and scratched themselves against the wall of the massive stone building which stood right across the road.

'What is it, this big place?' I asked Tam.

'The tollbooth, dearie. A grim old pile of stones, eh? I should know. I've passed a night or two in it myself. A good thing your uncle's off and away up in the countryside, wouldn't you say?'

The sinister fortress, with its small barred windows and heavy iron-bound door, made me shiver. I heard again the clang of the prison door in Rothesay as it slammed behind Granny and me, and felt the clammy chill of its dripping walls against my skin.

I looked up towards the building's high roof. It took

me a moment to recognize the blackened and grinning balls, jammed on the tops of poles, as heads that had once belonged to living men. Tam heard me gasp and looked up too.

'Are they Covenanters, Tam?'

He pulled at my hand.

'Come away from here. How should I know who the gentlemen are? Leave them to the crows. Let's go up the town and look at all the sights. A little caution, that's all we need, in case there are some who might be more pleased to see me than I am to see them.'

I forgot to be self-conscious as we walked up Edinburgh's great street, and felt even less so as I noticed, among the bright clothes, some plain brown coats and simple grey gowns like those my uncle and aunt wore. One of the Puritan men even bowed at me gravely, and I felt comforted, in an odd way, as if I'd received a sign from Uncle Blair.

'When are we starting out for Dunnottar?' I asked Tam. 'How long will it take us to get there?'

He looked dismayed.

'Maidie, we've only just arrived in Edinburgh! This poor old man needs a little time to rest and recover himself. Old Virtue will keep us a day or two longer. She'll feed us well and set us up.'

'And give you too much whisky,' I said severely. 'How are we going to pay her?'

It was mean of me to ask, I suppose, when I'd heard him talk about the purse he'd stolen, but I knew Tam. If I gave him the chance, he'd settle down happily in

Edinburgh to drink away all the money, and I'd never get him to help me find my uncle.

Tam looked confused for a moment, but he recovered at once and waved an airy hand.

'Virtue won't ask us for money. She's an old friend. Heart of gold. You wouldn't believe it, Maidie, but she was as beautiful as a spring morning once, before her husband caught her with – well, never mind that – and threw a pan of boiling oil at her face.'

'Is that how she became so scarred?'

'It is. And there's a good lesson in that, as your minister friends might say. It's best not to nag a fellow. You might make him lose patience, and drive him to violence.'

I couldn't help laughing at the neat way he'd turned me.

'You'd never be violent to me, Tam, I know that, however much I nagged.'

'No more I could, darling, but don't try me, eh?'

'But what about Uncle Blair?' I said, serious now. 'Think of him, Tam! He might be starving and ill. He might be dying!'

Tam gave a gusty sigh.

'Oh aye, well, you're right. We'll have to go on and pursue the man. But one more day, eh, Maidie? Just give me another day.'

'Tomorrow's Sunday anyway. Uncle Blair wouldn't want us to set out on a journey on the Sabbath Day. We'll go on Monday. Agreed?'

But Tam didn't answer. He was looking over my

shoulder. I thought for a moment that he had seen an old persecutor and was about to dive off down the nearest wynd. Instead his mouth opened in a grin.

'Here's a thing! What a stroke of luck! It's Mr Bannantyne himself, if it's not his ghost or his twin.'

I spun round. Coming down the High Street towards us was a short, red-faced man in a blue coat. It was easy to see, looking from his wig to his buckled shoes, that he was a gentleman, but as he came nearer I noticed that his cravat was old and torn and the heavy cuffs of his coat were frayed, with buttons missing. He was deep in conversation with a tall spidery man, all dressed in black, who was carrying a leather satchel under his arm.

Tam stepped out into their path and bowed, flourishing his dreadful old bonnet.

'Laird Bannantyne!' he said. 'You won't remember me, but I'm a fellow countryman of yours. From the Isle of Bute!'

Mr Bannantyne frowned, then nodded, and a grim little smile tightened his lips.

'A Bute man indeed. I'd know that from your accent. But I do remember you, as it happens. And I remember that fine trout you poached from my stream. Or was it a salmon? Not to mention the hares and partridges and goodness knows what else of mine that ended up in your cooking pot.'

'Oh no, Mr Bannantyne. You were good to me that day, and I repaid you in kind. I never poached from you again.'

He looked so sincere that even I believed him.

'I'm glad to hear it,' Mr Bannantyne said drily. 'But I have business with my lawyer. If you would step out of our way—'

'Business!' cried Tam. 'That's the very word. This young lady has some business with you, sir. Maggie, tell Mr Bannantyne.'

He drew me forward. I stood blushing like a fool, tongue-tied, not knowing what to say.

'Her name's Maggie Blair,' Tam said helpfully. 'Her father was Danny Blair, the drover who used to take your cattle from Keames to Dumbarton.'

'Stop! This is outrageous!' A thunderous scowl was dragging Mr Bannantyne's brows together. 'How dare you, sir? How many more impostors are going to come crawling out of Bute? I'll have you taken up, the pair of you.' He turned a furious face to the lawyer. 'What punishment does the court impose for fraud, Mr Shillinglaw? It's severe, I hope. Don't you ever, either of you, dare to approach me again, or by God, I'll have you!'

He stalked off, the curls of his chestnut wig bouncing in indignation against his shoulders.

'What was all that about?' I said, bewildered. 'What put him in such a temper?'

Mr Shillinglaw coughed, and when he spoke his voice rattled in his long throat, which was as pink and raw as a plucked chicken's.

'Mr Bannantyne dislikes to be imposed upon,' he said, 'and so do I. Good day to you.'

'Stop!' Tam darted to block his way. 'I know you!

You're wee Timmy Shillinglaw, from Kilmichael on the west of Bute. Your daddy was murdered, poor fellow, by the Highland hordes when they came raiding. Don't you know me, Timmy? I'm the piper who played the lament at the good man's burial. You were crying so hard I thought your little eyes would pop out.'

The lawyer, who was as tall and thin as a birch sapling, rocked on his feet, recovered himself, and poked his head forward, frowning at Tam.

'Maybe you are who you say you are,' he said huffily. 'I don't remember. In any case, "wee Timmy" is not the name I'm known by in Edinburgh. "Mr Shillinglaw" is a more common form of address for a Writer to the Signet at the Court of Session.'

'Aye. Quite right. So it would be,' Tam said, looking abashed. 'My memory of that sad day and of your noble father carried me away. It's a long time, after all, since you left the island and became so fine a gentleman. But since we're old friends, in a manner of speaking, do please tell me why Danny Blair's daughter is a sight so upsetting to Mr Bannantyne?'

'Firstly,' said Mr Shillinglaw, ticking his point off on one stick-thin finger, 'Danny Blair had no living children at the time of his death, as you well know. And moreover –' he ticked off the second point – 'this is the second young woman to claim that honour and to approach the Laird of Keames to settle on her a debt which he owed to her father.'

His words struck me like a dash of freezing water.

'What are you saying? That I'm not my father's

daughter? I know my mother died when I was born, but my daddy was mine! He – I remember him throwing me up in the air. He wouldn't have done that if I wasn't his, would he, Tam? Tam!'

Mr Shillinglaw wagged a finger at me.

'You can't deceive me, young woman. When Daniel Blair died Mr Bannantyne wrote a letter to the farmer at Scalpsie Bay, who also owed the man some money, asking him if he knew of any heirs to whom the debts to Mr Blair should be paid. The farmer answered categorically that Mr Blair's only child had died along with its mother at the time of its birth, and that consequently no debt was still owed.'

He glared at me triumphantly. I could say nothing. Mr Shillinglaw's words were spinning round my head like objects tossed in a whirlwind. They settled only slowly to form a pattern that I could understand.

'The farmer at Scalpsie – that must have been Mr Macbean. The letter Annie found and read – it must have been the one from Mr Bannantyne. Mr Macbean lied about me when he wrote back, so that he could keep the money. And Annie – she pretended to be me so she could steal it for herself!'

Mr Shillinglaw pursed his lips, shook his head and turned his back on us to stride on up the street. I felt a rush of rage so great I hardly knew what I was doing.

'Wait!' I shrieked. 'You! Lawyer!'

He quickened his pace. I raced after him and grabbed his arm, forcing him to spin round.

'I've been tricked, swindled, lied to, stolen from and

insulted. You can tell Mister High and Mighty Laird Bannantyne that he can keep his stinking money. But if he gives a groat – one *groat* – to Annie, I'll tear that stupid wig from his head and rip it to pieces. And if anyone ever again dares to tell me that my name is not Margaret Blair, and that Daniel Blair of Ladymuir was not my father, or that Mary Wylie was not my mother, I'll – I'll . . .'

I couldn't go on. Sobs had cut my voice. People were staring at me, and a crowd was starting to form.

'Come on, Maidie, come away,' said Tam, taking my hand. 'We don't want all the loons of Edinburgh knowing our business.'

I let him lead me away through the crowd but I turned back to glare at Mr Shillinglaw. He was standing looking after me, frowning.

My cooling temper left me feeling sick and shaky. By now I knew to expect any trickery and meanness from Annie, but the revelation that Mr Macbean had sent false information to Mr Bannantyne set painful new thoughts running through my head.

'That must have been why he was so keen to get me hanged with Granny,' I told Tam. 'He was afraid I'd find out what he'd done.'

'Could be, darling. More than likely,' said Tam, who was too busy looking over his shoulder to listen to me.

'Do you think Annie's still in Edinburgh, Tam? If she is, I'm going to find her, and when I do—'

I'd caught his attention now. We'd arrived at Mistress Virtue's cellar and he was hurrying me inside.

'No, please, Maidie! No more fusses and bother-ations. Just think, if Annie finds out that you're here, she might report on you to the military, to that fancy fellow of hers. She'll get you taken up.'

My stomach lurched.

'You're right, Tam. What'll we do?'

'Only one thing for it,' he said dolefully. 'We must take to the road again. I'm not sure that I trust Timmy Shillinglaw either. The man's a lawyer, after all, and his daddy was awfully sharp on any birds that went missing from his dovecote. We'll set off as soon as we can. There's to be no rest for poor Tam after all.'

Chapter Twenty-Two

We didn't set out for Dunnottar the next day, or even the day after, because that night Tam fell ill. I couldn't rouse him from his pile of rags in the morning. He stared up at me unseeingly, his cheeks sunk, his lips cracked and his tongue as dry as a piece of felt.

'Old fool,' Mistress Virtue said crossly, standing with her hands on her hips as she looked down at him, while I knelt on the floor, anxiously holding one of his hot, trembling hands. 'He'd better not die on me. I should never have taken the pair of you in.'

But she pulled some old dried herbs from a niche in the cellar wall and made up a concoction with them. I expected her to mumble spells as Granny would have done, but she only held the bad-smelling mixture to Tam's lips. I was surprised to see how patiently, even tenderly, she helped him to sip, though all the time she was muttering, 'Stupid old Tam. Daft old man. You think you can get round Virtue, but you can't.'

When the beaker was empty at last, she noticed me watching and stabbed a finger at me.

'What are you staring at, miss? There's not much I don't know about him. He's done more sinning than half the prisoners in the tollbooth, but he's more of a saint than all your prating Presbyterians.'

325

'I – yes, I know,' I said, taken aback.

'Well, get on with it,' she said, rising to her feet with a creak of bones.

'Get on with what, Mistress Virtue?'

'If you want to stay here till he's out of the fever, you'll have to earn your keep. Get up to the pump and fill up these buckets. There's washing to be done, in case you hadn't noticed.'

I hardly stirred from Mistress Virtue's dreary cave for the next two weeks, except to run up the wynd to the pump in the High Street to fill her buckets and carry them down to her cellar again. My back ached every night, and my arms felt as if they'd been stretched by inches, but the pains of my body were nothing compared to the worries in my mind. What was happening to Uncle Blair? Was he still alive? How were they all managing at Ladymuir?

At least after the first two dreadful days I could feel easier about Tam. Whether it was Mistress Virtue's remedies, or the rest he so badly wanted, or his own will-power, he came back from what had seemed like the brink of death, and at the end of ten days he was sitting once more on a stool by Mistress Virtue's fire, drinking too much whisky and spinning outrageous stories, accepting her scoldings with meek nods of his head.

I've asked myself over and over again whether things would have turned out differently if we'd stayed a week longer in Edinburgh, or if I'd had the courage to go north to Dunnottar on my own. But there's no going back to remake the past. What's done is done.

In the end, it wasn't even I who got us on the road at last, but Tam himself.

'If I stay another day in this airless hole, I'll turn into a goblin,' he whispered to me at the end of the second week. 'I feel like a worm that's been too long under a stone.'

We set off the next morning. There must have been more money in the purse that Tam had stolen than I had realized, because Mistress Virtue grunted with surprised gratitude when Tam pressed a yellow coin into her hand.

'And there's to be no more skulking about on the moors and mosses on this journey,' he told me proudly as we walked, at a slower pace than usual, down the road out of Edinburgh towards the port of Leith. 'We've no need to hide now. Presbyterians aren't so hot and strong over in Fife, and the soldiers won't be so keen to know everyone's business. And anyway –' he patted the pocket of Uncle Blair's coat and winked at me – 'we've money enough to pay for our food and our beds, like gentle-folk.'

I can't remember much about our slow progress to Dunnottar, only that I burned with impatience to hurry on but often had to wait for Tam, who was still too weak to walk fast or go far in a day. It was already after the middle of July. The road, which must have been churned to a bog of mud in the winter, was thick with dust. It blew uncomfortably into our eyes in the east

wind. There were many travellers going in both direc-
tions, mostly peaceful folk on foot, like ourselves, but an
occasional troop of soldiers clattered by on horses. The
first time I saw red coats, I dived down into the ditch at
the side of the road, expecting Tam to do the same, but
to my surprise he stood boldly in full view to let them
past, and even waved his bonnet.

'Weren't you scared?' I panted, scrambling back up
the bank to join him.

He shook his head, unconcerned, and I was shocked
to see how crumpled he looked, how worn and bent,
with his old sharpness and spring-like quickness gone.

He took my arm to lean on as we walked on.

'You think of them as enemies, Maidie, but every
one's a mother's son. Think of that. Every one of them.
A mother's son.'

I was so irritated by his tolerance that I dropped his
arm and hurried on ahead, and it was at the top of the
next rise that I caught my first glimpse of Dunnottar
Castle.

I had never seen, nor could ever have imagined, a
place so wild and cruel and desolate. I know that it was
God's hand which had, in the days of creation, thrown
up the mountains and poured forth the sea, but surely it
must have been the Prince of Evil who had vomited up
this vast black rock and cast it away from the land. It
reared up out of the creaming waves with only one
narrow spit connecting it to the land. And it must have
been the sons of Satan who had chosen this place on
which to build their castle, piling massive walls of stone

328

above the edges of the rock, and making the only entrance at the bottom so steep and narrow that no enemy would dare to approach it. Even the screams of the gulls and kittiwakes circling round the dank black ledges were more mournful than the calls of any birds I had ever heard before.

Perhaps they're the souls of the damned, I thought with a shiver, *or of poor prisoners who've died here*.

Tam had caught me up by now. He looked at the castle, then sat down heavily at the side of the road. He had turned pale.

'Are you all right?' I said, worried by how ill he looked. 'Is it the sight of the place? It scares me, Tam.'

'Scares you, aye. It puts the fear of death into me.'

'What do we do now?'

'We sit here for a moment so that I can get my breath back. I'm tired to my bones.'

I felt guilty.

'I'm sorry. I shouldn't have hurried on. I shouldn't have made you come at all. You ought to be resting still.'

He patted my knee.

'Time enough to rest in the grave, darling. I'd rather be out in the open, anyway, breathing the good air, than stifling to death in poor old Virtue's dungeon.'

I was still feeling bad, and defeated as well.

'I've made you hurry here, and worn you out. And all for nothing. Look at this place. However could I get my uncle out of there, assuming he's still alive even? It's useless, Tam. We might as well go back to Edinburgh.'

His lashless old eyes, red and sore from the dusty road, opened with astonishment.

'Go back? After we've travelled right across Scotland? Before we've even tried to find him? What are you thinking of, darling? When did Tam ever let you down? When did he ever fail to find a way?'

'It's true, you've been wonderful, but—'

'Did I or did I not get you out of the tollbooth in Rothesay under the nose of Donnie Brown?'

'You did, but—'

'Who got you in through the city gates of Edinburgh without a pass?'

'I know. It was you. But—'

'Who whipped you out from under your granny's nose that time when you broke her jug and she was going to beat you black and blue? Who hid you till she'd calmed down, eh?'

I had to laugh. 'I thought she was going to murder me.'

'Not as much as I'll murder you if there's any more talk of giving up and going back to Edinburgh. Here, help me with this strap.'

He was struggling to take off the sack that contained his bagpipes.

'What are you doing now?' I asked, as he removed the pipes lovingly from the worn old bag. 'You're never going to play them here?'

'It's just what I'm going to do, girl. A lament. For the poor souls in that horrible place. Music solves many a

330

problem. It'll make things happen. You'll see. And it'll help me clear my old head and think straight.'

He stood up, walked across to the edge of the cliff, which fell away in a sickening drop to the crashing sea below, and put the chanter to his lips.

'No, Tam!' I cried, running after him. 'There are soldiers down by the gateway. They're looking up at us. They'll hear you. They'll come and get you.'

But it was too late. He had filled the bag with air and the first notes of his wild, mournful lament were already echoing back to us from the grim rock walls. The music was so sad, so piercing and beautiful, so lonely and grand, that the breath caught in my throat and I stood unable to move.

Can you hear it, uncle? He's playing it for you, I thought.

The path that ran from where we stood down to the castle entrance was so steep and winding that most of it was hidden, so neither of us saw the two men coming up it until they were right in front of us. I stepped back, my heart pounding in fright.

They were a savage-looking pair, their hair long and rough, their leather jerkins open in front, their legs bare from the knee down and streaked with mud. I stepped back, nearly stumbling over a stone, but Tam played on regardless.

To my relief, the men didn't seem interested in me. They stood listening to Tam, frowning with concentration. Tam finished his lament on a sudden cut note, and the echo died away from the castle walls.

'He's a good piper, isn't he, Wully?' said one.

'He is that. Play us a jig, Grandad.'

As Tam played, I could see that the effort was making him even more exhausted. He gasped for each breath needed to fill the bag, and sweat beads formed on his dreadfully white face, but his fingers flew over the chanter holes as fast as the feet of scampering mice, and the tune was so lilting and catchy that the two men began to hop about, and even I, scared as I was, couldn't stop my foot tapping.

When at last the jig was finished, one of them took Tam by the arm.

'Come on,' he said. 'You're just the man we need.'

Tam gently shook him off.

'Hold on, son. What do you want me for?'

'We need you in there.' The man lifted his chin towards the castle. 'Our stupid piper went so hard at the bottle he fell halfway down the cliff. Broke his head and his right arm. He'll be weeks mending. The Earl Marischal needs piping into his dinner, and the lads are down without a note of music. There's not even a fiddle in the whole lousy place.'

'Well,' said Tam, with a show of reluctance which made me hide a smile, 'I don't know. What terms would you be offering me?'

'Terms?' They both burst out laughing.

'A draughty old hayloft to sleep in,' said one.

'Your food, and it's not bad either. There's meat every day and venison sometimes.'

'And we won't throw you off this cliff.'

332

There was a pause as the menace of this threat sank in.

'Plenty of whisky. It's good stuff too.'

Tam grinned then with what I could see was real pleasure.

'Now you're talking, lads. But I'm not going any-where without the lassie.'

Both men turned in my direction, and I felt hot at the way their eyes crawled over me.

'She's my granddaughter,' Tam said hastily, 'and if any harm comes to her, I'll play *The Unlucky Soldier*. Last time I had to do it, the plague struck the camp within the week. I felt bad about it, as a matter of fact. Twenty. Dead. In days.'

The tune of *The Unlucky Soldier* was a new one to me, as I was sure it was to Tam, but the two men's mouths had fallen open, and they were looking at Tam with respect.

'It's a deal,' one of them said. 'We'll warn the boys. The girl's not to be touched. They'll find a job for her in the kitchens.'

And so Tam and I walked boldly under the portcullis, through the archway, past the throng of guards and into that fearsome place as easily as if we'd walked out on to the beach at Scalpsie Bay. I looked back when we were through the entrance, across the narrow land bridge and up the cliff beyond. It had been almost too easy get-ting in. It might be much harder getting out.

There were steep steps rising from the gatehouse.

Halfway up them, Tam stopped and clutched at my arm for support.

'It'll end here, Maidie,' he said hoarsely.

'What will end? What do you mean?'

He seemed to give himself a shake. 'Your search for your uncle! He's here, I'm sure of it. Admit it, darling. Clever Tam got you in here as easy as a flying bird.'

I squeezed his arm and smiled, but a knot of dread was tightening my throat.

'I do admit it. I can never manage anything without you.'

He gave me a quizzical look, then struggled on up the steps.

It was easy to forget, once you were inside the castle, the terrifying rock on which it stood. The enclosing walls surrounded dozens of buildings, so that it felt almost like a town. There was a noble-looking keep, and grand lordly houses, stables, pigsties, hen-coops, workshops, open grassy spaces, stairways, passageways, and men everywhere. Some, in their shirtsleeves, were going in and out of the bakery and cellars and kitchens. Some, in leather aprons, were shoeing horses at the forge. Many, in soldiers' gear, were leaning against doorways, yawning and picking their teeth. There were men mending cartwheels, men sawing timber, men carrying baskets of fish on their heads.

I lost sight of Tam almost at once. He was borne off towards a beefy sergeant, who clapped him so hard on the shoulder that the old man nearly fell over. One of the soldiers who had brought us in told me to follow him to the kitchens.

I hesitated, scared of being separated from Tam.

'Follow him if you like,' jeered the man. 'But it's only whores who go into the barracks.'

I blushed and hurried after him, lost at once in the maze of passageways that led to the kitchens, which seemed to be on the furthest side of the castle, facing out to the open sea. My eyes darted everywhere, but I saw no sign of a prison where a large number of people could be held.

A huge man came out, responding to the soldier's call. He was naked to the waist, and wet with sweat. He frowned at the soldier's explanation, but nodded in the end. He pointed to a corner where I was to put my bundle, and told me to follow him.

The heat from the roaring fire and gaping bread ovens nearly knocked me over, but I had no time to get used to it.

'Peel that lot and chop them up,' the man said curtly, pointing to a huge stack of onions. For the rest of the day I was kept hard at work with no break to eat or drink. But a kitchen isn't a bad place if you're hungry, and I managed to sneak an oatcake or two, and even picked a few scraps from the carcass of a roasted chicken before it went into the stockpot.

The kitchens were full of people, working furiously under the eyes of the mountainous chief cook, but no one asked me about myself or exchanged any words except for curt commands.

'There's a new piper. That's his granddaughter,' I heard someone say. 'Till old Angus's bones have mended.'

'That'll be the day,' a scullion sniffed. 'The man's going so hard at his bottle that his bones'll be liquid before they grow back together.'

My heart sank.

We might have to stay here forever, I thought. *If there's no other piper, they'll never let Tam go.*

I didn't dare ask anyone about the prisoners. The clatter and bustle in the kitchen was so great anyway that the talk was all in snatches. I heard a bit about the Earl Marischal's tempers and whims (he seemed to be the hardest of taskmasters), and some cursing over the Countess's little dogs (though she seemed to be a kinder sort of person), and the soldiers' appetites (which were unreasonably huge, according to the head cook), and the poor quality of the rabbits delivered from the Marischal's mainland farms. But there was not one word about Presbyterians or Covenanters or prisoners.

Perhaps they're not here at all, I thought. *Perhaps we've come to the wrong place, or they've been taken somewhere else.*

Then, as the afternoon began to end and the light through the narrow windows began to dim, I was sent on an errand to the storeroom at the far end of the kitchen. The door into the passage beyond opened and a servant came in. He brought with him a stench so appalling that I rocked back.

'Bah! Close that door!' bawled the master cook.

'What is it?' I dared to ask Agnes, a thin, spotty girl, who had smiled shyly at me once or twice as she'd hurried past, and was now reaching over me to fill a pot with salted herrings from a barrel.

'Don't you know? It's coming from the prison.'

'What prison? Who's in there?'

'The Presbyterians. The Covenanters. There's nearly two hundred of them. They're all crammed into a little cellar. There's not even space for them all to sit down. I know they're wicked, and against the King and all that, but I feel sorry for them really.'

My heart had begun to pound.

How dare you call them wicked? It's the King who's wicked! I wanted to say. But I bit my lip, and asked instead, 'Have you seen them? Have you talked to any of them?'

She looked shocked.

'Why would I do that? They're traitors! I couldn't anyway, even if I wanted to. There are soldiers guarding the door all the time. The only window's at the back, right over the cliff, and it's really small.'

The door opened again and the stink was making me retch.

'Why does it smell so bad?'

Agnes had clapped her hand over her mouth and nose and I could hardly make out her words.

'Nowhere in there for them to do their – you know. Been locked up for weeks, and they have to do it where they stand. Serves them right, I suppose, but it's disgusting when you think about it.'

337

'But they must be getting sick! They must be dying!'
I was trying to stop my voice rising in distress.
She shrugged.

'They do bring bodies out sometimes. I've seen them. Pah! I can't stand this stink any longer.'

She took her pot filled with herrings, and hurried back into the kitchen.

Then, above the banging of cooking pots, the shouts of the cook and the ever-present crash and suck of the sea on the rocks below the kitchen windows, came the sound of singing. It was a faint sound, tremulous, mournful, and full of longing.

> *Lord, from the depths to Thee I cried,*
> *My voice, Lord, do Thou hear!*

Tears pricked my eyes as I recognized a psalm, one that I had sung often on dark winter evenings and in the last blush of summer nights at Ladymuir.

> *I wait for God, my soul doth wait,*
> *My hope is in His word.*
> *More than they that for morning watch,*
> *My soul waits for the Lord.*

'You! Girl! Come back here!' came an angry yell from the kitchen, but as I hurried back into the blistering heat I felt a new certainty. Uncle Blair was close by, I was sure of it, and though thick walls of stone and armed guards stood between us, I would find a way to carry out my promise, and reach him, and give him help.

The chance I had hoped for came that very evening. The grand people in their stately rooms above the kitchens had had their luxurious supper of roasted beef and smothered rabbits, and the soldiers, servants and workmen had gobbled down hearty stews and mounds of bannocks. The day's work in the kitchen was done, and it was time for the cooks and scullions to eat.

I made a sudden decision.

'Where do you go to pee?' I asked Agnes.

She jerked her head towards the entrance to the kitchens through which I'd come.

'Up there, then down to the right.'

I took a few steps, saw that her back was turned and hesitated, as if I was confused. No one was looking at me. I slipped down to the far end of the storeroom and opened the door into the passageway, biting my lip at the creak of the heavy hinges. The stench was so awful that I was afraid I would be sick, and I was glad I hadn't yet had supper, as I might have lost it all. To my left, I could hear men's voices, and guessed they were the guards. To my right was an archway, and beyond it, in the near darkness, I saw far below the white crests of waves rolling in from the sea to break thunderously on the rocks below.

The prison has a window, Agnes had said. It's right above the sea.

I was lucky, I suppose, that the light was now so bad,

because if I had been able to see the sickening drop, I might not have had the courage to set out along the little ledge that ran between the castle wall and the cliff edge. It was just wide enough to walk along, but crumbling in places, and a single false step would have sent me hurtling down on to the rocks below. I came at last to the window, a small, square hole at the height of my shoulders. The walls were so thick that I had to peer in to see anything. But then something white and living moved inside it, startling me so much that I nearly took a disastrous backward step. It was only a face, a man's face, pale and gaunt, the eyes wide and staring. He looked more terrified at the sight of me than I was of him.

'Please,' I said, 'are you one of the Presbyterians?'

'I have that honour.' He licked his dry lips. 'Are you an unearthly being? Have you come with more mockeries to torment us? I say unto you, *Get thee behind me, Satan!*'

'No!' I looked back along the way I had come, scared in case my voice could be heard. 'I'm looking for my uncle, Mr Hugh Blair of Ladymuir in Kilmacolm. Is he here?'

Two other faces were squeezing beside the first to look out through the small space. I heard interest and even excitement ripple back through the dense mass of humanity, and could sense rather than see the close-packed crowd of bodies inside shift.

'Who is it?' voices said. 'A girl? What's she doing out there? She's asking for Hugh Blair? Where are you,

Hugh? Come over here. There's a lassie asking for you.'

The displacement of bodies inside the vault stirred the foul air and it poured out of the window in a nauseating cloud. And then Uncle Blair was suddenly, unmistakably there, inches away from me, and though his lower face was covered with a beard, and his head had become as thin as a grinning skull, I knew his eyes, and his voice, as he cried out, 'Maggie! Dear girl! Are you real or a dream? Oh take care! Don't step backwards. There's a terrible drop behind you.'

I heard a heavy door crash shut in the castle, and with tense fingers I fumbled for the coins which I had kept and carried so carefully for this moment. I thrust them through the bars.

'What's this? Where did this silver come from?'

'From home. From Ladymuir. Ritchie borrowed it from the laird. I came to give it to you.'

He gave a shaky laugh.

'The Lord heard my prayer and answered me in my distress. There are poor souls here, faithful to Christ, in more severe trouble than I am. This will go some way to—'

'No, Uncle, please!' I spoke too sharply, scaring myself, and lowered my voice again. 'I came here for your sake, and for the family at home.' I couldn't bear to think that this precious money might not help Uncle Blair after all. 'I – I risked everything to come here. This money is for you.'

It was too dark to read the expression on his face, but

I knew that knots of moral struggle would be creasing his forehead.

'It's time to move on, Hugh,' came a quiet voice at his shoulder.

'I must go back in, my dear.' Uncle Blair's hand reached out and for a moment our fingers touched. 'We must take turns to breathe at the window, or we suffocate. My brethren have already been too patient. I will use these precious coins to buy food, Maggie dear, and I promise I will eat some of it myself.'

The pale face of another man took his place, his mouth gaping open, a black hole, sucking in the few precious gasps of fresh air. Behind him came a murmur of voices.

'Your uncle wishes you to know,' the man at the window said, 'that your coming has cheered him like a shaft of light direct from Heaven.'

He moved, and the next man stood at the window. There was more murmuring behind him.

'How are his wife, and the children? He has been tormented by fears for them.'

'They're well,' I whispered. 'Ritchie borrowed enough from the laird to pay the fine. They're managing.'

Another face appeared.

'Your uncle wants to warn you that you're in great danger if the enemy discovers that you came here as our friend. Others who have done so have been thrown in here with us.'

'Tell him,' I said, 'that I'll be safe. The piper Tam brought me. They think I'm his granddaughter.'

I wished at once that I'd held my tongue. Uncle Blair wouldn't like to know that a lie had been told.

But the next man, having listened to the voice behind him, said simply, 'Your uncle thanks you from his heart. He will call upon the Lord to help you, and see you safe home.'

Another door banged somewhere behind me, and voices came floating out from the passageway. I edged back along the ledge, ran through the arch into the passageway, and made it almost to the door that led back into the storeroom.

'Hey! You!' shouted a rough voice. 'Where do you think you're going?'

A guard was hurrying towards me, and I caught the glint of a dagger in his hand.

'I'm sorry,' I said hastily. 'I'm new here. I work in the kitchen. I'm looking for the latrine.'

'Up there,' the man said, pointing behind him. Then he peered closely at me through the gloom. 'Don't come this way again.'

'I won't.'

He put out a hand, as if he wanted to touch my breast. I slid past him and ran on up the passage.

Back inside the storeroom, I stood against the door for a long moment, my eyes shut. The horror of what I'd seen had shaken me so much that I was trembling uncontrollably.

He can't survive much longer. He looks like a corpse already, I thought. *And I can't help him any more.*

'There you are!' Agnes had come in search of me. 'Got lost, did you? Took me ages when I first came to find my way around. I kept some supper for you. You'd better come and eat it quickly, or they'll clear it all away.'

Chapter Twenty-Three

Work in the kitchens in Dunnottar Castle was so hard, so hot and hectic and exhausting, that for the next week I hardly had time to think of anything except how to relieve the ache in my back from hauling heavy loads, or how to avoid the curses and blows of Mr Haddo, the endlessly infuriated master cook.

I had no other chance to go to the tiny window of the prisoners' vault, and in my heart of hearts I felt relieved. The thought of looking once again into that pit of horror filled me with dread. But at least I'd carried out my task. I'd given Uncle Blair the money Ritchie had entrusted to me, so that he could buy food (though I'd learned by now that the soldiers charged exorbitant sums for small amounts of bread, and even for water). The best thing was that I'd discovered he was still alive.

Occasionally, above the mundane noises of the castle, I heard the faint sound of singing, as the Covenanters comforted themselves with the psalms they all knew by heart. Often their music was silenced by threats and jeers from the guards. I was guiltily relieved when the singing stopped. It made my throat tighten with sorrow and my heart thump with anxiety every time I thought of their suffering.

At night, though, I often heard another kind of

music. The garrison was working Tam hard. I'd grown up with the sound of his piping, but I'd never heard him play as he did on those nights in Dunnottar. He seemed to be inspired by the spirit of music itself, as if his soul was reaching out to find it.

When my work in the kitchens was over at last, and the last glow of the summer light was fading from the castle walls, I would stand drained with weariness at the edge of the green space in front of the barracks to listen to Tam's piping. His jigs and reels bore in them an almost unbearable gaiety, and his laments carried a world of suffering. Against the music I would hear the shouts and laughter of the men. Slowly, as the night went on, the notes would become a little less rhythmic, a little more blurred, and so it would go on until he let the air out of his bag in a final hideous wail. I knew then that he had drunk himself to silence.

In the first couple of weeks he came often to the kitchen to see me. He would stand in the doorway peering in, and if I saw him before anyone else did I would be able to run across to him. We never managed more than a few minutes, though, before the master cook shouted at me to get back to work. After the third or fourth visit, Mr Haddo lost his temper completely and told Tam not to show his face again if he didn't want me to get a beating.

I'd been able, even in those short visits, to see that Tam was looking different, though I wasn't sure if he was better or worse. The dreadful grey tinge in his face was not so noticeable. The drink had reddened it, and his cheeks had filled out a little.

'It's not that terribly bad here after all, Maidie,' he told me cheerfully. 'The lads are great ones to listen to a tale or two, and they're not stingy with the bottle either.'

'No need to tell me that,' I said severely. 'I hear it in your piping every night.'

'Well now, darling, an old man must have his comforts.'

When I told him I'd seen Uncle Blair, and how dreadful his situation was, he shook his head, and his eyes, dulled and softened after nights of drunkenness, filled with tears.

'Cruelty,' he said, squeezing my hand sympathetically. 'Unkindness. That's a thing I could never abide. I've been thinking and thinking, but there's no trick that even old Tam could pull to get the good man away from here.'

I worked hard in the kitchens. There wasn't much chance of doing otherwise, but in fact I wanted to. The work took my mind off my worries, and I even earned the approval of Mr Haddo, who began to send me out of the kitchens on errands to the stores, or called me to go with him up to the green to check over the fresh supplies brought in daily from the mainland. I didn't tell him that I could read and write. I was afraid he would become suspicious of me.

Whenever I left the kitchens I kept my ears and eyes

open for anything that might tell me how the prisoners were, but it was if those cruel grey walls had swallowed them up. They were a dark secret, a dreadful horror at the heart of this fearful place, which everyone seemed anxious to ignore.

I learned, after a while, that the female Covenanters and even some of the men had been moved to other rooms in the castle, but I had no way of knowing if Uncle Blair was among them. I took comfort, though, from the fact that they must now have a little more room in which to move around, and more air to breathe.

There had been uproar one day when a group of the prisoners had wriggled out of the tiny window over the cliff. One at least had fallen to his death. A few had got away but most had been rounded up and caught. Even behind the thick walls of the kitchens, on the other side of the castle, we heard the poor souls cry out in agony at the tortures that had been inflicted on them.

Uncle Blair can't be one of them, I kept telling myself. *He's too big. He'd never have got through that tiny window.*

But doubt nagged at me. I was wound up with anxiety all day, and woke each night in the grip of nightmares. I prayed constantly and fervently, as I knew that the Covenanters would be doing.

I longed for the certainty of their faith. I wanted to stand on the sure rock of conviction on which they were grounded, but under my own feet I could feel only shifting, sinking sand.

I'm not one of the Elect, I told myself miserably. *I can't be one of the saved. God hasn't chosen me for His own. He doesn't hear my voice.*

My worries were all centred on my poor uncle, but I didn't know – how could I have known? – that it was my dearest, my oldest friend, Tam, who should have been in my thoughts and prayers.

I won't forget a single detail of that dreadful day. I was hurrying back to the kitchens from the cowshed with a pail full of cream when a man came out of the door to the soldiers' quarters and called out to me, 'Hey, girl! Aren't you the piper's granddaughter?'

'Why? What do you want?'

He came over to me, and I stepped back warily. There was no threat in his manner though, only a kind of rough sympathy.

'You'd better come. You're needed.'

I looked at him stupidly, not understanding.

'Come where? I've got to take this cream to the kitchen.'

He took the pail from my hand.

'I'll take it. I'll tell them. Go in there, lassie. He hasn't got long. See Musketeer Sharpus? He's standing by the door. He'll show you the way.'

A chill of dread froze me.

'What do you mean? What's the matter?'

'Just get in there.'

I ran towards the barracks. The soldier, Musketeer Sharpus, had been watching. He beckoned me to the door. He didn't say anything, but nodded to me to follow him, and so I did, up a narrow stone stair and into a small dark loft, into which only a little light could struggle through the cracks in a shutter that covered the window at one end.

Tam was lying on a heap of straw. Even in the dim light, I could see death staring at me from out of his frightened blue eyes.

'Tam!' I dropped down on to my knees beside him. 'Tam, no! It's me! Please, Tam.'

He opened his eyes and with what seemed like an extreme effort turned his head to look at me.

'Maidie!' The word was no more than a breath.

I picked up his hand. It was horribly cold. I rubbed it between my own. I was shaking with terror.

'I can't manage without you, Tam,' I cried. 'You mustn't die! What will I do?'

How could I have been so selfish? How could I have thought, at that moment, only of myself?

He tried to say something, and I leaned forward but couldn't catch the word.

'Water,' he mouthed.

The musketeer called out, 'Bring the old fellow some water!'

There was a clatter on the stairs, and a moment later a beaker was put into my hands. I lifted Tam's head and held the water to his mouth. Even the effort of swallowing seemed too much for him, but when he'd managed it his eyes were a little clearer and he was able to speak more easily.

'I'm frightened,' he whispered. 'I'm a sinner, Maidie.'

'No, no! Never to me, Tam.'

'I stole that money in Edinburgh.'

'I know. It doesn't matter.'

'I've lied and cheated all my life. I'm a thief. I'm a—'

'You never hurt anyone. You risked everything to help people. To help me.'

'I'm going to Hell, Maidie. I'm going to burn for ever and ever.'

I tried to think of words of comfort.

'God loves a sinner who repents, Tam,' I said at last. 'You repent, don't you?'

A tear trickled out of the side of one eye. I wiped it away with my finger.

'Aye. If I've harmed anyone, I'm sorry, right enough. But I can't be sorry for the drinking, and the dancing, and the joy of all that.'

'I wish I knew what to say!' I cried, desperate to comfort him. 'I don't know what's a sin and what isn't! But maybe if you just say, *Jesus, I'm sorry for all my sins, and please let me go to Heaven*, that will make it all right.'

He managed to turn his head, and in his eyes I saw helpless doubt and fear.

'Would I not be out of place in Heaven, Maidie, among all the ministers and preachers?'

'No,' I said, suddenly inspired. 'My mother's there. She'll be your friend.'

The worry lines left his forehead as he relaxed into a trembling smile.

'Oh yes, right enough. Say the words again. I'll say them after you.'

I repeated my pathetic little prayer, and he mouthed each word after me. Then he turned such eyes of love on me that I felt my heart ache with sorrow and gratitude. I wanted to tell him everything I felt, but my throat was too tight. I couldn't speak. Anyway, he was struggling to say something.

'You've been the joy – the joy of my . . .'

He never finished. His eyes, which had gently closed on this last sentence, flew open, and his breathing changed, coming fast and rattling in his chest.

'Tam! Listen to me! Tam!'

I was holding his hand tight, and shaking it.

'He can't see or hear anything now,' said Musketeer Sharpus. I realized then that he'd been standing beside us all this time.

I watched, my heart in my eyes, waiting, until Tam took a last, shuddering breath, and then no more.

I saw, I felt his soul leaving. As it took flight, his eyes glazed, and his body seemed to shrink in lifelessness.

'Open the shutter!' I cried out. 'Let him out!'

The man had done so already.

I knelt and kissed Tam's cheek, which had greyed at once to the colour of stone.

'You've gone to Heaven, Tam, I know you have. Straight as an arrow. Jesus loves you, because you loved me.'

I didn't cry. Not then. I felt frozen. I rocked back on my heels, staring at all that was left of Tam, and would have been there for hours if the musketeer hadn't shaken my shoulder.

'We'll look after him now,' he said kindly. 'I'll come and tell you where he's to be laid. Don't come unless it's me who calls you. Neil Sharpus. Remember the name. Now you'd best get out of here.'

He almost dragged me to my feet, and pushed me towards the stairhead. 'You'll need to watch out for yourself,' he warned me. 'The old man protected you more than you know. There are too many sparky lads here who like a pretty girl.'

And he was right, because before I was out through the barracks door, there came a chorus of whistles and guffaws, and hands reached out to paw at me.

'Come on, boys, have a heart, will you? The lassie's just lost her granddaddy,' said Musketeer Sharpus, hustling me through.

'Yes, and he can't curse us now. He can't play *The Unlucky Soldier* now,' came the laughing answer.

My grief was swallowed up in a red tide of rage. I turned on them. I felt in my voice and in my face the power of righteous anger.

'He can haunt you,' I hissed at the mass of greedy, stupid faces. 'He can come at you from beyond the grave. He'll be in your nightmares, he'll infect your blood, he'll drive you mad . . .'

I stopped myself. Their mouths had fallen open and they were backing away from me, afraid.

Be careful, a little voice inside my head warned me. *Don't use the power of anger or they'll take you for a witch.*

353

Somehow I stumbled back to the kitchen, and there I was surprised. Agnes and the scullions and even Mr Haddo himself showed me such sympathy and gruff kindliness that for the rest of the day I was overwhelmed, and the sorrow came, and I was allowed to go and huddle in the corner by the salt box, and cry and cry until I had no more tears.

They laid Tam to rest in the little cemetery within the castle walls. The minister who attended the Marischal said a perfunctory prayer, yawning as he did so. I wanted to shout at him, *Make sure he goes to Heaven! Ask the Lord Jesus to take him in!* But I knew that no one could help Tam now. He must stand alone before the Throne of Grace while God weighed his sins in the great balance.

Musketeer Sharpus stood beside me at the open graveside. He was holding the bag in which Tam had kept his pipes.

'They're yours, I suppose,' he said, handing them over.

'They're his to take,' I said, and I leaned over the gaping hole and laid the bag on Tam's crude coffin.

The musketeer was silent as we walked away. At the entrance to the passageway leading to the kitchens I touched his arm.

'Thank you. You were kind to him, and to me. I don't want to lie to you. Please don't tell anyone, but Tam wasn't my real grandfather, only he looked after me all my life, and rescued me, and he was all I had.'

I couldn't go on.

'No need to cry,' he said gruffly. 'What are you going to do now?'

I was tempted for a brief moment to confide in him, and ask for his help in rescuing Uncle Blair, but I could see that he was impatient already and wanting to be off.

'I don't know. I'll see,' I said. 'I don't have any money.'

I saw a struggle in his face, and then he reluctantly put his hand into the pouch hanging from his belt and pulled out a little leather purse.

'I found this under your – under his pillow,' he said. 'I was going to buy whisky for the lads to raise a toast to the old man, but I suppose by rights it belongs to you.'

He dropped into my hands the purse which Tam had stolen at the city gate of Edinburgh, and was gone before I'd had a chance to thank him.

I have never felt so alone as I did in the weeks that followed Tam's death. The last link with my childhood had been cut. The last person who had truly loved me had gone.

As the days passed I started to feel as if I, too, was a prisoner in Dunnottar. The kitchen walls were as thick as a dungeon's, and the endless routine of work had closed round my mind, trapping me in a kind of dull helplessness.

I'd been surprised, at the end of my first week at work, to be given a couple of coins as wages, and my little hoard began to grow until they jingled satisfactorily in my pocket. The weight of Tam's purse, though, weighed heavily on my conscience. When the soldier had given it to me it had felt at first like a gift from beyond the grave, but every time I heard the sound of singing from the prisoners, the thought of the stolen money made me flinch with shame.

Uncle Blair would never have touched it, I told myself. *If he was me, he'd have flung it straight into the sea.*

But I kept the money, all the same.

As usual, the first that we in the kitchens heard of visitors to the castle was an order for a special banquet. The Countess sent for Mr Haddo, who came hurrying back down our steps, wiping his brow, which was furrowed with anxiety, repeating under his breath the long list of dishes that she had ordered. We were sent scurrying to pluck geese and ducklings, top and tail gooseberries for the sauce, shell crabs, knead the bread dough and clean the spit for the haunches of venison, while Mr Haddo made up the stuffing for the woodcock and tossed up a fry of cockscombs.

'Who's it all for? Who's coming?' I asked a scullion, without much interest.

'How should I know? Here, you've to gut this salmon.'

But as I passed a pair of men bringing in fuel for the roaring kitchen fires, I heard one of them say, 'It's the Lords Errol and Kintore, from Edinburgh. They've come about the prisoners.'

My hand, already greasy with fish guts, slipped on

356

the knife I was holding, and I almost cut myself. I strained to listen.

'Let's hope they're taking the fools away,' grumbled the second man. 'The way they drone on with their psalms gives me the creeps.'

'Are you sure?' I dared ask. 'Are they really coming about the Presbyterians? Are they going to take them away?'

'No point asking me,' he answered. 'Move, will you? How am I supposed to get these logs past with you standing there like a stone?'

They brought the prisoners out on to the castle green the very day after the banquet for the two noble lords. Mr Haddo, exhausted by the effort of preparing the great feast, had relaxed his grip on the kitchens and didn't even try to prevent his minions from pouring out of the bakery, brewery, dairy and storerooms to stare and wonder at the people they had only heard singing, and smelt, until now.

The sight of the wretched crowd of skeletons, with matted hair and clothes that had become no more than filthy rags, silenced everyone. The whole castle had come out to look. Maids hung out of upper windows, grooms emerged from the stables, and even the soldiers stood quietly, looking almost ashamed.

The murmur of shocked sympathy died away almost at once to leave an uneasy silence. Then one of the stable boys shouted out, 'Serves you right, you stinking traitors. God save the King!'

It was as if the others had been waiting for their cue. The lad's high-pitched voice had hardly died away when a chorus of jeers and catcalls broke out. Voices from all round the green yelled, 'Get them out of here! String them up! Where's your precious Covenant now, you fools?'

Suddenly I saw him. Uncle Blair was standing in the middle of a group of what looked more like standing corpses than living men. He was shading his eyes, as if blinded by the daylight after so long in the darkness of the dungeon. He was as thin as a pike-shaft, and as waxy-pale as a mushroom. I saw him stagger and clutch at the arm of the man beside him. I thought he was on the point of death.

I lost all sense of danger. I threw away my weeks of caution in one scream of anguish.

'Uncle Blair! Oh, please! Uncle!'

I didn't even reach him. A soldier grabbed hold of me and clipped my arms tightly behind my back.

'Well, well! So the piper's little girl is a damned Presbyterian after all!'

His voice was grim. He fumbled at his waist and I heard a rattle as something cold and hard snapped round my wrists. Then I knew what I'd done and shuddered with dread. The soldiers were working round the hundred or more prisoners, wrenching their bone-thin arms back and clamping on heavy manacles. A few moments later I found myself chained to a woman who was so weak that she could barely stand, and we were walking forward under the lash of a shouted command.

I had to help her even to stand upright, and as we were herded down the steep, rough-hewn steps to the narrow castle entrance, she leaned on me so gratefully that I ended by almost carrying her.

I managed to twist my head round as we turned the last corner, and caught sight of Mr Haddo in the middle of a group of kitchen workers. They were staring at me in shocked surprise, shaking their heads in disapproval, and making no effort to rescue me, though Agnes lifted her hand in a daring wave. I turned my back on them, lifted my chin and marched out of that dreadful place with as much dignity as I could, though my throat was tight when I thought that Tam could not leave with me. He would lie in Dunnottar Castle forever, and I hadn't even stood by the little mound that marked his grave one last time to say goodbye.

Was it by sheer chance that Neil Sharpus was one of the soldiers sent to escort the prisoners on their long, miserable march back to Edinburgh? Uncle Blair would have thanked the guiding hand of Providence. Granny would have congratulated herself on the success of one of her lucky charms. At any rate, it was a good thing for me that he was there.

The prisoners were so weak with lack of food and their long imprisonment that many of them could barely walk, and we went only a short distance that day. Once we had been herded into a barn commandeered from a grumbling farmer, our manacles and chains were removed, so that we could at least ease the cramps in our shoulders and move around among ourselves. At last I was able to go to Uncle Blair,

'Maggie,' he croaked, laying a trembling hand on my shoulder, 'dear child. I hoped you'd escaped from that dreadful place weeks ago.'

'I found work, Uncle. In the kitchens. I was never far away, but I couldn't find a way to speak to you again.'

He looked round vaguely.

'Where's your friend, the piper? He should have looked after you better. He should have got you away.'

I frowned at the criticism in his voice.

'Tam's dead, Uncle. He – I didn't realize how sick he was. I shouldn't have made him come with me. He was good to me. Always.'

'I'm glad to hear it. The man didn't seem up to much to me. A lightweight kind of a fellow.'

I was stung.

He came to save you, I wanted to say. *It was for you he died.*

But I could see that Uncle Blair's mind had moved on.

'Is there news from home? Have you heard from Ladymuir?'

As I shook my head there was a buzz of voices from the big barn doors. Someone even laughed.

'They've brought fresh water for us, Hugh!' a man called out. 'Without charging for it. And there are oat-cakes and even cheese, at a reasonable price.'

'Praise the Lord!' said Uncle Blair, his face lighting up with childlike delight. 'Today has brought such happiness! To smell fresh air again, and see the green grass, and the sky, and to see you again, my dear girl, so well and bonny. I've been tormented with fears for you! And on top of all this, a real supper!'

I swallowed my disappointment. The two halves of my life would never be brought together, I could see that clearly now. I felt in my pocket for my precious hoard of coins and threaded my way through the exhausted Covenanters towards the soldiers lounging by the door. Musketeer Sharpus caught hold of my arm and spun me round.

'So, piper's girl, you're a traitor after all. And to think I put myself out to help you. A fine fool you've made of me.'

I shook my head earnestly.

'I didn't mean to make a fool of you, sir. It's true that Tam and I came to Dunnottar in search of my uncle, but I'm not a Covenanter, not really. I don't understand about all that. I don't know what I am. I wish I did. I just want to do what's right.'

He loosened his grip.

'There's no making you out, girl. I keep tripping over you all the time.'

He sounded more perplexed than angry. Encouraged, I smiled at him.

'Please, will you let me walk free tomorrow? I won't run away. I want to stay near my uncle, that's all.' An inspiration came to me. I felt in my pocket again and pulled out the pouch of stolen money. 'You can have this if you'll let us both go, me and my uncle.'

He snorted with scornful laughter.

'What do you take me for? I'd never let a prisoner go. He's an enemy of the Crown. His name's written down on the list. I'd be arrested too.'

But his eyes were on the money. I began to return it slowly to my pocket.

'Tell you what.' His fingers were reaching out to twitch it away from me, and I snatched it back just in time. 'I could get *you* freed. It should be easy. Your name's not down on the charge sheet. A word with the captain should do it.'

'If it's so easy, it's worth less than all this money,' I said, jingling the coins, and thinking out the bargain. 'Look, I'll give you half the money now, if you can free me, and the rest when we get to Edinburgh if you'll make sure that my uncle's not driven too hard, and gets some decent food.'

He laughed.

'You're a one, you are. Give me a kiss and I'll throw in some wine for the man as well.'

I drew back.

'I don't sell kisses,' I said, my cheeks on fire with blushes as I dropped the coins into his outstretched palm.

I was afraid, as I went back through the throng of exhausted prisoners, that my uncle might have seen me talking to the soldiers, and would question me. He would have been disgusted, I knew, by my attempt to win him special treatment with the help of stolen money, and in fact my conscience did prick a little as I saw the desperate state of some of the other prisoners.

To my relief, someone started to sing before I'd reached our corner of the barn, and by the time I'd arrived, Uncle Blair was already joining in:

> *But blessed be God*
> *Who doth us safely keep*
> *And hath not given*
> *Us for living prey*
> *Unto their teeth*
> *And bloody cruelty.*

Some people were already asleep, their mouths open, making vacant, black holes between their hollow cheeks. Others were too weak to make a sound, but they were mouthing the familiar words, and I saw tears slide out from under closed eyelids.

> *Ev'n as a bird*
> *Out of the fowler's snare*
> *Escapes away,*
> *So is our soul set free.*
> *Broke are their nets*
> *And thus escaped we.*

Uncle Blair and I were lucky to have a good corner, beside a pile of hay bales against which we could rest our backs. He put up his hands to rest them on the front of his filth-encrusted coat, and I saw with a shock that they were roughly bandaged with strips of torn linen.

I put out my own hand and he flinched, as if afraid that I would touch him.

'What happened, Uncle?'

He shook his head.

'It's best forgotten.'

'No! Let me see.'

He hesitated, but allowed me to unwind the bandages, biting his lip hard with the pain. I had to suppress a gasp of horror. His fingers were a pulpy mass of raw flesh, deeply ulcerated. Yellow pus oozed out.

'How did this happen?'

He had lain back against the hay as if the sight of his own hands had exhausted him.

'It was one of their punishments,' he murmured. 'I spoke out in anger when one of our sisters was forced to give birth in that – that place. She died under their cruel neglect, with the babe. They – put lighted splinters of wood between my fingers and blew on them till they had burned away. Oh, don't look so upset, my dear. The Lord has been good to me. One of the brethren lost all his fingers that way. As the Lord Jesus said, *Blessed are ye, when men shall revile you and persecute you for My sake.* If He asks me to suffer, I must do it gladly. Only think of His sufferings for us on the Cross! How little this is to bear for His sake.'

'It seems rather a lot to me,' I muttered crossly under my breath, then bit my lip, afraid that such a thought was sinful.

Aloud, I said, 'You must let me care for them, Uncle. I know how to treat this kind of injury.'

He smiled at me.

'Thank you, my dear. If you would add your prayers to mine they will rise as a sweet odour to the throne of the heavenly grace, and surely the Lord will hear us.'

I nodded, but thought, with another little spurt of rebellion, *Prayers are one thing, but healing herbs are another*.

My poor uncle would have recoiled from any remedy if he'd known it had been learned from my grandmother. He would have feared enchantments and spells, and sniffed the sulphurous presence of the Prince of Darkness.

He had closed his eyes. I watched him for a few moments, till I was sure he was deeply asleep. Then I got up and tiptoed through the now silent prisoners to the barn door. Luckily, the man on guard duty was Musketeer Sharpus.

'Let me out for a little while,' I begged.

To my surprise he didn't look at me, and seemed embarrassed.

'You'll run away.'

'You know I won't. I told you, I'm here to be with my uncle.'

He hesitated, then jerked his head.

'Away you go then. But don't be long. My time's up in an hour. The next fellow mightn't look so kindly on comings and goings.'

I wished, with all my heart, as I darted away into the twilight, that I'd taken more notice of Granny's work with herbs. It was true that she had never tried to teach me. In fact, if I'd looked too closely at anything she was doing, she'd driven me off with a curse. But I could remember some things, and knew now what I was looking for.

When I was eight or nine years old, I'd burned my foot badly, stumbling into the fire. Granny had said nothing to comfort me, but had gone outside, coming back a while later with burdock leaves, which grew near the path on the way to Kingarth. She'd broken an egg, grumbling at the waste, and had crushed the burdock leaves into the slimy white before spreading it on the burn. I'd never forgotten how cool and good it had felt on the painful place, and how quickly it had healed.

But my burn was a small one, and fresh, I thought anxiously. *And there wasn't any pus coming out of it. Anyway, I don't know where to look for burdock. And how can I possibly get hold of an egg?*

I'd been walking too fast and aimlessly, and forced myself to slow down and think. In Scalpsie Bay, there had been clumps of burdock growing along the track underneath a stone wall. I'd seen a wall not far back along the way we'd come. Perhaps there would be burdock growing there too.

I found my quarry more quickly than I'd expected, and pounced. Then, as I'd seen Granny do, I studied the plant, and chose carefully from the leaves, only picking the big, healthy-looking ones.

Success gave me a jolt of confidence. God must have guided me to this precious plant. Perhaps He had listened to Uncle's prayers. Perhaps He would put an egg in my hands too.

Eggs meant hens, and hens meant farms, and farms meant people, and dogs, and trouble. Tam would have known what to do. I'd seen him many times, slipping shamefaced from a farmstead with a couple of oval bulges in his pocket.

And then I heard it. The track I'd been following ran close to the sea, near the top of the cliff which dropped away down to the rocky shore. The murmuring surge of the waves against the rocks was so familiar that I no longer noticed it, and while I'd been in Dunnottar I'd become just as used to the shrieks of squabbling kittiwakes and the wails of soaring gulls. But I was suddenly, sharply, aware of them. They were close by but out of sight. They had to perch on the rocky ledges of the cliffs overhanging the sea. The chicks would have hatched and fledged by now, but there were always a few eggs abandoned by their parents, or ones that had never had a chick in them at all. It was unlikely I would find one, but it was worth a chance.

And then my knees felt weak.

I can't, I thought. *Not down the cliff. I can't.*

But my feet seemed to be moving of their own accord.

I didn't dare walk right up to the crumbling edge, so I lay down on my stomach and crawled forward, till I could look down from the top of the cliff. It fell in one dizzying swoop to the black jagged rocks below, against which the waves hurled themselves in clouds of dazzling white spray. The drop was so terrifying that my limbs felt weak and my head began to spin.

The cliff was alive with gulls and kittiwakes, the whole face of it fluttering with white wings. The birds had not quite settled yet to sleep, but were taking off and landing, restless and quarrelsome.

It was hopeless, I knew it was. Surely the ledges would all be empty. Surely this was a waste of time. But then I saw it. An egg – large, spotted and unbroken – lay on a ledge below me, just beyond my reach.

I stretched my arm down as far as it would go and wriggled a little further forward. A great white bird came flying at me like a dart from the sea. It shrieked, its neck thrust out, trying to snap at my fingers. I beat at it, and lunged for the egg.

There was a terrible shriek and a confusion of flapping wings. As the bird tumbled backwards into flight, its foot dislodged the precious egg, which flew off the ledge and shattered on the rocks far below.

As I watched it go, I felt as if I was falling with it. My whole body began to shake with fright. I'd reached too far, and didn't see how I could haul myself back. My hands had nothing to hold on to. My legs were beginning to slip. I didn't dare try to wriggle backwards. The slightest movement, I knew, would tip me irretrievably over the edge.

'Jesus!' I whispered. 'Granny! O Jesus!'

And then I felt a pair of strong hands grasp my ankles, and I was being wrenched back from the cliff edge.

'What do you think you're doing? Whatever were you thinking of?'

Musketeer Sharpus flipped me over so that I was lying in a heap on the heather, looking up at him. I scrambled to my feet. He grabbed me again and dragged me further away from the hideous drop, as if he was afraid that I would run back to it and throw myself over.

'Are you crazy?'

His eyes seemed to be almost starting from his head with shock and anger.

I struggled free. I tried to speak, but I was shaking so hard my teeth were chattering together.

'Th-thank you,' I managed to say. 'I would have fallen if you hadn't come.'

He took hold of my arm again and shook me roughly.

'Don't you know that self-murder is a mortal sin? You would have gone straight to Hell.'

'I didn't – it wasn't – I didn't want to kill myself!'

'Then what were you doing?'

I swallowed, knowing how silly I sounded.

'I needed an egg. I was trying to take one from the ledge there.'

He stared at me, incredulous, then burst out laughing.

'You silly girl! If you wanted an egg, why didn't you ask me? I could have got you one from the farmer. You can't eat gulls' eggs, anyway. Any that haven't hatched will be rotten by now.' His eyes suddenly narrowed.

'Unless you wanted an unborn chick for some uncanny purpose. You don't make spells, do you? You're not experimenting with unholy things?'

'No!' I almost choked in my eager denial. 'I'd tell you but you wouldn't like it.'

'Try me.'

I saw that I had no choice.

'My uncle's hands are burned. I heard from . . . somewhere that if you crush burdock leaves into egg white it's good for healing burns.'

'Oh.' His voice had changed. I dared to look up at him and was surprised to see that he was frowning. 'I never liked that business of burning hands. It seemed – well, I never did it myself. Keeping traitors close in prison is one thing, but torture and starvation – they're not right, to my mind.'

He had one hand in the small of my back and was steering me back towards the barn.

'I'll get you an egg,' he said. His voice was soft and gruff. 'I'll bring it in to you. Go on in, now.'

Another soldier was guarding the door. He raised his eyebrows at the sight of us and dug Musketeer Sharpus in the ribs.

'You're a sly one. Up for it, is she? Let me have a go and I won't tell the sergeant.'

'You won't tell anyone anything, my lad,' Musketeer Sharpus said severely. 'Not if you don't want everyone to know about the musket you lifted from the guard-room and sold to that poacher. You won't take any liberties with this girl either. She's respectable.'

Inside the barn, not one of the exhausted Covenanters seemed to be awake. I slipped across to the far end and sank down beside Uncle Blair. How still he was, his chest barely moving as he breathed. He looked sad in his sleep, and much, much older. His injured hands were lying by his side.

I felt a wave of anger.

Why did You let them do this to him, God? I thought. *These people are only trying to be faithful to You. Why are You treating them like this? You said,* Blessed are the persecuted, *but they don't look blessed to me.*

My mind reeled back to the terrible moment on the cliff. I could see again the waves dashing on to the rocks below and hear the screaming birds. What had really happened then? Had Jesus heard me, and sent Musketeer Sharpus to rescue me? But I seemed to remember that I'd called out to Granny too. Had she used some strange power to reach out to me from beyond the grave?

Something had happened, I felt sure, that I didn't understand. There had been a kind of power there among those beating white wings.

He will give His angels charge over thee, I had heard Uncle Blair quote. *They shall bear thee up in their hands, lest thou dash thy foot against a stone.*

I thought I'd seen an angel once before, but it had only been Tam, when he'd opened the door to rescue us from the tollbooth in Rothesay. I couldn't imagine Musketeer Sharpus as an angel, any more than Tam, but God's ways were mysterious, I'd often been told. Maybe

Neil Sharpus was a messenger from Heaven, in spite of being a servant of the tyrant King, and so plain and awkward as well.

I wanted to thank Jesus, but I didn't know how to do it properly. While I was thinking about this, I saw Musketeer Sharpus stepping through the sleeping people towards me. I watched him carefully as he approached, wondering if the light round his head was shining from him, or if it was the glow of moonlight that was now coming in through the barn door. As he came nearer, I smiled at my silliness. There was nothing angelic about Musketeer Sharpus. He was just a soldier, with a scarred face, and a broken nose, and thin, straggling fair hair. Then I saw that he was holding an egg in his hand. I began to fumble in my pocket for a coin.

'No need for that.' He was frowning down at my uncle's hands with shocked pity in his eyes. He gave me the egg, and hurried away.

I don't know if my remedy really did have the power to heal, or if it was the fresh air and the better food which Musketeer Sharpus helped me to provide for my uncle, but at any rate, as the days passed and the sad cavalcade of prisoners straggled down the road to Edinburgh, Uncle Blair's hands began to heal. I could see that they would never be quite right. The flesh was too twisted and distorted to mend completely. But at least he wouldn't lose his fingers.

Slowly, our company grew. A few other friends and relatives of the prisoners, hearing of their departure from Dunnottar, had hurried to meet them and help them if they could. They paid for better food, and washed some of the stinking clothes. One or two prisoners were even spirited away, to disappear to freedom in the hills.

Most of the Covenanters were farmers like Uncle Blair – men used to hard work, to the rain and the cold. I watched them as they trudged stoically on, thin and ragged, their arms bound, unable to brush the tormenting midges from their faces or ease the ache in their shoulders.

'Why?' I burst out one morning to Uncle Blair as I watched a soldier kick at a man who had stumbled to the ground and was trying to get up without being able to use his arms. 'How can you bear all this? How can it be worth it?'

He turned shocked eyes on me.

'Do you still not understand? After all this time, don't you see what wickedness God is asking us to resist?'

I kept my head down and swiped rebelliously at the bracken growing by the path. Uncle Blair sighed and said patiently, 'Who is the true head of the Church, Maggie? God or the King?'

'God,' I said unwillingly.

He nodded, but said nothing more. I looked sideways at him, and saw that his thoughts had moved on, to some painful place of trouble.

'What is it, Uncle?' I asked at last.

He sighed.

'The worst is yet to come, dear girl. At Leith, when this journey is nearly over, we will all be asked once again to take the Test.'

My heart sank. I said nothing. I knew what this meant.

'One by one,' he went on, 'they'll question us again. How many times have they asked us, and how many times have we refused! *Do you accept that the King's Majesty is the only supreme Governor of the Church?* That's what they'll ask. *Do you swear allegiance to him in all matters temporal and spiritual?*'

'And if you don't swear?'

He hesitated.

'I didn't want to tell you this, my dear. After all you've done for me I fear your efforts will have been in vain. We are to be banished, on a slave ship, to the plantations in the New World. There will be no return, on pain of death.'

'No!' I cried, so loudly that heads turned to stare at me. 'Uncle, you can't! Think of them at home. At Ladymuir! They need you there. How will my aunt manage without you?'

He shut his eyes.

'I think of them all the time. But where does a man's true duty lie? To serve God and to be true to Him, or to succumb to the world of the flesh and the ties of human love?'

I didn't even try to answer his question. There was no doubt in his mind, I knew. But in my own head there was a tangle which I could not unravel. I longed for my uncle to go home safe and sound, to be the father and the husband in the happy family which had so warmed me in my loneliness. But how could I wish him to betray the truest part of himself, and live with shame and guilt for evermore?

The dream of the good life at Ladymuir was the strongest in me, and I began, almost unintentionally, to work on his resolve. Was I wrong? I only wanted to save him from the horrible fate that awaited him if he stayed true to his Covenanting principles.

'That's a decent crop,' I would say, as we walked past a team of men scything the ripe barley. 'I wonder if Ritchie's got the harvest in yet at Ladymuir?'

Or, 'See that butterfly? I wish Martha was here. She always runs after the big blue ones and tries to catch them.'

Uncle Blair never asked me to be quiet, but I think I must have tortured him, and I'm sorry for it now.

A quiet anguish had descended on the prisoners by the time we reached Burnt Island. Only the narrow waters of the Firth of Forth now separated us from Leith, where the Test would be taken. Some of the Covenanters, even after all they had suffered, seemed unshaken in their rock-like convictions. They would, I was sure, suffer torture, banishment and even death rather than bow to the tyrant King. But I sensed that others were weakening. They had drawn into themselves and walked apart, not singing the psalms in the evening with the same hearty confidence, knowing how bitterly their betrayal would be condemned.

What would Uncle Blair do? I watched him anxiously, and saw in him the signs of an inner struggle. At night, as we lay out in an open field, or sometimes in a welcoming barn, I heard him groan and grind his teeth as he slept, in an agony of mind.

Chapter Twenty-Four

They were waiting for us as we stepped off the boats on the cold grey stones of Leith harbour. No time was wasted. The Covenanters were herded at once inside the courtroom.

'Prisoners only,' a soldier said, barring my way as I tried to go in with Uncle Blair.

I had no choice but to join the crowd of anxious relatives waiting by the door. It was a hot day. A haze hung over the spires of Edinburgh on the hill a mile or two away. A few fishing smacks were tied up at the quayside, their catches already unloaded, and the fishermen were peacefully working on their nets, mending the rips in them. Smirking boys strutted mockingly behind a grand gentleman, and some little girls squatted in a doorway, playing with a kitten.

Don't they know what's going on in there? I thought, my heart pounding with anxiety. *Don't they care?*

I saw that some of the relatives were huddling beneath a high open window, trying to hear what was going on inside. They made room for me, and we stood with our faces turned up, straining to hear.

'Let George Muir stand forward!' called out an official-sounding voice.

There was a clank of manacles inside as the prisoners

shuffled about. The judge began to read out the Test. Fragments floated out to us.

'George Muir, do you swear . . . the true Protestant religion . . . educate your children . . . affirm the King's Majesty . . . the only supreme Governor . . . do you judge it unlawful to enter into any Covenants . . . to take arms against the King . . . is this your solemn oath?'

I couldn't make out the confused murmur from within, but the man nearest the window jumped up on to a barrel to see into the courtroom.

'He refused. He's refused it. On pain of banishment,' he reported down to us.

A woman standing by me cried out, 'Well done, George my man! The Lord is with you!'

Then she fell sobbing into the arms of another.

I listened with every nerve straining to hear my uncle's name.

'William McMillan . . . Peter Russell . . . Robert Young . . .'

The crowd by the window was shifting. Those whose relatives had refused the Test and been sentenced to banishment had already drifted away. They stood by the edge of the quay, talking quietly.

'Was that Hugh Blair? Did they call out Hugh Blair?' I called up to the man at the window.

He waved a hand to silence me.

'Shh. I can't hear. No, it's John Blackburn. He's broken! He's taken the Test!'

A man emerged from the courtroom a few moments

later, rubbing his wrists from which the manacles had been struck off.

'Bessie!' he called out. 'Are you there? Bessie! I can't – I couldn't – O God, help me!'

A woman ran up to him. As she passed the others, they turned their backs on her.

'You should be ashamed,' a man called out. 'You have betrayed your Saviour!'

The woman called Bessie turned on him fiercely.

'Hold your tongue, Simon Ballingall! Hasn't the man suffered enough? Come away, John. The children are waiting for you.'

Hostile muttering broke out as she led him away. He was weeping uncontrollably, like a child.

I twisted my hands together. Which was the worse fate? Banishment and slavery, or shame? I couldn't bear the thought of either for Uncle Blair.

The long afternoon wore on. Several more distraught men and a few women slunk out of the courtroom and hurried away to freedom. One or two, with rich friends behind them, paid for a bond, and were freed with honour, but it was clear that most of the prisoners were refusing the Test and accepting their fate with defiance.

They must have called him, I thought. *I must have missed hearing his name.*

In spite of myself, I felt a surge of pride. Only those who had taken the Test had been let go. He must be one of the brave ones.

There were only a few of us now under the window.

The man on the barrel had gone. I scrambled up in his place, and could at last see inside the courtroom.

The judge, under his heavy robes and with a great wig on his head, was red-faced and sweating in the heat of the close-packed, stuffy room. He was taking frequent gulps from the wine glass by his elbow, and was clearly tired and impatient with the slow proceedings. Below me, the prisoners who had already refused the Test were standing under close guard, but their backs were turned to me and I couldn't see their faces, or tell if Uncle Blair was among them. The ones still to be tried were out of sight.

In front of the judge's great chair was a row of clerks sitting at a table. Some were scratching away with their quills, but the one at the far end was holding what looked like a list. And leaning over him, stabbing at a name on the list with his forefinger, was Musketeer Sharpus. The clerk was shaking his head. Musketeer Sharpus whispered in his ear. The clerk hesitated, then picked up his quill and drew a line through one of the names. Musketeer Sharpus stepped back, and as he did so he glanced up at the window and saw me. A tight smile creased his pitted cheeks, which he quickly suppressed, but then he gave me an unmistakable wink.

I didn't dare to interpret what I'd seen, but a flower of hope burst open in my chest.

'What's happening in there? Have they called Janet Holm yet?' a man below me asked.

'Look for yourself if you like,' I said, hopping off the barrel.

A quarter of an hour later my uncle suddenly appeared at the courtroom door, chafing his wrists as the others had done.

He broke. He said it, I thought, my heart illogically dropping with disappointment. Then I saw that Musketeer Sharpus was pushing him forward.

'I keep telling you, man, your name's not on the list. You're free to go,' he was saying.

Uncle Blair was shaking his head, bewildered.

'But the Test! I haven't been called yet. How can I be free?'

Musketeer Sharpus prodded him sharply.

'That's enough. You're wasting the court's time. Get out of here.'

Musketeer Sharpus beckoned me over.

'Take this man away, for Heaven's sake,' he said loudly. 'He's making a nuisance of himself.' Then he leaned over and said quietly in my ear, 'Will you be in Edinburgh later?'

I hadn't dared to think ahead.

'I suppose so. Is he really free to go?'

'Yes! But take him away quickly! Meet me at six in the evening, at the door of the High Kirk. I'd like to tell you . . . I need to ask you . . .'

He looked down, unable to meet my eyes.

Another guard was coming to the door.

'Come on, Uncle,' I said, tugging at Uncle Blair's arm. 'It's over. It really is over! Quick, let's go before they change their minds and call you back inside.'

*

It was the strangest thing, to be walking freely beside my uncle out of the town of Leith and up the hill to Edinburgh. The hot sun was tempered by a cool wind from the sea, which sparkled in the distance. Larks rose from the stubble in the harvested fields. Ahead, a golden mist was forming round the crown of Arthur's Seat, which rose on the far side of the city. I had the oddest feeling that I had left Hell behind me, and was walking up to Heaven.

'Isn't this wonderful?' I burst out, facing my uncle again. 'You can go home, Uncle! You're free! And there's no shame to you. They never asked you. You didn't betray anyone.'

I saw with dismay that he didn't share my joy. He had stopped to lean against a wall.

'I must sit for a minute.' He sank down on the bank. 'How did this happen, Maggie? Why did they let me go? I didn't offer money for a bond. I couldn't have afforded it anyway.'

I longed to tell him what I suspected, that Musketeer Sharpus had persuaded the clerk to take his name off the list, but I held my tongue. I didn't understand myself why he would have done such a thing, and anyway, I thought it would be dangerous to let Uncle Blair probe too closely. His tender conscience might oblige him to return to Leith and give himself back into custody. I said nothing, and waited to see which way his mind would turn.

'This is the Lord's doing,' he said at last, to my relief. 'But why have I been singled out for this great blessing?

Why has He chosen me for freedom, and sent my poor brethren far away into foreign lands?'

I saw that I didn't need to answer. He was lost in his own thoughts.

'I'll never know!' he cried out. 'I can never be sure!'

'What do you mean, Uncle? What won't you know?'

He sighed.

'As I stood there in that awful place, waiting for my name to be called, I was in such an agony of spirit, Maggie. I heard the voice of my Saviour urging me to be faithful even unto death, but at the same time I could see the face of my dear wife, calling me home. My courage was weakening. I saw several fail, and submit, and in my heart I despised them. But would I have been one of them? If I had stood before that proud and sinful judge, the instrument of our cruel King, would I have had the courage to stand firm?'

'Well,' I said briskly, jumping to my feet and putting a hand under his elbow to help him rise, 'if God had wished you to be put to the Test, He would have let it happen. But He has freed you, and you should be glad and rejoice.'

He gave me a wavering smile.

'Oh, my dear, how wise you are! How easy it is to forget to offer praise and thanks to our Heavenly Father for the blessings He showers upon us!'

'And anyway,' I went on, 'we'd better keep going, because we have to find somewhere to lodge tonight.'

I didn't tell him that I'd spent the last of my Dunnottar earnings and had handed the rest of Tam's money in payment to Musketeer Sharpus for the food he'd helped me procure along the way. I knew what I had to do. After all this time, when I'd held on to it through thick and thin, the moment had come to sell my father's buckle.

But Uncle Blair surprised me by saying tranquilly, 'We'll have no difficulty over lodging. I have a cousin who lives in Bells Wynd. He'll be pleased to take us in.'

I was startled. A cousin of my uncle's must be a cousin of mine. My family was unexpectedly expanding once again.

I was so intrigued by the idea of these new relations that I gave no thought to the problem of how we were to get in through the city gates until we were almost at them. But I need not have worried. No papers were being asked for, now that the invasion panic was over.

Uncle Blair surprised me by walking straight up the High Street of Edinburgh and turning into a narrow close without hesitation.

'You've been here before?' I asked.

'Aye, in my youth. When my father – that was your grandfather – died I had to come here to sort out the title to Ladymuir. It's a fine city, no doubt, but awfully stinky.'

We had to flatten ourselves against the wall of the narrow canyon-like close to let a couple of laden pack-horses squeeze past.

My grandfather! I thought. *Another relative!*

'And your mother,' I said. 'What was she like?'

I'd never thought of my other grandmother. Granny had been more than enough for me.

He seemed to find the question difficult.

'She was a good woman,' he said at last. 'She loved the Scriptures. She spared not the rod on her children.' He smiled suddenly. 'Your father, Danny, he was a rascal. She never managed to beat the spirit out of him. A rover he was, by nature. Full of mischief. I miss him to this day.'

The horses had passed by now. We went on down the close, trying to avoid the worst of the putrefying slime under our feet. Uncle Blair turned in through a low entrance and I followed him, hardly noticing the narrow stone stairway we were climbing.

Uncle Blair was knocking on a door. It swung open. A short, red-faced woman stood gaping at him, wiping her hands on her apron.

'Hugh!' she said at last. 'What brings you here? We heard you'd been taken prisoner.'

She was looking anxiously past him as if she feared to see a cohort of Black Cuffs at his heels. Her eyes came to rest on me.

'Praise the Lord, Sarah,' said Uncle Blair cheerfully. 'I'm a free man. He has delivered me from the pit and the miry clay. And this is your wee cousin Maggie. Danny's daughter.'

'Danny!' Sarah's face lit up. 'I heard he had a daughter. I can't believe she's grown up already. Come away in, dear, and let me see you. There's a look of your

385

father, maybe, around the eyes.' She turned to call over her shoulder. 'Thomas! You'll never guess who's here!'

They were kind people, Cousin Thomas and Cousin Sarah, but they made little impression on me. They were more concerned with their tailoring business than with matters of religion. They were alarmed at first to be harbouring one of the notorious Covenanting prisoners of Dunnottar, but when Uncle Blair had explained that he'd been freed, and that no more charges stood against him, they were reassured. They listened, horrified, to his account of the prison vault, tutted over his hands, deplored the state of his clothing, then moved the subject on as if to dwell on such things was somehow indecent.

'You're not the first I've heard of, to slip out of their clutches,' Cousin Thomas said with a nod. 'There's quite a few who have passed money into the right hands and have been let go. There's a price for everything, if you know how to go about it. How much did the Laidlaws pay to free their brother, Sarah?'

They began to discuss the price of freedom as if it was a length of woollen cloth. Uncle Blair sat by in polite silence, but I could see that the conversation troubled him as the puzzle of his release weighed on him again.

I didn't know how late it was, but through the narrow window I could see that the shadows were lengthening towards sunset. Cousin Sarah was busy at the table, rolling out the oatcakes for our supper. I tugged at Uncle Blair's sleeve.

'There's a person who helped me that I promised to call on when I came back to Edinburgh. May I go out, Uncle? I won't be long.'

Uncle Blair nodded, but Cousin Sarah raised her eyebrows. Before she could say anything, I had fled down the stairway and was running up the close.

Musketeer Sharpus was waiting for me. He stepped out of the High Kirk's great doorway so suddenly that I was startled. I'd been trying to frame my gratitude into suitable words, but at the sight of him I found I couldn't say anything. He was ill-at-ease, and under my gaze his face was turning an uncomfortable shade of red.

'I don't know how to thank—' I began.

'I did it for—' he said at the same time.

We both stopped, and there was an awkward silence.

'Listen,' I said, seeing that he was tongue-tied, 'I saw through the window that you were talking to the clerk. It was you, wasn't it, who got my uncle's name taken from the list?'

'Yes.' Beads of sweat were breaking out under the wisps of greasy fair hair that fell over his forehead, and when he spoke, his voice was hoarse. 'It was for you. I did it for you. You got under my skin. I never knew anyone like you. Any girl. I gave the clerk all the rest of the old man's money. Thirty silver shillings! He struck a hard bargain.'

'You're a good man,' I said lamely.

He grabbed my hand and held it. His own hand was trembling and clammy with sweat.

'Maggie,' he said. 'Maggie.'

I was feeling more and more uncomfortable. I wanted to pull my hand away but I was fearful of appearing ungrateful.

'I'm a soldier,' he said. 'I haven't got much, just a bit put by. But I'd leave the army. My father's a stonemason. I'd work with him. Get a little place of our own.'

He stopped. Gently, I pulled my hand away.

'Will you?' he said desperately. 'Will you?'

'I can't. I'm sorry.' I was scarlet myself now with embarrassment. 'But I'll never forget you, Musketeer Sharpus.'

'Neil. Call me Neil.'

'All right then. Neil. I'll be thankful to you forever, for what you did. I'll pray for you.'

He crossed his arms over his chest as if to draw his feelings back into himself.

'I knew it wouldn't be any good. I knew I didn't have a chance with a girl like you.'

'It's not your fault. It's mine. I'm sorry,' I whispered.

'I'm glad I did it, anyway. Free your uncle, I mean. I didn't like what they did to his hands. And I didn't want to keep the old man's money. It had a taint on it somehow.'

I stood on tiptoe and reached up to kiss his cheek.

'I'll never, never, never stop thanking you for the rest of my life,' I said, and I turned and ran back down the street, knowing that his eyes were on me as I fled.

*

388

I lay that night in the little corner bed in the kitchen, more comfortable and safe than I had been at any time since I'd left Ladymuir. But I couldn't sleep.

These past weeks, I'd tried not to think about the future. The thought of what might become of me was too unsettling.

When Uncle Blair's free, I'd told myself. *I'll think about it then.*

I'd often imagined how grateful everyone would be to me for all that I had done, and how much they would admire my courage and cleverness. But now I realized that I would never be able explain how it had all happened. Uncle Blair had been bought with stolen money. His freedom had been arranged by an enemy soldier, whose motive was only to please me. If he had known all that, Uncle Blair would have been disgusted.

He assumed that I would return with him to Ladymuir and take up my old life as a member of the family. But now that the time had almost come, I could see with painful clarity what it would mean. Aunt Blair would be good to me at first, but she too could never know the truth. Her old dislike would soon take over, and I would feel it daily in a hundred little ways.

And then there was Ritchie. He liked me, I knew. He might ask me to marry him, and one day Ladymuir would be mine. It was a golden prospect for a girl who had grown up in a half-derelict cottage at Scalpsie Bay. I ought to have reached out to seize it with both hands.

Why didn't I want to? What other choice did I have?

Uncle Blair's words floated into my head.

A rover he was, by nature.

And I was a rover too. If I stayed at Ladymuir, I would be restless and unhappy. My spirit would rise up in revolt.

I wish I was a boy! I thought, remembering the freedom of the days on the drove, when I'd walked with bare legs, unmolested, through the hills.

There was no purpose in thinking that way.

Perhaps I should stay in Edinburgh. Find work. Be a servant. Wash clothes. I could . . . I could . . .

Tiredness overwhelmed me and at last I slept.

Perhaps because they had been too afraid to help Uncle Blair when he had been imprisoned in the Edinburgh tollbooth, our hosts overwhelmed us with their hospitality. Cousin Thomas insisted on making new suits of clothes for each of us, fussing over which of his best woollen stuffs to use. He measured us and did the cutting out himself, before setting his apprentices to do the stitching. Cousin Sarah sent for the apothecary, who shook his head over Uncle Blair's hands, though he commended me for the use of burdock. He made up a salve, but predicted that the fingers would never recover their full sensitivity and agility.

'You'll be able to steer a plough and grasp a scythe,' he told him. 'It'll be just the fiddly things that'll give you trouble, but your good lady, I'm sure, won't mind doing up your buttons for you.'

I could tell that Uncle Blair was longing with all his being to start the journey home to Ladymuir, but even he had to admit that he wasn't strong enough to walk the distance. He submitted with as good a grace as possible to a few days of Cousin Sarah's nursing, though he was sorely tried by the interminable talk of French silks and Italian velvets that flowed from Cousin Thomas. Fortunately, after a day or two, word spread of his presence in Bells Wynd, and a succession of plainly dressed kindred spirits found their way up the narrow stair to visit him. They exchanged news eagerly of friends who were still in prison, or were on the run, or banished, and spoke severely of those who had given in and taken the Test. There was much talk of the great lords of Scotland, the hangings of the Covenanting leaders in the Grassmarket, and most of all of the new King James.

'A papist king!' one would start, shaking his head. 'He's set up an idolatrous altar in the palace at Holyrood not a mile from here!'

'There's a picture in it, so I've heard,' another would add, 'of a dove that's supposed to be the Holy Ghost. If that's not blasphemy, I don't know what is.'

'Monks droning out masses . . .'

'The Beast of Rome . . .'

'The sorceries of the harlot Pope . . .'

I didn't follow it closely, but I pricked up my ears at the news that Mr Renwick was still free, still gathering the faithful out on the hillsides, preaching, praying and dodging the Black Cuffs, who were still in hot pursuit. The memory of him confused me. I could resurrect the flutter in my heart when I thought of his smile, and something of the exaltation I had felt as he preached,

391

but I resented, too, the trouble his presence had brought to Ladymuir.

I offered constantly to help Cousin Sarah, but she wasn't used to another woman in her kitchen and drove me away.

'Run up to the Luckenbooths, dear,' she said one day, as if I was still a child. 'A young girl likes a bit of finery. Here's a penny to spend.'

I refused the penny, but was glad to go out into the street. There was someone I wanted to see.

The steps down to Mistress Virtue's dungeon were more heaped with refuse than ever, and to my surprise the door was shut. I knocked on it, but no strident voice shrieked out an answer. I stood, wondering what to do, when a window opened above my head.

'Gardy loo!' came a cry, and I jumped aside as a chamber pot was emptied over the spot where I'd been standing. As the hand holding it disappeared back inside I called up, 'Excuse me!'

A woman looked out.

'What do you want?'

'I'm looking for Mistress Virtue. Her door's shut.'

'She's dead,' the woman said shortly. 'And good riddance,' and she pulled her head back in and slammed the window shut.

A pair of ragged boys had followed me down the steps, their hands held out to beg.

'No point asking me,' I said. 'I haven't got any money.'

They scowled.

'Old Virtue a friend of yours, eh?' said one of them.

'*Virtue, Virtue, dirty old hag, penny for a rag, sold her soul, died in a hole!*' chanted the other.

More children were appearing and I was starting to feel uneasy. I backed up the close to the safety of the High Street.

'*A witch! A witch! Died in a ditch!*' they yelled after me.

Passers-by were stopping at the noise and peering into the close.

'Old Virtue used to live down there,' nodded one.

'Was she really a witch?' said another. 'I often wondered.'

'So they say. She died in a fit. There were stories of a tall man in black clothes who came to her that night. He cast a chill around him.'

'Satan! Lord have mercy.'

They hurried on.

I went on up the street. I was sad for Mistress Virtue. I drifted towards the windows of the Luckenbooth shops and stared unseeingly at the displays of ribbons and lace and buttons. Had Mistress Virtue been alone at the end? Had anyone been there to hold her hand at her passing, as I had held Tam's? Would there be anyone to hold mine, when my turn came?

Yes, I told myself firmly. *I'm going to marry someone, a rover like me, who'll love me always. And we'll have children, and live . . .*

'Why, it's Margaret Blair!'

The voice behind me made me spin round. Mr

393

Shillinglaw, tall and angular as ever, stood behind me. I felt a rush of fury. I'd had enough unpleasant surprises today and had no wish for another.

'Oh, it's you,' I said brusquely. 'The lawyer.'

'You're very elusive, young lady.' He was ignoring my rudeness. 'I've been searching for you everywhere.'

'I've been with my *uncle*, Hugh Blair. The brother of my *father*. But then, according to you, he wasn't my father, was he?'

He looked uncomfortable and swallowed. In spite of myself, I couldn't help being fascinated by the way his Adam's apple rose and fell in his long thin neck.

'I owe you an apology.' He nodded solemnly, as if conferring on me a rare privilege. 'I know now that you are indeed who you claim to be.'

His condescension enraged me even more.

'I'm glad to hear it. I'm afraid I've got to go.'

I tried to move past him, but he blocked my way.

'What made me believe you first of all,' he said, looking suddenly more human, 'is that I remember your grandmother. To be frank, she terrified the life out of me when I was a little boy. When you lost your temper with me, you looked exactly like her. As a matter of fact, you look rather like her now.'

'Oh!' I didn't know whether to laugh or be angry. I laughed.

He smiled in response and offered me his arm.

'Will you come with me to my premises, Mistress Blair? There are matters to discuss which are better spoken of in private.'

No one had ever called me Mistress before. In spite of myself, I was charmed. No gentleman had ever offered me his arm, either, and I was grateful to Cousin Thomas for my new gown and shawl. On our slow progress down the High Street, every gentleman we passed bowed to Mr Shillinglaw, and ladies waved to him from their sedan chairs.

Mr Shillinglaw's office was panelled in wood and there were windows with glass panes in them, instead of wooden shutters. I tried not to look too impressed, and sat on the edge of the chair that he drew forward for me with my hands clasped tightly together.

'The sum of money which Mr Bannantyne owes you is not large,' he stated. 'I wouldn't want to raise your expectations. Macbean of Scalpsie Bay owed your father rather more. He was always reluctant to pay the drovers, and used to hold the money over from one year to the next. It might not be easy to recover it from him.'

'I couldn't, even if I wanted to,' I said. 'I can never go back to Bute.'

'Ah. The trial. We heard all about that.'

Now for it, I thought. *Here comes trouble. All this soft talk's a trap. He's going to have me arrested again.*

I looked towards the door, but Mr Shillinglaw was sitting close to it. My heart began to thud painfully.

'The general opinion,' Mr Shillinglaw went on, his voice as dry as straw in August, 'is that an injustice was performed against you. Your grandmother's case, of course, was another matter.'

'Granny wasn't a witch!' I burst out. 'I don't care what anyone says!'

He didn't meet my eyes.

'Be that as it may. But as far as you are concerned, there is no doubt of your innocence.'

'How do you know all this?' I demanded. 'What's it to do with you?'

He lifted a hand.

'There's no need to bite my head off, Maggie, every time I open my mouth. I'm trying to tell you what's in your interest.'

'All right.' I knew I sounded ungracious, but I didn't care. 'Go on.'

'Sentiment on the island changed almost immediately after your grandmother's execution. When the girl Annie disappeared, and was known to have joined forces with a disreputable vagabond . . .'

I wanted to interrupt again, to defend Tam, but even I had to admit that Tam had been extremely disreputable, so I held my tongue.

'. . . Annie's evidence was called into question. Other examples of her untruthfulness and even instances of theft were brought to light.' He dropped his grand manner and said simply, 'Everyone on Bute is ashamed of what happened, Maggie. They know you're not a witch. They were glad that you got away. You ask me how I know. I was in Rothesay myself a couple of weeks ago, on business for Mr Bannantyne. They still talk of you. They want to make amends. You would be welcomed back.'

I didn't know what to say. My head was spinning.

'Don't you even want to know,' Mr Shillinglaw was saying, 'how much money is owing to you?'

'Yes. I do.'

'Mr Bannantyne owed your father three pounds sterling, and Mr Macbean owed him four pounds, I believe.'

Seven pounds! My mouth fell open. I could never have imagined that such sums of money could possibly be mine.

From far away I heard Mr Shillinglaw say, 'A very respectable dowry. Your husband will be a lucky man. If you would like to return here tomorrow morning, I will have Mr Bannantyne's money ready for you, and will ask you to put your cross on a document in receipt.'

'I can write,' I told him haughtily. 'I'll sign my own name properly. And I haven't got a husband, thank you very much. What's mine will be mine.'

I stood up and walked to the door. Then a thought struck me.

'Annie. Do you know what's happened to her?'

'I wondered if you would ask.' He had picked a quill from his desk and was twirling it between his fingers. 'The young lady won't be troubling you again. Mr Bannantyne was greatly angered by her attempted fraud. He had her arrested. She had been living immorally with a succession of soldiers. Other matters – thefts, frauds, slanders, crimes of one kind and another – were proved against her. She's in the tollbooth at present, awaiting transportation on a slave ship to the colonies.'

397

'She'll get away from there,' I said bitterly. 'She
make up to the guards. She'll wheedle her way out of i
'I don't think so. She has been branded, you see, c
the cheeks, and her ears have been cut off. No man w
look twice at her now.'

My journey with the drovers from Bute to Dumbarto
had been quiet and slow, dictated by the leisurely pac
of the cattle. On the flight from Kilmacolm to Edir
burgh, Tam and I had been fugitives, fearfully dodgir
Black Cuffs and stealing to survive. My progress fror
Edinburgh back towards Kilmacolm with Uncle Bla
was quite different. We walked in the open along th
public highway, a respectable pair of travellers, Unc
Blair raising his hat courteously to passers-by. We pai
for our food and lodging with the pennies that Cousi
Thomas had pressed upon us.

Uncle Blair was stronger in body now, but his min
was troubled. Often we walked in silence, but from tin
to time his thoughts would boil over in impassione
speech.

'I've always been a peaceful man!' he would cry ou
'I've only wanted to do what's right, and look after m
family, and work in my fields, and worship my Saviou
in the true Presbyterian way! Why? Why has all th
persecution happened to us? Why have such wicke
men been unleashed against us?'

And he would go over, again and again, the crueltie
and slaughter he had witnessed.

They're not all wicked, I thought. *Not Musketeer Sha*

*s, anyway. You can't condemn them all. Tam didn't. He
as sorry about the ones who died on the other side too.*

Uncle Blair spoke of Tam only once, after the sound
f a bagpipe had wafted to us on a distant breeze.

'I couldn't get the measure of the man at all,' he said.
A rascally kind of a fellow, I suppose.'

'He was good,' I said lamely. 'You didn't know the
alf of it. He helped people. Even thieves, and poor
eople that no one else noticed.'

Like Jesus, I nearly added.

Uncle Blair was following his own train of thought.

'He wasn't a man of the Covenant, now, was he?'

'No, Uncle. I never heard him talk about that.'

'And on the subject of man's free will, were his views
und?'

'He didn't know what it meant.'

Uncle Blair walked on in silence.

'I sometimes think,' he said at last, with a kind of
ondering in his voice, 'that we judge wrongdoers too
arshly, and forget the message of love in the Gospel.'

I admired my uncle for the strength of his convic-
ons, but it was when he softened into a kind of doubt
at I really loved him.

While he'd been talking about Tam, the inner strug-
e which had been going on inside me ever since we
ad walked out through the gates of Edinburgh had
een resolved. I knew what I was going to do. I put my
and into my pocket and fingered the little leather
urse in which lay the precious coins Mr Shillinglaw

had given me. They rattled against my father's silv
buckle. Their jingle seemed to say, *You're free. Free to g*

If it hadn't been ~~such a fine day, with~~ the sun warn
ing the stones, and the rowan berries turning scarlet o
the trees, I think my resolve would have weakened. B
as we approached the turning that would lead to Ki
macolm and Ladymuir, I steeled myself to walk past i
and go on to the west, until I reached the sea and th
boat that would take me home.

Uncle Blair was about to turn down the famili:
path, and was speeding up with joyful anticipation of h
homecoming, before I plucked up the courage to te
him my decision. He stared at me, appalled.

'Go back to Bute? After all that's happened? Ar
travel alone? A young woman? You can't! I can't allo
it!'

'I'm sorry, Uncle,' was all I could say. 'I can't g
home with you.'

'Maggie, dear girl.' He put his hands on my arms an
looked earnestly into my face. 'I know that your aur
hasn't always – that she doesn't find it easy to – but i
her heart she values you, I know she does, and she wan
you to be with us.'

I reached up and kissed his cheek, from which th
beard, scraped off by Cousin Thomas, was already bris
ling out again.

'It's not my aunt,' I said. 'She's always done her be:
with me. But I want to go home! I told you what th
lawyer man said. There's no danger for me now. I hav
to face my accusers. I can't go on running forever. An

400

must thank Mr Robertson for trying to help me, and
ve got to see if my old cow is all right, and – and – oh,
 many things.'

'You mean,' he said, his brow wrinkling, 'that you
el duty bound to return? That it's the Lord who's
 owing you this path, and not some girlish wilfulness?'

There was such simple goodness and honesty in my
ncle that it was impossible to lie to him. A glib answer
 se to my lips, and died there.

'I'm not sure if that's it, exactly,' I said at last. 'It's
hat my heart is telling me to do. Is that my conscience
 eaking? And if so, is it the voice of the Lord?'

He nodded slowly.

'With you, Maggie, I believe it is. Your heart is pure.
 our courage is proven. But I don't like it. I'm afraid for
 u. And they will all be disappointed at home.'

They won't think of me at all, I thought. *Not once they've
en you. Except for Ritchie, perhaps, and Martha.*

Aloud I said, 'You don't need to worry about me,
 ncle. It's only a few miles from here to Largs. I'll be
 ere by tonight. And boats go across every day to
 othesay.'

'Well,' he said reluctantly, 'you've a strong mind, my
 ar, and you've achieved harder things than this. I sup-
 se I must let you go. But you'll come again soon to
 adymuir? We'll not be happy till we've seen you there
 ain.'

'I will. I promise.'

He had given in.

'I shall remember you daily in my prayers,' he sai
and kissed me fondly on my cheek.

I almost wavered when I saw the love and concern
his eyes, but I steeled myself for a last goodbye, an
once he had set out down the track he didn't look bac
I knew that every bit of him was yearning for his hon
and family.

For a moment I was horribly lonely, but straig
afterwards came a wave of joy. I jumped, and twirle
about, and began to almost run on towards the sea.

Fortune smiled on me that day, because half an ho
later, as I marched along the road, swinging my arms,
farmer and his wife offered to take me up in their car
I sat on the back of it dangling my legs all the way
Largs, where the masts of ships bound for the islan
were bobbing about on the quayside, casting long shad
ows across the water in the evening light.

The farmer let me sleep in his barn that night, an
his wife called me into her kitchen for a bowl of stean
ing porridge in the morning.

'There's a boat going over to Bute in an hour or two
she told me. 'My man's asked the skipper for you. He'
give you a passage for a couple of pennies.'

I thanked her, surprised by her kindness and intere
in me.

'What did you say your name was?' she asked, watch
ing me as I ate my breakfast.

'Maggie. Maggie Blair.'

'I knew it.' She clapped her hands down on to he
apron in triumph. 'I said to Nicholas last night, she'll b

at girl, I said, the one who was taken up for a – you
ow what I mean – over in Rothesay, and who got out
 the tollbooth.' She paused, her eyes on me, bright
th curiosity, and when I didn't say anything she
·dded, satisfied. 'There were all kinds of stories at
st, about the Devil flying away with you over the
imneys. Of course, I didn't believe them. Supersti-
·us nonsense! But then it got out about the gaoler
inking himself stupid, and how your granny shooed
u out on your own. How did you do it? How did you
t off the island without being seen? Everyone won-
rs. You must have been that scared!'

 She had been so kind, and seemed so excited to meet
·, that I felt obliged to tell her my story, though I
ln't want to. The memory of that awful time still
ide me shake inside. Luckily, before I'd had to say too
ıch, the farmer put his head round the door.

'If you want to get to Rothesay today, you'd better
n down to the shore now, miss. The sails are up.
ıey're about to cast off.'

ıere was a fresh wind blowing, filling the boat's sails
d making me shiver and pull my shawl close around
√ head. Slowly, very slowly, the Isle of Bute, lying long
d low on the horizon, grew up out of the sea, and as
e hours passed I could make out first the shapes of the
ys, and then the outline of trees, and then the long
ips of field at harvest, lying in brown and yellow lines
coss the hillsides, and then the farmhouses themselves

403

with their ragged thatched roofs. At last I could ma
out people, walking about on the foreshore.

It looks so small, I thought. ~~Even the castle. It's nothi~~
compared to Edinburgh. I'd always thought Rothesay wa.
grand big place.

Though my heart thudded with fear, I felt an une
pected longing as the boat's prow creamed through t
final stretch of water to tie up at the jetty. I'd nev
known until this moment how much I'd missed r
island.

I'd had no clear idea of what I'd do once I arrive
though I'd planned first to walk down to Kingarth
seek out Mr Robertson and thank him for the help he
given to Granny and me. But I hadn't bargained for t
stir my arrival would cause.

I'd hardly taken my first steps ashore when a wom:
carrying a basket of oysters on her head cried out, 'Lo
who it is! The Blair girl! Maggie Blair!'

Heads swivelled round. The miller, loading sacks o
of the boat on to his horse, almost let one drop as
turned to stare. A couple of fishermen, who were wor
ing over the upturned hull of their boat, dropped the
tools and came over for a better look. A moment late
a crowd had gathered.

I felt a surge of terror. Had Mr Shillinglaw told n
the truth? Or was I walking straight back into the o
nightmare?

Then someone called out, 'So you've come ba
then, Maggie. Good for you!'

He spoke with self-conscious bravery, as if he was
afraid he might be going against the general opinion.

'Aye, welcome home, girl,' said another, more confi-
dently.

'Look at her! She's grown! Hasn't she grown?' marvelled a woman.

'Aye, you always were a bonny lass,' another said, her
voice almost sickly with affection.

Inside me, something that had been pulled as taut as
a fiddle string relaxed so suddenly that I was afraid I
would slump down, and be overwhelmed with tears.
Only Granny's voice, loud inside my head, stopped me:
Hold your head up, child. Where's your pride? Don't let the
hens see you down.

'Well,' I said, swallowing hard, 'I see they've not
mended the castle walls yet. And the tollbooth looks
about the same too.'

There were a few uneasy laughs, and someone said,
'Look, here comes Mr Robertson,' and there was a
murmur of relief as they stepped back to let him past.

Mr Robertson raised his hat to the crowd, and was
about to hurry by when he saw me. He stopped, and his
face broke open into a smile so frankly joyful that I had
to smile back at him.

'Here's someone I'd never hoped to see again!
Maggie, it *is* you! Oh, this is wonderful. You've come
back, I hope, in a spirit of forgiveness. We know, all of
us, what a great wrong was done to you.' His gaze swept
round the ring of faces. Eyes dropped and feet shuffled.

'I'm sure I speak for everyone when I say we want make amends.'

At that moment a couple of boys, who had be chasing each other down the hill, burst into the crov They saw me, and the first began to chant, '*Witch g witch hag, hang and burn her, till she's—*'

Before he could finish, a giant of a farmer turned a swiped at him, catching such a clout on the side of t head that the boy went sprawling in the mud.

'Hold your tongue, you wee scunner,' he snarled.

It's still there. Under the surface. It always will be thought, a chill in my heart.

But Mr Robertson was talking to me again.

'You'll come home with me to Kingarth, I hop You'll take your dinner with us, perhaps. Where are y sleeping tonight?'

'I – I'm not sure. I hadn't thought.'

'Mrs Robertson will be delighted to meet you. M wife, you know. I was married last December.'

He looked self-conscious, and actually blushed. noticed then that he was no longer the thin, gangli young man I had known before. He had filled out, a the buttons of his long black waistcoat were actua straining across his stomach.

'Thank you, Mr Robertson,' I said gratefully, wis ing to get away from the ring of onlookers as much anything else. 'I'd be grateful.'

It was a relief to leave Rothesay behind, and Mr Rober son kept blessedly silent until we had gone past the gri

406

llbooth, and climbed the hill towards St Mary's
urch. But as we passed the door I was hit by such a
rong memory of the day when Granny and I had
ood there in sackcloth, as the good people of Bute,
led with hate, spat at us, that I began to tremble and
el sick.

'It's over, Maggie. It's all over now,' Mr Robertson
id kindly, seeing how white I had turned.

I couldn't help it. I started crying then. He stopped
d made me sit down under a tree in the churchyard,
d passed me his kerchief to wipe my nose, and waited,
iet and patient, until I had managed to pull myself
gether with a last hiccup.

It was five miles or so to Kingarth, nearly two hours
walking, but even that wasn't time enough for all the
estions he asked me, and his expressions of astonish-
ent at my answers.

'So you've been aiding the martyrs of Dunnottar,' he
pt saying admiringly. 'That was a terrible thing, so
e heard.'

There were questions I would have liked to ask him,
t we reached his manse at Kingarth before I had the
ance.

I hung back at his solid front door, afraid that Mrs
obertson might not be as pleased to see me as her hus-
nd had promised. I needn't have worried. Mrs
obertson was as clean and pink as her husband, but
all and round, with bobbing curls and a tendency to
ugh at the smallest thing. She seemed a strange kind
wife for the earnest young minister, but I could see

that she had done him good, softening his austerity a
giving him a greater ease.

Although I felt shy in her neat kitchen, I smil
inwardly at how much more nervous I used to be. I s
myself as I had once been: a wild, dirty child, wi
ragged clothes and unkempt hair, ignorant, illiter:
and fearful. I caught a puzzled look on her face as s
appraised the good woollen cloth of the gown tl
Cousin Thomas had given me, and watched me fold 1
shawl neatly and lay it aside, as Aunt Blair had alwa
done, before I sat at the table and folded my hanc
waiting for Mr Robertson to say grace.

Is this really the girl you told me about? she seemed
be asking her husband.

I couldn't help showing off a little as the meal pr
gressed. I told Mrs Robertson how Mr Haddo dress
cockscombs in the Marischal of Dunnottar's kitchens
explained to her Aunt Blair's method of salting beef, a
began to describe the fashionable dresses of the high-1
ladies of Edinburgh, though I stopped before I had to
her of the craze for ribbon knots when I noticed th
Mr Robertson was frowning with displeasure at tl
show of frivolity.

'So, Maggie,' he said at last, 'you'll do us the favou
I hope, of reading to us tonight's passage from the Goc
Book before we go to our beds.'

He took a large Bible down from the shelf in tl
alcove by the fire, opened it, and laid it front of me.
was gently done, but I could tell that he was setting n

a test, and my pulse quickened. I hadn't read a word since leaving Kilmacolm all those months ago.

It was fortunate that the story he chose was the Good Samaritan, a favourite one that I had read many times before.

'*A certain man went down from Jerusalem to Jericho, and fell among thieves*,' I began.

I read on, faultlessly, and when I had finished the chapter I looked up to check if he wanted me to carry on. As I did so, I surprised the Robertsons exchanging a look. He was mouthing a question to her. She was nodding with enthusiastic consent.

'That was well done,' he said, taking the book and replacing it on the shelf.

He sat down again at the table and cleared his throat.

'I have an idea for you, Maggie,' he began, nodding solemnly. 'It's a kind of – a proposition.'

'Oh, do tell her, Matthew!' interrupted Mrs Robertson, her shoulders heaving with her customary laughter.

'We're trying to set up a school here,' Mr Robertson said, suppressing her with a look. 'The teacher has been found, but he can't start until after this coming winter. I believe you could stand in for him, and teach the little ones their letters. There's a cottage for the teacher, you know, and a kail-yard. You would earn some pennies, enough to live on in a simple sort of way.'

His words seemed to buzz in my ears. The idea was too absurd. Impossible.

'I couldn't do that,' I said. 'I wouldn't know how to do that.'

'Say yes, dear! You'd be perfect!' said Mrs Robertson, clapping her chubby hands.

What do you know about it? I thought, with a little spurt of irritation. *The last child I saw in Bute was calling out to me, 'Witch girl! Witch hag!'*

'I don't know.' I shook my head.

'You must have time to think it over,' said Mr Robertson. 'Let us sleep on the matter prayerfully, and in the morning, God willing, wiser counsels will prevail.'

'Amen,' giggled his wife.

I fell into a deep sleep as soon as I had lain down on the small truckle bed they set out for me by the kitchen fire, but I woke very early in the morning. It was still dark, but the faintest glimmer of early dawn was creeping through the cracks in the wooden window shutter.

I had been dreaming uncomfortably of a kind of prison, a vault with a small window, from which a cliff fell away to the sea raging on rocks below. The vault was full of children tugging at me, pulling at me, calling me names as I shouted to them the letters of the alphabet.

The Robertsons' strange proposition came back to me with full force.

Me! A teacher! Right here, in Kingarth! How Granny would have laughed. How bitter her laughter would have been, and how triumphant.

You show them, girl, I seemed to hear her say. *You're better than the lot of them.*

410

But the dream of prison was still upon me, and the air in the little kitchen was close and stuffy. I got up and crept to the door, lifted the latch and stepped outside.

There is no air like the soft air of Bute, crisp with the tang of the sea, laden with the richness of the earth and the fullness of grass and trees. I breathed it in, long and deep, remembering the stench of Edinburgh, and the foulness of Dunnottar, and the lighter air of the moors and mosses of Kilmacolm.

Almost of their own accord my feet began to move, and I was walking, and then running, up the hill from Kingarth and down the long, long lane to Scalpsie Bay.

The sun had risen by the time I had rounded the last bend. I stopped, the familiarity of the place clutching at me. Every twig on every tree was known to me. Every stone in every ditch. Every pebble on the sweep of the beach.

The tide was out. The bones of the whale still lay on the sand, clean and whitened to a stark frame. Beyond the water rose the mass of Arran, touched with pink in the morning light.

And there was the cottage. Our cottage.

Smoke was rising through the thatch. I watched it for a moment, without understanding, then a howl of rage tore out of me and I raced down the last stretch of lane.

I reached the gap in the hedge. Robbie Macbean was squatting in the dirt by the kail-yard, his breeks round his ankles.

'Get out! What are you doing here? Get out of my house!' I shrieked at him.

He looked up at me, his mouth open, terror in his eyes. He tried to stand, but tripped on his breeks and fell on his face in the mud, letting out a wail of anguish.

Someone appeared at the cottage door. It was Jeanie Macbean.

She saw me and flinched, putting out both hands as if to protect herself.

'You've come at last,' she said. 'I knew you would.'

I'd been so hot with rage a moment earlier that I might have rushed at her and attacked her with my fists, but the distress of little Robbie was distracting me. I couldn't help myself. I went over to him, picked him up and set him on his feet.

'Stop that noise, you silly wee man. I'm not going to hurt you.'

He ran to his mother, clutching at his breeks, and clung to her skirts, staring at me wide-eyed.

The sight of Mrs Macbean standing in my own doorway, where I'd seen Granny stand so many, many times, made my fury rise again, but it was cold rage now.

'You took it then, our cottage, like you always wanted,' I said bitterly. 'I hope Mr Macbean's pleased with himself. I hope he's happy now.'

To my surprise, Mrs Macbean let out a shriek of laughter that was wild to the point of madness.

'Happy? In Hell? *Happy?*'

Before I could say anything, the laughter left her and she seemed to shrink within herself. She put a weary hand up to her head.

'You'll be wanting to put us out. I won't make a fuss.

Give me a day, Maggie, that's all I ask, to find another place.'

'What do you mean, another place?' I couldn't understand. 'Go home, to your nice big farm up there on the hill.'

She stared at me.

'You don't know then? You'll not have heard?'

'Heard what?'

She turned away, as if she was ashamed.

'Come inside for a minute. I'll tell you. You'll be happy enough to hear it, I don't doubt.'

I went into my old home with odd reluctance.

The vile toad, Granny had said. *The cold snail.*

And there was something vile and cold in that familiar room, where the floor was unswept, and Jeanie Macbean's little girls looked at me from thin, pinched faces, their eyes wide with fear. There was a chill of misery, a despair that not even Granny had spread around her.

'He hanged himself,' Mrs Macbean said baldly. 'From the old ash tree out by our barn.'

'*What?*'

I had to put a hand down on to the old table to steady myself.

'After you – after the trial, and all that, it came out. About him and Annie, and the child, and the lies he'd told. The lies! They stripped him of being an elder, of course. He was up before the Kirk Session. He had to sit for four Sundays on the stool of repentance, in the same gown of sackcloth, no doubt, that you wore. They said he'd lied at your trial. That he'd perjured himself. That he was practically guilty of murder. No one would speak a word to him, or to me. They all turned their backs.'

Her voice, thin with anguish, was making the hairs stand up on my arms and legs.

'He'd never been a drinking man, Maggie, you know that, but he started on the whisky then. He stopped working on the farm. He drank every night on his own. He'd get violent, and hit me. And the children.'

She stopped. I didn't know what to say. I just waited for her to finish.

'He had the drink badly on him one night, and he hit Robbie so hard that he knocked him right out. John thought he'd killed him. His own son. He did love his children, you know. He really did.' For a moment, her voice had lightened, and there was a spark of warmth in her eyes. 'I don't think he could bear the thought that he might have murdered his own child. I found him in the morning, hanging from the tree.'

'Oh,' was all I could say. 'Mrs Macbean, I—'

'His brother came, and took over the farm. It was his right, I suppose. He said we could live here, in your old place. He's a mean man, but he lets us have a sack of oatmeal from time to time.'

She licked her lips.

'I found the letter, about the money John owed your father. I'd give it to you if I had it, Maggie, honestly I would. But you can see how it is with us.'

414

She stood up, picked up a cloth that lay crumpled in a corner and began to fold it.

'I'll just put our things together,' she said. 'Please, Maggie. Just today. Give us today. I don't know who'll take us in now.'

I stood in silence, unable to speak. Known things from the past were shattering to pieces, and the fragments were falling about me. New patterns were being made that I could only dimly see.

Mrs Macbean was bending down to collect up her pots that surrounded the unswept hearth.

'Stop,' I said. 'You don't need to do that.' I took a deep breath. 'Never mind the money. You can't pay it anyway. And you can stay here. You can have this place. I don't want it any more. I couldn't live here alone, anyway.'

She sank down on to Granny's old stool. A pewter plate fell from her hand and rolled across the floor. I wasn't sure, though, if she had heard what I'd said.

'The house is cursed,' she said. 'She cursed it. Nothing good will happen to anyone who lives here.'

The memory of that dreadful morning, when they had come to the cottage with soldiers and weapons, their faces alight with cruel glee, was on us both. I seemed to see Granny kneeling by the hearthstone, her eyes darting with malice, her voice cracking with hatred.

The man who takes this place from me and my granddaughter will be cursed, she'd said. *His cattle will die, and his children too.*

I sat down on the other stool. My old stool.

'Listen, Mrs Macbean.' I wanted to touch her hand but was afraid she would recoil from me. 'You must believe what I'm telling you. My grandmother wasn't witch. She wasn't. She didn't kill your baby Ebeneze She saw he was sickly at his birth. She knew he wouldn live long, by her knowledge of these things. She was angry, and lonely and cruel, but she had no dealing with the Devil.'

Mrs Macbean shook her head.

'Maybe so, Maggie, but I told you, this place cursed. I know it is. Can't you feel it yourself?'

And then I felt a strangeness in me, a power tha frightened me. I didn't want it. I tried to push it awa But I heard myself say, 'Then I'll lift the curse, Jean Macbean. I'll bring a blessing here instead.'

I knelt on the hearthstone, where I'd cried myself t sleep so many nights as a cold, lonely little girl, an words came to me from some old corner of m memory:

> *God bless this house*
> *From beam to wall*
> *From end to end*
> *From floor to roof.*
> *Floor to roof.*

I paused. It wasn't quite enough.

'I lift the curse from this dwelling place. Go, vil toad. Flee, cold snail.'

I knew it had happened. A kind of warmth, a kind of peace, had stolen into that tumbledown cottage, like the first rays of a summer's sun. Jeanie Macbean had dropped her head down on to her arms, resting on the table, and her shoulders were shaking with sobs.

'Don't cry, Jeanie. Don't,' I said. 'I'm telling you, there's no curse now. You have no more to fear from my granny or from me. And the cottage is yours to keep.'

And I stepped out from that old doorway and ran down the path I'd followed a thousand times before, till I was standing on the beach at the water's edge. Under the clear sky, the sea lay flat and calm. There were no black and silver clouds to break open, as there had been on that day so long ago when the whale had come up there to die. There was only a haze, soft and blue, which seemed to lift the distant Isle of Arran, making it hover above the water as if it was floating gently down from the sky.

A white shell, perfectly grooved, was lying on a rock near my feet. I picked it up.

What shall I do? I thought. *Where shall I go?*

Would it be the schoolroom in Kingarth? Would I seek work elsewhere? Would I go roving again, to places I'd yet to see? Would Ritchie Blair come for me one day? And if he did, would I welcome him?

'Where's the answer?' I called out. 'Who's going to tell me?'

I lifted my arm and hurled the shell away from me, across the water. Ripples spread out from the place where it had sunk, then merged with a wave which broke in foam around my feet, as if the sea had flung my questions back to me.

I had known the answers all the time. I had no need to shout them out. They were there in my head, and in my heart.

I'll go where I choose, and I'll be who I am, and I'll rise up to meet whatever comes my way.

A selected list of titles available from Macmillan Children's Books

The prices shown below are correct at the time of going to press. However, Macmillan Publishers reserves the right to show new retail prices on covers, which may differ from those previously advertised.

Elizabeth Laird

A Little Piece of Ground	978-0-330-43743-1	£5.99
Crusade	978-0-330-45699-9	£5.99
Jake's Tower	978-0-330-39803-9	£5.99
Lost Riders	978-0-330-45209-0	£5.99
Kiss the Dust	978-0-230-01431-2	£5.99
Oranges in No Man's Land	978-0-330-44558-0	£4.99
Paradise End	978-0-330-39999-9	£4.99
Secrets of the Fearless	978-0-330-43466-9	£5.99
The Garbage King	978-0-330-41502-6	£5.99

All Pan Macmillan titles can be ordered from our website, www.panmacmillan.com, or from your local bookshop and are also available by post from:

Bookpost, PO Box 29, Douglas, Isle of Man IM99 1BQ

Credit cards accepted. For details:
Telephone: 01624 677237
Fax: 01624 670923
Email: bookshop@enterprise.net
www.bookpost.co.uk

Free postage and packing in the United Kingdom